PENGUIN BOOKS
THE POLITICIAN REDUX

Devesh Verma was associated with TV journalism for over twenty-two years before he turned to fiction writing. In 2004, he received the Sahitya Akademi Award for his translation, from Urdu to Hindi, of *Sakhtiyat, Pas-Sakhtiyat Aur Mashriqi Sheriyat*, an important literary and cultural theory text. His first novel, *The Politician*, was published by Penguin Random House India in 2021.

PRAISE FOR *THE POLITICIAN*

'Every bit a twenty-first-century Indian English novel, it neither tries to write back to a centre nor cares for a Western reader. The novel captures both the energy and the chaos that characterize life in small towns in Uttar Pradesh . . .'—Scroll

'Devesh Verma's debut novel, *The Politician* . . . exquisitely upends [the] dominant model of the political novel that oscillates between fact and fiction and highlights the success and skulduggery of corrupt and ruthless politicians. With well-fleshed-out characters, Devesh Verma weaves a gripping narrative around a flawed hero's quest for unbridled power'—*Frontline*

'From Jawaharlal Nehru's subtle handing over of the political mantle to his daughter Indira Gandhi to B.R. Ambedkar's fight for the untouchables, or his proposed Hindu Code Bill being seen as "wicked interference with the age-old Hindu personal laws of divine provenance", there is hardly any political event of significance that has escaped Verma's attention . . . The gentle and effortless unravelling of these complex minds, and the timelessness of this tragic-comic novel by Verma, who won a Sahitya Award for a translated work in 2004, deserves praise'—*Hindustan Times*

'At several points in the novel one felt the echoes of the plenitude of Hindi and Urdu voices that Devesh must have absorbed through his intellectual journey. That he can make us feel and smell those writings in an English novel is a singular achievement . . . This is a remarkable debut and one eagerly looks forward to the second instalment of what promises to be a colossal trilogy'—*Biblio*

THE
POLITICIAN
REDUX

Odyssey of
Chance

DEVESH VERMA

PENGUIN BOOKS
An imprint of Penguin Random House

PENGUIN BOOKS

Penguin Books is an imprint of the Penguin Random House group of companies
whose addresses can be found at global.penguinrandomhouse.com

Published by Penguin Random House India Pvt. Ltd
4th Floor, Capital Tower 1, MG Road,
Gurugram 122 002, Haryana, India

Penguin
Random House
India

First published in Penguin Books by Penguin Random House India 2024

ISBN 9780143463658

Typeset in Bembo Std by Manipal Technologies Limited, Manipal
Printed at Manipal Technologies Limited, Manipal

www.penguin.co.in

MIX
Paper | Supporting
responsible forestry
FSC® C043100

To Bhavna

And to the memory of my parents: my father, Braj Lal Verma, and my mother, Rama Verma; it's because of them that I started believing, for better or for worse, that there was something noble, something sublime about the business of imaginative writing, even when it is as unworldly and impractical as romantic love

'It's my opinion that men will gamble as long as they have anything to put on a card. Gamble? That's nature. What's life itself? You never know what may turn up. The worst of it is that you never can tell exactly what sorts of cards you are holding yourself.'

—Mr Ricardo in *Victory*

'Truth, work, ambition, love itself, may be only counters in the lamentable or despicable game of life, but when one takes a hand, one must play the game.'

—Heyst in *Victory*

ONE

'If I may ask you, Kartik—'
Before the question could be completed, some in the assembly erupted into laughter, those familiar with *The Politician*, my first novel, which had come out the year before and whose release was held up for over eleven months by the cataclysmic outbreak of COVID-19. Now I was working on its sequel and, since I am an inveterate dawdler, a friend of mine offered by way of a solution to organize at his place a gathering every two–three months, where I would read whatever I would have accomplished in the interim, a gathering of friends who were into books. A very senior official in the Rajya Sabha, my friend lives in a big government accommodation in Chanakyapuri, one of Delhi's most exclusive neighbourhoods, and the first such gathering took place on the terrace of his house one balmy February evening. His reputation as a good host ensured a good turnout.

The guest who had addressed me as Kartik didn't get it at first. He looked puzzled. Then, before his neighbour could correct him, he realized his mistake. 'Oh, I'm sorry. I finished reading *The Politician* just yesterday and—'

'You're not wrong to assume that. After all, Kartik, the narrator, is my alter ego. Just like some of the characters in my novel owe some of their attributes to real persons.'

'This sequel that you're working on, how many of the characters from *The Politician* are going to be in it?' This was another guest who too had read it.

'I'm glad you asked,' spoke up my friend. 'Today, he's going to discuss something like that.'

'Yes,' said I and took out the sheets from the manila envelope I held. 'I've written it down. Here you go:

'Before taking the story forward, let me talk about the chief protagonists from the previous book who will feature in *Odyssey of Chance*. It's not that one can't enjoy it without reading *The Politician*. One can, because it will also make for a stand-alone novel.

'This story basically is of Ram Mohan and his family and their vicissitudes of life. Of farming stock, Ram Mohan has neither social nor economic means to help his aspirations. What he does have, though, is no less important. He has mighty drive and a positive outlook, an outlook so positive it verges on pathology. He can't be without some goal to achieve or some problem to solve. No matter how difficult a challenge, he's game. He succeeds through guile in landing a lectureship in Hindi literature at Kanpur's DAV College, a reputable institute of higher education in the state and goes on to occupy a position of importance in literary and social spheres. Also drawn to politics, he weighs his chances in it, and a chance meeting with Tiwari-ji decides him and a lifelong bond comes to be forged between them.

'Ram Mohan is already a dominant figure in the region he hails from. Not only because of his education and knowledge but because he can also employ violence if warranted. He has a friend in the person of Gulab Singh, who ensures that there's no resistance to his writ in the area. No sooner does an upcoming local politico, Shukla-ji, introduce him to Chaudhary Baran Singh, a powerful state politician, than Ram Mohan's political venture takes off. That doesn't mean he's willing to let go of the place he has carved for himself in the state's literary realm. No. He tries to strike a balance between the two, politics and literature.

'Ram Mohan's behaviour at home is that of a tyrant. While his wife Kanti is all for their daughters being allowed enough freedom to spread their wings, he scoffs at the idea of girls planning a career before marriage. Particularly bitter on this account is Nisha, his eldest child, who thinks that given the opportunity, she can go places. When Ram Mohan decides to marry her off, Mahavir Wilson, a close family friend who disapproves of the former's views on the matter, consoles her that she should be better off married because then she might have more freedom to follow her heart. Sandhya, the younger of the two daughters, isn't as loud but she has the potential to achieve much in life. Her aspirations too fall by the wayside. It's not much different for the boys in this household, barring Mayank, the youngest, who's the cynosure of Ram Mohan's eyes. Nishant, who is younger only to Nisha, is his own man. He seems emotionally detached and remains outside of the close bond between Nisha, Sandhya, Deena and Mayank. Deena is the black sheep of the family. Not only is he low on scholastic ability but also bunks off school regularly and lives in the fantasy world of movies and storybooks. To satisfy these desires he steals money from his father's wallet.'

I stopped to take a swig of beer.

'Can I ask something?' said the person who had called me Kartik.

'By all means.'

'Is the character of Deena based on someone real, someone you knew or were friends with, who committed suicide as Kartik mentions in the beginning of *The Politician*?'

'Yes, but his name wasn't Deena, obviously, and the basic material for these novels I got from his VIP suitcase filled with

diaries and notebooks that he had left me to use for this very
purpose. To write the story he couldn't . . . Okay, let me finish
the summary:

'Because of a sudden turn of events and because of his own
follies, Ram Mohan's political ambition remains far from being
realized. Had he persevered with Chaudhary Baran Singh, he might
have got somewhere. Yet his decision to become Saansad-ji's acolyte
isn't bad. Saansad-ji joins hands with Baran Singh but later returns
to the Congress under Indira Gandhi and is made a minister. When
Saansad-ji's attempt to have Ram Mohan sent to the Rajya Sabha
is thwarted, he, as UP's chief minister, tries to include him in his
cabinet but his detractors in Delhi have Ram Mohan's name crossed
out on the list sent for Indira Gandhi's sanction. Saansad-ji makes yet
another attempt. To no avail. Nothing working out politically, he
appoints Ram Mohan as Member, UP Public Service Commission,
not the upshot Ram Mohan had been anticipating of his endeavours
in politics. He listens to Mahavir Wilson who says, "The position
isn't political but enjoys much social prestige." Tiwari-ji concurs,
"And it's just the beginning. Let's regard it that way."

'"Yes, the beginning of something bigger," says Ram Mohan.
"Given Saansad-ji's affection for me, it wouldn't be the end." Deena
was to comment later: Once aware of the constraints on his ability to
manoeuvre, Baabuji would demonstrate a remarkable capacity to adjust his
ambition accordingly.

'That's how The Politician ends, but the story continues in
Odyssey of Chance,' said I, putting the sheets back into the envelope.

Just as my friend, gesturing towards the well-laid table under
an awning on the far side of the terrace, announced, 'It's time for
dinner,' his wife said to me in everybody's hearing, 'You'll read us
the first chapter the next time we meet?'

'I guess so. Now that I have a kind of deadline!'

* * *

That's how I finished *Odyssey of Chance*, the book you are reading. If it hadn't been for this deadline thing, it would have taken much longer. Okay, that's about it. Let's roll on.

* * *

Soon after Ram Mohan's appointment as Member, Public Service Commission, his family moved from Kanpur to Allahabad, to the Commission's guesthouse, where they were to lodge till an official residence was available.

At first, he had had no clear notion of the importance of this appointment. Deena's admission to the Government Inter College with no hitch was the first instance of its high social status and the ease with which he could get things done now. Any school worth its salt, let alone the best Hindi-medium school, would be indisposed to give admission directly to the tenth or twelfth grade. The reputation of these schools was built around how well their pupils did in these two board exams. Not only had Deena done his ninth grade from another school but had barely managed to pass. When the principal of the GIC got a call from Ram Mohan, he came galloping and at his behest Mayank too, who had been admitted to Kendriya Vidyalaya, was shifted to the GIC.

Nishant and Sandhya had matriculated at Allahabad University. The former was doing an MA in English literature, the latter her BSc. Nisha too enrolled. She would be better off with an MA in Hindi literature followed by a PhD; then Baabuji could help her secure a lectureship at some girls' degree college. Teaching was the ideal job for women keen on something other than just minding the household, to say nothing of an additional income coming in.

The British era guesthouse in the Commission compound had decent-sized rooms built in a single row with a wide portico braced by big columns at the front, each with a large window and a spacious alcove at the back. Out front, a little distance off, was the low boundary wall edged with tall trees, through which one could survey from the guest house the street and its sparse traffic. The compound was dotted with trees of all sizes and undergrowth. The bungalows located within also had trees, and lawns and yards of various proportions, along with flowerbeds and vegetable gardens tended by official gardeners. Ram Mohan's family couldn't wait to move into one of these bungalows. That seemed unlikely anytime soon. Not for a year, at least, when two members would retire. Sent to the Commission, together with Ram Mohan, was one more loyalist of Saansad-ji, Munni Prasad, who was in no immediate need of official accommodation. A lawyer by profession, he had been practising at Allahabad High Court for years and had his own house in the city. He had joined a day later than Ram Mohan, so on any such available house, the latter would have first call.

Just as Ram Mohan looked settled for an extended stay at the guesthouse, he heard the story, part of the Commission lore. The bungalow at the extreme left-hand corner of the compound, though meant for members, had long housed officials of much lower ranks. Ram Mohan listened to the matter-of-fact tone in which the score was defended. Why no member wanted to live in that house was based on good sense. Those who had stayed in it had died in office—two in office and the third soon after retirement, but he, too, got co-opted. How the rumour started off no one knew, the rumour that the bungalow was haunted and only members were targeted! Other officials who lived there were spared.

Ram Mohan forthwith told the concerned department of his desire for the said house. The current occupant, a joint secretary, would have to go. Soon, an official accompanied by the caretaker came to request him to think it over. Their professed unease at Ram Mohan's readiness to live in a place with such a dire past savoured of design, hardening Ram Mohan's resolve to restore the house to those entitled. He didn't laugh off the ghost story. He just said, 'I've never heard ghosts harming one of their own'. The caretaker and his senior were stumped. 'I'd like to move into this house inside of a month.'

The joint secretary had no choice but to vacate. Ram Mohan sent Kanti, Nishant, Sandhya, Deena and Mayank to have a look at the house. It had four bedrooms, each with attached latrine and bath, a drawing-cum-dining area, a loggia at the back facing the garden that had a lawn and flower beds. On one side of it was a vegetable garden, on the other some beautiful citrus trees and lying between the portico and the boundary wall was the front lawn, the pillars supporting the portico clothed in ivy. They were going to live in such a big place and could enjoy comforts identified with a certain class! It took some time to grasp.

Articles of furniture such as a sofa set, a centre table, a dining table, two double beds, three steel almirahs (one that of Godrej), appliances like fridge, and cooking gas and pressure cooker, things of which they could formerly only dream would become part of their household. Yes, Ram Mohan used to have cars, one at a time, at various points of his stay in Civil Lines, Kanpur, but each one of them, after showing an initial breath of life, would run out of steam. To keep any of those beat-up things in action had been beyond Ram Mohan's means. For mobility, he had his Rajdoot, an unflashy but dependable motorcycle back in the day.

Now he had to have an operational car, accordant with his new status. Only some among the salaried people could get their hands on a car. To pay for a brand-new thing, one would have to save for ages. No, hold on! Even having the requisite money wasn't enough for the fulfilment of this dream. One had to first book the Fiat, the most sought-after car for personal use, then settle for a wait that could take years because of limits set on the production of four and two-wheelers, the most popular among which had an endless queue of prospective buyers. Ram Mohan didn't have to fret on that score. In a country romancing with socialism, there were hardly any rules that those with influence couldn't circumvent.

Ram Mohan had the resources to help him jump the queue for a new car. What he didn't have was the ready cash. Finally, an old Fiat was bought, which looked desperate for an overhaul and was sent immediately to a mechanic. In a week it came back, mended and done up.

Apart from other amenities, they also had a four-wheeler now, something that was still a big leap for the majority in the Indian middle class. It made such a difference that Deena and Mayank feared the prospect of being driven to their school, and when it happened, they would implore Zameer, the driver, to drop them outside the school gate but he would drive right through it and inside the GIC compound. To be seen climbing out of a car was mortifying. They didn't have the stomach for something that might be viewed as showing off, let alone that students who came in a four-wheeler were thought somewhat sissy. Sandhya, too, cringed at catching people's attention in this fashion. Nisha and Nishant were the opposite. They would bask in people being awed at whatever they could put on display, be it their talents or possessions.

The relocation of Ram Mohan's family to Allahabad was a glorious improvement on their lifestyle in Kanpur, to say nothing of the high social standing the Commission had conferred.

* * *

There had been signs of popular unrest and political turmoil across an enormous chunk of India, and the way it came to grow in scope and intensity was staggering. Ram Mohan was thankful to Saansad-ji, the Chief Minister, for sending him to the Commission.

Handpicked by Indira Gandhi, no Congress CM had the resources of his own to handle a crisis of this nature. It had all begun in the state of Gujarat, this flaring up of popular rage at inflation, where, incensed at their increased mess bill, students at an engineering college assaulted a college official, and put the canteen to the torch, following it up with another bout of destruction of college property. The trouble metastasized to other educational institutions. Students were baying for the sacking of the state government led by one of the most corrupt Congress leaders, Chimanbhai Patel, who had procured massive funds for the party through questionable means. That inflamed the situation on the price rise front. Then, Jayaprakash Narayan, an esteemed socialist figure, decided to lend his support to the agitation in Gujarat. Having been associated with the freedom struggle, he had once been invited by Nehru to join his cabinet. He had declined and quietly settled down in his home state, Bihar, emerging now and again from his retirement to pick up odd causes. Soon to be known as JP, he hailed the Gujarat students' angst, seeing it as a force that could bring about the redemption of the country from the corruption infesting the Indian polity.

With the students' anger winning public endorsement, the situation in Gujarat became one of pandemonium. Violence and vandalism were rampant. The opposition latched on to the agitation, and Indira Gandhi had had to remove the chief minister, placing the state under President's rule while the opposition clamoured for the dissolution of the assembly and fresh polls. She was unwilling. Forcing her hand was a fast unto death to which her old foe Desai, the tallest leader of Gujarat, had resorted. Meanwhile, students in lawless Bihar had put together their own movement with the opposition in tow, the grievances being the same as in Gujarat: corruption, price rise, unemployment.

With rioting, arson, vandalism becoming the order of the day, Bihar was thrown into anarchy. There was also this strike by railway workers when hundreds of thousands of them stopped work, demanding pay parity with other government employees.

A little prior to this twenty-day-long, debilitating strike that had to be broken up by the government, JP had agreed to take up the reins of the Movement. Sensing general discontent, he resurrected his old idea of 'total revolution' and, with the opposition rooting for him, took the Movement beyond his home state, appealing to people, chiefly the youth, to rise against the misrule of Indira Gandhi. In the meantime, Saansad-ji's reputation took a knock when the Congress lost a by-election for Allahabad, the parliamentary seat from which he had resigned to become a member of the state legislature.

It was against this backdrop of the growing bitterness against the Congress rule that Ram Mohan went to see Saansad-ji in Lucknow. He wanted to thank him for the Commission that had inaugurated a delightful chapter in his life.

'This was the best I could do in the circumstances and take my word, it's one of the most coveted non-political positions. As member, Public Service Commission, you'll have a term of six years during which nobody can touch you, whereas no political office can be immune to instability.'

'Yes, I have a large family to provide for. I need stability. But whenever I'm needed in active politics, you'll find me standing right behind you.'

Saansad-ji laughed. A listless laugh. His heart wasn't in it.

'You'd remember that within four months of my taking over as CM, Jayaprakash-ji came to UP to campaign for his total revolution. I didn't try to stop him. I declared him our state's guest, arguing that not only was he a renowned freedom fighter but a crusader for the good of the common man. This I did to restrain the rabble-rouser in him. Look at the response he's getting wherever he goes! But Indira-ji listens to Shukla-ji's wily Uncle Uma Kant Shukla and the like. These two things, the way Congress was licked in the Allahabad by-poll and the welcome extended to JP by my government, didn't go down well with her. There's something else. She hasn't taken kindly to my style of functioning . . . No Congress CM is supposed to govern in a manner that casts him as a leader under his own steam. Your only objective as minister or chief minister should be to keep the masses glued to the thought of her person,' Saansad-ji paused to sip his tea.

'JP is heading a movement out to undermine the Congress regime, and my action was nothing but a calculated move, a gambit. That's what I tried to explain to her coterie. Some agreed. What I should worry about most, Ram Mohan, is the misgiving she might have about my motive. That's why somebody advised me to avoid the trap of going after personal popularity.'

'If she's really upset with you, then?'

'I'll have to go.'

Ram Mohan's eyes widened.

'And nobody can foretell the outcome of the ongoing volatility. Even JP, who's so enamoured of his own rhetoric, his blanket statements, even he has no idea what he wants to accomplish by all this. This way you can only have one regime supplanted by another. For any systemic change to happen, requires rigorous engagement with workable ideas and willingness for a long-drawn-out struggle. Desai thinks JP an utterly confused man. I'm glad you're safely ensconced in a place sheltered from this turmoil.'

* * *

The room Ram Mohan chose for himself in the Commission Bungalow was the one that would afford him a good vantage point for keeping an eye on his children. It had one door opening into the loggia at the back and the other into the room that had five doors, occupied by Kanti, Sandhya and Mayank. Deena had no fixed corner to himself. At first, Ram Mohan thought that his being in this room would ensure there wasn't much intermingling among his children. Later he realized its disadvantage. The room, being

the farthest from the main entrance, didn't allow him to monitor
the activities out front, in the area around the portico and the road
just outside. He wouldn't know if Nishant or Deena sneaked out
and met someone there. Even Kanti or Sandhya could tiptoe to
the other side for a quiet chat with Nishant, whose room was one
of the two on the left side of the narrow hallway. The first room
on the left was by the front door and had front and side windows,
facilitating a clear view outside.

Ram Mohan shifted to this room. Sandhya and Mayank got
the room he vacated. Their mother now had the room with five
doors to herself. No, not entirely. Most of the time, Deena also
hung out there and would repair to the dining area at any sign
of Baabuji approaching. They all, in that part of the house, were
pleased to acquire some physical distance from Baabuji and would
sometimes laugh at his attempt to keep them from each other's
company. Nishant once said, 'Does he think we stay the way he
thinks we should when he isn't around?'

'He knows that. And that it can't be helped,' said Kanti. 'He
can't afford to shun his own interests just to keep you all rooted to
your designated areas at home. He must go out and visit friends,
attend functions—'

'Baabuji won't forgo his own happiness merely to ensure
our unhappiness. That's something to take heart from,' remarked
Nishant. Everybody laughed. Nisha, who was there when this
conversation took place, laughed the loudest. Her visits were
frequent. After each fight with Shekhar, her husband, over his
smoking, she ran to the Commission Bungalow. Later, he would
come to buy peace, pledging to try and swear off the habit. Apart
from her concern about Shekhar's health, she couldn't stand his
breath laden with tobacco. Their quarrels made Sandhya, Deena
and Mayank wretched. Kanti would plead with her to avoid letting
their differences escalate into something so caustic it might lead to
them getting physical, as it indeed did sometimes.

Kanti also drew her mind to how pleasant and jovial they looked when not arguing. Yes, they all—Sandhya, Deena and Mayank—looked forward to Shekhar Jijaji's visits, who, being a kind of VIP, could talk to Baabuji on an equal footing and was exempted, like Mayank, from the usual curbs that stayed in place for others. He didn't have to alter his demeanour according to Baabuji's location in the house.

Then came a spell of jocundity between Nisha and Shekhar, due, perhaps, to the counsel of Kanti. They all luxuriated in the development. Nisha had eased off piling it on and would gently remind him of his promise to fight the urge to smoke, reducing the number of smokes a day, then quitting the damn thing altogether. What's more, he got some money from his elder brother in the village, and they decided to buy a scooter, a Bajaj at that, making them mobile as well as moving their station up a notch.

To own a Bajaj, the dream two-wheeler, would take donkey's years for an ordinary citizen. Even after making a booking, it would be a long time before your number came. If one had money, one could buy it in the flourishing black market at more than double its showroom price. Shekhar made enquiries and found a second-hand one in good condition, which, though four–five years old, would cost him more than the original price for a new one. Ram Mohan would have none of it. 'Just book a new Bajaj and I'll pass the details on to one of Saansad-ji's secretaries. He'll know how to get an out-of-turn delivery. Politicians and bureaucrats have all kinds of privileges to ensure they don't find themselves in the common man's shoes.' But the dealers of Bajaj scooter in Allahabad had exhausted their quotas of fresh bookings. It would be months for the process to restart.

'Leave it to me,' he said to Nisha and Shekhar. 'You both in the interim start learning how to drive a car. Nishant has learnt it . . . Scooter's fine to begin with, and it's a good job that you want a Bajaj, but in a few years, you should aim at owning a car.' He asked Zameer, his orderly-cum-driver, to start giving them driving lessons. Nisha and Shekhar were euphoric. If you could drive a car, it was something to flaunt, even if you didn't own one.

Nisha, in about three weeks, was able to drive and could now teach the skill to Shekhar who, apt to tense up at the wheel, sometimes mistook the gas pedal for the break. Once, making a left at a crossing, he put on a spurt, though he meant to slow down. The man he hit wasn't hurt, but his bicycle was damaged. Some passers-by were yelling. A traffic constable appeared and asked Shekhar to get out of the car. An enraged Nisha took over the scene with her ringing voice and robust delivery. 'You have the gall to speak to us like that! Do you know who we are?'

'Even if you were from the governor's family, should it matter? Would that give you licence to drive as you please? You almost crushed him,' said the constable, struggling to hold his own, pointing to the man who stood gripping the handle of his cycle, its front wheel badly bent. Nisha took the wheel herself as the protesting constable made a feeble attempt to stop her.

Ram Mohan blew a fuse. He had his PA, Jaan Mohammad, make some calls and find out about this madcap, the traffic constable. Nisha and Shekhar didn't know his name, but the hour and location of his deployment was enough for the traffic police chief's office to identify him. After being pulled up by his boss for his misplaced sense of duty, he was asked to go seek Ram Mohan's pardon. Shekhar and Nisha were present when he presented himself at the Commission Bungalow, wearing an apologetic look, and listened to Ram Mohan as he told him off. 'Do you have any idea of the importance of what members, Public Service Commission do?'

'Sahab, it was a mistake, I've come to apologize.'

'We're the people who select your bosses.' Then, as if pleased with the man's mien, Ram Mohan offered him tea as Jaan

Mohammad, the PA, undertook to flesh out some other attributes of his boss's personality.

'During my fifteen years at the Commission, I've seen some remarkable individuals. But none comes close to the calibre of Dr Sahab,' he waved a hand towards his boss. 'Linguist, scholar, poet, politician, orator, he's all of these and—'

'My village Parsadpur was recognized as the first model village by the state government.'

'Dr Sahab has authored a book on village development, a trenchant treatise on the subject!' The constable respectfully nodded. They all—Shekhar, Nisha and Nishant in the drawing room and Kanti, Sandhya and Deena at the dining table behind the curtain— loved every word Baabuji's PA mouthed. The most learned of all the personal assistants at the Commission, Jaan Muhammad had a master's in history and would have gone on to do a PhD if not for economic hardship. When a relation had offered to pull strings and get him a clerical position at the Commission, he couldn't decline. In time, his overall awareness of things and ability to write good English set him apart from his colleagues and helped him to join the ranks of personal assistants. Even there he was the pick of the bunch. Ram Mohan was proud as well as fond of Jaan Mohammad whose peculiar take on many a grand question would crack him up like nothing else. Jaan Mohammad had next to no regard for political correctness.

* * *

Before long, Shekhar would become the proud owner of a Bajaj. One of Saansad-ji's men in Lucknow made this happen. Some people booked these scooters as a long-term investment, using names of relations and friends, and kept getting deliveries throughout the year, making easy money in a booming black market for the most sought-after brand of two-wheelers. One such person was close to a local MLA who, on receiving word from Lucknow, asked him to forget the profit on one of his scooters. Thus, Shekhar got a new Bajaj without paying one rupee over its original price.

This was, as I've mentioned, a delightful period in their togetherness, Nisha and Shekhar. To keep his word, Shekhar was trying and had succeeded in reducing by half his daily smokes, and then, as if to crown this run of gaiety, Baabuji came up with an enticing idea, even at the risk of sounding a bit off the wall.

Shekhar's job at the Indian Telephone Industry (ITI) was one of the most agreeable ones for someone with his qualification. To quit it for the purpose of doing research to obtain another degree would commonly be seen as idiocy. But Shekhar and Nisha were taken with the idea. They couldn't have enough of the way Baabuji viewed the prospect of Shekhar doing a PhD at the Indian Institute of Technology (IIT) in Delhi, the national seat of power, which he thought was the only city in India worth coveting. The idea had a dreamy air to it. Something akin to going abroad—London, Paris, New York.

Armed with a PhD, Shekhar would more than likely find a teaching position at IIT Delhi itself or any of the other four IITs. It was settled then. Baabuji had Shekhar do a trip to the great city with no more dallying and arranged for him to stay at an MP's flat. At IIT, Shekhar met two professors of his subject, one of whom so impressed with his academic record he guaranteed him admission to a PhD programme with a monthly fellowship.

Now Shekhar spent much time at the Commission Bungalow. He had intimated the office of his plan. Deena, like everybody else, would love to have him around. Not only was his company fun—he told them stories from his childhood and anecdotes from his time at the engineering college and how he had overcome his jitteriness to ask his friends to help him with spoken English—his presence also moderated the fraught atmosphere caused by Baabuji being home. Then, he did something that shattered Deena's faith in his otherwise warm manner.

Till Shekhar tattled on him, the impression was that Baabuji's words had made an impact on Deena. 'This new phase in our life is an opportunity for you to leave all your previous tomfoolery behind, stealing money, not studying, not attending school. You can turn over a new leaf here.' But Deena had been drooling to resume his cinema-going in Allahabad. His being on the day shift in school and Mayank on the morning shift had advanced his cause really and truly. He could now indulge his passion for movies with no apparent danger of discovery.

Watching a noon show was in tune with his school timing, and Allahabad, being a much smaller city than Kanpur, its cinema halls posed no difficulty in terms of distance. It posed another kind of problem. Deena had to remain extra vigilant, as running across some family friend or acquaintance was more likely here. One day, he and his friends were cycling back to school after a noon show at The Palace in Civil Lines when Shekhar's new Bajaj, with Nisha riding pillion, overtook them and pulled up on the side of the road. Deena was stupefied. His friends turned tail.

He begged them not to tell Baabuji. Nisha held his hands and implored that he must mend his ways and become a good boy like Mayank. Deena was relieved, too relieved to notice the dour demeanour of the man still straddling his Bajaj. Later, Shekhar talked Nisha around that by not reporting it to Baabuji, they would encourage such failings in him. Later that day, Deena would get his first pounding in Allahabad.

* * *

These were the most tempestuous times in India. The movement led by JP raged unabated. Large crowds cheered him wherever he went. When a meeting between him and Indira Gandhi came to nought, she raised the spectre of foreign hand, outside forces out to get India. JP, in his speeches, urged government servants to defy their political bosses. Then something occurred that would take the movement to its height. Raj Narain, the oddball politician and Indira Gandhi's opponent in the previous general election, had taken her to court for electoral wrongdoings, seeking to have her election countermanded. Now, four years later, she had to appear in the High Court. A historic and proud moment for the people of Allahabad. That Indira Gandhi was forced to come to the High Court in their city to give evidence! The event occasioned the arrival of many VVIPs. Saansad-ji along with his ministers had come a day earlier to inspect the preparation for her visit. Nishant drove Ram Mohan to Saansad-ji's, but he had gone to the circuit house where the PM was to freshen up and rest before heading to the court.

The day after her appearance in the High Court, the city was abuzz with whatever could be learnt about the case from the local papers, with all titbits related to the PM's presence inside the court for about five hours. How and where she was seated, her comportment before the bench, the way the two counsels had sparred and all! This was also the day when Ram Mohan met three men who would become his closest friends. They were part of the group of eminent citizens attending the function held to felicitate Saansad-ji before his departure from the city They, these three personages, were impressed with the way the CM called Ram Mohan aside for a word.

Chaturvedi-ji and Sinha Sahab were criminal lawyers at the High Court and had long been friends, while Tandon ji, the third one, the most distinguished and the oldest of them, had been a freedom fighter, a journalist, also the author of several books based on his reminiscences about some famous people. He had done a long stint with the *National Herald*, thanks to his closeness to Nehru. Had also dabbled in politics and been minister of information in the Kamlapati Tripathi government in UP, but most worthy of note among his credentials was that he had taught Indira Gandhi how to ride a bicycle, something that, when mentioned by Sinha Sahab, grabbed Ram Mohan hook, line and sinker. Sinha Sahab's family had traditionally been attached to the Congress. His late father's closeness to the Nehru household was well known. Sinha Sahab was personally known to Mrs Gandhi, a fact that had drawn Chaturvedi-ji, a much more successful lawyer, to him.

From the function, Ram Mohan brought them straight to his place for a chat. Chaturvedi-ji and Sinha Sahab stayed on for dinner. Tandon-ji, who needed to finish an article, had to be dropped back home, but Ram Mohan sensed he wasn't quite comfortable in the company of the other two. A man of modern sensibility, Tandon-ji was a gentleman, courteous and cultivated. What was certain to get under his skin was people's tendency to talk through their hat.

Tandon-ji didn't approve of the way Sinha Sahab stormed against the JP Movement, imputing it to one man's frustration in life. He called JP names. 'Indira-ji's right. The bastard's playing the CIA's game. America wants to get rid of her Soviet-friendly regime, while JP's mad with political jealousy born of his own confusion and inability to identify a cause that would make him a Gandhi-like figure.'

Tandon-ji, too, was opposed to the JP Movement, to its leader's personalized politics and laughed about JP's goal—the total revolution. Nothing of enduring significance could be achieved through these methods. Rather than exhorting the state employees to rebel and students to give up their studies for a year and fight for something as horrendously amorphous as total revolution, JP should put his energies into forming a party and take Indira Gandhi on at the polls. But Sinha Sahab, Chaturvedi-ji and Ram Mohan were getting a buzz out of the drama of rapidly unfolding events, having little patience for the way Tandon-ji viewed them, the gravity of his opinion. After his departure, they had a roisterous conversation.

The case against Indira Gandhi per se didn't hold people's interest. The charges were so flimsy that the dismissal of Raj

Narayan's petition was just a formality. The most discussed thing
about the affair remained her court appearance, not the case. About
three months later, the unimaginable happened. Allahabad High
Court invalidated Indira Gandhi's election, pronouncing her guilty
of unfair means in the conduct of her campaign in Raebareli.

Legal experts held that she was convicted on mere
technicalities. Even the vacation bench of the Supreme Court,
which she petitioned against the High Court decision, gave her
partial relief. She could remain PM and attend Parliament but
was forbidden to vote or receive salary as an MP, pending a final
judgement on her appeal.

Ram Mohan could gleefully behold, from the safety of his
position at the Commission, all the political tumult that wasn't
without threat of violence. The year had begun with the violent
death of Mrs Gandhi's railway minister, Lalit Narayan Mishra, one
of her closest acolytes and the most corrupt among her men, who
had, for years, kept her party's coffers topped up. He was killed in
a bomb blast. About two and a half months later, an attempt was
made on the life of India's Chief Justice. The hand grenade thrown
at his car had failed to go off. Justice Ray had been hand-picked by
Indira Gandhi to take the helm of the Supreme Court, passing over
three judges, leading to their resignations.

'Nobody had the remotest idea that an appeal such as the one
filed by this clown Raj Narayan would be upheld by the High
Court. Look at the charges against her! A bunch of frivolities,'
fulminated Tandon-ji to whose house Nishant had driven his
father. The Supreme Court's conditional stay of the Allahabad
High Court's order was the shot in the arm for the JP movement.
The opposition parties became more strident in their demand for
the PM's resignation, resorting to rallies, picketing and gheraos
in the coming weeks. JP and his followers vowed to stop the
government from functioning, bringing the nation to a halt. The
day after the SC ruling, JP was to address a big rally in Delhi and

issue an ultimatum to Indira Gandhi that if she failed to resign in four days, they would embark on making all their threats good.

'Look where Justice Jagmohan has got us with his one reckless judgement, opening the floodgates to further disorder.'

'But the Supreme Court could have set it right by staying his verdict,' said Ram Mohan, 'staying it unqualifiedly till the time its full bench deliberated on the matter. After all, the allegations of electoral malpractice against her lack in substance. Didn't she have the final court of appeal at her beck and call?'

Tandon-ji laughed, 'That's the ideal they've been working for, she and her adherents. Remember the uproar when she had Justice Ray elevated to the top, disregarding the seniority of three judges? She was denounced for her attempt to emasculate the judiciary and make it compliant with her wishes.'

'I wonder at the audacity of these mere judges! They have the face to go head-to-head against the PM.'

Tandon-ji smiled and said, 'It'll help her if she has the Lok Sabha dissolved and seeks a fresh mandate.'

'It doesn't augur badly for Saansad-ji, does it? All this political turbulence!'

'Oh, I forgot, I was talking to a journalist friend from my *National Herald* days, who's close to some Congress leaders. Saansad-ji's in trouble. He's going to get his marching orders. The reason? He's been trying to build a political base of his own, using the position he owes to Indira-ji.'

'He'll go back to the Union Cabinet, if Indira-ji can ride out the present crisis.'

'You don't get it. He's no longer in good odour with her. It's curtains for him.'

Ram Mohan gazed at Tandon-ji before sighing and saying, 'At least I have full five years at the Commission.'

'You're lucky to have escaped the current rumpus.' Ram Mohan nodded and rose to take his leave. As they walked towards the gate of Tandon-ji's snug little bungalow, the latter put his arm around Nishant, 'What do you want to do after your MA in English?'

'LLB,' straight off came the reply.

'You want to become a lawyer! What place could be better than Allahabad for that?' said Tandon-ji, impressed at the young man's clarity of purpose. His father was taken by surprise.

'I thought you wanted to pursue English, given your passion for it. If you wanted to study law, where was the need to do an MA? You could have done your LLB after BA.'

Chuckling, Tandon-ji said, without taking his eyes off Nishant, 'I know what enkindled his interest in law . . . Didn't the idea occur to you after all this drama surrounding the case against Indira-ji, the way this profession has become the centre of attention of late?' Nishant smiled. He neither confirmed nor denied the veracity of Tandon-ji's surmise.

* * *

The day after the SC's conditional stay of the HC verdict, Indira Gandhi had the country placed under a state of emergency. The measure was warranted as 'internal disturbances' presented a danger to India's democracy. It was the day when JP was slated to address a rally in Delhi, to instigate the police and the armed forces to mutiny. In the small hours of the following day, all opposition leaders were put in jail. Press censorship came in force. The idea of the 'foreign hand' would gain ground.

'If I were still with Chaudhary Sahab, I'd be in jail, not sitting here, enjoying the spectacle from a beautiful distance,' said Ram Mohan to Sinha Sahab and Chaturvedi-ji who had called in for a chat.

'With the JP movement decapitated and opposition leaders behind bars, that spectacle's history now,' said Chaturvedi-ji. 'No more agitations, rallies, slogan-shouting, nothing of the sort. This is the perfect moment for Congress workers, government servants and people close to the party to have a ball.'

'Especially for people linked with institutions as esteemed as the Public Service Commission. These are the best times to enjoy life, Dr Sahab,' said Sinha Sahab, his eyes twinkling cryptically. Chaturvedi-ji squirmed in his seat to remind his friend of the presence of Nishant and Deena. Ram Mohan sneaked a glance towards his sons.

Assuming a look of sobriety, Sinha Sahab went on, 'Those saddled with the task of enforcing the provisions of Emergency might feel a bit pressured, but—'

'No, all these people have become a lot more powerful,' Chaturvedi-ji put his oar in, 'they have the common man at their mercy now. No one's there to question their actions. In the name of implementing government policies, they can get away with anything. The only thing left to the public is to lump it.'

'No need to be so earnest,' said Sinha Sahab irritably. 'I'm talking about us and Dr Sahab, not the masses. What I was trying to say is that those involved in the day-to-day administration might feel stretched, but not the VIPs like Dr Sahab, who can just sit back and savour their position. Just look at the positive side of what the Emergency can mean even to the common man. It's only three or four days and there are signs already of things changing for the better. I hear trains have started running on schedule. Situation on the law-and-order front has improved. The Maintenance of Internal Security Act (MISA), passed by Parliament a few years ago, is now the most effective weapon in her administration's hand.'

'Yes, MISA will be—'

'And no grounds are needed to make arrests under this Act,' said Sinha Sahab. 'I can't praise enough the way she broke the railway strike, using this law. That's beside the point. What I was saying was that VIPs like our Dr Sahab can now, with no political racket, indulge his other hobby horses.'

'I've nothing to do with active politics while here, so it doesn't affect me in the manner that I can be kept from my other interests! People like JP, Desai or Baran Singh being in jail is of little consequence to me. I'm thankful for not being out there with them.'

'I know what Sinha Sahab means,' Chaturvedi-ji said, grinning broadly. 'He said to me months before the Emergency, "I wonder how Doctor Sahab must feel when the clash as intense as the one between Indira Gandhi and JP has reached the point of no return." He thought you must miss all that.'

'That's right,' cried Sinha Sahab, 'and now with the Emergency pulling the plug on all political activity, you must feel free, if a bit perversely, of any sense of deprivation on that account.'

'And can enjoy life with no political itch in the way,' said Chaturvedi-ji.

'That's probably right,' said Ram Mohan. 'It was hard to think of anything else in the midst of all that drama outside, and I can't say for sure if I didn't miss being part of it,' he paused and continued, 'I haven't been able to tend to my literary interests of late. Now is the time for that. My job at the Commission allows me lots of free time. I don't even have to write letters myself, physically I mean. I dictate them to Jaan Mohammad. So, yes, with all this free time and no other distractions because of this political quiescence, I can turn my mind to reading and writing, to attending literary gatherings.'

'That's what I meant,' said Sinha Sahab.

'Sometimes the death of possibility does you much good, the death of the possibility of things you have desired in vain. It relieves you of the need to struggle, relieves you of the pain of not being able to make sufficient effort.'

'And you can give your mind to things still obtainable,' said Sinha Sahab.

I would quote Deena from one of his notebooks: *What Sinha Uncle had in mind when he said, 'These are the best times to enjoy life,'— which made Chaturvedi Uncle shift in his seat—had nothing to do with the meaning they hastened to give to the remark unguardedly made in front of Nishant and me. I was to discover later, the precise nature of enjoyment Sinha Uncle may have suggested.*

It so happened that one day Baabuji went with them somewhere in the city and on returning, their manner spoke of an unusual hilarity. Over tea and snacks they kept chuckling and chatting in the drawing room. I was sitting at the dining table behind the curtain. To eavesdrop on Baabuji and his visitors was usual for me. Sometimes, others too would avail of the opportunity, but mostly it was I who, on hearing anything interesting, would broadcast it to everybody else. Yet that evening, what I learnt wasn't something I could share with anybody.

Their tone was lower, but they giggled loudly. I got the drift of their conversation. It was some woman they had met, who was into singing or dancing and had an inflated notion of her facility for Urdu poetry. She could render a raft of couplets from memory. I surmised she was someone fetching, maybe someone belonging to the fast-dwindling breed of courtesans whom I often came across in Hindi films. When Chaturvedi Uncle, apparently an old admirer of her charms, pitted his friend's stock of Urdu couplets against hers, she affected to be offended. She had yet to meet someone who could get the better of her cache of couplets. That was her proud boast.

But she met more than her match in Baabuji. Awed, she asked, was there anything she could do to show her admiration? And prompt he asked for a kiss. To a teenager like me, such people, people capable of behaviour like this, outlandish and wacky, existed only in films as villainous characters. Is that what Sinha Uncle had meant by 'enjoying life'?

'This position couldn't have come to me if I hadn't been politically active,' went on Ram Mohan, 'but now, active politics doesn't interest me. Given my familial responsibility, I don't want to look for an electoral adventure anytime soon, not till I've fixed each of my children with employment.'

'They'll turn out fine,' said Sinha Sahab.

'You don't have to worry about Deena and Mayank. It's too early for that,' added Chaturvedi-ji.

'Mayank won't need my help. He can achieve whatever he sets his sights on. I'm concerned about Deena. He's indifferent to the importance of passing exams.'

Deena had flunked in his tenth board. He had worked hard to prepare rolls of cheating material in advance, which sadly, had gone to waste, most of it, thanks to the watchful invigilators. He couldn't crib the answers beyond a few lines to each of the three or four questions he had managed to attempt.

'Even I, with all my influence, can't get him a job, if he doesn't get these certificates, tenth, twelfth and BA. He needs to get through these exams. I can take care of the rest.'

'I wonder about his aversion to whatever little effort that's needed to pass these silly exams,' said Sinha Sahab.

'I wasn't a good student either. My friends performed better in exams. But unlike Deena, I forced myself to make an endeavour to clear my exams. I knew if I failed to find myself a situation in the city, I'd have to go back to my village and settle for a career as a farmer.'

'Times have changed Dr Sahab,' said Sinha Sahab. 'It's much easier now, for someone with your clout, to find a way to get round the rule-bound manner of realizing ends. There must be a way to see to Deena's success in his exams.' That set off Ram Mohan thinking as Chaturvedi-ji and Singh Sahab took their leave.

* * *

With Shekhar pursuing his PhD in Delhi, Nisha was staying at the Commission Bungalow. She had scarcely passed her MA first year in Hindi. Ram Mohan was alarmed. If she didn't do better in her final year, a third division was all that lay in store. Maybe worse!

With a few marks less than what she got in the first year, it would be all over. The prospect of her flunking out of the university was real. Ram Mohan decided to go in for some remedial course of action.

Though in terminal decline, Allahabad University had still left in its faculty scholars, just a few of them, reminiscent of what had once earned it the epithet 'Oxford of the East'. The Hindi Department, too, had a representative sample of this soon-to-be-extinct species. Ram Mohan knew them all and they him. His work on the poet-saint, Saalik, occupied a place of importance in the world of Hindi scholarship. To manipulate these Hindi professors into helping Nisha shouldn't be all that hard now that he also held this position at the Commission.

He learnt from his sources about the make-up of the two main camps in the Hindi Department, vying for getting the upper hand. The idea was to work on those who counted in their respective groups and one by one, he began to invite them over for a literary chat. They were appreciative of his gesture, and he found these interactions entertaining, as none of the professors belonging to the fading tradition of Hindi scholarship had trouble opening out to him. Yet, while getting to hear all the gossip related to their department, he sensed he had to tread cautiously, given their entrenched rivalries.

During one such meeting he learnt about Nisha's growing closeness to this woman, Dr Moon Aggarwal, a faculty member and an adherent of the professor who led the rival camp. Ram Mohan was perturbed. He had a word with Nisha.

'How hard I'm trying to make sure you pass your MA with at least a second division! Why did you have to get in the way of my dealing with the issue?'

'What did I do?'

Why then this woman . . . What's her name? This Aggarwal lady.'

'Dr Moon Aggarwal!'

'Yes, Dr Moon Aggarwal,' he paused. 'Why do you think she's suddenly showing interest in you?

She knew who Baabuji's source was. Deena had told her about the visitor.

'Suddenly? She's been kind to me from the start.'

'But surely, she'd have known who your father is!

'No. What first drew her attention was that I'm married. She herself did her MA after marriage and went on to do a PhD. That's how we began talking more and more. Then, because of my Hindi pronunciation, she became curious about my family background. She said she seldom found people who spoke Hindi so elegantly. When I told her about you, she was more impressed by your literary attainments than the Commission.'

'Yet I suspect she'd have found out about my being a Commission member, before singling you out for special attention. That's fine if she can help you do well in MA final . . . What kept her from helping you in the first year?'

'She didn't know I'd do so badly in the exams.' Nisha tittered.

'I leave it to you then to see that nothing goes wrong this time. You shouldn't just pass in MA final but pass with a second division.'

Presently, Dr Moon and Nisha grew close. They also talked on the phone. It was the former who had started making calls, prompting Baabuji to declare that his suspicion held good after all. She was trying to be friends with the family of a Commission member. Nisha wished Moon Auntie wouldn't call when Baabuji was home but didn't know how to tell her. How to tell what kind of a creature their father was? That he was hostile to them being called upon or visited by their friends or relations. Nisha had become an exception after her marriage. Not that he approved of her enjoying these liberties. His behaviour would change in line with his cognizance of the limit to which he could go to impose his wish. It didn't take Moon Auntie long to sense there was something peculiar about the relationship between Ram Mohan and his children. Because of her fondness for Nisha, she thought it fit to make his acquaintance and have him over some time.

One Saturday, Moon Auntie called and wished to speak to him. Looking good-humoured, he announced afterwards, 'Dr Moon has finally invited me, all of us, to lunch tomorrow.' His emphasis on 'finally' wasn't lost on Nisha.

Ram Mohan took Kanti, Nisha, and Mayank to Moon Auntie's place. Deena, to his dismay, was ignored. Sandhya didn't mind being left alone, while Nishant kept aloof from such occasions. Plus, the thought of descending together on the house of Moon Auntie, whose own family comprised just three, was embarrassing. On their return, Nisha and Mayank recounted what a nice little bungalow Moon Auntie's family lived in, which had two small lawns, one at the front and the other at the back, a well-tended garden studded with flower beds, and trees of guava and shahtoot (mulberry). What impressed them the most was its elegantly organized interior. Even their daughter's room was so neat. Shampa was about the same age as Deena, who, listening to Nisha's account, was left smitten. He pictured her as a young graceful beauty.

Yet there was something in Nisha's description of Shampa's room that made Deena despair. Beside her bed stood a bookcase, each shelf filled with novels by children's authors. It was intimidating that someone of her age read fiction in English. Even the titles of such books, to him, were no more than randomly collected letters of the English alphabet. Not only was she a devourer of English story books but was one of the brightest students in her class at St Mary's Convent. Adding fuel to the flames of his anxiety, Nisha didi mentioned that she was the same vivacious girl who presented *Baalsang,* a popular radio programme for children, broadcast live every Sunday morning from AIR Allahabad. A renowned announcer was her co-host.

That meant they all would have heard her on radio. Deena was charged with a yearning to lay eyes on her.

Nisha's visits to Moon Auntie's place became a regular affair. Once when Baabuji went out of town, she took them along, Sandhya, Deena and Mayank, and Deena found the mental image he had of Shampa quite close to the real thing. She was confident, full of verve; she was curvaceous with a tiny waist that accentuated her seductively rounded derrière. But her assiduous avoidance of looking at him would soon fill him with a sense of desolation. He shared it with his best friend in school, whose precocious expositions of things were lapped up by him. This friend-cum-philosopher put down Shampa's behaviour to her being shy with him. 'She finds you attractive. That's what it means. She's too conscious of her feelings to openly look at you. Yet she would have seen you more than you saw her. It's just that she didn't want to be caught.' He related a similar experience he had had. The girl he thought was indifferent to his fervid glances would later write a love letter to him.

In time, Sandhya and Deena and Mayank became struck on their visits to Moon Auntie. Just being at her place soaking up its free and friendly atmosphere was such a pleasure, not to mention the warmth of her hospitality. Shampa continued in her apparent lack of interest in Deena. He played it cool after his friend's explanation. Then one day, he got a chance to impress her. It was the time when *Sholay* was the talk of the town, and Shekhar, during a trip to Allahabad, had taken them to see it. Deena could afterwards reproduce many of the dialogues delivered by Gabbar Singh, a diabolical character with mannerisms that would make him the most talked-of baddie of Hindi films. Everybody marvelled at Deena's memory, unaware that he had seen it several times during school hours. What amazed them was his ability to imitate, an ability of which they had had no inkling

When told, Moon Auntie said she wouldn't believe till she saw it. He dithered. Shampa was watching her mother, then tried to steal a look at him and was caught. For the first time, he espied in her manner, a shimmer of interest or curiosity or whatever it was, some favourable emotion, a twinkle of it. He got up and enacted all his favourite sequences from *Sholay*, featuring Gabbar Singh. Everybody laughed. Shampa whispered something in her mother's ear and just as he sat down, Moon Auntie said she wanted Deena and Mayank to be part of a live audience of 10–12 children in the AIR studio for the programme *Baalsang*, towards the end of which, they would be asked one by one to render something into the microphone in the way of a joke or a poem or whatever.

'Deena should start taking part in plays, and in a few years, he can seek entrance to the National School of Drama in Delhi,' said Moon Auntie's husband, a government advocate at the High Court, a very jovial fellow. Shampa studied her father, who wouldn't advance an opinion unless he meant it. Deena was in seventh heaven.

On Sunday, Nisha took them to the AIR station. Shampa explained how the programme was done, looking at Mayank, avoiding Deena's gaze.

It all went well. Shampa's silvery laugh was all that Deena could hear when he told a joke in front of the mic. Mayank had memorized a Hindi poem for the programme. In the corridor outside the studio stood Moon Auntie and Nisha didi, their faces full of praise.

As they approached the Commission compound—Moon Auntie was dropping them off—Nisha noticed Deena turn grim. He was in the grip of that familiar sinking feeling, the same as he had while leaving a cinema hall. Though Baabuji had given his consent for *Baalsang*, thanks to Mayank, Deena was filled with dread.

Nisha insisted on being dropped at the compound gate but Moon Auntie, innocent of the reason for her pleas, drove straight through the gate. Now Nisha had to guide the Fiat to their bungalow. She desperately wished they wouldn't run into Baabuji. That wasn't to be. Just as Nisha and Deena were getting out of the car, he emerged in the portico and walked over to them. He had heard and glimpsed the Fiat through the window of his room. Moon Auntie and Shampa also climbed out. Seeing the latter, Ram Mohan lost some of his exuberance, something noticed fearfully by Deena and Nisha. She hadn't told him that Shampa was the co-presenter of the programme. He invited them, a bit lukewarmly, to come in and have tea. Moon Auntie declined. She was expecting guests at home. Deena braced himself for something nasty to happen.

Soon Ram Mohan sauntered into Kanti's room and sat down on the bed in the middle. Nisha, Sandhya and Mayank were in the adjacent room. Kanti, who was on the veranda outside the kitchen, hurried in. 'Deena!' he yelled. My friend, who sat at the dining table, his usual place of refuge from being seen by Baabuji, lurched to his feet. 'Come fast,' Ram Mohan bellowed. Deena hastened, his insides throbbing with fright. Nisha, who had steeled herself for something like that, also appeared.

'You don't want to pass your tenth board ever?' Deena was shaking. 'How to make you realize the importance of these certificates?', then turning to Kanti, 'Have you ever thought about what he'll do in life? Isn't it your responsibility too, to see that—'

'I always tell him to study. He wouldn't listen.'

'He listens to me.'

'Yes, you find him gawping at some textbook of his when he's not kneading your legs or serving tea to your visitors! That's a sham. That's because he's scared of you.'

'Even that's better than him being up to some mischief, a capital discipline for learning to sit quietly at one place. The best way to put him to rights is not to put temptation in his way.'

'What temptation?'

'Don't put it on; you know what I mean,' Kanti thought better of responding.

Nisha stood quietly in the doorway. He gave her a black look. 'I wonder why you took Deena to the AIR. These distractions keep him from his textbooks. You've no notion of how serious the problem has become. If he goes on like this, he'll end up being a labourer.'

'Keeping him home is the solution! That's how he can be made to pay mind to his studies!'

'You had better mind your own married life and let me handle things here, my way. Look at your own scholastic record! And you're going to top it off with a dazzling performance in MA final.'

'I'll pass my MA with good marks.'

'Don't be too assured of Dr Moon's help. Let's see what happens once she senses the futility of her aim to become entitled to my attention . . . Through her professed concern for you!'

'She'll cease to exist for me the day I learn of any such intent on her part . . . Had you not agreed to my taking Deena and Mayank for *Baalsang*?'

'Such a schmuck! Can there be any comparison between the two? Mayank's bound to do us proud one day while Deena's set on bringing shame on the family. Shouldn't you yourself have thought better of taking him along, the weed!' Ram Mohan looked around before calling out, 'Where's he?' Deena, who had hurried back to the dining table, returned, pale and distressed. Ram Mohan grabbed him by the neck and snarled, 'I know why you're so eager to be with this Moon and her daughter.' Then, noticing Deena's thick, curly hair, now disarranged with a lock flung over his left eye, he ordered Sandhya, who sat petrified in the next room to get him scissors. Shortly, a head blessed with such luxuriance lay reduced to its ugliest look possible.

* * *

Ram Mohan shouted that from then on, Deena wasn't to be taken to Dr Moon's. Looking in the mirror, Deena felt numb with a sense of estrangement from the thought of Shampa, and the thought of going to school in this state mortified him. He announced with devil-may-care finality that he wouldn't step out of the house till his former look was restored. Ram Mohan sent for the blackguard but seeing him, his anger gave way to remorse. He asked Nishant to take him to a barber.

Even the barber couldn't put the mutilation out of sight. 'His hair's hacked too badly to be tractable.' Deena remained in a wretched state of mind the whole week. Whoever saw him would look intrigued. Only petty criminals were known to receive such treatment at the hands of either the police or the public, something unthinkable in Deena's case. It had to be his father.

TWO

Three months into the Emergency. The rains all but gone. Ram Mohan gets a call from Lucknow. The CM wanted to have a natter over tea with the members of the Commission during his forthcoming visit. Ram Mohan, on his own initiative, began meeting fellow members to discuss things to be raised with the CM, things for the sake of the greater efficiency of the Commission.

On learning that the CM's office was being selective about whom to invite to tea, he cried in righteous anger, 'What are these people playing at?' He was at the house of the member who hadn't got a call from Lucknow but was the one he was most friendly with. They both had a political background and were once close to Baran Singh. Mr Indrajit, too, had an aversion to making money though dishonest means. While Ram Mohan made great play of his hatred for bribery, Mr Indrajit wasn't so strident. He would rather have others talk about his uprightness. But Kanti believed that her husband's warmth towards Mr Indrajit stemmed from something else. That he fancied Mr Indrajit's wife, his second wife, over twenty-five years his junior.

Members invited to tea with Saansad-ji happened to be only those appointed by him. Whether the omission of Mr Indrajit

and two others was intentional was hard to say, but it gave Ram
Mohan the opportunity for some grandstanding, some drama, to
help him take on the role of their leader, to achieve pre-eminence
at the Commission. It would also furnish him with something
to brandish, in the face of attempts to paint him as Saansad-ji's
loyalist, to wreck his chances of currying favour with Indira-ji.
That Saansad-ji had got on the wrong side of the PM was preying
on Ram Mohan's mind. He wasn't eying any political office but
something like his present position, though more notable: the
Union Public Service Commission in Delhi that selected officers
for all-India civil services.

Ram Mohan decried the selective invitation to tea with
the CM as 'a brazen attempt to undermine the integrity of the
Commission'. To help his colleagues see the light, Ram Mohan
hinted at Saansad-ji's precarious political future and got them—
except the chairman and Munni Prasad, both Saansad-ji's
appointees—to sign the letter that explained why the members
had to decline the invitation. Saansad-ji called off the meeting but
not before the letter, leaked to the press, was splashed across the
front pages of all the three local dailies.

Chaturvedi-ji and Sinha Sahab applauded Ram Mohan.
Nothing could be more emphatic to scotch the perception of his
being Saansad-ji's adherent. The only person taking a dim view
of Ram Mohan's stance was Tandon-ji. Saansad-ji couldn't have
been behind such a horrid idea! Ram Mohan should have told him
about it before adopting the posture he did, seizing the high moral
ground. Ram Mohan, Chaturvedi-ji and Sinha Sahab laughed up
their sleeves at Tandon-ji. 'He has little understanding of realpolitik.'

A few days later, one of Saansad-ji's ministers telephoned the
Commission Bungalow to regret that Ram Mohan didn't bother to
inform the CM of the bungle perpetrated without his knowledge.
Some bureaucrats in the CM's secretariat might be in league with
certain personages in Delhi.

'Saansad-ji's on the slippery slope, no two ways about that!' said Ram Mohan to Nishant, after that call. Yet he couldn't help feeling a twinge of remorse. If not for Saansad-ji, the man subjected to such a slight at his hands, he would be leading a limited life in Kanpur, teaching Hindi literature at DAV College. On Tandon-ji's advice, he went to see Saansad-ji's wife, who mostly stayed in Allahabad, nurturing her husband's constituency as well as serving as the elected president of a local body. She was courteous, though vexed. She heard him out. He expressed his regret at allowing himself to be taken for a ride by some of his crafty colleagues. She said, 'He was hurt and wondered if you were looking to distance yourself from him. You should meet Saansad-ji.'

That wasn't to be. In a sudden development, Saansad-ji made a dash to Delhi and sought an audience with the PM. That she couldn't spare a few minutes for him was lost on no one. She couldn't be more explicit. Saansad-ji had no desire to sweet-talk her into changing her mind but wanted to present his side of the story. Finally, he resigned. When he came to Allahabad to spend some time with his family before looking at whatever political options he had left, Ram Mohan met him and apologized for being so naive as to go along with his fellow members' decision. 'Had I known it would be passed on to the press, I'd have backed out.' That he sought to apologize even after Indira Gandhi had cast Saansad-ji aside, signalling his political wilderness, was enough to restore the latter's trust in Ram Mohan.

The man succeeding Saansad-ji as CM was none other than Shukla-ji, who had known that whenever there was a vacancy, he would be in the reckoning. Still, given the fact that among the probable, there were two men more illustrious than him, he couldn't be sure of being the pick, his Uncle's influence in Delhi notwithstanding. Yet he swung it. Not for nothing had he been sucking up to Indira-ji's heir apparent, Sanjay Gandhi, whose only

source of power was his mother but for all practical purposes, he
was more powerful than her.

He held that to make Indians get their act together warranted
a decisive leadership. With sceptics, he had little patience. That he
had his mother's blessings to his bossing everybody was learnt the
hard way by a cabinet minister, who had the gall to decline to take
orders from him, resulting in his being divested of the Ministry of
Information and Broadcasting, a job that required someone with
no qualms about the gagging of the press. Saansad-ji had run afoul
of the young man too. Despite all her distrust of Saansad-ji's style
of functioning, Indira-ji might have given him some more time
and more time to herself to know for sure he was up to something
she wouldn't endorse. Sanjay would have none of it, none of his
mother's propensity for being troubled by occasional doubt.

Yet to be thirty, he was a man in a hurry and would let
nothing get in his way of getting things done. Political propriety
was a luxury the country could ill-afford, sticklers for which
would rattle his cage. Anyone reluctant to fall in with his ideas
was a liability. Sanjay wanted to jolt his countrymen out of their
lethargy, their indifference to problems impeding their own cause,
problems threatening to sink India's prospects of ever getting out
of the mire, problems he had singled out for being tackled head-
on: problems of overpopulation, indiscipline, squalor and so forth.
He demanded that people associated with his mother's regime get
down to business like never before.

Ram Mohan's image of the youth leader, till then, was that
of a spoilt brat, a rogue, part of whose idea of fun had once been
to steal cars in Delhi, his and of the son of Muhammad Yunus, a
close henchman of his mother. While studying in London, Sanjay
Gandhi was picked up several times for flouting traffic rules.
Tandon-ji told Ram Mohan that for a person of his background,
Sanjay was hardly educated. A car enthusiast, he had joined an
iconic automaker in England as a trainee but didn't finish the

programme and returned with the dream of setting up a car manufacturing company in India. He wanted to produce a purely Indian vehicle, small and low-priced. To help him in the venture, his mother's administration had gone out on a limb, winking at all rules and objections. He was given land almost for free by the bootlicker CM of a neighbouring state.

As it turned out, nothing would come out of the effort. The project was still just a name, Maruti, when Sanjay moved from his ambition of car-building to that of nation-building. Maruti would become a reality but only after his death, a few years into that, though nothing would be Indian about it, save the name, of course. Every single part of it would be manufactured in Japan.

What changed Ram Mohan's perception of him was the kind of power he came to wield during Emergency. He was impressed by the way everybody, regardless of their position, truckled to him. Ram Mohan often had a friendly exchange with Tandon-ji, who frowned on Sanjay's high-handed approach to the question of India's enduring distress. 'The speed with which he wants to accomplish things is unsettling, this obsessive pursuit of his hare-brained plans!' But that's what Ram Mohan found so attractive. 'I see nothing wrong in his resolve to take India forward.'

Tandon-ji argued that whatever Sanjay tried to do, before getting into politics, had fallen flat. 'God knows what else he did in London besides not studying, and mind you, he was no less single-minded about his Maruti project,' Tandon-ji stopped as if something had occurred to him. 'But then, whatever we know about Sanjay and his behaviour, his way of doing things and all, most of it can just be idle talk! Who knows? Sanjay has never elaborated on his plans for the country in public. He never speaks to the press. He's a shy person. The other day I was talking to an old acquaintance who's in and out of 1, Safdarjung Road; he told me that Sanjay had nothing to do with the imposition of Emergency. It was Siddharth Shankar Ray's idea, backed by the

likes of Barua and Pant. Sanjay wanted his mother to hand over the
job to Jagjivan Ram, till the Supreme Court gave its verdict on her
appeal. Ray and others convinced her that once Ram got her chair,
she wouldn't get it back.'

What mattered to Ram Mohan was that Sanjay was the most
powerful figure in the country. His mind was busy trying to think
out a way to approach him. Just one faint nod from him would
be enough to have him settled in Delhi as Member, Union Public
Service Commission. He sent for Tiwari-ji.

* * *

Ram Mohan's absence from the arena of active politics had enabled
Tiwari-ji to stay in his village for extended periods. Just once had
he been to the Commission Bungalow. That Ram Mohan needed
his counsel on something crucial, electrified him. He set out with
Zameer, who was sent to fetch him.

Together, he and Ram Mohan cast about for a way to meet
Sanjay. Ram Mohan needed just a few minutes to make their
meeting stick in the young leader's mind. The only man they knew
among the Congress politicians who could make this meeting happen
was Shukla-ji. Ram Mohan had sent him his greetings after he had
taken up the reins of the state but had received just a formal reply,
exploding his hope that Shukla-ji would add a few words in his
own handwriting to the brief-typed text of his letter of thanks. To
keep brooding on it was self-defeating. 'Shukla-ji can't be faulted.
I'd made my choice clear by throwing in my lot with Baran Singh.'

'It was Shukla-ji who had introduced you to him in the first
place,' said Tiwari-ji.

'He did it for my sake. Baran Singh was a much bigger name
in the state Congress and in a better position to help. It was I who
chose to remain with Chaudhary Sahab, even after he turned his
back on the Congress, to carve his own political territory.'

'Shukla-ji thought it made better sense for you to be with Chaudhary Sahab, a non-Brahman leader, one of the very few in the Congress, who was also known to have farmers' interests uppermost in his mind.'

'Yes, and that was kind of Shukla-ji, because my being with Chaudhary Sahab at the time was full of promise, for the reason you mention. But who would have thought he would leave the party and I'd tag along?'

'That's how it's supposed to be. Being close to someone means you'd stick up for them. That wouldn't have irked Shukla-ji. Even if you'd stayed on in the Congress, Shukla-ji would have been hard pressed to help you, hard pressed because of your caste. How could a prominent Brahman leader afford to be seen promoting someone like you? That's possible only at some risk to his own standing among his people, the Brahmans, who have had a proprietorial grip on the Congress.'

'What about Harijans and Muslims—the other two major constituents of its huge political base?'

'Brahmans don't mind putting up with Harijans and Muslims, whose support's vital to the Congress. Shukla-ji wouldn't lose face by helping advance the political career of his myrmidon Liyaqat Argali who's an MLA because of him, and going by the buzz, he'll soon become a minister. By promoting certain persons from these two main vote banks, Congress leaders look to help their own as well as the party's cause.'

'You're not suggesting that my idea of approaching Shukla-ji for help is pointless?'

'Not in the least! I just wish to dismiss your notion that Shukla-ji might have felt betrayed when you'd walked out of the Congress.

Tiwari-ji stopped, as if he had lost the thread, then going on, 'My point is that Shukla-ji would have been loath to have you on his hands for the simple reason that you belong to a caste that has little significance to the Congress that boasts three major vote banks. On top of that, Baran Singh had already taken the farmers' fancy.'

'Saansad-ji, too, is a Brahman, who'd almost got me nominated to the Rajya Sabha.'

'Saansad-ji can't be compared with the likes of Shukla-ji or his Uncle. He's different from the general run of politicos. Certain things, he wouldn't give up. Would resist to the last any pressure to compromise them. I think it's a good idea. Let's try and meet Shukla-ji and see how it goes. Since we're not looking for anything political, he might be of help. Even if he's hesitant to let you meet Sanjay Gandhi, he himself can recommend you for this Commission in Delhi.'

The day they reached Lucknow, Shukla-ji met the Governor to discuss the expansion of his cabinet, leave for which had been granted, but due to Sanjay Gandhi's tour of the state, the swearing-in of new ministers was to be put off. Shukla-ji had his hands full. They couldn't get an appointment.

While in Lucknow, they met some of Ram Mohan's old acquaintances, one of whom had previously been a minister but tagged as Saansad-ji's man, he had no chance of making it to Shukla-ji's cabinet. It was he who confirmed that Argali was on the list of those to be sworn in as ministers.

'It's time we stopped resenting Argali's success,' said Ram Mohan to Tiwari-ji. The next morning, they went to see him. Surrounded by his supporters, he received them warmly and after the usual civilities, Ram Mohan put both his hands on Argali's shoulders and said, his voice laced with emotion, 'Kindly allow me to confess that Tiwari-ji and I had no inkling of you making such a capital politician. Not many in UP can match you at electoral politics. That's a fact of which I became aware a bit late in the day.'

Argali was moved. He embraced Ram Mohan before signalling everybody to sit down. His men beamed. He said, casting a glance about him, 'Your words embarrass me Dr Sahab. Few would be comfortable contesting against you in Fatehpur. Whether you run as an independent or on some party's ticket, the fear you invoke in your rival's mind remains the same.'

'Yet the fact is, I've yet to win an election and you've yet to lose one.' Argali groped for something gracious to say as Ram Mohan pressed on, 'I've had enough of active politics, Liyaqat bhai. It's not that my ardour for electoral battle has waned. It's only that I'm fed up with giving a good fight to the winning opponent.' There was a burst of laughter in Argali's room at the MLAs' quarters.

'If a person of your calibre becomes exasperated with fighting elections, where a winning candidate doesn't mean someone able and deserving, it's not surprising.'

'That's what has got my back up . . . These caste and communal factors and the role they play in your prospects! It was frustrating. Still, I find myself reluctant to let go of the excitement of a poll campaign.'

Argali gave a puzzled look.

'But I've found a way,' Ram Mohan went on. 'Tiwari-ji and I agree on that.' All eyes turned to Tiwari-ji, who, taking the hint, straightened himself up in his chair but before he could say anything, Argali spoke up, 'If you ask me Dr Sahab, your present job comes close to what would ideally be suited to an educated man like you, or something to do with higher education, the position of vice chancellor, for instance.'

'You can say that again!' said Tiwari-ji. 'Dr Sahab can have his fill of electoral thrill by lending a hand to a friend in the fray, for instance, to you and Shukla-ji. He can speak to people in small groups in your respective constituencies, people who'd listen to him, people of his own caste.'

'I can't but marvel at the idea.'

'It was Shukla-ji who introduced Dr Sahab to Baran Singh, through whom he met Saansad-ji and Saansad-ji, having nothing else to offer, sent him to the Public Service Commission, which

Dr Sahab, instead of feeling short-changed, finds agreeable. His familial duties were at odds with the uncertainty of a political career, though the fact remains that if Saansad-ji had wanted, he could have included him on his cabinet.'

'When Saansad-ji had become CM, Shukla-ji had said Dr Sahab would become a minister,' said Argali.

'We also thought so. Later Saansad-ji said he wouldn't get clearance from Delhi.'

Argali pursed his lips, then shrugged and said, 'That's hard to believe. Every Congress CM must get the list of his ministers approved by Delhi, but they do let you decide on some of them.'

'You're right, Liyaqat bhai,' said Ram Mohan. 'It sounded like a piece of fiction even then, but I kept my doubts to myself, though I did nurse a bit of a grudge against Saansad-ji and no sooner did an occasion present itself than I got back at him.'

Argali looked mystified.

'That's why I persuaded my fellow members at the Commission to turn down Saansad-ji's invitation for a meeting.'

Argali's face lit up. 'Oh, yes, it was in the paper.'

'It was politically judicious too, a smart way to declare his independence from Saansad-ji,' Tiwari-ji halted, smiling, then gazing at Argali, said, 'Isn't it interesting, this denouement? The fact that Shukla-ji, whom Dr Sahab credits with starting him off on a political life, should also now rescue him from it, from its uncertainties. That—'

'Hold on! Dr Sahab's already been bailed out of active politics. He occupies a position which has nothing to do with politics.'

'Let me explain,' said Ram Mohan. 'I've four more years at the Commission but after that, what?'

'I've seen your book on Saalik, the poet-mystic. You can—'

'These scholarly works are of little use to me monetarily. I need to have a regular income.'

'You already have something,' and reminded of others in the room, Argali walked them out, across the corridor to the parapet, leaning on which, he resumed, his voice dropping to a whisper, 'One should make hay while the sun shines. You must not let your current position fritter away. You've four more years left at the Commission! That's a hell of a lot of time to become financially secure.'

'Something that's not negotiable to Dr Sahab is financial probity,' said Tiwari-ji.

'I've heard of his hostility to bribery.'

'He's no longer against giving it, but enriching himself this way is a no–no.'

Argali chuckled. 'What world are you living in, Dr Sahab? Those who still fuss over making money this way, suffer from nostalgia for the Raj. Something that's dead and buried. Don't you see the trend? The further that era gets removed in time the closer we move to our own sense of right and wrong.'

'Are you saying there shouldn't be laws against making money through corruption?'

'That's all fine, all that high-minded talk about these modern norms, laws, rules, all that sermonizing! It's nothing but posturing. Look how the encounter of Indian ethos with that of the West has led to a separation between our words and intent. Most of us behave that way. Why to stay committed to your hostility to this so-called corruption, which is so pervasive that no wonder you had to modify your stance by becoming receptive to the idea of giving bribes? It's time to go in for another revision of your stand—'

Right then one of Argali's men came out and gestured that tea and samosas had arrived. 'Give us two minutes,' he said and motioned Tiwari-ji to move closer as he began to address Ram Mohan, 'Listen up, Dr Sahab! People crave the jobs for which your Commission makes recruitments. People will pay big sums to get them. To enter our bureaucracy is to enter the world of lucre and influence. Here's my suggestion: let me find someone. I have someone in mind. He'll get you the candidates, just their names, candidates who need to clear this last but decisive hurdle—'

'The interview.'

'Yes. That's when you have the power to decide their fate. Like I said, it's time you made further adjustment to such a rigid notion of rectitude, something out of sync with the times. Don't close your mind to what I suggest, and I don't suggest you become rapacious like this colleague of yours, also a Saansad-ji appointee . . .'

'Munni Prasad.'

'That's him. You don't have to become a mercenary like him. I know you can't. Here's how you can further adapt your sense of probity to suit the India we live in. You don't have to come into the picture. My man will handle everything. He'll be given the brief of quoting no sum to the interested parties, who'll be free to pay as they please, and that'll set you apart as an honest and good man from the generality of bribe-seekers.'

'Makes sense,' said Tiwari-ji. 'Anyone allowing me that freedom—a policeman, a government clerk, a court official, anyone, even a rickshaw-puller, a railway porter or just an ordinary labourer—anyone allowing me to pay as I please, warms the cockles of my heart, leading me to pay more than what they deserve for the service rendered.'

'Absolutely,' cried Argali. Ram Mohan glanced at Tiwari-ji, alerting him to the danger of getting side-tracked, but before the conversation could be nudged back into what they wanted to talk about, Argali led them back into the room to tea and samosa. That he was sure of Ram Mohan being won over to the relatively civilized way of making money, could be sensed from his light-hearted manner, as they joined others discussing the importance of the education portfolio that their leader was likely to get in Shukla-ji's government. Ram Mohan reached out his hand to grasp Argali's with profuse congratulations.

As Argali listened gleefully to his men discussing his rising stature, Ram Mohan signalled they would take their leave. The room quieted down. They all rose. Argali walked them to the door where they paused for a last word.

'Liyaqat bhai, I'm still not comfortable with the idea of securing my financial future this way,' then, adding hastily, 'but your candidates will be selected if I happen to interview them. You just send word before the interview.'

Argali grinned.

'Let me explain how I propose to make do with a life outside active politics,' continued Ram Mohan. 'I need Shukla-ji's help. Everybody knows who the real ruler of India is, and in UP, our Shukla-ji is closest to him.'

'It's Sanjay Gandhi who's given us the throne of the largest state.'

'Earlier, I thought if Shukla-ji introduced me to Sanjay-ji, I could make an impression on him, making it easier for Shukla-ji to push my name for the Union Public Service Commission. But now—'

'That's the body that selects IAS, IPS officers!'

'Yes, and they rank the highest in Indian bureaucracy,' said Tiwari-ji. Argali nodded and said to Ram Mohan, 'Please complete your thought, Dr Sahab!'

'I was saying if I get the UPSC, it'll be only because of Shukla-ji; so where's the need for me to meet Sanjay-ji unless—'

'I haven't met him yet. Where's the need, as you said!'

They exchanged farewells and left.

* * *

Tiwari-ji extended his stay in Allahabad to make another attempt to meet Shukla-ji after Sanjay Gandhi's UP tour. The plan didn't come off. After his first cabinet expansion, Shukla-ji was summoned to Delhi. One of the biggest political figures put in jail was said to have softened towards Indira Gandhi, expressing his wish to attend a Congress function to be held to hail her leadership and of her son and make a speech supporting the Emergency. No way could Ram Mohan meet the CM any time soon. When he called Argali to congratulate on his joining the state cabinet, he was assured of a meeting with Shukla-ji during their visit to Allahabad next month.

'I'll need you here again in a few weeks,' said Ram Mohan to Tiwari-ji. They were having lunch just before the latter was to leave.

'Our Lucknow trip wasn't a waste. Without making amends to Argali, we could never find favour with Shukla-ji.'

'Can we count on him?'

'It was obvious that he'd appreciated this climb-down on your part, and your willingness to help his people to government jobs leaves no room for him to distrust your intent.'

Just as Deena replenished their thalis with fresh chapatis from the kitchen, the doorbell rang. Ram Mohan asked him to get it. 'Deena's grown quite tall,' said Tiwari-ji as if he noticed the fact at that very moment.

'I'm concerned about him.'

'You're concerned about his height!' Tiwari-ji quipped.

Ram Mohan brushed the joke aside, 'His antipathy to his studies, to the question of passing the key exams, is the cause of some serious headache for me. I'm concerned about what he's going to do in life.' Deena returned. It was Zameer, the orderly-cum-driver, who was to drop Tiwari-ji at the bus station.

'He's failed in high school once and will fail again in the ordinary course of things,' said Ram Mohan, carrying on with his train of thought.

'How can you let that happen?'

'You know how bad he's at studies! You give him newspapers, magazines, story books, he'll read everything. Except for what he really needs to read: his textbooks. He'll read even the textbooks, but only for pleasure, with no thought of exams. That's a hindrance to his notion of pleasure from reading.'

'That's fine, but why should he lose a year, at this stage?'

Ram Mohan felt relieved, sensing a solution at hand to the seemingly intractable problem, as Tiwari-ji continued, 'A relation of Pratap Singh's is the owner and the principal of a higher secondary school in Dhata. I know they help students pass the board exams. That's where Deena needs to sit his tenth board next time.'

Pratap Singh, the strong man of Dhata in Fatehpur, whose support was the chief factor in getting Ram Mohan 80 per cent of the votes from his area in the elections the latter had fought.

'Next time? Exam forms for tenth board will be out shortly. You tell me how to go about it. I'll task Nishant with it.'

'First, Nishant should find an obscure school from where Deena can, as a private student, fill up the form. Better if the school is some distance from the city. After his exam centre is announced, you can have him transferred to this school in Dhata.'

Nishant found one such school on the outskirts of Allahabad. The filling of the exam form was done soon after and once the exam centres were announced, Ram Mohan spoke to some official at the UP Board of High School and Intermediate Education and secured Dhata as Deena's exam centre.

* * *

A few days before Nishant was to chaperone Deena to Dhata, a virulent exchange occurred between Ram Mohan and Nisha, leading to something none of them could have envisaged. If Sandhya had had the slightest notion that her wish to take lessons in painting could cause something like that, she would have kept it to herself. She had a flair for drawing and the university's Fine Arts department was holding a painting workshop for students from other disciplines during summer vacation. Those with promise would be eligible for some more lessons. Kanti and Nisha thought it a wonderful opportunity for her. Moon Auntie, too, said that a bit of a formal training in the art of painting would give Sandhya a measure of the artist in her and some grounding in its technical aspects to help explore her creativity. But Sandhya had to get Baabuji's permission.

One day, just as he had returned from the office, she approached him timorously. He heard her out and said he would come to their side after he had changed. He came. His face was a picture. Kanti glanced at Sandhya, who looked crushed. Sitting down on the bed in the room with five doors, he said, 'Won't you people ever understand the importance of what I expect from you?' then turning to Sandhya, 'You've been a disciplined girl, focused on your studies, always obtaining first-class marks.' Nisha, who was in the adjacent room, emerged in the doorway. 'It can't be your idea, I know.' Nisha bristled. He went on, 'Drawing, sketching, painting, these things are for kids. One should grow out of them as one grows up. If anything, a camera is what one needs, not a paintbrush.'

Nisha couldn't hold back, 'What about all those articles in newspapers and magazines, discussing the works of Indian artists?' She mentioned two famous Hindi litterateurs, one of whom was Mahadevi Verma, a big name in Hindi literature, who, known for her exquisite poetry and prose, was also fond of drawing and painting. Her books carried her sketches in tune with the themes of her verses. What got Ram Mohan miffed was the mention of this other personage, a professor of Hindi at the university, who, while visiting the Commission bungalow, was stingy with his praise for his host's various gifts.

Mahadevi Verma's interest in painting or sketching one couldn't laugh off. She was too formidable a name. Ram Mohan had great regard for her achievements. 'Exceptions are always there. No great intellect would seek to make a name solely in painting business. I find little difference between these painters and those who do cinema hoardings. Even Tagore drew sometimes, to delight the child in him. But it's the world of literature, where his triumphs lie. The same's true of Mahadevi-ji.' Then he denounced the other fellow Nisha had referred to, who, according to him, used the paintbrush to hide his inadequacy as a poet. Nisha said that in the class he sounded deeply knowledgeable and others, including Moon Auntie, regarded him highly. Ram Mohan saw red.

'This Moon's illiterate. I know the likes of her and how they land these jobs! Through coquetry and all!' He paused. 'You're married and have your own family. What business do you have to—'

'I've every business to help Sandhya decide what she wants to do in life.'

'Help her decide what she wants to do in life! It's my job to help her get educated and then married. If she wants to do anything afterwards, anything in addition to looking after her family, she can do it then . . . Do not mess around here. Your own dependency on me is far from over.'

Nisha's face lost colour before becoming florid and warped with rage.

'Get stuffed, I won't stay in this house beyond today.'

Ram Mohan couldn't believe what he heard but stopped short of sounding conciliatory. No way that she could leave that very day to join Shekhar in Delhi.

'You're making a drama out of it,' he said and returned to his room, thinking the issue would pass. He was in error. They all were. The moment he left in the late afternoon to join Chaturvedi-ji and Sinha Sahab somewhere, Nisha rang Moon Auntie and began packing after that, sobbing, as Sandhya, Deena, Mayank, and Kanti watched, protesting tearfully. Nishant was flummoxed. She asked Deena to get a rickshaw. Knowing Nisha didi, any attempt to make her change her mind was useless. She wouldn't back down from a showdown with Baabuji.

'I know how you all look forward to being at Moon Auntie's place. Come as often as you wish! Whenever Baabuji's out of town,' she said before climbing on to the rickshaw.

This busted Ram Mohan's notion that his position was the reason for Moon Auntie's affection for Nisha. He was astounded. Moon Auntie could have the temerity to displease him in this manner! 'This woman, she could be so wicked I had no idea. Rather than talking some sense into her favourite student, she's teaching her how to insult her father,' said Ram Mohan when he returned in the evening. 'It speaks of her frustration. Her ploy to cosy up to me didn't work. She's found a way to get back at me . . . So long as I'm here, she'd never become part of the panel of Hindi experts at the Commission.'

The atmosphere at the Commission Bungalow became strained. Deena was thankful to leave for Dhata with Nishant. The board exams were about to start, but he had nothing to worry about. He wouldn't be required to be fretfully alert all the time to the location of the invigilators while trying to use his cheating material. He didn't even have to prepare that material this time. What a relief! Ever since this idea had taken wing, he had awaited his sojourn in Dhata.

* * *

Pratap Singh had to be called from the fields when they reached this nondescript dusty settlement. Nishant gave him their father's letter, which he read with absorption. Folding it back, he called his son over, 'Tell your mother not to bother about sherbet. We're going to the school first.'

Ghanraj Singh, his relative and the principal of Jawaharlal Nehru Intermediate College, received Nishant and Deena heartily and dispatched a man to the local sweetmeat shop. Pratap Singh took Ghanraj Singh outside to have a word. Nishant and Deena sat in his room, the only plastered room in the school building. When they returned, followed by the sweets, Ghanraj Singh made plain to Deena the import of the board exams, beginning just a day later. He asked him to come prepared, carrying all the necessary material to be able to answer all the five questions properly and fast, fast because they would be allowed no extra time. Even the examinees in the VIP room had to finish the question paper in the stipulated three hours. What marked the VIP room off from other rooms Deena and Nishant would be enlightened by Pratap Singh's son.

Examinees in this room were given carte blanche to use their books during the exam. Not many could afford that room. Money or influence was the sole criterion for being eligible to the privilege. Other rooms had limits set on the examinees' freedom to crib. Crib they could, but only on the sly. They had to be heedful of the presence of invigilators and couldn't use entire books. Only torn pages. Or it had to be handwritten material. Also, they were required to preserve something of the gravitas of the occasion and the sanctity of the idea of invigilation. If any examinee became too audacious, he would be reproached. If he persisted, he might have his precious cheating material taken away. Things rarely came to that pass. The invigilators would stick to their brief of keeping the mass copying in check. If done discreetly, they feigned to not notice. Nothing was charged for allowing this latitude. Ghanraj Singh was applauded for his effort to promote higher secondary education in the area. If not for such schools, many youngsters would remain deprived of the distinction of being the proud possessors of class ten and twelve certificates.

The first day when Nishant walked Deena to the school, the exam centre, a crowd of students had already gathered along the dirt track leading to the yet-to-be-opened school gate. Nishant and Deena hung about outside, by a tea shack under a neem tree. Two men and two boys were having tea. Nishant also ordered tea and fell into conversation with the two men who belonged to two different villages near Dhata and were the guardians of the two boys sitting the board exam. They had shelled out a considerable sum for the VIP room.

No sooner was the gate opened than they all made a rush for it. Inside, the fortunate ones were separated from the less so and were led by a school help to the VIP room, a thatched brick structure standing at a dusty corner on the far side of the school compound. Deena located the desk with his roll number on it. Armed with two books, he was confidence incarnate and couldn't wait to lay his hands on the exam paper. It was light years from those furtive attempts at copying from the rolls of narrow strips prepared so assiduously and kept hidden so carefully!

Just before handing answer-sheets, the invigilators, one after another, commanded something so terrible it didn't get through to Deena at first. The moment it did, his mood of elation took a nosedive. He sat petrified. His co-examinees were doing what was asked of them. 'What're you waiting for?' one of the invigilators yelled. Then the order was repeated, 'Turn everything out, any books, or notes, or pieces of paper of any kind, whatever material you have on you. Turn it out. If caught with anything like that, then don't complain you weren't warned.' His innards reeling, Deena rose and walked to the hillock of books and notebooks in the corner by the door. He wished he had made provision for something like this. But that would have made an out-and-out nonsense of the VIP room. It was none of his fault.

No way Deena could intimate the catastrophe to Nishant. He felt like crying. The invigilators began to distribute answer-sheets for them to write their roll number and other information, and when the gong rang, they quickly handed out the question paper. Deena sat still. He could write nothing that resembled the answer to any of the questions. He surveyed the VIP room. Many of the examinees were perusing the question paper. Some sat with their gaze fixed at the invigilators. When one boy rose and took a tentative step forward, one of the invigilators cocked an eye at him but said nothing and began to talk to his colleague.

The boy strode to the pile, fished out his book and got back to his desk. Two more took courage. Then there was a scramble, prompting a warning against being unruly from the invigilators, one of whom sounded particularly irate. When he saw Deena watching the spectacle, confused, he shouted, 'Don't just sit around or you won't be able to finish on time. Principal Sahab will blame us for your incompetence,' then a bit sarcastically, 'Or you wish me to find and bring your books to you?' Euphoric, Deena rushed and picked up his books. He could have been spared the momentary shock and agony if somebody had told him that invigilators in Dhata too followed the norm of instructing the examinees to turn out any cheating material they might possess. 'It's just a ritual, going through the motions, nothing else. Sorry, I forgot to mention,' Pratap Singh's son would tell him later.

Just as they all settled down to locating the portion in their books from where to start copying, the second invigilator, more genial than his colleague, declaimed, 'You boys are the most privileged lot at this centre. Be thankful and don't blow this glorious opportunity by being reckless. Make doubly sure you copy the correct answer to every question you attempt. Last year, three boys messed up and could barely pass. This kind of sloppy approach to such an important occasion is unpardonable. Not only does it ruin the chances of your doing well in the exam but is a disgrace to the VIP room!'

To answer all the five questions to his total satisfaction, three hours weren't enough, but Deena was jubilant. So was Nishant, as he listened to his account of the first day in the VIP room. He advised him on how to do better in the remaining papers. 'Keep your answers short so you can do justice to all the five questions.'

Proud of his role in the venture, Nishant headed back to Allahabad. He couldn't wait to relate it all to Baabuji.

* * *

Deena was enjoying his stay at Dhata, at Pratap Singh's place. He befriended his son, three years older than him, whose stock of stories was inexhaustible. The stories that explored various facets of Pratap Singh's clout were especially entertaining. Deena felt thrilled at being the strong man's guest, and Pratap Singh's son was proud of hosting the son of Ram Mohan, a figure known to all and sundry in Dhata.

With so much to share, Deena, at the first opportunity, by way of several days' gap between his two papers, set out for Allahabad. The narrow road to the nearest bus station was in a perpetual state of disrepair and an hour-long ride on a horse-drawn thing called *ekka*, would be an exercise in discomfort, a bone-breaking experience, but compared to the luxury of the VIP room, this inconvenience was nothing. What he found hard to bear, though, was the sight of the underfed and frequently whipped mare, farting every now and then, pulling a packed ekka on a broken-down road, a life-and-death struggle for her.

Ram Mohan wasn't home when Deena arrived. 'Where else could he be?' Kanti said when he enquired. She didn't know that Deena knew what her scornful tone implied. That Baabuji was at Indrajit's place, chatting and making everybody laugh, especially his favourite colleague's wife. To Ram Mohan's children, what mattered was the absence of their father, not the reason for it. Ignoring their mother's insinuation, they focused their attention on Deena, who felt like a hero returning from an adventure. They revelled in it. The entire sequence of events that Deena dished out with brio. The drama of the first day in the VIP room brought the house down. The only thing missing was the laughter of Nisha didi, whose stay at Moon Auntie's place was a settled thing now. Even Baabuji had softened towards it, towards her. He had spoken to Moon Auntie, over the phone, thanking her for all the care she was taking of Nisha, though they knew he was on the lookout for a chance to get Nisha back at the Commission Bungalow.

* * *

Even conscientious students had an attack of exam nerves. To those who abhorred exams, the occasion presented the most fraught situation. For Deena, it was a magical moment. Free from reading for the exam. Free from the pain of pretension to reading. He had never felt so good before. It had given Ram Mohan a lift too, the success of Tiwari-ji's idea, the idea of Dhata. Before leaving for Kanpur, as was his practice every other Saturday, he gave Deena some extra money, more than needed for Dhata.

This, combined with Baabuji out of town, made every moment of his remaining two days in Allahabad delightful. He listened to his favourite radio programmes, read Hindi thrillers, went to the movies, and visited Nisha didi at Moon Auntie's house along with Sandhya didi and Mayank. None of their friends or acquaintances knew about Dhata and his confident response to Moon Auntie's query about his board exam made Nisha didi titter. He scowled. Right then, Shampa, who had slunk away, re-emerged titivated.

Deena's heart missed a beat. While he was away in Dhata, she had seemed someone unreal, illusory. Now, in the face of the truth of her existence, Dhata itself appeared remote and absurd, and then, before he could locate his own reality between Shampa and Dhata, a stab of the farcicality of his yearning shot through his heart. He was still floundering when Mr Aggarwal, looking fresh from a bath, materialized and greeted them. When told Deena was doing well in his board exam, he said, 'Good, keep it up,' then added in the same breath, 'And don't forget what I said the last time. That your aim, in the end, should be the National School of Drama.'

'Is this the time to bring that up?' Moon Auntie chided her husband. 'Let him focus on his exams for now. It's early days for him to think about a career in theatre!'

'Hardly four or five years!' Mr Aggarwal was serious. 'Once you have a BA, you become eligible to go to the NSD, though it's not as simple as that. If I'm not mistaken, you should have some prior experience of acting in plays in school or elsewhere. I have a lawyer colleague who's serious about sending his son to the NSD.' Before Moon Auntie could respond, Shampa whispered in her ear and Nisha, sitting close to them, caught it and gaily asked Deena to enact his favourite scenes from *Sholay*, scenes featuring Gabbar Singh, among others. Shampa glanced at Deena, as if acknowledging his gift. He felt lifted out of the abyss of hopelessness. Now Dhata seemed nothing but a fictional scene in his life, invented to help him deal with some requirements of the world out there.

He was to go back to Dhata on Monday. Nisha didi asked them to come again on Sunday, the day following, the day Baabuji would also be back, but thankfully not before the evening. 'We'll have lunch together,' declared Moon Auntie. Deena felt delirious with a newly discovered sense of self-worth. That was the day he began fancying himself as a future film actor, and soon after getting back to the Commission Bungalow, he sat down to write a letter to his favourite movie actor, the reigning star of the day. To play it up, his devotion to him, he decided to make it into a kind of verse and succeeded after labouring awhile. Everybody was impressed. Kanti couldn't have thought Deena capable of using Hindi so well!

The moment they stepped into Moon Auntie's house the next day, Mayank cried out to Nisha didi, who had answered the door, 'Deena's written a poem.' Shampa, who was right behind her, couldn't suppress a laugh, which Deena thought was at his expense. He was abashed.

The kerfuffle brought Moon Auntie into the drawing room. Mr Aggarwal followed soon. 'Who has written what?' said she before asking their maid to serve water.

'We're in for a hot summer this year,' grumbled Mr Aggarwal as he sat down. Moon Auntie repeated the question, her face bright with curiosity. Nisha looked towards Sandhya, who said it was a letter to Rajesh Khanna, written in the form of a poem by Deena. 'So, our friend here wants to become a film actor himself!' exclaimed Mr Aggarwal.

'Many boys of his age dream of that,' said Moon Auntie, apparently in Deena's defence, which disheartened him instead.

Looking at him, Mr Aggarwal said, 'No, you can't class him with the crowd of boys enchanted by the glamour of the cinema. Deena has a flair for acting. With some training at the NSD, he can well be in with a chance of making it as a film actor,' then with a tilt of his head, 'provided he's willing to gird up his loins when the time comes for a gruelling struggle in Bombay.'

'Fine, let's hear the poem or the letter,' said Moon Auntie. 'I'm more interested in Deena's ability to write.'

'He has it in his pocket,' blurted Mayank.

'You're more excited than anybody else,' said Nisha, reaching out her hand to ruffle his hair, then turning to Deena, prodded him into taking it out, the piece of paper.

Shampa was waiting. He forced himself to recite it but was too self-conscious to bring the poem alive. His hurried manner interfered with its rhythmic rendition. Moon Auntie asked him to give it to his Nisha didi, who then read it aloud and what a difference her style and confidence made, rendering the poem indistinguishable from its earlier delivery by Deena. But his ability to write impressed Moon Auntie who thought his poem showed promise. 'Deena's literary gift puts his talent for acting a bit in the shade. I'd say he had better take to writing. He can make a name for himself in literature,' she declared, looking at her husband, who

seemed at a loss what to say at first, then said, 'Yes, it's hard to
know with conviction about his true calling, where it lies, in acting
or literature. And yes, I'm amazed by his skill in handling Hindi
words, the way he's done in this letter in verse.'

'Let's say he has talent for both. Yet there should be no
difficulty in deciding which road to take. That would be writing,
the greater calling of the two!' said Moon Auntie. Known for her
fascination with poets and writers, she was close to one of the two
tallest literary figures. Pant and Mahadevi lived in Allahabad and
were part of the legendary quartet, the pioneers of the Romantic
Movement in Hindi poetry. The other two were dead and gone.
Though she hardly wrote anything herself, Moon Auntie was all
for spotting and encouraging literary talent. 'Once he's composed
a few poems, I'll show them to Pant-ji,' she said to Nisha, sending
a ripple of delight through Deena. Later, as they had lunch, Mr
Aggarwal said, 'His linguistic flair is compatible with his talent
for acting.'

Moon Auntie said to Deena, 'For now, you just keep your
mind on your board exam. Don't let anything distract you. There'll
be plenty of time to talk about it.' And just as they were leaving,
Shampa spoke to him for the first time ever, smiling bashfully, 'All
the very best for your remaining papers.'

That day marked the decisive moment in his life. That was
the day when he felt a revulsion against his habit of stealing from
Baabuji's wallet, as he experienced that peculiar sensation, the
sensation of falling in love, distinct from the desire for raw sex,
though the idea of coitus, the idea of being that intimate, formed
the very basis of it, which would be elaborated later by his friend-
cum-philosopher. How enigmatic he found the condition that
made everything else seem so very ordinary, dulling his appetite
even for something to which he had been addicted since before
reaching puberty: a craving for onanism. He tried to make sense of
the phenomenon, the peculiar sensation, that took the immediacy

out of the yearning for coupling. What consumed him now was the desire to spend some time with her, chatting, leading to the flowering of romance, to the beginning of the delicious wait, to the savour of making out and the certainty of finally making love.

* * *

Dhata had worked out fantastic for Deena. Results were still some way off, but that he wouldn't fail this time was just a matter of course. He could now enjoy popular Hindi fiction, his ideal occupation after the movies. That had to change. The commitment he had made of his time and energy to being absorbed in Hindi literature was sacrosanct. He stuck at it. Albeit Hindi thrillers he couldn't eschew. He would go to them but only after having immersed himself for some time in poetry and literary fiction. Without movies however, he couldn't do for long. At every opportunity, he rode his bicycle to a cinema hall, sometimes he took Mayank along, but only occasionally. He was a bad influence on his brother, and Baabuji who, though appreciative of their closeness, accused him now and then of being bent on spoiling Mayank's chances in life as well.

Deena had now turned the corner. He pored over Hindi literary texts for hours on end, making everybody at home alter their opinion about him. His industry impressed Baabuji, who wasn't given to feeling the anxiety parents feel for their children to do well in school. Nor was he the one to be charmed by someone's scholastic feats in the form of certificates. His notion of an authentic personality was that one's true talents didn't require a piece of paper to vouch for them. They should be demonstrable in one's linguistic command, one's ability to write or speak or both, one's knowledge, one's ready wit and intellect, one's flair for music and things like that, things obtained independent of scholastic education, an education that, in the main, was to do with the passing of routine exams, whose importance though Ram Mohan wouldn't disparage, for no decent employment was possible without a formal education, but unlike other parents he wouldn't lose his sleep over his children being unable to perform well in exams. When Deena had failed in high school board exam, Ram Mohan had laughed it off, assuring him of success the next year if he made just a little bit of effort. Once Tiwari-ji furnished him with the solution to the problem, Ram Mohan's worries in that respect dissipated.

He felt vindicated by the way Deena was taken up with Hindi literature. Worthy of praise was Deena's assiduity. That, along with his other passion for movies and reproducing dialogues from them, strengthened Baabuji's opinion of him as being gifted. He would have him enact Gabbar Singh and recite his poems—which Deena awaited to being shown to Pant-ji on his return from Kausani, his hometown in the hills—in front of his visitors.

Meanwhile Baabuji toned down his antipathy to the bond between Nisha and Dr Moon, of which Kanti, Sandhya, Deena and Mayank were glad. They had no inkling, till then, of this incredible ability of his, the ability to alter his approach to a situation over which he had little control. He wouldn't sulk or be put out when faced with something like that. Not only did he soften towards Nisha and Moon Auntie but appreciated the warmth they shared and was gracious in climbing down. He called Dr Moon and thanked her for being kind to Nisha and was invited to dinner at her place. He took Kanti, Sandhya and Mayank along. Deena didn't mind his omission. Was rather relieved because the sight of him with Shampa in the immediate vicinity would trigger something dreadful in Baabuji.

Whatever left of his earlier contention, that it wasn't Nisha but his position that had caught Dr Moon's attention, was knocked down soon. He had said to Nisha, 'Now that she's failed to ingratiate herself with me, Dr Moon won't help you offset the effect of your poor showing in the MA previous.' But that's what

Moon Auntie did, rather went out of her way to do, and proved Baabuji wrong. Nisha's eligibility to enrol in PhD after her MA had looked unattainable until then. No longer so. Her making the grade was a sure thing now, for in two of the four papers her marks were the highest in the class. Moon Auntie had seen to that.

She had procured one of the question papers of the MA Final in advance so Nisha could prepare all the answers well in time. The next paper was even easier. She just had to while away the three hours, sitting in the exam centre, writing nothing. But she tried and wrote, taking her own time, the answer to the question relatively manageable. Most of the time, she only went through the motions of it, faking the seriousness of someone taking an exam. This exam paper was to come to Moon Auntie for marking. Barring a couple of pages, all of it was left blank to be filled later and that she did neatly and beautifully, copying the answers, sitting at Moon Auntie's dining table, unrushed.

What a difference it all made! Not only did Nisha get a first division but moved from the bottom to being one of the star performers in MA in Hindi literature that year, capturing third position on the merit list. Moon Auntie was exhilarated. Yet she couldn't help bemoaning that her ignorance of Nisha's plight in MA Previous had cost her the top position. Oh, before I forget—Deena too passed his tenth board, though only with a second division, a good second division, just a few marks short of a first. Ram Mohan was relieved. Dhata had helped Deena break through this great hurdle, the tenth board.

* * *

Still no hint of Nisha moving back to the Commission Bungalow despite the rapprochement with Baabuji. She stayed put. It was no longer an issue they thought, Nisha and Moon Auntie. How mistaken they were! Wary of people thinking Nisha could thumb her nose at him, Ram Mohan's propitiatory gesture was to prompt her return. Making matters worse was the fact that now even Shekhar, while in town, stayed at Moon Auntie's place, though he and Nisha did visit the Commission Bungalow. The situation was a disgrace to Ram Mohan, who said to Kanti one day, 'I did my bit. Now it makes sense Dr Moon does hers and sends Nisha back to her parents' place.'

Just when he thought of letting Dr Moon know that to not appreciate his predicament was unbefitting of her, a chance came his way to make another attempt to have Nisha shift back.

Ram Mohan had endeavoured to keep Kanti, Nisha and Sandhya from getting to interact with his male visitors. Yet some among his friends did succeed in occupying a tender place in the consciousness of the women in his family. Of that he had been sensible. Aware too was he that heading the list of such persons was the one who was his favourite too: Mahavir Wilson. The reason for his absence till now had to do with the absence of a situation pertinent to the narrative. That too thanks largely to his being abroad all this while. After Ram Mohan's appointment to the Public Service Commission, Wilson had won a full-time research scholarship for the faculty of Language and Cultures at the School of Oriental and African Studies (SOAS) in London. The research proposal in which he had outlined his take on the genius of Kabir was, in fact, a kind of synopsis of the book he had roughed out. Rather he was well into writing it when the idea of applying to SOAS for a research degree had occurred to him, the idea of obtaining a PhD and publishing the thesis as a book.

His PhD thesis was all but ready while he still had a few months left at SOAS. To put this time to good use, he began to rework the text a little, with a view to making it palatable to the general reader. From London, he would write to Ram Mohan, keeping him clued up on how his work was progressing. It was on the latter's advice that he made an unscheduled trip to India, when he could also approach the Oxford University Press with a basic abstract of the proposed book.

Eager to finalize the text of his *Kabir*, before the end of his stint as a research scholar at SOAS, Wilson's chief purpose of this trip was to fine-tune its structure and arguments with the help of Ram Mohan. He also wanted to visit Benaras to meet Hazari Prasad Dwivedi, Hindi scholar and author, the brilliance of whose works, both critical and creative, had stopped in their tracks many a leading light of Hindi literature. The book that had taken the cake was his *Kabir*, which was also the book Ram Mohan had recommended to Mahavir, who had earlier been left agog by Tagore's *Songs of Kabir*, along with its penetrating introduction by Evelyn Underhill, a novelist and writer on mysticism. Underhill had collaborated with Tagore in translating those verses of the mystic, one hundred of them. In fact, these writings, Underhill's piece and Dwivedi-ji's *Kabir*, about which Ram Mohan had said, 'This is the book that's taken the wind out of the sails of the hitherto commanding critical approach to Hindi poetry,' were what had stirred Mahavir's abiding interest in Kabir.

This unscheduled trip of Mahavir Wilson's provided Ram Mohan with the chance to lure Nisha back to the Commission Bungalow. He called in on Moon Auntie, taking Mahavir along. What a surprise it was to Nisha, who hadn't seen Mahavir bhaiya in almost two years. They were received warmly by Moon Auntie and Mr Aggarwal. Nisha had made them familiar with her Mahavir bhaiya.

Once introductions were made, Ram Mohan told them about the reason for Mahavir's visit. Moon Auntie sat up. She enquired what drew him to Kabir. He looked at Ram Mohan, who said, 'Yes, you can answer in English.' Though not good at conversing in English, Moon Auntie had no trouble understanding it. She, her husband and their daughter, they all listened to him with awe, his choice of words, pronunciation, style and all. Nisha felt proud of him. Then Ram Mohan suggested that Nisha accompany them to Benaras. 'Since she wants to do a PhD in Hindi,' said he, addressing Moon Auntie, 'It's a marvellous opportunity for her to meet in person, this pre-eminent literary giant.'

Nisha was blown away by the suggestion. Moon Auntie, glancing at her, said, 'Yes, she should go. To get to meet someone like Acharya Dwivedi is something to be proud of, something to treasure. Scholarship of this calibre would die out soon.' She turned to Nisha, 'Show your Baabuji and Mahavir bhaiya the book Pant-ji gifted you. He's written such beautiful lines for her.' Nisha rose, all pepped up. Moon Auntie said, 'I know you have *Chidambara* in your collection, Nisha told me but—'

'But it's a gift from the poet himself with his words scribbled especially for her. It's not the same thing!'

Moon Auntie grinned with pride.

Nisha returned with the book and gave it to him. He read in admiration, what Pant-ji had written, then passed it to Mahavir, who nodded at Nisha before looking at the book, as Ram Mohan said to Moon Auntie, 'Nisha should come to the Commission Bungalow tomorrow. We'll be leaving for Benaras the day after. I think it'll be nice if you all come and have dinner with us.'

Moon Auntie looked at her husband, who said, 'Well, yes. We'll come, bringing Nisha along.'

'I'm so happy Nisha has two caring families in Allahabad.'

'No two ways about that,' Moon Auntie intoned.

'You'd agree then that she should stay at the Commission Bungalow with her mother and siblings for some time. She's free to come to your place whenever she wants.'

Nisha smiled in agreement.

Ram Mohan offered another incentive. 'We'll be travelling by car, and I'd like you to drive most of the journey, which isn't long. Zameer will be there, just in case!'

Ram Mohan instructed Santosh, the cook-cum-manservant, to prepare an elaborate meal under Kanti's supervision. They were all excited. Sandhya wanted to tidy up the house, a task best performed in Baabuji's absence, and he wasn't going to be home for a few hours in the daytime. He was invited to lunch at Chaturvedi-ji's. Sinha Sahab was also coming. On learning about Mahavir Wilson, who he didn't know, Chaturvedi-ji asked Ram Mohan to bring him along. Chaturvedi-ji wanted his best friends to meet this new neighbour of his, who had just returned to India after being in England for nine years, and that was the reason for Chaturvedi-ji's excitement. The length of his neighbour's residency in England had made him a man of distinction.

By the time they got back, Sandhya, with the help of Deena, had neatened the house.

Not long afterwards, the guests of the evening arrived, and Baabuji, who sat chatting with Mahavir in his front corner room, opened the door himself. Deena, who had also come on the scene, grabbed Nisha didi's suitcase. Ram Mohan was gushing in his welcome. Nisha went inside. He had them seated in the drawing room and began to laud Moon Auntie. When she enquired about Kanti, Ram Mohan ordered everybody out in the drawing room. He was in his element, making them all shake with laughter.

Ram Mohan talked about his visit to his friend Chaturvedi-ji's place that day and about his friend's failed attempts to get his new neighbour to converse in English. 'When I told Chaturvedi-ji about Mahavir and his being a PhD student in London, he insisted on having him over too. Few chances he lets slip to befriend persons he can show off and this foreign-returned neighbour fills the bill perfectly. I could see how desperate Chaturvedi-ji was to get him to switch to English, eager to match Mahavir's two years in London with his neighbour's nine, or to pit a fully grown lion against a cub, his lion, that is.'

They all chortled. Mr Aggarwal said, 'People who have lived in either England or America for long tend to become oblivious of the prestige with which English is identified in places like India. They feel awkward to use it when they can speak in Hindi.'

'That's fine. But the truth is he doesn't know that my Mahavir was already a lion when he went to London, that he can teach English to many an Englishman,' said Ram Mohan, glancing towards an embarrassed Wilson.

It was one of those occasions when Ram Mohan's family loved every moment of his presence. His being in this mood was such fun. They were still laughing when Moon Auntie turned to Deena, 'Where are your poems and how many?'

'He's reading literature and learning to appreciate the likes of Pant and Mahadevi at his age. But, to me, he never shows what he writes unless asked!' said Ram Mohan feigning petulance.

Deena was on a high. It was something he had anxiously awaited. 'Four,' he said to Moon Auntie. 'Excellent,' said she and asked him to recite. His manner of recitation had improved as he tried to emulate Nisha didi in giving each phrase its phonetic due. He received much praise for his effort. Moon Auntie chose two of the poems she wanted to show to Pant-ji. 'Copy them on separate sheets and give me in a day or two.' Mr Aggarwal demanded that Deena do Gabbar Singh as well. Ram Mohan, who had no time for movies, had seen *Sholay* because of Deena's imitation of this famous screen baddie. 'Yes, without that, this gathering won't be complete,' he said, his voice tender and cajoling. Deena's performance was praised yet again.

Mr. Aggarwal said, 'Dr Sahab, you must send him to the NSD.'

Ram Mohan, who hadn't heard of National School of Drama, presented a bewildered look. Mr Aggarwal spelled it out.

All this was a pleasant surprise to Mahavir Wilson, Nisha being one of the toppers in MA in Hindi, and Deena developing a flair for acting and literature and Nishant aiming to become a lawyer. As for Mayank, Mahavir agreed with Baabuji. 'For someone like him sky's the limit.' It was only Sandhya, for whom Mahavir bhaiya felt sorry, as she, the most talented of Ram Mohan's children, had little to look forward to other than marriage. Something was cooking as regards Mahavir's marriage too. Of that, he would tell Ram Mohan through a letter from London.

'Drive carefully,' said Moon Auntie to Nisha before leaving. Ram Mohan said, 'Nothing's better than a long drive to smooth out glitches in one's driving.'

Deena in the meantime was busy stealing glances at Shampa, who had got into the back seat of the car. She looked at him, her lips flickering, sending Deena's blood berserk.

* * *

Among the well-known cities in India, Benaras was one of the dirtiest, the most congested and crowded. But Hazari Prasad Dwivedi's neighbourhood, a relatively new housing colony, was spared the city's general squalor. Touching seventy, he was a handsome old man. He was bald in front and wore a thick moustache, white as snow, just like his hair or whatever left of it. A few of his upper teeth were missing. With his aura of calmness, he looked like a sage to Nisha. To his admirers, he was an author of acuity and depth. He remembered Ram Mohan well, whom he had met twice before. He remembered him for his work on Saalik, the poet–saint, the compilation of whose verses was a challenge so daunting that no one before had had the spunk to take up. Not only had Ram Mohan been able to meet the challenge, but met it he had with academic rigour, making a splash in Hindi literature, pulling the creator of those verses out of obscurity.

Of particular interest to Acharya Dwivedi was Ram Mohan's book, his published thesis, which he mentioned glowingly to Mahavir Wilson as soon as they were introduced. He applauded

the idea of the book Wilson planned to publish following his PhD,
expressing hope it would be no less weighty than Ram Mohan's
fifteen or so years before, also dealing with an important figure
from India's Bhakti tradition. 'Dr Sahab's work was totally original.
My attempt doesn't fall into that category, so—'

'True,' said Acharya Dwivedi. 'He laid the foundation of any
further discussion on the subject, recovering a significant note of
the grand composition that our devotional poetry is.'

Ram Mohan was overwhelmed by the compliment. Then his
feelings became mixed as storming into them was a sad realization
that it wasn't just a compliment but an indictment too. The way
he saw it. Indictment of his decision to leave the path of literary
scholarship for the pursuit of political influence. Yet always one for
optimistic clarity, Ram Mohan, motioning Mahavir to wait who
was about to respond to Acharya Dwivedi, said, 'Pandit-ji, my PhD
topic had been suggested by an acclaimed scholar at the time. He
was also my supervisor. It was during the writing of my synopsis
that I grew conscious of the challenge. Most of the Hindi faculty
at DAV College would laugh up their sleeve at my choice of the
topic. Others saw some intrigue at work, a plot to undermine my
confidence, my ambition of making a mark. The purpose was to
either derail my PhD project or to ensure that if I did manage to
finish it, it should be sloppy enough to join the heap of theses
meant to get you just a degree. What these people didn't know was
that nothing dynamizes me better than a dare. Rather than scaring
me off, this gossip stiffened my resolve.'

'But just look at what you produced, a work of true scholarship.'
Then a bit ruefully, 'Yes, no sphere of activity is above petty
politics, not even our centres of learning—'

'Which was one of the reasons I chose to strive towards real
power, the kind that's feared and admired by one and all,' said
Ram Mohan. 'But thanks to the workings of the caste factor, I
failed to succeed in politics . . . What's also true is that if you

have the support of your caste, even when it's not enough to help you win an election, it gives you critical leverage in obtaining something else, something not overtly political but a position of power nonetheless . . . That's what, Pandit-ji, I've managed to achieve in the way of Public Service Commission. Now I get invitations to all kinds of social literary functions. Not to be in the audience. I'm there either as chief guest or to preside over the event. These requests come even from people who wouldn't have bothered earlier.'

Mahavir Wilson shifted in his chair. His unease at Ram Mohan's boastful tone didn't escape Acharya Dwivedi, who said, 'It's important that persons of academic and literary background, too, are appointed to these august positions,' and then without waiting for Ram Mohan's response, he turned his attention to the younger man, 'So, what's you take on Kabir, Wilson-ji?'

Caught on the hop, Mahavir Wilson took a few seconds to gather his wits. 'Pandit-ji, after going through his more popular verses and some rudimentary writings dealing with his person and poetry, I came to primarily focus on your book on Kabir and Evelyn Underhill's introduction to Tagore's *Songs of Kabir*.'

'That's capital, that long foreword of hers, very perceptive, of which I too have been a beneficiary.'

'It was the work of Acharya Kshiti Mohan Sen,' said Wilson, 'the scholar par excellence, to whom you've also dedicated your book, that had planted the first seeds of *Kabir* in your head. You've acknowledged as much in the preface.'

'Oh, yes! He was the foremost authority on the mystic tradition of medieval India. If it wasn't for his efforts, Indian culture might have missed something quite substantial. His work on mystic saints of that period, their poetry, led to in-depth research into the subject. The text he edited of Kabir's poems, the poems he had obtained from ambulant musicians and fakirs, that text was also the source for Gurudev's *Songs of Kabir*.'

'Yes, it's mentioned in your book as well as in Underhill's introduction . . . You met Sen—'

'I met him in Shanti Niketan for the first time. He was invited to teach there by Gurudev himself. That was just a year after I was born.'

Before Mahavir could respond, Ram Mohan said to him, 'You're going off at a tangent and haven't answered Pandit-ji's query about your understanding of Kabir.'

'I'm sorry . . . In *Songs of Kabir* Evelyn Underhill states, and I quote from memory: *In the collection of songs here translated, there will be found examples which illustrate nearly every aspect of Kabir's thought, and all the fluctuations of the mystic emotion: the ecstasy, the despair, the still beatitude, the eager self-devotion, the flashes of wide illumination, the moments of intimate love. His wide and deep vision of the universe, "the Eternal Sport" of creation, the worlds being "told like beads" within the Being of God, is here seen balanced by his lovely and delicate sense of intimate communion with the Divine Friend, Lover, Teacher of the soul.'* Noticing the awed look on Acharya Dwivedi's face, he halted, looking abashed!

Nisha laughed with delight as Acharya Dwivedi gasped, saying, 'My gosh, you know it word by word!'

'There's nothing so surprising in it, Pandit-ji. You know it. Anybody having read a text as often and as many times as I have can reproduce quite a bit from it,' then returning to the point, 'Pandit-ji, Underhill and you have addressed yourselves to the spiritual aspect of Kabir's creativity. Or more precisely, you both are of the view that he, at bottom is a Bhakt, a mystic. Underhill describes him as, I quote, *A great religious reformer, the founder of a sect to which nearly a million northern Hindus still belong, it is yet supremely as mystical poet that Kabir lives for us. His fate has been that of many revealers of Reality. A hater of religious exclusivism and seeking above all things to initiate men into the liberty of the children of God . . .'*

Acharya Dwivedi threw an approving glance at Ram Mohan as Mahavir carried on, 'And you, as if on cue, state: *Kabir has said many such things that, if used, can be helpful in social reform. Yet, to think of him as a social reformer because of that, will be a mistake. He was an apostle of spiritual endeavour at a personal level. Collectivism was not the natural attribute of his mind. He was individualistic. The strong reasoning for harmony between religions permeates all his poetry, which is selfless love for God and to regard all men as equal without distinction.*'

They all listened, speechless, as Mahavir added, 'You both are of the opinion that on the whole, Kabir was an exponent of "personal realization of God".'

'But you have a different approach to him!'

'I agree with most of your reading of Kabir, everybody would, but the bit with which I have issues is that it's wrong to view him as a social reformer—'

'That there's a strong element of social reformer in him I've acknowledged. But, yes, basically, he was a Bhakt, a mystic, bitterly opposed to all ceremonial observances in all religions—'

'*Thoughtless slavery to external religious practices he didn't like,*' Mahavir produced the exact line from Acharya Dwivedi's book. 'But my emphasis is on the aspect of his being a social reformer. I've argued that nearly all his admirers were marginalized people whose voice he'd become. This, I've presented as evidence of his being no less a social reformer, as most of his adherents, people looking for comfort and courage in his songs, are those who, for ages, have suffered at the hands of the customs against which Kabir speaks so strongly—'

'I agree with your argument, in a way,' said Acharya Dwivedi. 'But Kabir can't fit in with those who go by the term "social reformer" which is used to depict people who fight social ills primarily by means of reason and without invoking God. Many such voices were active during the last century.'

'Yes, during British rule! You're right. Kabir can't be bracketed with them. But then, before the advent of the English, there was no scope for such humanitarian voices, and I concede that Kabir doesn't fall into the category of the reformers you alluded to. But almost all these individuals owed their existence, broadly speaking, to the English, to the space, to the latitude made possible by the latter's presence, the latitude of which these reformers took full advantage to air their views, to reason out vicious, barbaric, heartless traditions and reason with their blind followers in general and their champions in particular, champions of those centuries-old customs, their apologists.'

Nisha couldn't take her eyes off Mahavir bhaiya. Ram Mohan listened with pride. The way he would switch to English whenever his Hindi failed to cope with what he wanted to say, while sitting gracefully in his easy chair was Acharya Dwivedi, his face wearing a patient and gracious look with no desire to disturb his interlocutor's flow.

'I'm not saying it lessened in any way the enormity of their challenge. My point is that they could confront the formidable odds because of the leeway available under British rule, something unthinkable for someone like Kabir, the nonconformist of his times.'

'I got it,' said Acharya Dwivedi, leaning forward. 'Other than to try and sensitize people to inane and unfeeling socio-religious customs, there was no way Kabir could look for any reforms in society, which he tried to do by nailing his colours to the mast through his songs, always finding a robust, vigorous idiom to serve his purpose.'

'Yes, that was the only way he could do that, unlike the reformers from our recent past who had the British to petition and seek intervention, besides trying to sensitize people to the societal horrors.'

'You surely have a case, Wilson-ji. I've argued that many a verse of Kabir could well be read as exhortations for social reform but that, as a matter of fact, is subsidiary to his being a mystic, a non-essential ingredient of his basic attitude. Whereas in your reasoning, it's the other way round. You hold, and quite cogently so, that Kabir, at heart, was a social reformer, the one unwittingly obliged to dress up his intent as mysticism. What an inversion of my thesis, which, from your perspective seems quite reasonable!'

'That's a shift of focus Pandit-ji, not inversion.'

'Your arguments are solid. Your questioning of the emphasis I've placed on Kabir, the mystic, does hold water. In taking up Kabir, my chief objective was to establish him as a pre-eminent thinker and poet, poet-saint, for after coming across Acharya Kshiti Mohan Sen's work, I had become conscious of the perfunctory way Kabir was treated in Hindi literature.'

'Mahavir,' said Ram Mohan, 'you should take these words as the ultimate compliment.'

'My confidence is going through the roof.' Wilson's voice quivered with emotion. 'I feel encouraged enough to ask something of you, Pandit-ji,' Wilson paused, looking tentative.

'By all means,' said Acharya Dwivedi, as he took off his glasses and fumbled, trying to put them on the stool by his chair and was saved from dropping them by Nisha, who sat close by, eliciting a thankful glance from him.

'Nothing can add more to my book than your foreword for my book.'

'Certainly, Wilson-ji, but it will be in Hindi.'

'Mahavir will translate it into English,' said Ram Mohan.

Acharya Dwivedi gave a yawn. Nisha glanced at her father, who said, 'Pandit-ji, it'll be kind of you to write a few words for my daughter!'

'Of course,' Acharya Dwivedi put on his glasses as Nisha, all perked up, handed him her notebook.

* * *

A few months later, Acharya Dwivedi would die, before Mahavir Wilson could finalize the manuscript of his book on Kabir.

THREE

Ram Mohan kept his word to Liyaqat Argali. None of his candidates failed to make it to the state civil services, if interviewed by the board chaired by the former. 'This man's making money,' said Tiwari-ji once, 'sullying your reputation.' The man in question was the one Argali had deputed to contact Ram Mohan with names of candidates.

'The last time on my way here, I met this person on the bus, he named you and Munni Prasad as the two biggest bribe-takers at the Commission. I said, "This's calumny. I've been told the opposite." He said, "Dr Ram Mohan doesn't meet the candidates because he wants them to approach his middleman."'

Not meeting candidates in person was an obsession with Ram Mohan. If anyone brought him or her along, before the interview, he would make a song and dance about it and tell the visitor to send the young man or woman away. Some took offence. How could they be faulted on something they didn't know! That plainclothes CID sleuths were deployed to keep an eye on the visitors to the members' bungalows was what Ram Mohan told them. No one in his family bought it. 'He's being fantastical,' was Nishant's refrain, who thought Baabuji was losing out on the gratitude the candidates must feel after their selection. They would come to hold crucial positions in the state bureaucracy but wouldn't feel indebted to Baabuji. The man who got Baabuji to select them would remain their sole benefactor.

After the initial shock and disbelief at what Tiwari-ji's fellow passenger had said, Ram Mohan recovered and said, 'Those with no power run down those who've got somewhere. Their cynicism renders them incapable of telling the wheat from the chaff.'

'That's right. To win everybody's approval is impossible. People would say what they like. That's how they cope with their failures. My concern is something else.'

'If you think Argali has broken his word, you're wrong. I got a call from him.' Tiwari-ji sat up, his face gleaming. 'He's already mentioned UPSC to Shukla-ji, who likes the idea. Not only that! Shukla-ji once came close to speaking to Sanjay Gandhi about it, but Sanjay-ji was in one of his moods. Argali wants to talk to me face to face.'

'You're thinking of going to Lucknow?'

'Shukla-ji and Argali are coming here to attend a wedding. Shukla-ji will leave after the wedding. Argali will hang around for two more days. He's the chief guest at some function here. I want to invite him over.'

'What if Saansad-ji gets wind of Argali paying you a visit?'

'I've thought of that. I'll tell him that someone close to Argali has cleared the written exam of the state civil services. His visit was in that connection . . . Saansad-ji isn't the suspicious type. Not like Shukla-ji or Indira-ji or for that matter Baran Singh.'

Things went as planned. Tiwari-ji was present when Argali came to the Commission Bungalow. Chaturvedi-ji and Sinha Sahab too were there. Ram Mohan was jubilant. He was back in favour with Shukla-ji. They hadn't talked so warmly in ages like they had that afternoon at the circuit house, just before the latter was to head back to Lucknow. 'I know you're keen on the UPSC, Ram

Mohan. If not for this thing cropping up, I'd have got the process started. Liyaqat would tell you. I'll get you this appointment.'

Ram Mohan couldn't wait to know what this 'thing' was. Leaving the other guests in the drawing room, he took Argali and Tiwari-ji to his room.

'Please mention it nowhere,' Argali said. 'Other than people close to Indira-ji and Sanjay-ji, no one else knows . . . Indira-ji's thinking of holding election—'

'Where's the need? The country's on course,' said Ram Mohan.

'She's under immense pressure from her friends, none of whom is into active politics. Sanjay-ji, on the other hand, thinks that the Emergency should be in place for an indefinite period. Setting things right will take a lot of doing. This country isn't amenable to measures other than coercive.'

'He's right, one hundred percent!'

'We all agree. His mother, however, can be made to feel qualms about the Constitution kept in abeyance. But we Indians, bound up in old ways, don't understand the true objectives of the Constitution. The rights and freedoms set down in it become apt to be misused to promote anarchy. The opposition knows the importance of a liberal Constitution but prefers to take advantage of people's ignorance to achieve its short-term goals. That's beside the point. The point is that Indira-ji, with Emergency on her conscience, might declare general election. We don't know when! It's a serious possibility or Sanjay-ji wouldn't feel so out of sorts and Shukla-ji wouldn't have desisted from making the request for you to be considered for the UPSC.'

'Now what, Liyaqat bhai?'

'Don't worry, Dr Sahab. Shukla-ji and Sanjay-ji are going nowhere. It might take some time, but you'll be given your due. Let's go back to the drawing room.'

* * *

The next day, Ram Mohan and Tiwari-ji went to meet Saansad-ji, who now stayed in Allahabad, barring occasional trips to Delhi. He didn't think much of Shukla-ji's right-hand man calling on Ram Mohan. 'If you're holding a critical position, they all would approach you. We, politicians, are barefaced when it comes to seeking favours.' When Ram Mohan told him what he had learnt from Argali, Saansad-ji began to speculate on the opposition's strategy, on the political equation likely to emerge.

To Ram Mohan's query about his options, Saansad-ji gave a shrug, 'If what Argali's saying is true, I don't know what I'll do. There's no place for me in the party that is under Sanjay's sway. Among the older lot who count are those who've won his trust through servility. With him in the wings, Indira-ji has settled the question of leadership for good. Congress is a family-owned venture, neither more nor less,' Saansad-ji laughed.

'About a year ago, Sanjay was informed that Baran Singh, being at the end of his rope, had raised the white flag and wanted to atone for his intransigence through a speech at some function, supporting the Emergency. He was released from prison and brought straight to this event,' Ram Mohan and Tiwari-ji listened spellbound, 'and before anything else, he shouted, "Jawaharlal Nehru". The crowd roared, "Zindabad". Then, "Indira Gandhi", which received a more vigorous response, enough to confirm Baran Singh's capitulation. And when he yelled, "Sanjay Gandhi", the audience exploded in "Zindabad, Zindabad". It was sensational. Someone like Chaudhary could be brought to his knees! Then catching them out, was the next name, "Rahul Gandhi", to which the response was the same, though a fraction subdued as those on the stage checked their enthusiasm. Baran Singh was quiet for a second before proceeding to speak in the same mordant vein, but before he could go too far, he was shouted down and whisked off.'

Ram Mohan was still laughing when Tiwari-ji said, 'But Saansad-ji, there's an anomaly here. Rahul Gandhi is Rajiv Gandhi's son, not Sanjay Gandhi's.'

Ram Mohan wiped his eyes as Saansad-ji said, 'So what? He and his younger sister Priyanka are the only grandchildren Indira-ji has. It's hard to think up a more ingenious way of saying that Congress belongs to the Nehru dynasty. Rahul Gandhi can well be viewed as next in line to the PM's chair after Sanjay. At least for now. Until Sanjay has a child of his own.'

When they took their leave, Saansad-ji, still chatty, came out and walked them to the Fiat.

A week later, Argali's information came true. Indira Gandhi announced an election for a new Lok Sabha, astounding the country, explaining what had warranted Emergency and why she decided against its continuation. It had served its purpose. The country was moving in the right direction. Even as she addressed the nation on AIR, political detainees were being released, who would later meet at Desai's place in New Delhi, not all of them, only leaders of the four major opposition parties. Baran Singh commanded the largest following among them.

These leaders agreed to merge their parties together and contest the general election under one symbol and one flag. Thus, in the crucible of the common opposition to the Congress, was born a new political entity: People's Party. The man behind the experiment was JP, who would later concede in an interview to a foreign publication, that his insistence on Indira Gandhi's resignation was an error of judgment. Had he had any inkling of her resorting to Emergency, he would have done things differently. He would have waited for the elections less than two years off.

Desai, the dogged practitioner of Indira-baiting, was at the helm of this assemblage, People's Party, which had less than two months to prepare for the polls. No way it could get in place an organizational structure of its own, at such a short notice and amidst such scorching political activity as had taken over the country. It had to make do with whatever was left of the electoral logistics belonging to the erstwhile parties that made up this straggly formation, of which Baran Singh's former outfit

and People's Union, the Hindu nationalist party, were the two
key constituents.

Ram Mohan went to see Saansad-ji again. It was the last month
of winter, and the grounds of his house were buzzing with visitors.
Some stood in a group near the gate. Some others occupied the
chairs placed in the sun on the lawn. Others hung about on the
driveway, while three or four of them had parked themselves on
the front veranda, waiting to be let in. This was only a shadow of
what it used to be when Saansad-ji visited his hometown as CM.
The present crowd consisted mostly of the politically orphaned,
after he had fallen foul of Indira Gandhi. Now that things were on
the move, they were eager to know what strategy their leader was
contemplating.

Ram Mohan didn't have to wait outside. A close aide of
Saansad-ji ushered him straight into the drawing room filled with
people more important than those outside. Engaged in conversation
with them was Saansad-ji's wife, who motioned Ram Mohan to
a sofa. Saansad-ji was closeted in the study with an emissary from
Delhi. What could have prompted the sudden move on the PM's
part was the question she was trying to address.

Just then, Saansad-ji and the emissary from Delhi came out
of the study. They all rose. Some touched Saansad-ji's feet,
including Ram Mohan whom Saansad-ji, holding by the elbow,
walked to a corner of the drawing room. 'I might soon have
some good news for you, something to revive your aborted
political career.' Everybody was still on their feet when they
returned. Saansad-ji asked them to sit as he took a seat beside
his wife. All were keen to share their reading of the situation.
Saansad-ji had no time for that. He had to make some urgent
calls to Lucknow and Delhi. Then there were others waiting
outside to see him.

* * *

That Saansad-ji wanted to involve him in some political venture didn't stir Ram Mohan. He was disconcerted. He wanted to play it safe. His new-found friendship with Argali had helped restore his old ties with Shukla-ji. He had said to Chaturvedi-ji and Sinha Sahab, 'I'll wager that Shukla-ji will get me into the UPSC.' Ram Mohan had little interest left in the hurly-burly of politics. His mind set on the UPSC as his next port of call, he couldn't afford his association with Argali and Shukla-ji to start unravelling.

One evening, Chaturvedi-ji rang up, 'Sinha Sahab has an explosive piece of news! We're coming to your place.'

'Jagjivan Ram has resigned from the cabinet and the Congress.'

Ram Mohan gulped. Sinha Sahab added, 'I've no reason to doubt my source.'

Jagjivan Ram, the tallest Harijan leader, had served in the Congress government since the first Cabinet of independent India. Had been one of the staunchest adherents of Nehru's daughter. His departure would be a monstrous blow to her.

Chaturvedi-ji questioned the time he had chosen to ditch her. Sinha Sahab was quiet. Ram Mohan said, 'Jagjivan Ram will regret his move. Congress is going to win this ballot.'

'Jagjivan Ram's decision can't be faulted,' said Sinha Sahab. 'He was loyal to the family for decades together and let himself be used as the party's mascot of its Harijan following. Yet while in the Congress there was no chance of him ever becoming PM. He might achieve this burning ambition of his in the new, rapidly emerging political scenario.'

'You think the Congress might go belly-up in the polls!' said Ram Mohan.

Sinha Sahab smiled and asked Nishant who was in the drawing room to go tune in to BBC on his radio. Nishant left. They went on with discussing the import of Jagjivan Ram's supposed defection.

* * *

It was on BBC Radio. Jagjivan Ram had quit. Leaving with him were three or four senior Congress leaders, one of whom was next only to the Harijan leader in stature: Saansad-ji. Ram Mohan recalled his words, 'I might soon have some good news for you.' He put two and two together. This, the talk about reviving his political career, was linked to the message the emissary from Delhi had brought.

The breaking away of Jagjivan Ram and others from the Congress was the banner headline in every newspaper. Congress for Democracy (CFD) was the name chosen for their new outfit with Jagjivan Ram as its president and Saansad-ji, sitting next to him in the picture taken of their press conference, as its general secretary. Then came the word that CFD would contest elections as an ally of the People's Party, the grand alliance, a mélange of anti-Congress forces led by Desai, blessed by JP. Ram Mohan held his breath.

Less than a week later, Saansad-ji's wife landed at the Commission Bungalow. The CFD and People's Party had reached an understanding on seat sharing. Ram Mohan was earmarked as CFD's nominee from Fatehpur. 'You get ready for taking on the Congress in your old constituency. It'll be to win this time,' she said and left, having no idea of Ram Mohan being in two minds about giving up his present position.

Excitement surged through the Commission Bungalow. It was the first time the prospect of Baabuji being elected to Parliament looked solid. To know his family's thoughts, he gathered them in the drawing room. They were all for him to contest. 'Is it worth the risk? My leaving the Commission to fight an election? To rush into such a critical decision without taking account of the stakes involved! Let's assume for a minute that I lose—'

'When any of us point out something like that, you say why argue against one's own self?' said Nishant.

'Nothing's without context. If I tell you to look on the bright side of a situation, that's because I don't want you to be daunted by the obstacles. I'm against quitting easily. Even if you fail, you won't regret you didn't make the effort. That's only when there's nothing much at stake—'

'Shekhar Jijaji had such a good job. You had him quit—' said Nishant before being cut short.

'He's an engineer. He can always get a job. Even in India where unemployment is rife. He can go abroad . . . Instead of being stuck with this job, he should explore other possibilities. A PhD in his field would put him in a different league from his ITI colleagues. Not counting the fact that to be able to live in Delhi is itself an achievement!'

'Chances of your losing must be close to nil. Or Saansad-ji wouldn't think of fielding you. He sent you here when security of the Commission seemed the best option. But now—'

'The victory will mean we can all live in Delhi,' said Nisha who was to go to Delhi to be with Shekhar for some time.

'Nobody can question my interest in politics. I fought three elections, but we had nothing to lose then—'

'In terms of money, we lost a lot,' said Kanti.

'If I hadn't fought those elections, we wouldn't be living in this bungalow. You can't see these linkages!' Then turning to Nishant, 'Unless you're an Indira Gandhi, a Baran Singh, a Jagjivan Ram, a Saansad-ji or Shukla-ji, unless you're a big politician, you can never be sure of winning a ballot. Suppose I lose! Where will we go? Back to Kanpur? That's why I'm reluctant. The risk involved is way too much. Before anything like that, I must ensure you're fixed up with a job . . . But, before anything else, I also have to find a boy for Sandhya. Leaving the Commission with nothing solid in hand can spell disaster. What about my newly revived alliance with Shukla-ji and Argali . . .? Losing an election now will mean losing so much else,' he paused and said to Nisha, 'I wouldn't have encouraged Shekhar to go to IIT Delhi for PhD, if I didn't have a good mind to find a way to move to Delhi myself. That day isn't far off. We'll all be living in Delhi before long. Not through getting elected to Parliament but through my appointment to the Union Public Service Commission.'

'The possibility of Congress's return to power is thin,' said Nishant, 'so even if we don't win in Fatehpur, Saansad-ji would be better placed to have you sent to the UPSC.'

'Can Indira Gandhi be defeated so easily? Look at this disparate crowd of politicos banded together to fight her and the son. Can such an entity as People's Party pose a threat to Congress, her ownership of which nobody can challenge? You can leave her like Jagjivan Ram and Saansad-ji, but at your own peril . . . These people have agreed to fight the polls under the leadership of Desai in deference to his seniority and to JP's wish. How long can an arrangement like this last? In terms of mass following, Desai's nowhere near the likes of Baran Singh. Jagjivan Ram and Vajpayee, too, have the backing of a certain section of society, but none can match Indira Gandhi as regards political legacy and personal charisma. And because of its unbroken stint at power, her party's coffers are full, let alone its vast organizational base inherited from the freedom movement. Considering all this, wouldn't I be justified in declining Saansad-ji's offer?'

* * *

Ram Mohan was racked with a dilemma. He couldn't let go of the security of the Commission for a venture whose outcome was hard to guess. Yet he didn't want to let down Saansad-ji, but for whom he would still be teaching at DAV College, competing with people who now looked up to him. He was anxious about how to convey it to Saansad-ji, his inability to rise to the challenge. A day or two later, as he still dithered over the issue, blew in K. Dwivedi, the man who would help set his mind at ease.

On the strength of his unalloyed sycophancy, K. Dwivedi had come to possess a special place among Ram Mohan's favourites. In his late thirties, he hailed from one of the villages in Fatehpur district and had supported Ram Mohan during an election campaign.

A lower division booking clerk in Indian Railways, stationed at Kanpur Central, he supplemented his paltry salary through bribes that people paid to travel on trains running packed. Most of these clerks kept some berths aside to be sold to the desperate at a premium. K. Dwivedi had got this job through some political connection, not long after his BA. Always a poor student, he could have passed none of his exams without the help of unfair means, a fact appreciated by the likes of Deena. Later, he obtained an MA degree in Hindi literature as a private student by means of an innovative way. A fulltime job and married life wouldn't allow him time or patience to prepare cheating material. This novel idea occurred to him because he was a railway employee.

Kanpur University was made up of an assortment of colleges located in various parts of the state. Its exam papers were sent to external examiners for marking and the chief means of transport employed for the purpose was by train. As an insider, it wasn't hard for K. Dwivedi to learn of the movement of the bundles of exam papers. He would go to where those big bundles were stacked before being loaded onto the train and write down the addresses, then armed with his railway pass, he would travel for free to each address.

Plied with entreaties, the examiner would be left with no choice but to melt. 'Sir, I come from a poor Brahman family. My father died when I was in class twelve. I somehow did my BA as a private student and got this job. Now I'm the sole earning member in my family. My father, who couldn't go beyond grade eight, wanted me to obtain an MA. Sir, it's just his wish that I want to fulfil.' At the first sign of resistance, he would hunker down before the examiner and catch hold of his feet. Not only had he passed his MA but done so with a second division.

On Ram Mohan's advice, he had kept his eyes peeled for certain positions in the state's administrative setup, appointments to which were made only through interview. No sooner did a suitable situation materialize than K. Dwivedi applied. Quite a senior post in the state's labour department, which would send him many notches up from his present low-grade position. Hence, K. Dwivedi launched into an argument against Ram Mohan resigning from the Commission.

'It's your call Dr Sahab. I, for one, would rather you declined to be drawn into the uncertainties of electoral politics again. You still have three years here. Congress may be on the slippery slope, but no guarantee your votes would increase enough to hand you a win.'

'How to say no to Saansad-ji! That might end our friendship.'

K. Dwivedi laughed and said, 'Dr Sahab, you'll soon have to choose between Shukla-ji and Saansad-ji.'

Ram Mohan's face lightened up. 'I won't squander my current relation with Argali and Shukla-ji.'

He went to see Saansad-ji's wife. She listened as he made plain how difficult it was for him to get into electoral politics now. 'It might blow up in the face! Yes, I appreciate your reluctance, Ram Mohan ji. But this is the chance of a lifetime. That doesn't mean your anxieties aren't reasonable. This is a contest after all . . . I'll let Saansad-ji know.'

When Saansad-ji called from Delhi, the excuse mouthed to his wife earlier was cut off when Ram Mohan tried to repeat it. K. Dwivedi, who sat there to provide moral support to his only hope of a better life, could hear the voice on the other side. Saansad-ji was agitated. Ram Mohan listened, looking contrite. An alarmed K. Dwivedi moved to the edge of his seat, gesturing that he shouldn't back down. Just as Ram Mohan made as if to respond, Saansad-ji hung up. K. Dwivedi was put at ease.

'It's thrown him. Fatehpur should be part of Baran Singh's share of seats. Saansad-ji bagged it by invoking my name. Baran

Singh couldn't suggest anyone with a better performance against
the Congress in Fatehpur. I can't but feel sad. I let go of them out
of expediency, first Chaudhary Sahab, now Saansad-ji!'

'No need to be sorry, Dr Sahab. Why can't we look at things
from our perspective? All that matters to Saansad-ji is that you're
the only one who can win Fatehpur for his fledgling party. Let's
not lament. Nothing in the circumstances is better for you than
the UPSC.'

Ram Mohan nodded.

Ram Mohan invited Chaturvedi-ji and Sinha Sahab to tea in
the evening. They talked about the upcoming election, about what
made the occasion so singular, about the presence of such diverse
political groups and personages on one platform whose hate for
Indira Gandhi's guts was the only force binding them. Sinha Sahab
endorsed Ram Mohan's decision. The only differing voice was
of Nishant's. Chaturvedi-ji also murmured that Ram Mohan may
well have missed out on an opportunity. K. Dwivedi laughed it
out of court.

The final straw in clinching the fact that Ram Mohan wouldn't
stand in the election was K. Dwivedi. Nishant wouldn't forgive
him. Then a remark of K. Dwivedi's made Nishant's dislike of him
visceral. It so happened that when the conversation turned to Ram
Mohan's personality, his varied talents, followed by the question
as to who among his sons looked like picking up his mantle, K.
Dwivedi said, 'None of them has it in him. Our Dr Sahab's in a
class of his own.' Chaturvedi-ji and Sinha Sahab remonstrated. This
wasn't the way to draw comparisons. Ram Mohan said nothing,
which Nishant took as his approval of K. Dwivedi's cutting remark.
As it is, Nishant didn't take kindly to Baabuji's assertion that he
would fit each of them with the wherewithal to lead a comfortable
life. Now, after that silence, he vowed he would rather remain
unemployed than secure a job with Baabuji's help. If bracketed
with Deena, who was helpless without Baabuji, Nishant felt

offended. Baabuji couldn't appreciate the nature of his ambition. He too liked to think big, and a job meant merely to sustain him, to help him see his existence out, wouldn't be good enough. A profession must allow not just a respectable income but also some influence. Without that, life wouldn't be worth your while, and Baabuji could do nothing other than helping him get some clerical job in some godforsaken government office.

Nishant wasn't so much averse to his father's help as to his idea of employment for him. But with the kind of influence Baabuji had, nothing better was possible. Only successful politicians had that power to help you to something important. That's why Nishant didn't approve of the turning down of Saansad-ji's offer, because once elected, Baabuji could become a minister. If not for K. Dwivedi, he could still have been persuaded to stand in this election.

But yes, Ram Mohan would open the way for K. Dwivedi to prosper unbelievably. Given a single vacancy, only one interview board was formed, and Ram Mohan got to preside at it by the courtesy of the Commission chairman.

* * *

Electioneering had entered its crucial phase. All the biggies of the Congress and People's Party were furiously addressing public meetings. Asked by Shukla-ji to supervise the Congress campaign in all the three parliamentary seats in Allahabad, Liyaqat Argali, who had made the city his interim base, swung by the Commission Bungalow. Ram Mohan was thankful for not succumbing to Saansad-ji's offer as Argali said, 'Shukla-ji has spoken to Sanjay-ji. You'll be sent to the UPSC after Congress returns to power.'

Argali was lodged at the Circuit House. His immediate task was to mind the preparations for Sanjay Gandhi's rally two days later. He had asked Ram Mohan to keep the coming week free. 'You wanted to be part of the poll excitement! Here's this constituency where you can be of help.'

The area in question had significant votes of Kurmis, among whom Ram Mohan was held in high regard. It was rare for anyone of their caste to occupy such a prestigious place in a constitutional body like the Public Service Commission. He had also attended several weddings and social functions in this area.

If Sanjay Gandhi's rally in Allahabad was anything to go by, the ragtag group called People's Party had no chance of besting the Congress. Nishant and Deena were flabbergasted at the hordes of people pouring into the KP College ground to hear India's most powerful man. Even the neighbouring roads were bursting with crowds. Despite a heavy police bandobast, it took a while for the youth leader's motorcade to crawl to the venue. Amidst slogan-shouting, Sanjay Gandhi, Shukla-ji and others made their way onto the stage to be welcomed by Liyaqat Argali and other Congress leaders, including the party candidate for Allahabad City, Arimardan Singh. Indira Gandhi always looked on him with favour and had, during the Emergency, promoted him from deputy minister to Minister of State. Arimardan Singh was ever ready to suit his opinion to that of Mrs. Gandhi and her son and was one of the fawners they couldn't do without.

After the rally, Nishant admitted that Congress might not be in such a bad state after all. Ram Mohan was gracious to him, 'First, all the racket made by the JP Movement, and now all these people joining hands against Indira-ji, given all this, it was natural for you to draw the conclusion you did. Once Tiwari-ji arrives, you two can get down to the campaign work Argali assigns.'

Zameer left in the morning and was back with Tiwari-ji before the day was out. Ram Mohan updated his friend on the latest. Late in the evening, they went to the Circuit House. Argali was in the lobby, talking to local Congress leaders. They got up to greet Ram Mohan. Settling down, Ram Mohan said, 'I must congratulate you for the rally, Liyaqat bhai. What a smash hit!' Argali gestured towards the local party leaders, 'Credit goes to them.'

'To pull off something like that wouldn't have been possible without Liyaqat bhai's leadership,' said one of them. Then they left. Ram Mohan, Tiwari-ji and Nishant followed Argali into the dining room. They had had their dinner. He ordered tea for them.

'I'm so happy to see you, Tiwari-ji.'

'He'll be here all through the campaign,' said Ram Mohan. 'I'll take him and Nishant to visit some people, though Kurmis have long been voting for Baran Singh's party.'

'Baran Singh is now part of this new dispensation. Won't that dilute his influence?'

'It's hard to say!' said Tiwari-ji. 'He—'

'He's one of the several biggies in this new party, no longer the biggest leader that he was of his party,' said Argali.

'He's had a big say in ticket distribution in People's Party. At least in UP. But yes, the situation's different this time. No wonder if Congress eats into some of his following!'

'That's the spirit,' exclaimed Argali, then to Ram Mohan, 'I'd like to have Tiwari-ji with me during my stay in this area. I need someone with whom I can share my thoughts in confidence. Each of those who surround me here has an axe to grind.'

'No problem. Tiwari-ji's feedback should give you something to consider.'

'Okay, Tiwari-ji, tomorrow you can enjoy Dr Sahab's company. The day after when I'm travelling outside the city, you'll come with me.'

Then one day, while sharing his experiences of the campaign in and around Allahabad in the company of Argali, Tiwari-ji said something that dealt a blow to the buoyancy of Ram Mohan's drawing room, where they were having a good time speculating on the post-election scenario. Chaturvedi-ji and Sinha Sahab were also present. 'I don't think Indira-ji's coming back to power. People's

response to the opposition rallies is altogether different from that
of the crowds at the Congress meetings addressed by Sanjay and
his mother. Even Argali confided to me his grave doubts about his
party's victory.'

'Would she have gone in for election if that were the case?'
snorted Sinha Sahab.

'People's Party might get a surprising number of seats in UP
and some other states in this part of the country,' said Ram Mohan,
'but what about the South, where the JP Movement was virtually
non-existent? People's Party has a ghostly presence, if any, in non-
Hindi states.'

After that there was much debate on the issue, with Nishant on
Tiwari-ji's side and Ram Mohan on Sinha Sahab's. Chaturvedi-ji
found glimpses of truth in the arguments of both sides.

* * *

The poll results staggered everybody. For the Congress, they were
cataclysmic. Surprised too were People's Party leaders who, though
confident of their victory, had failed to get the true measure of
the intensity of public anger against the mother–son duo. Indira
Gandhi herself was defeated by Raj Narayan in Raebareli, so was
Sanjay Gandhi in Amethi, though the South stood behind the
Congress. That couldn't stop her foes being swept to power with
absolute majority.

In every single Lok Sabha seat in UP, the ruling party stood
smashed. People joked that even scarecrows for the opposition's
candidates would have won. A landmark election that dissolved
all identities. People voted as one on the deposition of Indira
Gandhi. Nishant felt vindicated. Even Ram Mohan, an optimist
of his calibre, reeled from the results. Staring in his face was
the fact that there would be no UPSC for him now that the
Congress was booted out, but taking heart from what he still

had, three years at the Commission, he recovered and turned his
mind to the shape of things to come, including the imminence
of the People's Party's government.

With Desai, Baran Singh and Jagjivan Ram being the leading
contenders in the new dispensation, PM's chair became a cause of
contention. Asked to intervene, JP picked the most senior among
them to lead the first non-Congress government of independent
India. Desai's age-old ambition was realized. Baran Singh and
Jagjivan Ram were thrown a bone each and made deputy prime
ministers. Elected to parliament from Lucknow, Saansad-ji also
got a prominent place on the cabinet. Ram Mohan recalled his
association with Baran Singh, talking nostalgically about the trust
the latter had come to place in him.

Soon, the People's Party regime dismissed Congress regimes
in various states where, given the general mood, Congress had
forfeited its right to remain in power. It was payback time for Indira
Gandhi, who had repeatedly abused the provisions of an article
in the Constitution to dismiss non-Congress state governments.
When fresh assembly elections took place, Congress was put to
rout again. People's Party captured power in all northern states.
Most of the new chief ministers were Baran Singh's men. The
one given the reins of Uttar Pradesh was truly undistinguished,
a lawyer from a small town. The installation of someone of this
stature showed that Baran Singh had no better choice among those
close to him. It had to be the farmer leader's hardcore man. The
choice cut Ram Mohan to the quick.

'You should have the courtesy to go meet Chaudhary Sahab,'
said Tandon-ji when Ram Mohan went to his place for a chit-chat
in the light of the altered political landscape. 'There's no harm in
that. Tell him how pleased you are to see him as deputy PM.'

One day, Ram Mohan got on an overnight train to New
Delhi. From the station, he went straight to Shekhar's lodgings.
He chose not to stay at the UP Niwas for fear he might bump into

some acquaintance of Shukla-ji's or Argali's. Shekhar took a couple of days off from his PhD work at the IIT.

Like some other politicians in office, Baran Singh too met members of the public at his residence every morning, for which no prior notice was needed. Anybody could walk in. Some came merely to make an acquaintance, while some others, who had met the leader in the past, would be there to remind him of their existence. A few others dropped in to do some bootlicking. Much of the crowd, however, consisted of people seeking relief from some injustice or crisis or disadvantage or hurdle that they faced in their respective areas.

'It's a good thing for those in power to make the time to have open house at their places,' said Shekhar as they made their way, sitting in a noisy but slow-moving three-wheeler, towards Lutyens' Delhi, the poshest, the most exclusive pocket in the country, the grandeur of which—its stately tree-lined avenues, majestic roundabouts with flowerbeds, big, awesome bungalows sitting in splendid grounds—the grandeur of the setting identified with India's most powerful, the grandeur so desirable, in form and substance both, that it could have solely accounted for the insistence of Nehru and his cohorts on seizing power from the British without delay. Some others were wary of the haste. Something to that effect had Jaan Muhammad said once, on a lighter note, during a discussion at the Commission Bungalow. But the observation made by the PA on a rather serious note, during the same discourse of which Shekhar's comment reminded his father-in-law.

'How vastly at odds two ways of looking at something can be,' said Ram Mohan, 'which amuses me no end. I agree with you that it's thoughtful of our political leaders to allow the common man a chance to seek justice directly from them. Many have got their grievances redressed this way, through these Janata Durbars, but Jaan Muhammad's take on the matter is the opposite of how you or for that matter I see it.'

'I've met him twice. He sounds intelligent.'

'That he is! Not many at the Commission can match his knowledge of English. He drafts letters for me. But he's a mortal dissenter. He delights in making a show of his hostility to fixed notions, to interpretations of things held as given. He feels aggrieved at being deprived of what he deserved. He'd had to give up on his desire to teach History at some college through the force of circumstances. Now he takes out his frustration on anything or anyone revered or idolized. I enjoy the way he rips into the arguments of the unwary—' Ram Mohan paused as Shekhar gave directions to the three-wheeler wallah.

'What problem can he have with politicians listening to complaints of people at their residence?' said Shekhar.

'He imputes it to the politician's attempt to benefit even from their failure to provide good rule—'

'I don't get it.'

'He says that rather than making themselves accessible this way to just a few amongst the multitude, these politicians should make accessible to people things for which they profess to seek power. Through tokenism, they try to hide their failure on a grand scale in almost everything, failure to deliver the goods: to empower people by means of education, and protection from violence, by strengthening democratic institutions, by efficient delivery of public services, by providing the needed infrastructure, by economic policies that should help generate employment and bring in revenue for social programmes and so forth . . . If the politician saw the public right, where would be the need for holding these Janata Durbars? Jaan Muhammad declaims. They're all for the bestowing of political patronage selectively yet keep spouting off about their being the common man's servant.'

'How can it serve the politician politically, this listening to the grievances of such a small number of people? So, why take the trouble?'

'That's what Jaan Muhammad means by tokenism. This is just one of the devices they employ to make a favourable impression on people in general, people who're not the recipient of such benevolence but get to hear dramatic versions of it and are likely to think better of these leaders.'

'Isn't Jaan Muhammad's reasoning a bit fanciful?'

'He overdoes it sometimes. But I love the way he locks horns with people who're no pushovers. The élan with which he dissects the issue under discussion leaves his interlocutors mumbling. I love it.'

The hubbub ahead marked the home minister's residence. A posse of policemen was trying to maintain order. Outside the small entrance gate beside the closed main gate, some volunteers were making feeble attempts to convert the throng into a queue. Suddenly, a middle-aged man in khadi strode towards Ram Mohan, who along with Shekhar, had quietly joined the visitors converged near the small gate. He was one of Baran Singh's aides, a small-time one for sure, as Ram Mohan failed to place him, but the man knew 'Dr Sahab'. He took them out of the melee, and away from the main gate, they followed him along the front side of the boundary wall, into the side lane leading to another entrance to the huge bungalow, meant for members of the home minister's staff.

The man said he was happy to facilitate Dr Sahab's meeting with Chaudhary Sahab for old time's sake and asked why Dr Sahab didn't request for an appointment. Ram Mohan said he wished to meet Chaudhary Sahab, first, just as a humble admirer at his Janata Durbar, and discerning even a flicker of his old affection, he would come again to solicit his indulgence. The man took them straight to the big lawn at the back, where many visitors stood in a line. Shortly, amidst a murmur of excitement on the back veranda, emerged Chaudhary Baran Singh, clad in white dhoti-kurta. Flanked by aides, he climbed down the steps to the lawn and walked over to the head of the line. His Janata Durbar was under way.

Standing before every visitor, he listened as one of his men scribbled down the points of the problem. Many visitors had their complaints in writing that Baran Singh would hand to another of his men. As Ram Mohan touched his feet, he gazed at him, then putting his hand on his arm, he steered him away to a secluded spot on the lawn. Ram Mohan hadn't expected Chaudhary Sahab to be so blunt. 'You left me, didn't you?'

'Chaudhary Sahab, I never left you, at least not emotionally, but—'

'You thought the Congress was a better option? Patience isn't a virtue by which you set much store!'

'That's not the case. In terms of time and money, I found active politics hard to sustain. If I'd had some additional source of income—'

'You never left me emotionally! What about those who have toughed it out alongside me? Look, I've nothing to say but this: if you'd stuck to your teaching job and stuck by me, you would be a central minister today.' Baran Singh turned and walked back.

Shekhar, who had stood by the hedge along the boundary wall, under the lone mango tree, was thrown by the abruptness with which Baran Singh had disengaged himself from his father-in-law. 'That's what I'd feared . . . but didn't wish to regret later that I didn't try to mend fences.'

* * *

Not long after his trip to Delhi, Ram Mohan rushed off to Lucknow with Tiwari-ji, to show solidarity with Shukla-ji and Argali by visiting them at the hour deemed best for introspection and knowing your friends. 'If there's no chance to ingratiate yourself with the winning side, it's better to find friends among the losers.'

'And deepen our ties with them,' said Tiwari-ji.

From the guesthouse where Ram Mohan stayed when in Lucknow, they drove to Shukla-ji's new bungalow, allotted to him as the leader of opposition. Like the houses of those dislodged from power, his too wore a forlorn look, with hardly any people around. But the former CM was in good spirits, and after Argali arrived, there began a hearty conversation, full of jokes, about the new dispensation and its members, many of whom, with no experience of governance, were out of their depth in their new positions. One anecdote involved Raj Narain, the vanquisher of Indira Gandhi, who now was a Union cabinet minister. When Argali related the anecdote, Ram Mohan and Tiwari-ji laughed their heads off.

Three decades of Congress rule had taught people that they had to approach the politician for everything—for roads, healthcare, schools, electricity, post offices, granaries, irrigation facilities, and protection not only from local thugs but also from the police and other civil servants. To confer privilege on those who counted and dispense largesse to the common man in critical moments was the Congress's mantra. 'That's the key to success in electoral politics,' a Congress leader had once said to Ram Mohan. 'If people are in serious trouble, if there are floods, a cold wave or heat wave, a calamity of some sort, you give them a glimpse of your kindness by providing some relief.'

No sooner had the People's Party leaders assumed office than they began to be flooded with all kinds of demands. Raj Narayan was no exception. Pestered for this and that, he once lost his cool when a group of people from his area came with the request for electrification of their villages. 'Just plug it into my ass. You'll get non-stop power supply,' he shouted.

The prime ministerial ambitions of Baran Singh and Jagjivan Ram, too, were mocked during their chatter. Shukla-ji opined, 'This motley assemblage has no future. Given all the rumblings of discords within it, the experiment's bound to come apart, making way for Indira-ji's return sooner rather than later.'

The next day, Argali dropped them off at the station. On
entering its concourse, Ram Mohan couldn't help surveying the
boundary wall on the left. Facing it, stood then as before, a few
men with their legs splayed. Further ahead in the corner sat the
same decrepit public urinal, soaring above which was the same big
billboard and beholding the scene from it now, was neither Nehru
nor his daughter but the bespectacled JP.

* * *

The People's Party had been in power for fourteen months when
I arrived in Allahabad, amidst blistering summer, having just
passed class eleven in Kanpur. My father wanted to send me to
Allahabad University after twelfth, but Ram Mohan Uncle made
my move advance by one year. That I should do my twelfth from
Allahabad's Government Inter College, made sense to my father.
The city, though variously in decline, still offered a good learning
environment.

I stayed at the Commission Bungalow for a few days before
moving into my rented room. Thanks to political quiescence, Ram
Mohan was often out of town, on literary and social tours, not to
mention his visits to Parsadpur and Kanpur, occasioning a relaxed
atmosphere at the Commission Bungalow, making our remaining
summer vacation full of fun. Nisha had gone to Delhi. Sandhya was
there and all four of us would make merry. I cycled down daily
from my place and sometimes stayed overnight and sometimes
longer, depending on the length of their Baabuji's absence. We
played carrom board, cards, ludo, listened to film songs on AIR,
went to the movies. We watched Sandhya draw and paint. We
read stories. Sometimes Deena read out his poems. That Pant, the
famous Hindi poet, who had died the previous year, had praised
Deena's poems made us proud. Deena couldn't conceive a life
without poetry and film acting, about which he wouldn't stop

daydreaming. His Gabbar Singh act was quite talked-of among the visitors to the Commission Bungalow.

One day, Ram Mohan returned from one of his trips a day ahead of schedule. I knew of his stifling grip on his family, barring Mayank, who could never know the fear their father evoked in his siblings, especially in Deena. Nisha was now spared from his bouts of fierceness because of her marital status. Nishant too, because of his mutinous disposition. Though I knew their Baabuji to be a martinet, I couldn't have known what it looked like till that day.

We had just finished playing cards and sat chatting in the room with five doors. There had been the first monsoon showers earlier in the day, bringing respite from the heat, and Santosh, the cook-cum-servant, always jaunty with the master not home, was making onion pakoras. No sooner did he bring the first lot of steaming things than the doorbell rang. It should be Nishant, who had gone to meet some friend. Deena went to answer the door. The rest of us carried on. Seconds later, walking in on us was Ram Mohan Uncle, who, on hearing the gaiety, had decided to catch us with our fingers in the till.

Mayank and Sandhya, sitting on the bed, were making a pitch for being the first to be handed the plate of pakoras, which Santosh held temptingly, standing at a safe distance, giggling, and dithering, deciding finally in favour of Sandhya, reasoning that she was older. Just as he stepped up to hand her the plate, Ram Mohan bawled from the doorway, 'What's going on?' It was tangible, the fright in that room. Seated on the edge, Kanti Auntie and I stood up while Sandhya, as if rendered immobile, stayed where she was. Ram Mohan glowered at Santosh, a picture of utmost pity, whose attempt at meaningful sound collapsed as Ram Mohan lunged at him. His claim, tearful and mumbled, that he didn't do anything, was drowned out by a barrage of oaths spewing out of the master.

I hadn't seen him in such a ferocious temper. My parents, at times, mentioned something to the effect that he had a thing about men and women interacting. No, not just interaction but their mere presence in geographical proximity had a suggestion of indecency. I had had some idea, even if kind of blurry, of his tendency to be suspicious this way. Now it all lay illuminated. The reason for his violent reaction to our being together in that room with Santosh jovially offering the plate of pakoras to Sandhya couldn't be clearer. Santosh was asked to collect his things and leave the same day.

We had left the room. Sandhya and Mayank were now in their room, next to which all the action was taking place. Deena and I had gone back to Nishant's room. Shortly, Ram Mohan Uncle came to our room and said to me, 'Kartik, you mustn't lose sight of your aim. Work hard and live up to what's expected of you,' then glancing at my friend, 'Deena's on the mend, though still far from being able to pass his exams on his own. Boys like him have it in them to impact the performance of diligent students like you more than the other way round. Mayank and you are alike in many ways. Still, I'm happy that Deena employs his time constructively now. His talent for acting and writing poetry has been a revelation. He reads Hindi literature and mimics Gabbar Singh so well. He's come a long way from what he used to be. Now I want to ensure he gets the educational certificates required even for a clerical job. Given his marks in class eleven, I can't take a chance. He'll have to be sent to Dhata for his twelfth boards.'

After a good second division in tenth grade, Deena had been admitted to class eleven at the GIC again to see if he could clear his exam with enough marks to testify to his likely success in twelfth boards. That wasn't to be. He scraped through the class eleven exam. Even that wouldn't have been possible without the active help of his class teacher. To explain that, I want to recount an interesting episode.

Having quit stealing money, the frequency of Deena going to the movies had come down to once in a week. That meant no increase in his attendance at school. He would rather be elsewhere than in the classroom. His favourite haunt was the nearby Company Garden, where, sitting under a tree or in the sun, depending on the weather, he read poems or stories, sometimes with friends, but mostly alone.

One day, before he could make good his escape from the classroom, the class teacher entered. They all stood up. 'Sit down,' he said, taking his place behind the desk, when his eyes fell on Deena. 'Wherever have you been, Dinkar!' It was the period Deena feared most—English. 'Meet me after the class,' the teacher said and asked him to stand up and read anything from the textbook. Deena didn't have the textbook. Was given a further dressing down. His neighbour handed him the book. Deena couldn't move beyond the first word 'The', cutting a pathetic figure! Later, the class teacher said, 'Get somebody from your family to meet me or your name will be struck off.' What to do! Baabuji couldn't know that he was at it again, cutting classes and all. A way out had to be found. He hit on an idea.

He took two sheets of Baabuji's official letterhead and envelopes, went to the Company Garden, prepared a rough draft of a letter to the class teacher. His friend-cum-philosopher suggested they get it converted to English. How to do that? None of his friends was capable of a feat like that. Yet it had to be someone trustworthy. The FCP came up with a solution. He knew a student in class nine, who was his English teacher's blue-eyed boy. A while ago, the FCP, while looking for a quiet place to masturbate, had come upon them, the boy, and the teacher, in a room located in a rather isolated old wing of the school building. The teacher, engaged in ravenously kissing the boy's bared butt, hadn't heard the FCP, who, glued to the spot, didn't know how to handle the sight before him. Once he collected himself and left, the boy came running after him and was all entreaties. He divulged how he was seduced by the teacher who had been so persistent, hinting at all kinds of help and favours he could bestow and was generous while marking his exam papers, even told him questions to be asked in the exam.

The boy and the FCP struck a deal. The latter would keep mum in return for being occasionally allowed to touch the former up. The teacher was relieved. He wouldn't be given away. The FCP got this boy to have the teacher render this letter in English. From a nearby market, they got the letter typed on Baabuji's letterhead, Deena forged his signature, put it in the envelope that too had the insignia of the state government. The class teacher read it twice and said he should start attending school. Deena resolved to increase his visibility in each period to ward off undue attention his long absence would draw.

The class teacher, as it turned out, would have felt ill at ease that Ram Mohan, a man of consequence, should have taken the trouble to write to him. One late afternoon when Ram Mohan had some guests and Deena sat at the dining table behind the curtain, eavesdropping, the doorbell rang. The announced visitor sent a chill through Deena. What a catastrophe! No way could he have foreseen it. The class teacher was warmly received by Ram Mohan, who introduced him to others present and enquired as to the reason for his 'kind' visit. Deena, with his heart palpitating, left the dining table to brace himself.

When summoned, he found they were having a good laugh about something. No, not about something. It was the letter that Baabuji held in his hand while teasing the class teacher for being duped. An intrigued Deena was told to sit down. 'It's amazing, isn't it, his cleverness!' Baabuji said and asked Deena how he did it. They were impressed when he told them. One of the guests said, 'And look at his courage!'

Just before the class teacher was to leave, Ram Mohan asked
him to help Deena clear his class eleven and let him know what he
thought of Deena's chances in the twelfth board.

* * *

With the help of the class teacher and his own long-honed expertise
in cheating, Deena got past class eleven, though barely, leaving
Ram Mohan in no doubt that left to himself, he wouldn't pass his
twelfth board. Pratap Singh and Ghanraj Singh, the principal-cum-
owner of the Jawaharlal Nehru Memorial Inter College in Dhata,
had to be alerted.

Nishant went to Dhata and reported back the same evening.
Pratap Singh's response had been lukewarm at best. No, that
wouldn't be accurate. Pratap Singh was lukewarm only to the
suggestion of putting up Deena at his place, citing a family function
as the reason. He said nothing against Dhata being Deena's exam
centre again. Pratap Singh's discontent was revealed towards the
end of Nishant's narrative. He was disappointed in his friend.

Earlier that year, Pratap Singh had paid a visit to the Commission
Bungalow, accompanied by a young man who had cleared the
written exam for the state judicial service. Ram Mohan asked his
friend to send him out of the Commission premises immediately.
Pratap Singh was startled at the brusque way the demand was made.
Ram Mohan clarified why he didn't meet candidates at his place
before the interview. 'There are sleuths here in plain clothes who
keep an eye on our visitors. Why take risk when all I need is the
candidate's name?'

Mollified, Pratap Singh said the boy was the son of a close
friend and just needed to jump over this last fence, the interview.
'There are two interview boards for the purpose. If I happen to
interview him, he'll be selected.'

'What if the boy has the misfortune to face the other board?'

'A favour of this nature I never ask of my fellow members.' It just so happened that this candidate couldn't get to be interviewed by Ram Mohan and failed to make it to the judicial service. That was it! Pratap Singh had taken it hard.

Nishant had also gone to see Ghanraj Singh. He had an important visitor at the time, the deputy inspector of schools of Fatehpur, who, at the mention of Ram Mohan, had warmed towards Nishant. 'I've met Dr Sahab once. It was nine or ten years ago, when I was posted to Kanpur district. Give him my regards, though I doubt if he remembers me.' He took their phone number. 'Whenever I'm in Allahabad, I'll call Dr Sahab.' On learning of the purpose of Nishant's visit, he offered to help in any manner possible. They, the deputy inspector of schools and the principal, also zeroed in on the school likely to have Ghanraj Singh's school as its exam centre for the twelfth board. From that school, Deena had to fill the form as a private student. 'If they change the centre by chance,' the Inspector of Schools said, 'Dr Sahab can get him . . . What's the name of your brother?' he asked. 'In that case, Dr Sahab can get Dinkar shifted to this centre, to our Ghanraj Singh's school.'

About a month later, the deputy inspector of schools was visiting Allahabad in connection with some official work. He called the Commission Bungalow and Ram Mohan invited him over. With Pratap Singh feeling hard done by, having an official like him on his side would place Deena handily for his Dhata venture. The deputy inspector of schools recalled effusively his only meeting with Dr Sahab. When Deena brought tea, Ram Mohan asked him to sit and said, 'This is my son, the one least inclined among my children to obtain scholastic qualifications. He's otherwise fond of reading. He composes poems and has a gift for acting. I had to see *Sholay* to know how well he takes Gabbar Singh off. He wants to be a film actor, but he should acquire all the necessary certificates, without which you can't hold your head up in society.'

'You needn't worry, Dr Sahab. He'll pass his twelfth. Ghanraj Singh's school being his exam centre is just the job, and there are few places that allow an easier BA and MA than our Kanpur University. Getting all these certificates isn't a big deal.'

'Last time, Deena stayed at Pratap Singh's house. This time, I'd like to spare him the inconvenience—'

'Please leave it to me. I'll arrange his stay in Dhata.'

* * *

When told that in the twelfth board Deena wouldn't be appearing as a GIC student, the class teacher lauded the decision. He couldn't vouch for his success in the crucial exam if left to manage by himself. Now free to do with himself whatever he fancied during school hours, Deena returned to his old lifestyle outside home— going to the movies, spending time in the Company Garden and so forth.

The freedom from the harrying thought of the twelfth boards opened the way for Deena to be shackled to another kind of distress, distress more profound than anything Deena had known, more of a metaphysical kind than mundane, this distress. It was love, an emotion he hadn't experienced this way before. With Nisha didi in Delhi, he hadn't set eyes on Shampa in a while.

Girls would attract him all the time. Two of them were the daughters of the Commission employees, who had lit his fire. That was totally physical. He lusted for their bodies, yearned to see them naked, beat the meat thinking of them. With Shampa's image in mind, he didn't feel like masturbating. All he ached for was to be with her, chatting softly and voicing his love in beautiful poetic phrases. 'That's to begin with,' said the FCP, as they strolled in the Company Garden. 'You couldn't feel love for those two girls without the immediacy of lovemaking. It's nothing but unalloyed physical urge at that age. Yet you can't confuse your current state with what you see in films either, romantic love infused with certain sacredness. The thing they depict as love between the hero and the heroine is so virtuous one thinks it has nothing to do with sex, and to prove that lovemaking is incidental to their being in love, they might be willing to let go of it altogether as their love is to do with their souls, not bodies. In real life, romantic love is nothing but a garnish on physical passion, the throbbing desire beneath.'

'That's right,' said Deena. 'With the possibility of sex gone, one can't stay in love. I mean romantic love.'

Delighted to elucidate this to his friend-cum-disciple, the friend-cum-philosopher said, 'To desire sex you don't have to fall in love. Falling in love denotes one's longing for it to last, to have someone in your life. That's for starters though, this kind of emotion, because nobody knows for sure what exactly lies ahead. If things went sour, they'd wonder how come they were so eager to be together! While carnal passion you can have for anyone with no strings attached—'

'How do I get to meet Shampa?'

'Meet? You two hardly speak.'

'That's true. Whenever I'm at her place, she avoids looking at me. She's mindful of my feelings. That I know. And that's enough to make my heart leap. I'm starved of laying eyes on her.'

They went to St Mary's Convent near Hathi Park and parked themselves at a safe remove from the school gate. There were trishaws, their specially built models to ferry children to and from school, and some Fiats, Ambassadors and two wheelers. The city elite sent their daughters to St Mary's Convent. Deena beckoned the FCP to move further down the road, away from the school gate, as lurking in the vicinity were two-three groups of eve teasers, waiting to ogle girls and pass lewd remarks. 'I don't understand what pleasure they derive from this,' said Deena.

'What are you doing here?'

'I'm here to see the girl I love. I never go stand in front of girls' schools to harass them.'

'I was joking. It beats me too. What satisfaction these louts get from making girls blanch this way. It just goes to show how frustrated they are at the impossibility of ever being able to romance these classy girls, much less see and feel and smell and lick their beautiful, fragrant bodies.'

'Then why Hindi-medium schools have more such rowdies hovering outside their gates?'

Loath to miss any chance to impress Deena, the FCP said, 'That's right. Girls in those schools are easy meat as they come from the lower class. If you dare harass someone from an influential family, you're done for. Look what happened to Nagina after he made the blunder of plumping for the wrong boy!' Notorious for his boy-love, Nagina, a petty local goon, would spot lads liable to be flattered by his attention, the attention of someone whom others feared. His gentle manner gave no hint of his intent. The object of his lust believed he had his protection. Nobody could bully him.

That Nagina had his wicked ways with young boys was known but nobody knew how he operated, except the FCP who had tricked a suspected victim into revealing it by his claim that he knew Nagina had buggered him. Shocked, the boy admitted to such an attempt on Nagina's part, but that he had forced the pederast to back off. The FCP was too smart to buy it.

Nagina would con the unwary prey into going with him to a designated place where he exposed his engorged manhood and bade him to hold it. If the boy demurred, Nagina would take out his Rampuri, the vicious flick knife. The boy would have no option, and then Nagina produced a blank sheet and dictate to him just one sentence: 'I have received twenty rupees from Nagina for agreeing to be sodomized by him.' No victim after that dared share his ordeal with anybody.

But Nagina had made a grievous misjudgement a while ago. He picked on a boy from an influential family that owned a posh cinema in the city. Struck on his adolescent beauty, Nagina made a move on him without enquiring about his background. The boy, with no clue what to make of Nagina's overtures, his sugar-coated words, had kept quiet, until one day when Nagina did what was in open violation of his own rule, the rule that he would do nothing to make his prey wary till he got him in his lair. Overcome by lust, he traced the shapely swell of the boy's bum that day.

The day following, during lunch break, under the big neem tree inside the school, where the paved path leading from the main gate terminated, Nagina was seen talking to the boy who, as would be revealed afterwards, had especially come there to snare him. In no time descended on the scene, four young men, making Nagina blanch, who recognized Ghanshyam, their leader, the man whose rise to the league of the most feared gangsters of Allahabad had been quick. He had only two murders under his belt. What had clinched it for him was the manner of the second murder, commissioned by Omji, one of the mob bosses in the city, who had taken him under his wing. It was a revenge killing.

The businessman whom Ghanshyam had slaughtered was said to be the one behind the killing of the journalist father of Omji, a directionless youth at the time of his father's death. As if given a purpose in life, he had killed one of the men who had shot his father a week before. Not to be messed with now, Omji formed a small band of his own, and when he threw his hat into the ring of the competition for government contracts, there were more killings, securing him a place on the list of a who's who of the city's mob, and catching his attention was Ghanshyam's skill in bomb-making, a cottage industry in Allahabad back then. Not only would his innovation make country bombs more effective but easy to carry and use. Departing from the usual way of making these bombs, using empty tobacco canisters or some other small tin or simply some paper and jute string, Ghanshyam was the first to employ cast-off torch cells, emptied out and filled with apt explosive. It was one of these bombs that Ghanshyam had hurled at the businessman, which landed near his feet and Omji's enemy was left only with his torso and head that Ghanshyam would crush with a stone.

One of Ghanshyam's men had grabbed Nagina's arms from behind while the other two frisked him, removing the Rampuri from under the shirt and handing it to Ghanshyam, they laid about him. His screams died away before long. He became the embodiment of bloody chaos, his shirt torn, the face and the front lacerating. Calling a halt to the pounding, Ghanshyam dealt a couple of blows himself to his belly before ending the operation. Deena and others thought Nagina would die, but he had been spared any fatal injury. Killing him wasn't part of Ghanshyam's brief. Though that certainly was the end of the GIC being a happy hunting ground for the inveterate pederast.

* * *

It was hard to pick out Shampa in the milling crowd of uniformed students outside the St Mary's gate. 'She'll be in one of those trishaws,' said Deena.

'Why don't we go somewhere near her house and wait there?'

Her house was less than two kilometres. No way could she beat them to it. They jumped on their bicycles and rode fast towards her neighbourhood. Lined with lush, tall trees, the street that housed her house was enchantingly peaceful, set back from which were many a British-era bungalow. A little ahead of her house, beside a tiny copse, they parked themselves. When the trishaw came in view, the FCP began to tinker with his bicycle. Deena walked to the edge of the road and caught Shampa saying something to the other girl, her neighbour, who then looked towards him. He had been made. Shampa said bye to her friend and just before swinging around to open the gate and go inside, she rewarded him with a lingering glance.

The FCP described their effort as successful. 'Did you notice the way she said bye to her friend? It was a bye to you as well.'

* * *

It wasn't that cold for the time of the year when Nisha returned from Delhi, happy, excited. She was pregnant. The baby was due in about eight months. Kanti and everybody else thought her stay with Shekhar in Delhi had helped smooth things out between them, which was true to a degree, though not the result of their staying together. It was their coming parenthood. Before that, they had fought bitterly on several occasions. What had got her steamed up at first, was that Shekhar was back to smoking.

'I gave it a shot. It was no good and it's no good when you behave like a harridan.' Nisha was at a loss how to handle him being so upfront about his inability to break the habit. It was no more an issue only about her concern for his health or about his mouth reeking of tobacco. It was also a blow to her self-esteem, her failure to prevail.

She said she would start smoking herself. Shekhar ignored her. No sooner had he come back from the IIT, than she lit a cigarette. He lunged and engaged in a scuffle till the cigarette between her fingers lay mangled. He slapped her. She remained calm. Was happy with his reaction. Now every day on his return, he found their ashtray full of cigarette butts. Their quarrels went on for a while, then the discovery of her pregnancy brought them down to earth. Shekhar became conciliatory and resolved once again to have another go at cutting down on the number of smokes every day.

Nisha found a new meaning, a new purpose in life. She talked about the kind of mother she would be. 'I'll never compromise on my child's education. Not less than one of the best schools in Delhi will suffice. Who knows better the pain of being deprived of English! What a limited version of life it clamps on you! There exists this larger world and we lack the wings of English to explore it, the world of books brimming with a variety of knowledge. A world full of fun and entertainment too. It lies out of our reach. Look at what Mahavir bhaiya has achieved through his exposure to English culture . . .'

'His father wouldn't stay content with him going to English school,' said Kanti. 'He made him work extra hard on the language. Mahavir didn't read just his textbooks but read so much else.'

'Given our Gabbar Singh's passion for fiction, how good at English he'd have become, had he been able to read English novels,' Nisha said, looking at Deena. 'Oh, I must borrow from Shampa some English story books for Mayank.'

Mayank's knowledge of English wasn't enough for him to enjoy even children's fiction, though compared to Deena, he was a hell of a lot better acquainted with English. He and Sandhya were good at swotting up for their exam in the subject. They also did well in the grammar section, so was Nisha, though with less scores. Nishant, who had been making a determined effort, couldn't be compared to any of them. Mayank and Sandhya could acquire English through some sweat. As for Deena, few students of his age could match his ignorance of English, ignorance so profound he wanted nothing to do with it. He was to write later: *With my desire to make a mark as a Hindi poet, I too, like a Hindi partisan, believed that with English around, Hindi couldn't spread the way it should. The point that no creative writing was possible in a foreign language resonated with me. That would cost me invaluable time. Mayank, who carried on doing well in exams, switched after his twelfth to English medium, and Kartik, though sympathetic to those baying for banishment of English, felt piqued at Hindi having ousted Urdu from its formerly dominant position. Urdu was Kartik's obsession. My aversion to English issued from my absolute poverty in it. The challenge to learn it as a grown-up was too exacting. Specially so when the efforts I was putting into Hindi literature were getting praise. This distaste for English disguised my rage against my innocence of it. I too, like many others, couldn't help being in awe of anyone capable of producing a sentence here, a sentence there in English. At least Nisha didi and Sandhya didi could fleck their Hindi sentences with English phrases.*

His illiteracy in English was the chief reason Deena would let go of the thought of Shampa. I wondered at this wonderful ability of my friend's, an ability I found so enviable, the ability to lose interest in his object of passion the moment it dawned she mightn't be inclined. End of story. With no heartbreak. No pining. He would rather be thankful to find his mind free of the anxiety integral to romantic pursuits. Yet on two occasions he slipped up and jumped the gun, as it later transpired that the girls were just playing hard to get. Still, these near misses wouldn't take away from the fact that this gift of an ability sheltered him from so much pain and turmoil that would be the lot of ordinary lovesick mortals whose distress would get worse if their advances were ignored by their quarries.

It was a pleasant discovery for Deena himself, this great gift of his, the way he was to cease to be in love with Shampa.

* * *

Deena's exam centre was Ghanraj Singh's school. Ram Mohan wouldn't have to get it changed. The Deputy Inspector of Schools had ensured that Pratap Singh's indifference didn't act as a fly in the Dhata ointment. Though, to show regard for the latter's sentiments, Deena wouldn't be seated in the VIP room. 'Last time, he instructed me to allot him the VIP room,' said Ghanraj Singh. 'Now that he isn't taking interest, I shouldn't give him reason to suspect my motive. This, however, won't affect Deena's performance. He'll be free to cheat as before. It's just that instead of copying from question-and-answer books, he'll use the pages torn from them. I'll tell the invigilators that in his case, the rule of the non-VIP seating won't apply.' Though invigilators in the non-VIP area ignored the acts of cheating, the examinees were required to observe some restraint. Their manner shouldn't look brazen.

Deena was fixed up with a place to stay in Dhata. His host-to-be, Netaji, had a relation who taught at a school in Fatehpur city and was happy to be of help to the Deputy Inspector of Schools. Netaji was no less enthusiastic about putting up Ram Mohan's son. Deena, who was in high spirits, said there was no need for anyone to accompany him.

He had no difficulty in getting hold of Netaji, a known figure in Dhata. The man he asked, showed him the way through the long, buzzing lane that was the main bazaar of Dhata to this little grocery shop whose owner was Netaji's friend, who then took him through a narrow passage off the main lane to the door of an under-sized dwelling.

The knock was answered by Netaji himself. It wasn't where his family lived. That house was located somewhere in the interior of Dhata. A large part of Netaji's day was spent at his friend's shop. This dwarfish thing served as a place where he and his friends, on occasion, enjoyed country liquor and things not possible in their homes. The chief source of his family's income was their fields that he gave to sharecroppers. He had lots of free time. A dabbler in local politics, he was opposed to the dominance of Pratap Singh but avoided any face-off with the big man.

His fond demeanour made Deena welcome. He was invited inside and told this was where he would stay during his board exams starting the day following. Ghanraj Singh had to be informed of his arrival. Netaji called out to one of his young lieutenants and asked him to tag along with Deena. Outside the school, there was a small crowd of examinees and their guardians. Unfamiliar with the exam centre, they had come to take a gander. Leaving the escort at the gate, Deena stepped inside. The place was full of activity. In the distance, outside his room, in the company of his close aides, stood Ghanraj Singh. Some junior members of staff scuttled about. Deena missed Nishant. Ghanraj Singh saw him 'Come, come!' Deena walked up to him. He introduced him to his confidants and breathed something into the ear of his deputy, who nodded, looking at Deena.

In the morning Deena was nervous. He wouldn't have the liberty to keep a whole book with him during the exam, the liberty associated with the VIP room and had to carry on his person so many leaves ripped from his question-and-answer booklet. How unwieldy, inconvenient! Damn Pratap Singh! When the invigilator gave him a smile while handing the question paper, he loosened up. He had to feign to be careful. Even when he became lost in locating the answers among his pages, the invigilators looked the other way. Others were warned if found cribbing too overtly.

* * *

All in all, Deena's second sojourn in Dhata was quite agreeable. He would meet a variety of people who dropped in on Netaji, whose friend's shop was the adda where they hung out.

Things were fine, until one day a sudden turn of events sent Deena into a cold sweat. He had hardly finished copying the first question of his history paper when somebody began hollering something. It didn't register at first. When it did, all hell broke loose. Ghanraj Singh leapt out of his room. The man had been shouting, 'Flying Squad'.

Several such squads were formed by the UP Board just before the tenth and twelfth board exams, each comprising teachers drawn from various schools with a Board official as its head. They showed up unannounced. In isolated instances of cheating, only those caught were punished. In case of mass copying, the school would face the music. The Board would take it off the list of prospective exam centres, a fearful prospect for school managements. It seldom happened, though. Members of these squads were liable to team up to milk the opportunity and could be kept sweet. The pay-off on these occasions would be quite a bit. Schools preferred to avoid this mishap.

Last time, nothing of the sort had happened, no flying squad, though the threat was always there, and Ghanraj Singh, a seasoned customer, had a team of two in place every year, for the express purpose of sounding the alarm so his people could sanitize the exam area before the Squad's arrival. So was the case this time. One of these two men armed with a double-barrelled shotgun would station himself near a broken-down culvert, a furlong before the narrow, battered road to Dhata petered out, while his partner cooled his heels under a banyan tree between the school and the end of that road. It was this man, who after hearing two shots one after another, had run to inform. Taking charge of the situation, Ghanraj Singh shouted not to panic. The dirt track leading off the road to their school wouldn't allow the squad a quick passage. They had half an hour to do the clean-up. All the examinees were asked to surrender whatever objectionable stuff they had. Misery was writ large in Deena's face as he parted with his pages.

Things were in limbo for nearly an hour. No sign of the Flying Squad! Ghanraj Singh sent for the duo that had raised the alarm. It was a false one. The man who had fired the warning shots couldn't be faulted. He did see a Jeep, the sighting of which was a rare event on that derelict road along which plied mostly ekkas—one-horse carriage—bicycles, motorcycles and dumper trucks. If the man with the shotgun took the Jeep bumping along that road towards Dhata to be the dreaded Flying Squad, it was in order. That exactly was his charge. At any sign of a Jeep at the crucial hour, he was to press the panic button. That Jeep, however, belonged to some official of the district administration.

No time to lose. The false alarm and its aftermath had taken much toll. To make up for lost time, the examinees would be allowed extra time. There was a scramble for repossession of the cheating material that had been bunged in jute sacks and hidden away; each now brought back to where it belonged and emptied in the far corner of every room. For those in the VIP room, it was easier because they could keep whole books. In the non-VIP zone, it was bedlam. Less-assertive students were close to tears. Deena, too, tried his luck with others as they frenziedly grubbed about for their pages in the heap. Then, they began to snatch up whatever they could. Some pages that Deena managed to grab, could supply the answer to just one question. Aided by the ongoing chaos, he folded the question paper, put it in his pocket, tucked the exam sheet under the shirt and sidled out of the school compound.

* * *

As he tried to slink into the passage leading to the house, Netaji, who stood bantering with some people outside his friend's shop, saw him. Something wasn't right. Presently he came in. Deena, perched on the *takht*, was turning the pages of a book in the fading light. Netaji picked the lantern from the niche in the wall and lit it. 'Let's not waste time. They must be looking for you. You locate the answers in your book. I'll dictate.'

They were on the last question when came a knock at the door. Netaji went to get it. It was dark now. He opened the door a bit and then let the visitor in. It was one of the members of Ghanraj Singh's inner circle, who, his amity with Netaji known, was deputed to go find Deena and retrieve the missing exam sheet. 'Why did you take flight? We'd have helped you finish the paper at any rate.' Netaji and the visitor stepped outside for a chat. Deena finished the remaining answer by himself. The situation stood resolved. Then again, about a week later, he had to spend an entire day in distress, the day before his third paper of English, the last of his twelfth board exams.

The first and second paper he had managed. There was no question-and-answer book available for the third one. There couldn't be. This paper consisted of questions pertaining to English grammar and to answer them, you must have some idea of the rules of the language, rules regarding its tenses, active voice–passive voice, direct–indirect narration, et al. Nishant, it had been decided, would go to Dhata to help him out, and the day Deena was so strung up was the eve of this feared paper. 'What if Nishant didn't turn up.'

'How can your brother forget something so crucial?' said Netaji.

Nishant didn't fail him. He arrived in Dhata and reached Netaji's place just as it was getting dark. Deena jumped for joy when he saw him, a small piece of luggage in his hand, talking to Netaji in front of the friend's shop.

For the first time Deena had to carry no cheating material to the exam centre, would even be spared the trouble of copying. Ghanraj Singh welcomed Nishant and directed one of his helpers to escort them to a separate room. This room, like most of the school building, was without plaster and had in its walls only gaps for doors and windows and had two charpoys and a scruffy desk with a wobbly leg. When the man who had guided them there made as if to go look for a chair, Nishant stopped him. 'I'll make do with a charpoy.' The man then brought them an exam sheet and the question paper.

Nishant was concentrating on the task at hand, while Deena, with nothing better to do, went off to sleep on another charpoy and was woken when it was over. On the way out, they stopped at Ghanraj Singh's room, who came out and walked them to the gate. 'I'll look in on Dr Sahab when in Allahabad.'

* * *

Ram Mohan embraced Deena. 'Ghanraj Singh didn't give Deena the VIP room but ensured he was none the worse for it. Now I can leave in a better frame of mind today.'

Ram Mohan was going to Bombay to attend a literary conference organized by an old friend associated with *Dharmyug*, a prestigious Hindi weekly, which came as the frosting on the cake of Deena's already euphoric state, a full week of freedom from restraints and a real possibility of letting Shampa in on his having lost his heart.

With Ram Mohan in town, though he was no more hostile to Dr Moon Aggarwal, Nisha wouldn't take Deena to her place. The terrible quarrel it once caused still rankled with her. The day after Ram Mohan left, Deena made a pitch for a visit to Moon Auntie's. 'I can't wait for the delicious snacks she serves.' Nisha laughed. 'We'll go in a day or two. You should be ready with your Gabbar Singh lines and poems.'

Deena wasn't home when Moon Auntie and Shampa picked Nisha up and took her to meet some senior official at the AIR, who, pleased with Nisha's voice and diction, got her name added to the panel of those invited to take part in a weekly programme dealing with women's issues. When she returned, Nisha was on a high. 'Tomorrow when we go to Moon Auntie's, Shampa will give you two books,' she said to Mayank. 'One is by Enid Blyton. I don't recall the name of the other author. . .' she chuckled, 'Shampa's put aside a book for Deena too, the one she's just finished.' Sandhya smiled. 'It really threw me. I didn't know what to say. Let's see how Deena handles it tomorrow.'

That was the moment Deena was disenthralled from the thought of Shampa, whom he couldn't do without until before that very moment. It was magical, wondrous, took his breath away, the sudden explosion of distance from her; the immeasurable remoteness of being in love.

He backed out of the plan to visit Moon Auntie. 'I must go get Kartik. He'll be off to Kanpur soon.' It was the summer break, and I was planning to leave in less than a week. Deena didn't tell me at the time what had happened. I recall him looking at the two books Shampa had given Mayank, both beyond him, the titles as well as the authors' names: *Five on a Treasure Island* by Enid Blyton and *James and the Giant Peach* by Roald Dahl.

I stayed at the Commission Bungalow for two days, during which I was captured by the beauty of the Urdu language. The ardour would blind me for a long while to things that, in terms of setting a course for my place in the world, deserved my attention infinitely more. The day before I was to leave for Kanpur, Jaan Muhammad came by to drop off an invitation to a grand *Mushaira*, a gathering of Urdu poets, to be held at the Sangeet Samiti Hall. Jaan Muhammad was a popular figure at the Commission Bungalow. Nishant invited him in for a cup of tea and we all trooped into the drawing room.

Jaan Muhammad talked with relish about the Urdu poets who would grace the *Mushaira* the next evening. Some of them big names, huge draws on the Urdu poetry scene. He recited couplets by each of these famous poets, one of whom was Firaq, the biggest name, the senior most, who had retired as a professor of English literature at the university twenty years ago. My interest in Urdu poetry, enkindled by Jaan Muhammad, became a roaring passion when I heard all those Urdu poets.

* * *

Ram Mohan's return from his out-of-town trips meant the return of an overwrought atmosphere to his household. Deena bore that so palpably it turned him into a mouse of a person. That's beside the point now that the long history of his fear of Baabuji was to give way to the beginning of a different narrative of his perception of Baabuji.

Ram Mohan couldn't wait to tell them what he had got for Deena from Bombay. Nothing could have been a greater gift to

someone dreaming of becoming a film actor. After a bath, he got
everybody in the drawing room. None had the vaguest notion of
what it was he sounded so excited to share. He was at his jovial
best. 'You're in a very good mood. I guess people were dazzled
by your eloquence at the conference,' said Kanti. He laughed,
'Yes, I sparkled there but about that later.' He asked my friend
to come sit beside him. 'My Deena might soon do us all proud.
I've seen that he gets his start in film acting before long.' They
were floored.

In Bombay, at his host's house, Ram Mohan met this gentleman
whom he thought a literature aficionado. That Uma Shankar was.
But basically, he was into film making. He had produced one by
the name of *Andolan*. Had also acted in it. As a producer, it hadn't
been a smooth ride for him. His film that had been ready for release,
could see the light of day only after power changed hands in Delhi.
During the Emergency, *Andolan* was thought sympathetic to the JP
movement and discomfiting to Indira Gandhi.

Ram Mohan couldn't have asked for more when his Bombay
friend had introduced him to Uma Shankar, 'Meet my friend, the
film producer and actor—'

'Not much of an actor. I just dabble.'

'Ram Mohan, you've made a great impression on Uma
Shankar. He rates your literary oration at the conference as one of
the best he's heard.'

'That was the moment when I felt thankful for my decision to
attend this conference,' said Ram Mohan.

'The moment you were told what an impact your speech had
made on the film producer,' Kanti said. Ram Mohan laughed at
her attempt to pull his leg.

'Not at all. It was the fact that if I hadn't made this trip, what
a chance I would have missed, the chance to meet Uma Shankar.
When I told him about Deena, he took no time in promising that
Deena would get to act in his coming venture.'

Uma Shankar had friends in Allahabad and was chummy with Arimardan Singh, a hardcore Indira loyalist, who had commiserated about his friend's film but couldn't have dared intercede with the information and broadcasting minister during the Emergency.

What had been a pure yen, a mere dream on Deena's part, with nothing to suggest it being realizable even remotely, was no longer so. Most of such dreamers who fled to Bombay were forced to take up menial jobs to survive, merging into the fringe of the great Bombay crowd. Some would plod back home, their spirit broken and hopes dashed. The resourceful few who could put up a fight for a while longer got landed with the job of extras or became small-time, piddling actors. That's why Mr Aggarwal, Moon Auntie's husband, stressed that Deena get into the National School of Drama first and then, after gaining a toehold in the world of acting, he could have a fighting chance in Bombay.

Now he needed nothing of the sort.

* * *

Dhata lived up to its reputation once again. Deena passed his twelfth board with a second division. Ram Mohan asked them to go out and enjoy their favourite snacks and sweets, but with Nisha expecting her first child, they decided to celebrate at home. Ram Mohan let Deena, to his delight, take the Fiat to get all that they wanted to eat. Though good at driving, he wasn't allowed to be at the wheel when alone.

When the baby was due, it was Deena who drove Nisha didi to hospital. What a heady feeling, the feeling of being in a position of responsibility, something he hadn't expected before! Even Moon Auntie took notice of his driving prowess, not to mention Shampa's look of admiration, and he couldn't but be amazed that her charms no longer troubled him, no heartache, nothing. How great it felt, free from that agony, from her thought!

And now he was going to get a role in Uma Shankar's film, who had written to Ram Mohan about his forthcoming visit to Allahabad. Adding to all that was the fact that he was done with the board exams. Baabuji wanted him to obtain the degrees of BA and MA also but didn't think Allahabad University was a good idea.

'Kanpur University is exactly right for my Deena.' Unlike the Oxford of the East, still haunted by the ghost of its former eminence, a burden most of the institutes set up before Independence were condemned to carry, unlike it, Kanpur University was free from any pretence to greatness. 'My alma mater understands what our students need. They need certificates and degrees that qualify them for government jobs, the kind obtained through influence or money, not through competition. Deena can do his BA and MA as a private student. Most likely, these degrees would be of ornamental value, now that he's going to act in films!'

Presently, Nisha and her baby were discharged from hospital. Ram Mohan named his granddaughter Shivika, and decided to celebrate her arrival by having a small party. He had been in a great mood lately. Reasons were obvious. First, Deena getting through with his secondary education was such a relief, then the advent of Uma Shankar, the film producer, who had promised him a start in films, the most unpromising of his children. Lending heft to Ram Mohan's confidence was this other development, the certainty of Tiwari-ji's son, Sukesh, being employed in the Railways soon. Ram Mohan's closeness to Shukla-ji and Argali was paying off. On his last visit, Argali had brought to the Commission Bungalow the chairman of the Railway Service Commission in Allahabad—there were four such bodies in the country set up to hire subordinate railway staff—and the suggestion that Nishant and Sukesh both should take up a job in the Railways came from the chairman himself. The jobs were for the asking. They just had to fill up the application forms. Nothing else. The chairman and the two members of the Railway Commission had joined hands to devise a way to make recruitments as they pleased. Their candidates didn't even have to sit the written tests. Their names would be there in all the documents related to the process. They would be called for the interview just to keep up appearances.

The job on offer was well below the station Nishant had in mind, not the kind that could induce him to disregard his pledge that whatever he strove to do in life would have nothing to do with Baabuji's influence. Everybody at home knew about the pledge, save Ram Mohan.

Nishant was still resentful that Baabuji had declared that none of his children would compete for any posts announced by the Public Service Commission so long as he was a member. When Nishant and Shekhar had questioned the need for such a declaration, his answer was, 'Nishant doesn't cut it. He isn't that focused . . . So why not distinguish myself from my colleagues by seizing the moral high ground.' When reminded of posts to which recruitments were made only through interviews, of which K. Dwivedi had been a big beneficiary, Ram Mohan had snapped, 'Why didn't you tell me then? You were taken up with law and English language! You gave me to believe that the only profession you had in mind was that of a lawyer.' That had silenced Nishant, who was absorbed in studying for LLB.

When Ram Mohan tried to hustle Nishant into accepting what was offered by the chairman Railway Service Commission, he showed no interest. Argali said, 'No need to hurry. Maybe he's serious about becoming an advocate.'

* * *

Things were looking up for Ram Mohan and his family. Given the pathetic state of the People's Party and its tottering government, Indira Gandhi's return looked all but inevitable. During his last visit to Lucknow, Shukla-ji had reiterated his resolve to have him sent to the Union Public Service Commission. Mid-term polls couldn't be far off. Before getting pulled into the rough and tumble of things, before the UPSC happening, Ram Mohan wanted to marry Sandhya off.

He invited the young man he had, for some time, been sizing up with Sandhya in mind, to the party he threw to mark Shivika's arrival. Nisha and Nishant kept wondering about the young man who didn't belong in the gathering of such worthies as the DM, the SSP, the chief development officer, the vice chancellor of Allahabad University, the editors of the two local Hindi dailies, let alone Ram Mohan's colleagues at the Commission. The occasion had filled the young man with such awe that the uncouth aspects of his person would become all too visible, his dress sense, manner of looking and speaking. His total comportment bespoke a plebeian background. Later when Ram Mohon revealed the purpose of his presence at the party, they were appalled.

* * *

The notion that education was the key to any advancement in life had lately been on the up amongst the intermediate castes. The Kurmis were no exception. Even those who could hardly afford sending their children to cities for higher degrees would do so. Many such Kurmi youths were studying in Allahabad. Those confident and enterprising, would come to meet Ram Mohan, an inspiring example of success for them, success in terms of fame and social prestige, not riches. There were so many Kurmis who were much better off than him. The young man in question had done his MSc from Kanpur University and moved to Allahabad to prepare for competitive exams. That's what had caught Ram Mohan's notice.

Sandhya was crushed. The prospect of being married to this man was nightmarish. Few, with his so-called degrees, could look more provincial. 'Everything about him is so nondescript, so drab, and he's better off with his mouth shut,' said Nisha. To complete the ghastly picture was the fact that he couldn't speak a word of English. Sandhya was snivelling. Kanti and Nisha and Nishant tried to reassure her.

When Nisha and Nishant told him what they thought of the boy, Ram Mohan gathered everybody in the drawing room and clarified why he was in a hurry to find a boy for Sandhya. 'My term at the Commission is due to end in less than a year. It might not come to even that. The People's Party regime is on a self-destructive trajectory. Mid-term polls are a solid possibility. That'll mean Mrs. Gandhi's return. The UPSC in Delhi should come our way soon after. Yet all that looks a few months away. I'm no pessimist, but who can be completely sure of the situation ahead? I must take advantage of the stability we at this point are enjoying. To put off Sandhya's wedding isn't prudent. Holding it in the Commission compound will save me money, something I don't have much of. This boy seems fine. If you all think otherwise, let me try and find someone that fits your notion of a husband for Sandhya. But I have no more than a month to spare for the exercise.'

Thanks to an old acquaintance of Ram Mohan, a suitable boy materialized soon enough. His father was about to retire from his job in the office of the state's Accountant General in Allahabad. A year ago, his son had, after an M.Com. and a short course in accounting in finance, found employment in a big steel plant in Jamshedpur. Ram Mohan went to meet the father who, dazzled by a Member, Public Service Commission coming in a Fiat to his house, looked dumbfounded. Ram Mohan explained the reason for his visit and handed him Sandhya's picture.

Nishant went to Jamshedpur to meet the boy who, Kanti and Nisha hoped, wouldn't be a disappointment. Sandhya, a bag of nerves, couldn't decide which of the two she feared more: the tearing away from all and everything she had known, from all that she thought was hers, the deep emotional bonds of kindred, of friends, and getting flung into a setting unknown, a territory controlled by strangers, or the possibility of being tied to someone with no mind of his own, someone with a received notion of a good wife, with an outlook that brooked nothing but conformity. Her face wore a constant morose look. Nisha's heart went out to her. 'Don't distress yourself. After marriage, you'd be able to enjoy more freedom, something not possible here with Baabuji around.'

'That's what Mahavir bhaiya had told you, when you were distressed, frightened of marriage.'

'He was right, to an extent. I've more freedom now than before.' Sandhya knew better. She knew of the fights between her and Shekhar Jijaji, not only in Allahabad but in Delhi too, several times at the Commission Bungalow itself, when a seemingly innocuous comment made by either of the two would lead to a fierce exchange. Sandhya didn't bring that up. Nisha didi only meant to pacify her fears.

* * *

Ram Mohan wasn't home when Nishant returned from Jamshedpur. He took out from his small suitcase an envelope and gave it to Kanti. All of them, barring Sandhya, drew closer to their mother, who now held two postcard-sized photographs in her hand. They were bowled over. Varun, the young man, looked like a film star. He wasn't just handsome, according to Nishant, but intelligent and well-mannered. 'The only thing that's a bit annoying is that he's quiet, speaking only when spoken to. Doesn't indulge in small talk. He isn't chatty like us,' said Nishant.

'To know whether a man will be a good husband isn't easy,' said Kanti. 'No matter how carefully you vet him. The real man will emerge only after you're well into the journey together.'

'His being quiet qualifies as a good sign,' said Nisha. 'He won't have the patience to get into long arguments that often result in more bitterness. I can tell from experience.'

'Yes, a husband who's quiet and possesses a cool head is any day better than the one who's testy. I think this boy's suitable for our Sandhya,' said Kanti as others continued to look at the photographs,

Without further ado, let me tell the readers that Sandhya and Varun were married within a month of Nishant's visit to Jamshedpur. They didn't even meet prior to the wedding. Given the fluid political scene and mid-term polls looming, Ram Mohan didn't want to delay it. All pre-wedding ceremonies were hurried through. The money for the main function, for the kind befitting his status, Ram Mohan didn't have but was confident all would work out well. It did.

No sooner did Gulab Singh learn of the upcoming wedding, than he rushed to Allahabad to inform his friend that he would pick the tab for the entire event. It turned out a decent and well-organized affair. The next day when Sandhya had to go away, the scene was poignant and heart-breaking. Kanti and Nisha kept weeping. The pain Deena and Mayank experienced was past expression, the magnitude of Sandhya didi leaving them forever. To Deena, the previous experience was of no use, the devastating emotional impact that Nisha didi's marriage had had on him.

Ram Mohan couldn't have asked for more. Having married Sandhya off and in the manner accordant with his social standing, was no mean thing. Many an esteemed personage attended the wedding, the most important of whom were Shukla-ji and Argali who had travelled from Lucknow.

The day after the departure of all the guests, he summoned them to the drawing room to share in his feeling of satisfaction, at how things were poised for the good of their lives. 'I couldn't have hoped to find such a fine groom for Sandhya . . . The way it all went off makes me doubly proud. Now we stand on the cusp of entering the most significant phase of our lives. Nishant's all set to obtain his LLB degree. Soon after he'll embark on a career as a lawyer. The most wondrous of it all is the possibility of Deena bringing us laurels. Once Uma Shankar witnesses his Gabbar Singh act, he'll know for a fact how talented he is,' then turning to Nisha, 'And we'll also be in Delhi soon!' Her face lit up as he went on, 'Given the current scenario, the throne of Delhi will fall into Indira-ji's lap again.'

A day later, Ram Mohan left for Lucknow. Shukla-ji wanted to discuss some serious matter about which he had given a hint during the wedding, something that had to do with some complex political skulduggery.

FOUR

In less than three years in power, the People's Party fell apart. The party and its regime had long become a conundrum, a battlefield of personal vanities and ambitions posing as ideological clashes. Indira Gandhi, hitherto sunk in gloom, was coming into her own.

Within months into the People's Party's rule, an opportunity had presented itself to her by way of a gruesome massacre of nine Harijans by upper caste landlords in a village in the state of Bihar, the birthplace of the JP Movement that had dethroned her. Treating it as a godsend, she dashed to the village, the site of slaughter, beating even the government to it. No less heroic was the way she, after flying to Patna, had made that journey into the bowels of Bihar. First in a Jeep along the broken-down road which, after it rained, became untraversable, forcing her to shift to a farmer's tractor, and to cross a small but swollen river, she rode on an elephant.

By the time she reached the village, it was dark. The villagers were terrified by the commotion, fearing another attack, but on realizing that the visitor was none other than Indira Gandhi, they rushed towards her and fell at her feet, the beginning of an upturn in her fortunes. The way she was hounded by the People's Party regime, through a Commission to probe into various atrocities during Emergency, helped oil the wheels of her comeback.

* * *

When fresh elections were declared, Mrs. Gandhi burst into extensive travels through the length and breadth of north India. There was a groundswell of opinion in her favour. She set off making every effort to sweep UP, where her party had failed to win a single seat in the previous election. During these trips, Shukla-ji was seen at her side. Sometimes Argali too. When she came to Allahabad, Ram Mohan deputed Nishant and Deena to take the Fiat and join her cavalcade.

After flying into Lucknow, she was driven to Allahabad, addressing groups of people along the way and could make it only in the late afternoon, three hours late for her scheduled press conference at Anand Bhavan. Flanked by Shukla-ji and the District Congress president, she answered the questions of excited scribes. She sat hardly a few paces from where Tandon-ji, Nishant and Deena stood in the aisle near the main door of the room, one of the several in Anand Bhavan, the house built by her grandfather, which she had donated to the nation. Full of her family memorabilia, Anand Bhavan stood as a memorial to its role in the freedom struggle, holding memories of several great figures it had hosted, figures from the National Movement.

Crowding the space in front of her were journalists, while local Congress leaders stood along the walls of the room, hoping to be noticed as she darted glances in every direction. Nishant and Deena expected her to greet Tandon-ji when she saw him, but there was no trace of recognition in her eyes when she did.

'She's tired and distracted,' said Tandon-ji. 'I'll come along when you join her entourage tomorrow.'

'I'm worn out,' she said and rose, bringing the press conference to a close. She was to stay at the Circuit House.

In the aftermath of her departure, in the melee, Tandon-ji ran into a former acquaintance, now an MLA. They walked to the edge of the bustling portico for a quick chat. The MLA, after being introduced to Nishant and Deena, said, putting his arm around Tandon-ji, 'Do you know who this great man is? He's the one who taught Indira-ji how to ride a bicycle when she was a small girl—'

'I'll try and meet her tomorrow. It's been a long time, though she always responds to my letters.'

* * *

Deena got up earlier than usual the next morning. He couldn't wait for their Fiat to join the vehicles following Indira Gandhi's Ambassador. He would also get a chance to drive outside the city limits for the first time. Ram Mohan had told Nishant to let Deena take the wheel on the highway, the same as passed through the constituency that boasted the largest number of Kurmi voters in the region. It had a Kurmi leader, Patel, as Congress candidate, to boost whose chances Indira Gandhi was to address two rallies before heading to Lucknow. It was one of the several legs of electioneering on her part before the polls.

When Tandon-ji, Nishant and Deena reached the Circuit House, it was bristling with people. She was closeted with Shukla-ji for a last-minute confabulation. On the front lawn, Nishant spotted Argali surrounded by a group of party workers. With Tandon-ji busy talking to someone, he decided to meet Argali but then erupted an excited whisper that Indira-ji had come out, breaking up all the big and small groups. Everybody hurried to the portico, a few steps above which, on the veranda, could be seen the former PM with her head tilted towards Arimardan Singh, who was breathing something into her ear. According to a rumour, he was eyeing the CM's chair in UP. Shukla-ji, who stood right behind Indira-ji, was frowning on Arimardan's attempt to corner their leader's attention. When Argali tried to approach, Shukla-ji made a sign to hold it. That's when Nishant caught Argali's eye, but before they could have a word, Shukla-ji succeeded in disengaging Indira-ji from Arimardan Singh by announcing they had to get a move on. All scampered to their vehicles.

Tandon-ji complimented Nishant on his skilful manoeuvring of the Fiat into a place not far from Indira-ji's Ambassador, only a few vehicles in between. As the motorcade passed through the arches, erected along the route, festooned with garlands, streamers and party flags, Deena felt oddly distinguished, didn't mind Nishant not letting him drive. Soon after crossing the bridge over the Ganges, a huge arch awaited Mrs Gandhi. To welcome her into his constituency, stood Patel with a posse of supporters. He was friends with Ram Mohan and had been to the Commission Bungalow. Nishant knew him. The motorcade had to halt for a few minutes. Patel introduced some people to Indira Gandhi—she looked smothered under garlands—people believed to control the electorate in their backyards. With some more vehicles added, the motorcade got on its way. Patel was in Mrs Gandhi's Ambassador, briefing her on the two public meetings she was to address.

Deena couldn't have enough of the way crowds of onlookers beheld the long motorcade, the passing of vehicles, one of which was the Fiat. During the first meeting, the smaller of the two, they kept sitting in the Fiat as Patel and his close confidants led her, amidst sloganeering and announcement as to her arrival, to the makeshift stage on a small dusty school ground packed with people. Patel took the mike. He exhorted the crowd to strengthen 'the great leader's hands', and shouted into the microphone several times, 'Indira Gandhi', the crowd responding, 'Zindabad'.

Making short work of her address, she spoke harshly of the People's Party. How its leaders, owing to the ferocity of their egos and ambitions, held their own government to ransom, their assemblage lying in tatters, most of whose constituents looking to recover their erstwhile identities. She asked the people to vote for the Congress, vote for Patel.

An hour later, the motorcade arrived at the venue of the second rally. Teeming with people, it was a big barren open space off the main road. A bit further away, a furlong from the main road, was Patel's own village, a big country settlement, dominated by Kurmis.

Indira Gandhi spoke for a good deal longer at this rally, adding detail to what she had merely touched on at the previous one. From here, she had to travel to Lucknow, carrying on along the same road. As she sat talking to Patel and others after the address, Tandon-ji took Nishant along and climbed on to the stage. Nobody stopped him. He walked straight up to her. She raised her eyes, smiled, and rose with her palms placed together. No time for a serious chat, she enquired about his health and writing, while he voiced his confidence that the country would soon be in her safe hands.

* * *

After her departure, Nishant caught hold of Patel, who touched Tandon-ji's feet and introduced Nishant and Deena to his close associates, one of whom was known to Nishant. Singh had been the first to visit Ram Mohan after his appointment. Patel insisted they join them for refreshments in his village. They all got into their vehicles and proceeded along the asphalt strip leading off the highway, but the Fiat wouldn't start. Singh, who sat with them, said, 'It must be the battery.' Climbing out, he ordered some young men loitering nearby to give it a push. It started but the engine kept

acting up as they crawled in fits and starts. 'It's not the battery. It's
the carburettor,' said Nishant.

Then the engine ceased running, the Fiat inched to a halt by
the wall of one of the houses at the edge of the village. Patel's
house was still at a little distance. Singh asked some youths to
push it off the main path and into the front yard of a nearby
house, whose owner was outside, standing deferentially. Nishant
looked rattled as they walked to Patel's house. Singh said, 'You
needn't worry. The problem will be resolved.' Other guests
were already sitting in faded plastic chairs and on the charpoys
in the front yard of Patel's house. It was suggested that Tandon-
ji and Nishant ride in one of the cars returning to Allahabad and
Deena stay the night in the village, putting up at Singh's house.
Patel's was buzzing with people involved in his campaign.
The next day, Zameer would come to bring him and the
Fiat back.

Like most Kurmis, Singh's family occupation was farming, left
in the care of his eldest son. He was looking to Patel, his political
mentor, to help him get the Congress ticket for the next assembly
poll. It was also through Patel's help that Singh's second son had
become the owner of a ration shop in the nearby bazaar. His third
son was active in local politics. A politically successful father meant
a politically successful son. Singh was proud of him. But, for any
aspirant politician it was imperative to be free from financial worries;
his family shouldn't suffer hardship on account of his ambition; at
least until he could make money from politics. It was something
Ram Mohan couldn't achieve. He blamed his scuttled political
vocation on his inability to be a full-timer in politics. Singh wanted
to give his third son enough economic freedom to become a full-
time politician. Patel had come up with the idea of a petrol pump
to help his protégé achieve this end. After Indira Gandhi's return
to power, he could help Singh's son to a retail outlet dealership,
something he had done for his own family.

It was this petrol pump, managed by his brother, that took care of most of Patel's needs. Few business ventures were more lucrative than the thing called petrol pump. You could make big profits by adulterating your petrol and diesel with kerosene, a heavily subsidized substance, a widespread practice among petrol pump owners. Singh's second son, who ran the ration shop, was already doing well. Like other fair price shop owners, he could divert a big quantity of kerosene to their own petrol pump, while diverting sugar and food grains to the open market for a much better price than what he would get from those entitled to these subsidized items under the Public Distribution System. The beauty of it all was that you just had to tell your ration card holders that what they wanted, sugar or rice or kerosene, wasn't in stock. Officials in charge of the system were suitably compensated.

'Once in power, you can make enough money to afford you a lifetime of luxury, the kind made by politicians and government officials, and can keep your family in comfort for generations to come.' With this, the third son of Singh ended the discussion taking place on the terrace of his house. He turned his attention to Deena, the VIP guest he had to look after, and explained to those present the importance of the position Deena's father held.

'I might be part of the cast of a film soon.' His host, the third son, eyed Deena curiously, looked at him with a new interest. This wasn't just the son of Ram Mohan but someone important in his own right, a future film actor. They all wanted to hear the story of how this dreamlike thing came about. Deena told them. They listened; their lips parted. When he referred to his ability to take off Gabbar Singh, the conversation turned to *Sholay*'s heroine. The belle of the film industry. The voluptuous pulchritude. The way she was made to dance on shards of glass by Gabbar.

The third son declaimed that all film heroines were intensely desirable, each in her own way, that Deena could, in time, goggle at these celestial damsels up close, make friends with them, something of which they, the third son and his friends, could only dream. They all became friskier. 'He might get to fuck some!' muttered one of them.

They were all rolling in the aisles, except the third son, who asked Deena, 'Have you ever had a girl?' The no-nonsense Hindi expression for the thing with its cold-blooded directness caused Deena a searing pang of lust. He tempted to lie but desisted. Any queries about the act of sex, would put him in a spot. He answered in the negative. 'If you want, I can arrange for you to have a girl tonight,' said the third son. 'You'll have a great time.' Deena's erection threatened to become all too manifest. He shuffled in his chair.

Too covetable to be true, the proposition, he was in a dream. The third son and others were talking in quiet tones. Deena's innards were quivering. Among the three such girls available, the one chosen for him was the best, the most succulent of them. The third son knew. He had savoured them all. One of his toadies was charged with the task of preparing a corner in a tube-well for the tryst. Deena was given a change of clothes for the night, a kurta, and pyjamas. The treat awaiting him made him feverish. After dinner, the third son with a torch in his hand, took Deena to the said tube-well in the middle of the fields.

* * *

The sky was a bit overcast. The night darker than usual. The brick structure that sheltered a big electric pump, some farming implements and sacks of fertilizer, was the size of a room. The corner earmarked for Deena to get laid had a thin cotton mattress rolled out over evenly spread hay on the floor, the corner where he would live through moments of such rapture and ecstasy hitherto unknown to him!

The girl had a slender frame, and no way one could guess at the shape her sari concealed. Her face, too, was covered, partially.

'From head to foot, she's good enough to eat,' the third son said. That was an understatement, Deena would discover that night.

The third son left a torch and a lantern behind and took his friends to another tube-well to sleep. Deena, in the grip of fierce yearning, couldn't stop trembling. He bolted the door and helped her onto the makeshift bed, and by the light of the lantern, he began to unwrap her, his hands unsteady, and the figure that emerged left him breathless with lust. No. With something past lust. He fell on ogling and tasting her deliciously firm body, firm and succulent, as the third son had put it, boasting conical breasts, a flat midriff, gorgeously moulded buttocks, enchantingly tapering legs. What a spread of charms! Deena stayed fortified against the ebbing away of ardour through the night, a wondrous night.

'I was so utterly bewitched by this most fetching sculpture,' he would say later and describe the encounter in all its sensuous aspects, describe the night during which the constancy of his tumescence was to leave him drowned in an aching delight, something that intrigued and overcame her too, his ravenousness. 'Are you a man or the devil?' she said bashfully. So exhausted was she towards the end that he had to beseech her, wheedle her into letting him enter her one more time, the seventh time.

Deena had been careful not to rush in. A little patience would add to the savour of the great moment. He wished her to know that he was a nice, considerate, well-behaved youth, the one conscious of his good fortune. She was dark-skinned, had rustic features with no finishing detail, a bit incomplete, as it were. He was struck by the ordinariness of her looks. Yet no one better looking could have fanned the flames of his passion more that night. With his gentle and solicitous manner, he had her open out to him—who she was and how she ended up being thus available to the third son and now to him—and was surprised at her being so expressive. She was illiterate but showed a spontaneous grip on the idiomatic local dialect of Hindi when she gave Deena an account of her family's precarious existence as he proceeded to trace and caress and kiss and lick the contours of her comely body.

This wasn't her parental village. She was married here into one of the six or seven Harijan families—her husband had died of some stomach disease—that lived in mud dwellings in the outermost part of the village. The funny thing was that in public, these women, like other outcastes, were required to keep a distance from people of other castes, but in private they could be touched most intimately in the most intimate parts of their person by them, by the strong among non-outcastes.

What an unforgettable night, unforgettable because of what it lavished on him, transports of rapture, a night that would serve for him as a touchstone for the quality of the pleasure from all such encounters in future, a night when he came to discover how erroneous was his assumption to view the prettiness of a girl as the key determinant of sexual merit. For starters, that was what made a woman desirable, her apparent beauty and charm, but alas, that wouldn't be the whole story. It had basically to do with the actual act. No. That mightn't always live up to its promise. It had to do with the kind of coupling that bestowed a breath-taking sensation of being snugly enveloped in the luscious wet warmth and being alive, to the core, to the entire length of oneself slithering in and out through the exquisite grip. That's what Deena experienced that night.

'It was the apotheosis of gratification. What an encounter, the recalling of which would invariably make me bring myself off. It was my first time. I thought it was usual. In time, I learnt it couldn't be taken for granted. Among several such escapades that I have had, only two or three can match the quality of that night, the night of intoxicating pleasure. That too when initially I found it hard to enjoy it with a clear conscience because of her story. It had affected my capacity to relish that night to the full. I couldn't help those ecstatic moments being threatened to be clouded by a sense of guilt. But, as the night progressed, I managed to extenuate my conduct by the fact

that I had no part in the way she and her family was treated by the powerful among the higher castes. Had I refused to sleep with her, it wouldn't have stopped her being had by the third son. If anything, by being tender and loving, I made the thing pleasant to her. More than that. My avidity made her achieve cascading orgasms. She admitted as much and was embarrassed by my expression of gratitude for the joy her person had bestowed.'

The next day Zameer came with a car mechanic. The problem was indeed the carburettor. Once rid of the dirt that choked it, the engine was up and running again. In the late afternoon, I pedalled my bicycle to the Commission Bungalow to find my friend in a state of excitement. He couldn't wait to share his fabulous time the previous night. That he was no longer a virgin. Years later at JNU, Deena, while discussing his erotic exploits, would write of that night, *'I still marvel at how a mundane adversity like the breaking down of our Fiat could have led to such a sublime treat, such a memorable episode of my life.'*

* * *

Two days after Indira Gandhi's campaign tour of Allahabad, Argali called. Saansad-ji might come back to the Congress! Ram Mohan rushed to Lucknow. 'Is it confirmed? It doesn't bode well for me.' Ram Mohan and Argali were sitting at Shukla-ji's place. The former feared that Saansad-ji's return might impair Shukla-ji's ability to manipulate the party high command.

'I don't know if it's been finalized,' said Shukla-ji.

'Why hasn't the press got wind of this?'

'Only those close to Indira-ji know,' said Argali. 'They don't want it to get out until a decision's been made. Indira-ji's spoken to Saansad-ji on the phone. She hasn't met him yet.'

'What about Sanjay-ji, is he party to it?'

'He'll be the last to agree. His dislike of Saansad-ji is no secret,' said Shukla-ji.

'Why does she want him back?' said Argali.

'That's exactly the point. Voters are going to return to Indira-ji in hoards. She'll sweep the mid-term polls.'

'She can't get over the way she was rejected,' Argali said. 'Doesn't want to take a chance on the support of Muslims.'

'Saansad-ji's one of the few leaders who enjoy Muslims' trust,' said Ram Mohan.

'Her fears are unfounded. Muslims are back,' cried Liyaqat Argali.

'Who can convince her of that,' Shukla-ji said. 'Sometimes she gets so paranoid, few would have the nerve to reason with her.'

Ram Mohan said, 'There must be others, apart from Sanjay-ji, who want to halt Saansad-ji's return!'

'That's right,' said Shukla-ji. 'These people, including me, will send groups of people from their areas to appeal to her and Sanjay-ji against the move. But she knows these methods.'

Argali said, 'Sanjay-ji remains our only hope. His aversion to Saansad-ji—'

'I've conveyed my concern to Sanjay-ji,' said Shukla-ji, then to Ram Mohan, 'I also want you to chip in. I'll give you the telephone number on which you can reach him. He might recall your name even. Tell him his supporters will feel let down if an opportunist like Saansad-ji is welcomed back in the party.'

'This I can do from here, this very moment.'

'Yes. The best time to get hold of him is before ten in the morning. Let me find out about his location.' Shukla-ji looked at his wristwatch. 'To catch him at home or in the office at this hour is unlikely, but we'll know when to call him.' He gave instructions to a member of his staff, who informed them half an hour later that Sanjay-ji could be reached between ten and eleven at night. 'We'll do it tonight,' said Shukla-ji, 'and listen, your call has nothing to do with me. You couldn't help calling Sanjay-ji after hearing the rumour.' Then Argali had Ram

Mohan move from the guesthouse into Shukla-ji's bungalow for the rest of his stay in Lucknow.

At about eleven, they got Sanjay Gandhi on the phone. After introducing himself, Ram Mohan said, 'Sanjay-ji, this rumour that Saansad-ji's returning, it's causing angst among Congress loyalists. There's no need for this. The party's coming back to power.'

'First, it's not a rumour, and yes there's disquiet among party workers in UP. Some leaders here too are upset, but Indira-ji thinks the move makes sense . . . Why don't you talk to her?' The mother and the son weren't on the same page on this.

'It's happening,' said Argali, 'Sanjay-ji couldn't have been more explicit. She is decided.'

'She thinks that not to pay heed to her son on the matter is for his own good,' said Shukla-ji. 'Who else will be the ultimate beneficiary but him if she ensures Congress's victory? Okay, let's have Ram Mohan speak to her in the morning. It'll be useless. But if that's what Sanjay-ji wants, so be it.'

At about half past six in the morning, Shukla-ji and Ram Mohan were sipping tea in the study, discussing how Saansad-ji's presence in the Congress could undermine their interests, Ram Mohan's in particular. A little later, Argali arrived. One of the staff Shukla-ji had asked to come early, booked an urgent trunk call to Delhi. Soon, Ram Mohan was speaking to Indira Gandhi. A minute later, he replaced the receiver. That she recalled his performance in the Lok Sabha polls in Fatehpur made his day, but couldn't neutralize his dismay when she, after listening to him, said, 'I appreciate your concern, Dr Ram Mohan. I'm sure you understand there are times in politics when one must take decisions according to the larger interest of the party, even when those decisions might militate against one's personal likes or dislikes. But old party friends and loyalists needn't worry on this account.'

Shukla-ji said, 'Let's wait and see how it all pans out.'

'In a few months my time at the Commission will end. With Saansad-ji in the party . . . If he gets a whiff of anything coming my way, his ears will start flapping.'

'You sound as if I'm nowhere in the scene. I've already discussed your case with Sanjay-ji. You just have faith in my standing in the party, my standing with Sanjay-ji.'

* * *

'Uma Shankar-ji called from Delhi. He'll be in Allahabad next week,' said Nishant to Baabuji, on the latter's return from Lucknow. Things were looking good. Ram Mohan summoned everybody to the drawing room. He had something important to share.

At first, the news dampened their mood, but when he got on with his interaction with Sanjay-ji and Indira-ji, and Shukla-ji's heartening words, the way Ram Mohan narrated it, the whole drama of it, they brightened up. 'Now Uma Shankar ji's coming,' Baabuji said and asked Deena to come and sit beside him. 'Even an optimist like me was close to giving up on Deena. To the extent that I thought he might be forced into manual labour for his livelihood. The prospect of such a life, a life beset by penury, would shake me to the depths of my soul. I took refuge in the thought that Mayank would look after his brother.'

'Why go to the extent of his being a labourer?' Kanti said. 'There are jobs less degrading. He can become a typist. Look at his Hindi, his knowledge of Hindi words. If it comes to that, he can distinguish himself in the field of Hindi typing . . . What about his poetic skill? Can you find a labourer with—'

'It was just to make a point. By the way, a freelance typist's hardly a notch or two above a labourer and can barely survive on what he earns.'

'What happened to your resolve to have all of us comfortably settled?' asked Nishant. That riled Ram Mohan.

'I was saying something else, but to let go of a chance to
be sarcastic is too much for you. I stick by what I said and have
achieved that goal to quite an extent. Nisha and Sandhya both are
married. The railway job Sukesh is going to get could have been
yours too. If you want to become a lawyer, that's fine. Mayank's
a few years shy of completing his education. In Deena's case, the
major handicap . . .' Ram Mohan paused, laughed, and said, 'Why
are we going into all that? Deena's going to become a film actor.
Imagine that! None of us would have thought it possible. What
a glorious future he might have . . . What do you think of my
getting hold of Uma Shankar?' Nishant looked beaten.

Ram Mohan called off his visit to Kanpur. 'I'll stay put and
wait for Uma Shankar-ji to show up.' He did show up. Two days
later, when he called, Ram Mohan invited him over to dinner
that very evening, sending a ripple of anticipation through Deena.
Sandhya, who was at the Commission Bungalow for a few days
before moving to Jamshedpur, spruced up the drawing and dining
area. As the time of the expected arrival drew near, Deena put on
his best pair of bellbottoms and a bush-shirt with an exceptionally
long collar, clothes in fashion back then.

At dusk, an Ambassador car drew up outside the gate. Ram
Mohan came out onto the front veranda followed by Nishant, who
ran to the gate to guide the car into the portico. The man at the
wheel was a relation of Uma Shankar's host. This host of whom
the film producer seemed so proud, was Arimardan Singh whose
brother Udai Pratap Singh had defeated Ram Mohan twice in
closely fought elections in Fatehpur. Though Ram Mohan kept up
his warm manner, the surprise put him off a bit. His visceral dislike
of the two had its genesis in the fact that they, chiefly Udai Pratap
Singh, had, after Saansad-ji, his former mentor, having effectively
pleaded his case, forestalled his nomination to the Rajya Sabha by
furnishing false information to Mrs. Gandhi. Ram Mohan thought
Arimardan a wily and slick customer, whose brother, on the other

hand, was forthright and direct, traits that hadn't gone down well
with Indira Gandhi. That's why he, despite being more deserving
than his younger sibling, was never made a minister and kept
languishing in Parliament.

As the guests settled down, Kanti and Sandhya peered through
the chinks in the curtain into the drawing room. Lean, fair, of
average height, dressed in a silk kurta and stylishly tied dhoti, Uma
Shankar didn't disappoint them. He came close to how they had
pictured him. After discussing politics and the probability of his
friend Arimardan contesting from Allahabad, he said, 'Where's my
young friend, the actor?' Ram Mohan called out to Deena. In the
meantime, Uma Shankar cleared up the mystery to his puzzled
escort, Arimardan Singh's relation.

Deena came, his heart racing. Uma Shankar-ji looked him up
and down and had him sit beside him and said, 'If he can act, which
he can, from what you told me, he'll have a good screen presence.'

'I seldom see Hindi films,' said Ram Mohan, 'but seeing him
enact Gabbar Singh, I had to see *Sholay*.'

Deena's performance did make an impression on Uma Shankar-
ji, who said, 'He'll get to act in my film. I'll tell the director. He'll
have to come to Bombay for a screen test, which, as far as I'm
concerned, should be just a formality. I know what part he'd play
in the film, the part of the hero's young friend, his sidekick.' He
gave them an outline of the story. The script was almost ready,
needing just a few final touches.

* * *

Arimardan Singh, who had been made the state Congress chief,
was indeed contesting for the Lok Sabha from Allahabad. He
was out on the hustings forthwith. A small army of his friends
from Delhi and elsewhere descended to give him a hand with the
campaign, people not in politics, Uma Shankar being one of the

more prominent among them. Learning of his friendship with Ram Mohan, a key member of Arimardan Singh's campaign told him that his friend could help bring in some extra votes. A segment of the Allahabad Lok Sabha seat was home to a sizeable number of Kurmi voters. Though his position barred him from political activity, Ram Mohan could do it discreetly through some leading Kurmi locals who held him in esteem. Uma Shankar undertook the task of getting Ram Mohan on board.

Ram Mohan was glad about Uma Shankar in town but resented his friendship with Arimardan Singh. Uma Shankar didn't know of Ram Mohan's antipathy to his friend. When he rang up and said he wanted to discuss something, Ram Mohan asked him to dinner again. He also invited Chaturvedi-ji and Sinha Sahab, who knew he was going to fling open the gates of the dream world to Deena.

His second visit so soon had to do something with him, Deena thought. So sold was he on the idea that everything else—other people's lives, their aims, excitements, concerns—seemed humdrum. He couldn't have suspected what infernal despair lay in wait for him.

Arriving earlier than Uma Shankar, Sinha Sahab and Chaturvedi-ji had time to go at Arimardan Singh. His quick ascent to being one of Indira Gandhi's most trusted men was put down to his ability to cater to her constant need to be humoured. 'In that, he's way ahead of his fellow aspirants to her attention,' said Sinha Sahab, who was bitter about not being rewarded for his family's loyalty. His attempts to obtain a position in any of the non-political government bodies had come to naught. After his father's death, his family had lost access to Indira Gandhi. To break through the cordon of the crowds of her sycophants, looked beyond him.

'Forget about me,' went on Sinha Sahab, 'a person like Tandon-ji, who could have been made governor of some state, stands banished from her thoughts, someone of his standing!'

'Not only that,' said Chaturvedi-ji, 'much of his writing is about her family and its greatness.'

'And he had taught her how to ride—' Sinha Sahab's sentence was cut off by the doorbell. 'It must be him,' Ram Mohan said. 'We won't say anything negative about Indira-ji! You can direct your barbs at Arimardan Singh—' Right then, Nishant ushered Uma Shankar into the drawing room. They all rose. After introductions and all he said, 'I got late because Arimardan's leaving for Delhi tonight. He also gave a hint that—' Uma Shankar stopped and eyed the two whom he barely knew. Ram Mohan assured him they were close friends, that Sinha Sahab was a hardcore Indira supporter.

His mind set at rest, Uma Shankar went ahead, 'Arimardan has been sent for by Indira-ji, who's having second thoughts about his role after the polls. She's realized that handing over the control of her government to Sanjay wasn't okay. He got surrounded by people who, through calculated inputs and doctored information, misled him. She wants to get the message across that she'll be in charge now. Sanjay shouldn't be hurried into anything. He should be allowed to grow into a politician, and when the time's ripe, he'll slip into her shoes. No need for any ballyhoo before that. Arimardan is one of those who'll see that Sanjay isn't led up the garden path by vested interests. It was in Hindi states that she was dealt such a blow, and many blame the party leaders in charge of these states at the time—'

'That includes Shukla-ji,' said Sinha Sahab.

'Yes, of course,' said Uma Shankar. 'Things were mishandled in UP. She was misinformed about the ground realities, about the fact that public sentiment had turned totally against her regime. That's why she made an honest and upright man like Arimardan UP Congress chief, ignoring the wishes of Shukla-ji and others.'

'How can they be blamed for that debacle?' said Ram Mohan. 'Whatever they were doing or saying, was in line with Sanjay-ji's social, political and environmental agenda. Let's assume for a minute that some of these leaders were indeed in the know of things and might have sensed the looming catastrophe. Let's assume that. But who could have dared stick his neck out? Any opinion conflicting with that of the young man would be to their disadvantage.'

'Let's not go into all that,' Uma Shankar said. 'It's not for us to muse on these details, and I'm not qualified to comment on these matters. I'll just say that Arimardan is the most trusted man of Indira-ji in UP. My primary concern is to do whatever I can in my own small way to add to his vote tally, for which I've come to seek help from another friend.' Uma Shankar smiled at Ram Mohan. Before the latter could respond, Chaturvedi-ji said, 'Since you're close to the man who's close to Indira-ji, are we to understand that Shukla-ji has fallen from favour—'

'In that case, Arimardan might be her choice for chief minister when Congress returns here,' broke in Sinha Sahab.

'That I don't know. What I know is that he's her man at present, but to write off Shukla-ji as the next CM will be too early. Shukla-ji remains the favourite of Sanjay-ji, and if she wants to realign her forces in the Congress, that's only to ensure Sanjay's ascent to the throne.'

'What help can I offer to your friend?' asked Ram Mohan.

'If you could speak to Kurmi leaders—'

'Kurmis vote wholesale for Baran Singh's candidates. Even if I speak to some of the leading voices among them, it won't help. They'll say, "Dr Sahab, if you were the Congress candidate, our people might be persuaded to support you." To ask them to reject Chaudhary Sahab's man in favour of Arimardan Singh would be a sell-out in their eyes, a sell-out to the Congress. We'd be dubbed as its agents.'

'What about this Patel fellow, the Congress candidate from Phulpur, the constituency that used to send Nehru-ji to parliament? Patel too is Kurmi and is popular in his area.'

'I'm sceptical about his chances in this election,' said Ram Mohan. 'Regardless of the general sentiment in favour of the Congress, I'll be surprised if Patel wins. Baran Singh's candidate is also Kurmi. Most of these votes will go to him.'

'I should have talked to you before declaring our friendship to Arimardan's campaign managers. Can we do it for the sake of appearances? If you could invite a couple of people from Phulpur and ask for their support in front of me and someone from the campaign! That'll save me face.'

Chaturvedi-ji and Sinha Sahab laughed. Uma Shankar grinned. Ram Mohan's face grew grave. 'Your ambition lies in the realm of filmmaking. I don't belong to that arena, hence in no position to help you with your movie ventures. I can appreciate you trying to help with your friend's campaign. And you should also appreciate what I think of Arimardan Singh as a politician. I've fought three elections—'

'You fought twice against his elder brother,' said Sinha Sahab.

'Yes, and I believe that even in politics, there's room for people who want to win elections without resorting to unfair means or crafty behaviour.'

'I agree,' Uma Shankar said. 'I'm proud that my friend Arimardan's one such politician. He's well-meaning, honest and wants to work for the public good.'

'That's the reason I said it's not your field. You're friends with Arimardan Singh, the man, not the politician. Forgive me for speaking my mind. I've yet to see a politician foxier and more devious.'

'That're quite harsh words. I know enough of him as a politician to stand by what I just said.'

'Please take no offence, but you know nothing, Uma Shankar-ji. Arimardan felt no twinge of conscience while serving under Indira-ji when her administration was unleashing all kinds of monstrosities during the Emergency. When it comes to abuse of power, that period's a benchmark. But as a reward for his solidarity with the Emergency, your friend was promoted to the rank of minister of state. He's seen that the political career of his own brother, who once was close to Indira-ji, remains at a standstill. Yes, Udai Pratap Singh was my adversary. Yet no denying he's a better person than Arimardan, to whom you're close. But so am I to Shukla-ji. If your friend's made CM, that'll be at Shukla-ji's expense.'

Chaturvedi-ji said, 'Uma Shankar-ji, in the present scenario, any attempt to persuade Kurmis to vote for Congress will go by the board. Even if Dr Sahab does make such an attempt, just for show, it might well jeopardize his friendship with Shukla-ji.'

'Unlike you, Uma Shankar-ji,' said Ram Mohan, 'I have a big stake in my political associations. I don't see much difference between you asking me to help your friend in his electoral battle and my asking you to hire someone of my choice to direct your film.'

'That's a stretch . . . If it's come to that, it'll make better sense if I say that there's hardly any difference between my request in question and you wishing that I give your son a chance in my film.'

That was close to home. Ram Mohan kept silent. Sinha Sahab said, 'This is out of order. Let's drop the subject. It's getting personal.'

'I'm not getting personal. It's Dr Sahab making such a big issue out of a small request of mine, a request for just a symbolic gesture, nothing more. If there was a problem with that, he didn't have to attack my friend, laying it on too thick, calling him names.'

'Deena won't act in your film,' said Ram Mohan and asked Nishant, who was gobsmacked, to see Uma Shankar-ji out.

Deena was catatonic. Nothing worse could have befallen him. Sitting at the dining table behind the curtain, dressed up, waiting to be called, he had kept hoping, till the very last, till it was all over, for the situation to be retrieved. Yet what trauma he would have been spared, had he known that Uma Shankar wouldn't get to make the proposed film. That he was to remain a one-film producer before

being consigned to oblivion. He was to disappear from public life
so completely there would be no mention of him anywhere, in no
newspaper or magazine.

* * *

Indira Gandhi was at the apogee of her power again. Most of
her adversaries lay bleeding in the electoral battlefield. The outfit
coming next to her party was the one led by Baran Singh. That's
technically speaking. To call it even a distant second would be
a stretch. Baran Singh's MPs were less than one-sixth of hers in
the new Lok Sabha. Yet in some states, he was the only one to
weather the Indira gale and left standing. In UP, his party's tally
was half of that of the Congress. Patel had lost to Baran Singh's
candidate in Phulpur. From Allahabad city, Arimardan Singh won
by a big margin.

Indira Gandhi took office. Her cabinet consisted of those who
had stood the test of time with respect to their servility. What
came as a shocker were the omissions. Chiefly, two. Saansad-ji and
Arimardan Singh. Ram Mohan put through a call to Argali and was
taken aback when his buoyancy wasn't reciprocated.

Argali's mood was subdued. He made plain how Shukla-ji
looked at the two exclusions. After such a big win, Saansad-ji had
to be put in his place. She had wooed him back because of her
party's obliteration in UP earlier. It turned out a wave-election
in her favour. This was perfect time to get back at a turncoat like
Saansad-ji, the man who, along with Jagjivan Ram, had betrayed
her. How could she forget that? Now he was of no use to her.

'We can celebrate Saansad-ji being kept out of her cabinet,'
Argali continued, 'but Arimardan's exclusion is a matter of
concern.' Ram Mohan braced himself. 'He's heading the state
Congress and knowing Indira-ji, assembly polls in the states ruled
by non-Congress parties aren't far off. She wants her governments

in these states. UP's one of them, and Arimardan's going to head
the next Congress government here—'

'What about Shukla-ji?'

'He'd be inducted into the Union cabinet. That's what Sanjay-
ji told Shukla-ji—'

Shukla-ji would rather be CM than a minister at the centre.
But let me confess to being a little selfish here. As a Union minister,
he'll be in a better position to get me to the Union Public Service
Commission.'

'That no longer obtains, Dr Sahab. At least not any time soon.'

'I don't get it! UPSC's no longer possible?'

'Yes. Shukla-ji had raised it with Sanjay-ji, who spoke to his
mother only to learn the persons to fill the available two vacancies
had been identified.'

Ram Mohan recalled Sinha Sahab's remark. 'Indira-ji rewards
these positions to those who, before retiring from important
posts, were devoted to her cause. There are so many sinecures
that she, with a variety of socio-cultural outfits and a humungous
public sector under her command, can dispense to her yes-men
of all stripes: good-for-nothing politicos, inept bureaucrats, pink
academics and so forth. This's her way of saying to those holding
key positions that they shouldn't be above being partial towards
her wishes.'

'What should I do now, Liyaqat bhai? I don't have much time
left at the Commission.'

'I know. But rest assured, things will get better. A little patience
is all that's needed . . . If Shukla-ji were to be CM again, he'd make
you VC of some university, any university of your choice. That's
why we should resent his losing out to Arimardan. We'll have to
wait now. It's not going to be a long wait. Just as I said, things in
time will pan out well.'

Ram Mohan was tempted to ask if he might be considered for
the Rajya Sabha. If Shukla-ji could talk to Sanjay-ji! But forbore

from that. Didn't want to come over all desperate. When Tiwari-ji, who had, of late, been staying in his village, turned up to discuss Ram Mohan's chances in the altered scene and opined that giving up on the Rajya Sabha was a mistake, that he should speak to Shukla-ji, Ram Mohan said that with Arimardan Singh's rising stature, Shukla-ji couldn't be of much help; he himself was waiting to be accommodated on the Union cabinet. 'It would be much too high an expectation from him at this juncture.'

That was to stay that way. Because Sanjay Gandhi, Shukla-ji's chief source of power, would die, attempting some aerobatic daredevilry while flying an aircraft of Delhi Flying Club.

* * *

Ram Mohan replayed his conversation with Argali in his mind. There was nothing to give hope in what the latter had said, nothing but homilies to comfort him. 'Things will get better. A little patience is all that's needed.' It was nothing but an admission that things weren't OK, that there wasn't much they could do, save for riding it out. Ram Mohan didn't have that kind of time. He called Lucknow again.

Argali had little to add to what he had said. It wasn't Argali's fault that Ram Mohan found himself looking at an uncertain future. Yet he couldn't help being angry with him. Him and Shukla-ji. Why couldn't they have been more sentient of the coming upset; why couldn't they have read Indira Gandhi's mind; why couldn't they have discerned Arimardan Singh's rising stock and done something about it? When Argali said they hadn't bargained for Arimardan supplanting Shukla-ji, Ram Mohan was close to losing his rag but checked it, though couldn't desist from saying that because of Shukla-ji's assurance, he had let go of two big opportunities that were his for taking: the certainty of his election to the Lok Sabha from Fatehpur, which Saansad-ji had so solicitously offered; the second, when he could have joined Arimardan Singh's camp by supporting him during the recent poll. Not only that. He had to lose a friend like Uma Shankar in the bargain.

There was an odd pause on Argali's end. 'Dr Sahab, success, or failure of one's allies can't be measured against what one can achieve with or without them in the immediate future. Expediency has its benefits but mostly short-term. Such benefits can't match up to rewards for loyalty, rewards that aren't only more significant but last longer.' He let out a sigh, 'I won't ask you to wait for Shukla-ji to be able to do something. Please feel free to join hands with anybody who can help after you leave the Commission.'

'Had I felt this way, I'd have made a move quite a while ago. And without your advice. I valued our friendship so much that the thought never occurred.'

'That's very kind of you. But believe me, no one would be more pleased than Shukla-ji and I if you found someone else to help you get something from the Centre or from Arimardan's government here as and when it come into being.' With that, Argali excused himself. He had some visitor to attend to. The chilly impersonal note on which the conversation ended wasn't lost on Ram Mohan. His Shukla-Argali phase was over.

* * *

Assured of the UPSC, Ram Mohan hadn't thought of a house of his own in Allahabad. Returning to Kanpur wasn't an option. Nishant was to start practising at Allahabad High Court, and Mayank was to go to Allahabad University.

Whether they lived in Allahabad or went back to Kanpur, mattered little to Deena. He could live anywhere. There was nothing in the pipeline for him. With his dream of Bombay going up in smoke, he was back to Hindi literature and films. Then one mid-afternoon, when Ram Mohan summoned them all to the drawing room, his tone dripping urgency, Deena was startled out of his world of literature and films. He was missing his sisters. Nisha along with Shivika had moved to Delhi. Shekhar was about to get the married hostel on the IIT campus. Sandhya was in Jamshedpur with her husband, Varun.

Ram Mohan was quiet even after they had sat down.

'So, what's it about?' said Kanti, breaking the silence.

'I was trying to recall something, but you had to break in . . . I had a long conversation with Argali. It might be our last.' They were stunned. 'The UPSC's off and my getting any other position isn't in prospect either. Arimardan, being the next CM, signals the end of that,' then to Nishant, 'You were right. I should have grabbed it when Saansad-ji had offered his party's ticket. I erred on the side of caution.'

'That Lok Sabha lasted less than three years—'

'So what? I would have achieved a lot in that period. Not only would Saansad-ji have got me a place in their government from his party's quota, but I'd have been better placed to read the scene on the ground; to know which way the wind was blowing and take steps accordingly. I might have joined the Congress when People's Party was crumbling.'

'There's so much a politician can do to secure the future of his family,' said Nishant with a lament in his voice.

'That's all behind us. Let's confront the present. We haven't got much time left in this bungalow. We can stay here a little beyond the end of my term, but we must start looking for a house in Allahabad.'

'A house to rent?' asked Kanti.

'No, our Kanpur property can fetch enough for us to buy a house. We had better set about it.'

'What about our tenants in Kanpur?' said Nishant.

In one portion of their land in Kanpur, stood a double-storied structure built with the money from the selling of the copyright of Ram Mohan's two-volume book on Hindi language to the publisher. Each of the two floors, rented out to two families, had two tiny rooms, a kitchenette and a bathroom. Their old house was in a state of dilapidation. Ram Mohan's nephew, Sateesh, had stayed there before moving to his college hostel.

'You go to Kanpur and speak to the tenants. We must get them out. Tell them it's not negotiable. They must go.'

'Meanwhile, we should look for residential properties here,' said Kanti.

'Yes, we should keep an eye out for such houses. An active search can begin only when we start getting offers in Kanpur after getting rid of the tenants.'

'It might not be easy,' said Nishant.

'Give them a month. If they don't listen, we'll have to throw them out. Let's hope things don't come to that. It'll save us much trouble if they leave of their own accord. Take Sateesh along when you visit them. He's in DAV College and active in student politics. DAV College students are a feared lot,' he leaned back on the sofa, 'Now, what do you think of my decision to marry Sandhya off? Look at the situation . . .! Come to think of it, things aren't so bad as they seemed after that despairing talk with Argali. Soon we'll have a high court lawyer in the family—'

'First I need to serve under some senior advocate, as one of his juniors.'

'To learn the ropes! Do you have someone in mind?'

Nishant mentioned a famous advocate's name. 'When you come back from Kanpur, we'll go meet him.' Nishant smiled. This famous advocate wouldn't say no to his father.

Ram Mohan looked at Deena. 'I'm going to find Deena a job. He can do his BA as a private student from Kanpur University. It's important he starts earning some money. However small a sum to begin with. It's time he began getting to grips with the world out there.'

Deena's stomach lurched. Looming ahead was the end of his beautiful world, the world of poetry, fiction, of films. If not the end, then definitely the time he spent on these delights would shrink after being saddled with a full-time job.

* * *

Both the tenants in Kanpur expressed their inability to move out in a month. They needed seven-eight months. 'At first, they were staggered that Sateesh was a student at DAV College. No sooner did he try to reason with them than their combativeness returned.'

'Sateesh is hardly the stuff thugs are made of,' said Ram Mohan, 'I'm happy with the way he behaves. He can have others talk tough on his behalf. If I hadn't stopped him he would have become president of the students' union . . . Should I get Gulab Singh to—'

'No need of that. Sateesh has someone, some student, who can put the fear of God into these tenants.'

'I want you to be present when they go there, Sateesh and this boy. We must have that place vacated fast. Even if the matter went to court, the decision would be in our favour since we own no other residential property. But that'll take years if they want to drag it out.'

'Tenants do it to force landlords to cough up some money in lieu of their departure.'

'Yes, they might try to trade on our need. I don't have that kind of money. Even if I had, I wouldn't square these extortionists . . . If this friend of Sateesh's proves inadequate, I'll call in Gulab Singh.'

Two days later, Nishant popped over to Kanpur again to meet this youth by the name of Umesh, lined up by Sateesh to frighten the tenants. He was active in student politics at DAV. His appearance, though, was a disgrace. Nishant's mental image of him lay shattered, the image he had formed after listening to Sateesh. His slight build and boyish face with hardly any hair belied his twenty years. Nishant didn't know what to say, as Umesh stood grinning shyly before him. Sateesh took Nishant out of Umesh's hearing.

'Nobody can be a farther cry from being a bruiser than this boy. He looks just a tiddler, if anything.'

Sateesh laughed. Nishant went on, 'Just a look at him would encourage them to hold out.'

'That's good if they feel that way. For the impact of what comes next will be much greater then. You haven't seen him in action. His innocuous size, age, looks, these very attributes add to the maniacal menace he's capable of dispensing.'

Nishant darted a glance towards Umesh who, a red scarf round the neck and the same shy smile on the face, stood leaning languorously on the wall by the gate of Ram Mohan's property opposite McRoberts Hospital in Civil Lines.

'When he gives rein to his rage, it's no sham. It's not affected in the sense that he can't act on his threats. He can and will if the situation demands. His daring and fearlessness were a problem when he lived in his village. His parents were worried about his risk-taking. I brought him here. Under my tutelage, he's become sensible of the dangers of rash behaviour.'

Nishant was engrossed as Sateesh continued, 'If he'd stayed on in his village, he would be dead. He was a terror in his school and made quite a few enemies.' Then, the shocker Sateesh had kept for the last, 'That he'd have committed two murders is hard to believe.' Nishant eyeballed Sateesh as if aggrieved at the way the most crucial bit of the youth's bona fides was flung at him, casually.

'What murders?'

'He had this close pal, a punk, who, on the strength of Umesh's reputation, would strong-arm people who crossed him. About a year ago, this punk's family suspected his elder brother's wife of a secret affair in her parents' village. I don't know all the details except that the punk, with the consent of his brother, discussed it with Umesh. A plan was hatched to catch them in the act. When she went visiting her parents' next, this punk and Umesh set a trap. The moment her lover threw his arms around her, as she sat squatted inside the cornfield, their trysting place, he was in for the shock of his life. It was Umesh dressed up as woman.'

'He just murdered him, how?'

'Umesh had a big knife hidden under the sari. Both were later found headless and a field apart.'

'My goodness! Was she also there? How did he do in both without any help?'

'No, her brother-in-law, the punk, was holding her down somewhere nearby in the same cornfield when Umesh, after doing her lover in, took the blood-soaked knife to her. Her father couldn't name anybody in the FIR. The case went cold in no time. He might have inferred the truth later from the gossip which something like this always occasions.'

'Let's go inside,' said Nishant.

'Let's first be clear how to approach them. I think you should speak to them first, and then Umesh and I will take over.'

'No need to talk to them both. We'll shake one up and the other will get the message.'

It was Sunday. Both chief householders were home. They, Nishant, Sateesh and Umesh, entered through the small door in the big gate. The yard on the side of their now crumbling house, was thick with weeds and junk. Nishant strode down the narrow dirt strip along the yard, with Sateesh and Umesh at his heels, towards the front yard, most of which was taken up by this small double-storied structure. A middle-aged woman with a pinched face peeped from a window on the floor above. Nishant knocked at the door downstairs. Emanating from inside were the sounds and noises typical of families in cramped quarters. Nishant knocked again. A boy of ten or eleven answered and ran inside. 'That bhaiya has come again.' The tenant appeared and before he could ask them in, Nishant said, 'We'll talk outside,' and walked him a few paces towards the gate.

'What have you decided?'

'Decided what?'

'Don't act . . . When are you both vacating our flats?'

'I don't know about the man upstairs. As for myself, I can only repeat what I said earlier. Give me seven-eight months. Not before that. I've spoken to an advocate who's advised me against your demand. I'll stay put unless you come up with a better solution.'

'What solution?' yelled Nishant. Then to Sateesh, 'He thinks we should pay him to go—'

'Finding another place will take time and resources.'

'What're you playing at?' said Nishant before Sateesh took over, 'You've no idea who you're fucking with—'

'Look, motherfucker, you have no choice,' burst in Umesh. 'Once I put the screws on you, nobody can save your ass, not even your advocate. If any motherfucker dares, it'll be only to scurry off with a bamboo pole up his ass.'

A sucker-punch, hitting the tenant like a ton of bricks. Even Nishant reeled at the kind of filth Umesh spewed. And his voice! The way he could throw it, someone of his build! Sateesh nudged Umesh aside and told the petrified tenant that even the police couldn't save him, as Umesh was a student leader who, with his army of rowdy youths, would give him and his family hell on a regular basis. 'Your departure from here is a sure thing. The sooner you realize the better.' Casting a side glance at Umesh, he stepped back.

'Bhaiya, you leave it to me.' said Umesh and made as if to grab the tenant, who stood paralyzed with fright. Sateesh held him back and asked the tenant to beat it. Umesh screamed, 'Do not force my hand, you motherfucker, or you, your wife, your kids will be out on the street by tomorrow.' There was no holding him, his roar and thunder went on, even after the cowering figure disappeared into his rented hole. When Umesh trained his menaces at the second tenant, the faces crowding the window on the first floor dissolved.

Nishant, in the meantime, got engaged in conversation with some neighbours near the gate, who, brought out by Umesh's hollering, appreciated the need for such an action as Nishant explained the situation to them.

* * *

The progress made in Kanpur eased Ram Mohan's mind. He could get into action in Allahabad now. He met the famous lawyer who agreed to include Nishant in the team of his juniors. Mayank, who had to sit twelfth boards, got down to some serious study, while Deena, with the sword of some tedious daylong job hanging over him, couldn't freely enter the world of Hindi poetry and fiction.

That Baabuji would get him employed couldn't be wished away. But that happened sooner than expected. It was Sinha Sahab who brought to the Commission Bungalow this man by the name of Bachchu Pathak, who had recently been elected President of Allahabad District Cooperative Bank by its board of directors, who were voted in by secretaries in the cooperative societies in the district.

Once close to Saansad-ji, Bachchu Pathak had friends and foes across political affiliations. He had started off being a minor thug and come to Saansad-ji's notice for his contribution to the victory of the latter's man in an assembly by-poll, but after a run-in with Saansad-ji's son, he joined forces with Saansad-ji's detractors in the city Congress. That too wouldn't last. In the meantime, he had risen to the stature of someone people avoided messing with, a thug with political patronage.

When Deena was called to the drawing room, he didn't know why. He sat down, as Baabuji, Sinha Sahab and Bachchu Pathak were engaged in discussing the rise of Arimardan Singh in the

Congress and how Saansad-ji, once the tallest political leader in UP after Baran Singh, had been cast aside by Indira Gandhi. 'It was she who coaxed him back into the party,' said Pathak, who was all praise for Saansad-ji, for his administrative ability, his grasp of the issues at the root of UP's backwardness, and rued, 'I wish I'd stayed in touch with him. It wasn't his fault that his son had got up my nose. I'd try and make up with Saansad-ji. He'll bounce back.'

Sinha Sahab introduced Deena to Bachchu Pathak, who grinned and said, 'Congratulations, you've become a bank employee.' They all laughed. Ram Mohan beckoned Deena to come along as they all walked out. Waiting in the portico was Bachchu Pathak's Ambassador. Sinha Sahab was to leave with him. Ram Mohan asked him to stay back. He would have him dropped later. Pathak was about to climb into the car, when Ram Mohan ordered Deena to touch Pathak-ji's feet.

'You get to the head office of the bank tomorrow at about eleven and wait if I'm not in.'

To start working after twelfth meant a lowly status, a humiliating thought for someone whose father was Ram Mohan, who, even before coming to the Commission, was an important man, an academic, a speaker, a teacher of repute, a village-builder, a politician who had fought two Lok Sabha and one assembly elections. A son of such a worthy had to be worthless to have to start working after twelfth. Yes, as regards prospects and promise, he occupied the lowest rung among his siblings. To explain the reason to their friends for his lowly paid job in this bank would be a crying shame to Nishant and to Mayank, though chances of it being found out were slim as the two social worlds never met, the one in which belonged people working with outfits like this godforsaken bank and the other inhabited by their friends and acquaintances. That's how it would stay during the period that Deena would work at that bank, holding a position barely a rung above that of a peon. Few in their set would ever learn of the ghastly anomaly Deena was in his family. Nothing could make Nishant accept something like that, a job as demeaning as the one Deena was about to take up.

'One day, you have to cut it as someone who counts,' Ram Mohan would tell Mayank, his favourite child, which enkindled in the latter early on the desire to make a mark in life.

After Sinha Sahab left, Ram Mohan, noticing Deena's morose look, had him sit before him. 'Look, formal education isn't your bag. You can't pass an exam on your own. I've somehow got you past twelfth. It's important you start earning a little; that'll help you not only gain in confidence but feel a sense of responsibility towards your own life. Now cheer up and stop being downcast. You should be happy that you'll have money to spend whatever way you wish. You can indulge your passion for literature in your spare time. Read as much as you can. Write poetry! Why let this bank job become your identity when you can find a place in the sun as a poet, a writer? That should be your chief identity. I know people who, as regards their position at work, are nothing, but as men of letters, as artists, they're big. They command the esteem of many an esteemed personage.'

* * *

The next day, Deena rode his bicycle to the head office of the District Cooperative Bank. He was nervous at having to meet strangers or his colleagues-to-be in an office where he would stand out as someone who didn't belong there, didn't belong in a place crawling with the rabble. What would they think of him? How would they judge him? A bum of a son of his father! Hopeless! Embarrassment to his family! No, he shouldn't let his mind race that way. They might as well be awed, the staff at the head office. He could certainly expect to be treated a bit deferentially.

The building of the head office of the bank, situated close to an old cinema hall with which he was familiar, was yellowish and old, a low rundown boundary wall marking its precincts, and the iron gate through which Deena entered was partially resting on the ground, rusted and dysfunctional. Leaving his cycle at the bicycle rack, he walked up to the guard who, armed with a shotgun, was lounging in a scruffy chair in the shade of a corrugated iron sheet by the entrance of the main building, one half of which lodged the main branch of the bank, the other its head office that also had a separate entrance from the road on the other side.

Deena, the guard told him, could get to the head office through the branch using the door in the partition.

Right ahead, as he entered, sat a big slab of a counter where two men were busy arranging ledgers and stamps in front of them, getting set for the day's public dealing. Sitting in his cubicle on the far side to the left, the cashier, a middle-aged man, looked absorbed arranging bundles of notes of various denominations in two drawers. Occupying the space between the main counter and the strong room were two more tables. The bigger one that had a table cover, though variously stained, belonged to the branch manager, who sat there with his back to the partition, his face sporting an inexplicable frown. Before being mistaken for a customer, Deena told his purpose to the duo behind the counter. Both pointed to the door in the wooden partition behind them.

Moving towards the door in the partition he threw a glance around. The place was grimy and dingy. On the walls, the dull green paint was flaking off at places, and the corners and parts of the ceiling harboured cobwebs of varied sizes, while the white blades of the ceiling fans were thick with soot-like dust. The far corners, one near the cashier's cubicle and the other next to that of the branch manager, lay smothered in betel stains.

The same shabby, tenebrous conditions prevailed on the other side of the partition—the head office comprising the accounts, the establishment that is HR in current parlance, a separate room for the seniors, the chief accountant and the senior manager; a corner of this room also housed a contraption called cyclostyle, close to which sat a pale hollow-eyed woman typist with a small table and a ratty chair. Set apart from the rest by another partition were the rooms of the president and the secretary of the bank.

Bachchu Pathak wasn't in yet. His peon, who had taken up his position outside his room, said he was expected anytime and pointed out a man who, with a bundle of files in his hand, stood near the entrance to the head office, talking to the secretary, the top official of the bank who reported to the president. The man with files was the establishment head. Before Deena could reach him, he along with the secretary stepped out and stood at the edge of the driveway gazing towards the road to their right. The peon too hastened there.

A moment later, Bachchu Pathak's Ambassador pulled up just a step away from the establishment head, who opened the door, before anybody else could, for the president to disembark. Clad in starched white dhoti-kurta, Bachchu Pathak had to stand still as they all began touching his feet. Spotting Deena, he flashed a grin. After everybody was done, Deena too went ahead and stooped down.

Bachchu Pathak took Deena inside his room, signalling the Secretary and the Establishment Head to come in too, and with no preliminaries, asked that Deena be given his appointment letter fast. Pathak needed to be off to the circuit house to meet Komal Singh Yadav, the state's cooperative minister, who was said to be corruption itself.

'Please come,' said the establishment head to Deena, who hurried after him. People in the Accounts section eyed them as they walked past before disappearing into the Establishment room. Offering a chair to Deena, the head directed one of his two subordinates to ready an appointment letter. Deena was asked to give his educational documents to the man who was taking out the record books and registers, to get cracking on with the thing. On learning of the position of his father, the establishment head gave

Deena a broad smile, 'Oh . . .' The other two looked up to have a fresh look at him. The head said he was an erstwhile aspirant for a place in the state civil services and had almost made it once but his score in the written exam couldn't offset the deadly effect of poor marks in the interview.

'He can't be a regular employee! He's underage by a year and a half,' burst out the subordinate entrusted with the paperwork, showing the relevant document to his boss, who sprang to his feet, rushed out and returned with a solution. Deena, for now, would work on a daily wage of twelve rupees—seventy-two per week payable every Saturday—and on becoming eligible, would be made a regular employee.

On the carbon copy of the recruitment letter, Deena was asked to write 'Received' and sign it. He got terribly nervous. The subordinate watched. Deena, his insides shaking, wrote 'R' and stopped. What next, 'e' or 'i'? Certain to bungle it, he couldn't move further. To buy time, he affected to read the letter, perspiring all over. The subordinate smiled and glanced at his boss, who came and stood over Deena and asked him to write it in Hindi, telling him the official phrase. When done, he congratulated him on becoming a daily-wage clerk-cum-cashier at the District Cooperative Bank.

'Don't worry! Few of us here know any English,' said the establishment head, 'All ledger entries and vouchers are made mostly in English. That's nothing. A few technical terms and stock phrases, something anybody can learn.' With these words, he took Deena to introduce to his co-workers and seniors.

Later, Bachchu Pathak called up the Commission Bungalow to clear up the underage thing. That, a year and half later, he would make Deena a regular employee. Though piqued, Deena would come to see some merit in his changed situation. Things that put him at a disadvantage vis-à-vis his brothers fell away. No longer a dead loss, a wastrel, he was free to do what he liked in his free time.

He could read anything, go out, meet friends, go to the movies for which he now had money. Much of the donkey work he had to do earlier at home would cease to come his way, as most of the day he was at work. Baabuji looked on him as a responsible, gainfully employed young man. He would chat with him, cracking jokes and all, would also encourage him to write poetry. It was on his advice that Deena, to bolster his Hindi, picked up some Sanskrit. 'If you have some knowledge of it, nobody will mess with you,' said Baabuji. 'The moment you draw the sword of Sanskrit, those with no grounding in it would run for cover.'

Yet Deena had to spend hours at work, slaving away at the tedious task of filling up ledgers with debit–credit sums and tallying them, day after day, learning nothing of substance, nothing to help sharpen his linguistic skill or raise his literary sensibility, a fact at which he in time began to feel deeply aggrieved. Particularly so, when he would become determined to learn English, come hell or high water.

* * *

Umesh turned out to be their winning card in Kanpur. In less than the time they were given, both the tenants got out, opening the door for a stream of prospective buyers to look at the property located in one of the most chic and upmarket neighbourhoods of the city. The man who would buy it, lived in one of the localities that were nothing but labyrinths of dark, dirty, clamorous alleys. He was a big retailer of spices, whose innovative idea of mixing them with substances similar in texture and colour had brought him riches.

He had put something as worthless as horse dung to a lucrative use by melding its sun-baked desiccated version with coriander seeds at the time of their being ground. 'It's all a question of finding the right ratio, which he's worked out so well that unless you're an expert, it's hard to find anything wrong with his coriander powder,' said Khatri Sahab, their former neighbour, to Nishant as Ram Mohan finalized the deal.

'It was a bargain, the price at which I got it,' the businessman confided to Sateesh. Ram Mohan had agreed to a sum of three hundred and twenty-five thousand as the closing price, partly because of his impatience to be done with it and partly because they had identified a property in Allahabad up for sale. Ram Mohan wanted to pay an advance before other interested parties vitiated his chances of a reasonable deal.

He needn't have worried. The letter Nishant found waiting for him on their return changed the equation. Ram Mohan forgot about the property he was thinking of buying. It would have eaten up the entire proceeds of their Kanpur deal. With this letter to Nishant, the letter from a descendent of the Rajah of an erstwhile princely state not far from Allahabad, they came in sight of a much better property, promising a much better bargain.

A former classmate of Nishant's at the university had told him of a big double-storey building at the edge of classy George Town, not far from Moon Auntie's place. Ah well, Moon Auntie! I forgot to talk about the cooling of relations between Nisha and her. About that later. Let me get on with the matter at hand. The owner of this property was this middle-aged man of princely stock, who lived in his ancestral mansion in his family estate in Rewa. He owned several other properties in his own state, in Delhi and in the hills. On his Allahabad property, he seemed to have given up. Occupied by four tenants, two of whom had lived there for a decade, paying negligible sums as rent, the property was all but gone. None of the tenants could be persuaded to relinquish its possession, something they had almost for free.

Given the dice of the Rent Act loaded against houseowners, recourse to legal route was hardly an option for this heir to a former Rajah, to whom Nishant had sent a letter drafted with much deliberation and in English, as its addressee had been educated in England. It was a shot in the dark. But lo, here is the response from the landlord, resonating with Nishant's musings. His shot in the dark had hit the mark. He went through the letter several times before showing it to Baabuji, who was overjoyed and paid glorious tributes to Nishant's initiative, to his ability to draft such a letter in English, for which the man who had been educated in England had a word of praise in his reply.

He invited Nishant and his father to make a trip to his estate. They accepted. Nishant then took Baabuji to see the said property, a large, shingled building along with an annexe, standing on a big corner plot, putting all the houses nearby in the shade. A property of such a majestic presence lodged such commoners! The four tenants had nothing to make them stand out.

The ground floor of the main building was occupied by some engineer in the Public Works Department, while on the first floor lived a district court lawyer who, if he thought that with his sun-faded black jacket, yellowed white shirt, dusty white trousers and a face etched with stress, he could inspire confidence in his potential clients, was kidding himself. His wife taught at a government school and was the family's chief provider. They often quarrelled. Nishant learnt all this from his friend. Each of the two floors of the annexe consisted of two rooms, a bathroom, and a small veranda; the tenant on the ground floor was a Tamil couple, with the husband working as some sort of manager in the Indian Coffee House and the wife made idlis that she supplied to a vendor selling south Indian snacks at the university gate. The upper floor was in possession of the family of a lower division clerk in the district administration.

Soon, Ram Mohan and Nishant set off for the landowner's estate, a three-hour-long journey, in the Fiat, with Zameer driving. 'He can't wait to be rid of this property, going by the tone of his letter,' said Ram Mohan.

'Yes. Or he wouldn't have put us to the trouble of travelling to his place.'

'The property looks expensive! What should our offer be?'

'A hundred thousand! Doesn't matter if its market value is enormously more. Its tenant-infestation makes it worthless to this former prince. He'd be thankful for whatever it fetches him.'

Their host was courtesy itself, with nothing in his manner to suggest they had yet to talk it over. 'The day I received your son's letter, so nicely composed, I knew I'd found the buyers I was looking for. We all know there'll hardly be any takers for a property blighted by the presence of four tenants. The people who showed any interest were thugs. I didn't want to let them have the house where we, my elder brother who's no more, my two sisters and I, lived as school-going children. My brother and I were students at St Joseph School while our sisters went to St Mary's Convent. Our father had built it just for that purpose. He didn't want us to live in the boarding. Our father thought that after finishing school, we might go to Allahabad University, a reputable institute back then, but decided to send us to England . . . Our first two tenants were decent people. How I came to land myself with the present crop is a long story . . . You should be wary of this chap on the upper floor of the main building. He's the leader of the pack. They all listen to him because of his profession. You know lawyers are one of the most feared species, the others being politicians and students. Then there're local outlaws. I wonder how a city like Allahabad, a cultural, literary, and educational city, much smaller in size and population than the other four major cities of UP, I wonder how Allahabad came to be home to so many mobsters, small and big time.'

'Nishant's also setting out to make his name as an advocate of Allahabad High Court,' said Ram Mohan. The former prince of Rewa wished Nishant success, and when asked how much he expected for this property, he said, 'How much would you like to pay?'

'A hundred thousand.'

He agreed. Ram Mohan wished he had offered yet a smaller sum. 'He didn't even weigh it up,' said Ram Mohan as they left the next morning. 'He might have agreed to seventy-five thousand.'

'I'd have started with sixty-five thousand—'

'Let's not be fussed about it. We've got ourselves a wonderful deal.'

The property was secured within a week of their meeting with the owner, who came to Allahabad just for a day to sign the papers that Nishant had got prepared. The entire process took less than two hours at the sub-registrar's office. Once an agreement was reached about the size of the sweetener to be distributed among the staff in that office, they didn't create hurdles. The property was registered in the name of Kanti and their three sons. Ram Mohan kept himself out of it.

* * *

Before he could focus on their tenant problem, Ram Mohan was distracted by a prospect to politically redeem himself. Being no longer close to any politician of consequence was disquieting and the man he missed most was Saansad-ji, and couldn't help reproaching himself for ditching him, the man who had sent him to the Commission. Suddenly, here was his chance to revive the old bond.

Frustrated and jaded in the Congress, Saansad-ji had decided to quit it yet again. Not only had Indira Gandhi given him no responsibility but made it obvious that he was out of the loop. 'She's out to humiliate him,' Munni Prasad had screamed, his fellow member at the Commission. 'It was she who had invited him back into the fold.'

During this conversation with Munni Prasad, Ram Mohan had flashed on the idea. He called everybody to his room. 'I've something to discuss. It's a good idea, an idea well worth pondering.

'Nishant's well on his way to becoming an advocate, and Deena, though not out of the woods yet, is on track for a better situation in the bank. Bachchu Pathak isn't the man to loosen his grip on the District Cooperative Bank. So long as he's there, he'd confer whatever favours he can on Deena . . . Mayank, like I've always said, is the least of my concerns. He'll shine in whatever he chooses to do in life . . . With this property, we're rid of the problem of where we'd go from the Commission Bungalow.'

'First, we have to throw these tenants out, a big ask, bigger than buying a house,' said Nishant.

'That it is. And we're capable of tackling it. If they refuse to pay heed, they'll have asked for it. Let's leave it at that. We'll set our mind to it later. Today, I want your opinion on something else, something that's of utmost importance now. I didn't share it because I had yet to come up with a course of action to deal with it. I've thought up one now . . . Well, you all know that in about four months, my term at the Commission will end. But I'm not of an age to lead a life of retirement. It's the first time I'm faced with a situation when there's no political leader who counts to call my friend, I, who was close at one point of time or another to such illustrious figures as Dixit-ji, Baran Singh, Saansad-ji and Shukla-ji, each of whom played some part in the betterment of our prospects in life . . . The man to whom I'm most indebted is Saansad-ji, and it's him I want to make up with now, which isn't easy. I kind of betrayed him. To reignite his affection, I must make a gesture of goodwill. And in a manner that it's noticed by one and all. Something that would put paid to his loss of trust in me, and the sacrifice it requires isn't much compared to the stir it would cause,' he paused. His face wore an enigmatic expression, a smile lurking about the mouth. The face of someone who had hit on a way out of an intractable situation.

'Saansad-ji can quit Congress any day,' he forged on. 'Indira-ji's given him a raw deal. It was she who'd wooed him back, but then she hadn't expected such a big, definitive victory. With Saansad-ji of no use to her, she's intent on having his guts for garters, as he had shown the temerity to defect from the Congress.'

'What else could Saansad-ji have done!' said Nishant. 'After his removal as CM, his political life was put on hold.'

'You're not supposed to react in that manner. You should wait for her to take pity on you, wait till she looks kindly on your need to get back on her right side, but that's aside. What I'm thinking is that when Saansad-ji resigns from the Congress, I'll resign from the Commission. To show solidarity with him.'

'How would it make sense? I mean quitting your position from a constitutional body in support of Saansad-ji quitting a political party?'

'Who bothers about these things!'

It was thrilling, the idea of resignation, the idea of a kind of rebellion against someone as mighty as Indira Gandhi, the idea of affirming one's closeness to a political figure of stature no less than that of Saansad-ji, the idea of the decision making a splash.

'It'll cost me four months' salary, but that's worth it because Saansad-ji won't sit quietly. He may join forces with like-minded people and form a party of his own. Whatever he decides would keep me politically alive. We're not so well-off as to be able to bribe our way through a difficult situation. I've to have some standing in the post-Commission world. Without being part of something noteworthy, something loud, without being part of some action, one can't stand on one's dignity in life.'

'*Besotted with the drama of resignation, Baabuji couldn't look beyond,*' Deena was to observe later in his diary. '*We were taken in by its exciting prospects—the press coverage and people's open-mouthed reaction—with no idea of its brevity, the brevity of that moment. Barring Tandon Uncle, Baabuji's friends applauded the idea, including*

Chaturvedi and Sinha Uncle, who thought it would make their friend politically relevant.'

Saansad-ji left the Congress. A day later, Ram Mohan quit his position at the Commission. It was a front-page story in the local papers, also in national dailies as a small news item. Among a raft of calls that day, there was a call from Delhi too. Saansad-ji's wife was on the line. She was effusive in thanking him. 'When we come to Allahabad, we'll discuss our further plan of action.'

Bachchu Pathak phoned to congratulate Ram Mohan and said Saansad-ji was his leader too. For a week, Ram Mohan remained in the spotlight, receiving visitors, talking to people on the phone, was invited over by Saansad-ji when he and his wife arrived from Delhi. It was a good meeting, full of verve and energy. Ram Mohan explained away his supposed act of treachery and Saansad-ji was gracious enough not to dwell on anything hurtful from the past. Not now when Ram Mohan had resigned for his sake, laying all doubts about his loyalty to rest.

Saansad-ji's supporters held a public meeting to express their support. Bachchu Pathak was one of the speakers. Ram Mohan was at his rhetorical best. Saansad-ji mentioned his sacrifice, 'That he had only four months left at the Commission doesn't reduce its significance. The point of his gesture lies in the fact that he's chosen to stand by a man who's dared to cross yet again who else but Indira Gandhi, and Ram Mohan has shouted his preference from the rooftops.'

It had hardly lasted a fortnight, this enthusiasm and rhetoric, when the truth sank in. The truth that there wasn't much for Saansad-ji and his supporters to do, except wait for an opportune moment, the moment of the slackening of Indira Gandhi's grip on the public, on power. That seemed a long haul. Saansad-ji went back to Delhi to attend Parliament.

* * *

Once the brouhaha over his resignation tapered off, Ram Mohan, who couldn't do without some immediate goal, was lucky to have to attend to a pressing problem staring him in the face: how to free their property from the tenants. He got into gear to take the bull by the horns.

They had to draw up their plan for every stage of the campaign and the tenants mustn't be given reason to suspect that the new owners could employ physical aggression. Ram Mohan thought of his most trustworthy friend, and Zameer, though officially no longer with Ram Mohan, offered to take the message to Tiwari-ji.

Two days later, Tiwari-ji arrived, all perked up. The quarrel over the division of his agricultural property among his sons, that had threatened to snowball, had subsided. He could turn his attention to the battle in the wings in Allahabad.

He took a moment and said they should approach the most vulnerable of the four tenants first, vulnerable to the tactic they had in mind.

'That would be the South Indian on the ground floor of the annexe,' said Ram Mohan.

'Yes, he wouldn't want his family to get caught in a sticky situation. Did the previous owner ever ask them to leave?'

'He did, but that would have been a request that I'm sure was met with a rebuff from this lawyer who must have taken up cudgels on behalf of his fellow travellers. The lawyer is their leader. You should meet this South Indian and give him an idea of what to expect if he chooses to defy the new reality.'

'I'll take Nishant along . . . Can we offer him some money?'

'Considering what a wonderful deal we've got, I can pay some money to those willing to go with no fuss.'

'Five thousand should be OK!' said Nishant.

'We'll pay this much to any of them for their trouble,' said Ram Mohan.

'That's a reasonable sum,' said Tiwari-ji. 'We should try to get hold of one portion of the house first. Things would get easier then. That portion can be the South Indian's.'

* * *

The tenants didn't know the property had changed hands. The South Indian looked disconcerted. He eyed the visitors peculiarly. Dressed in khadi kurta and dhoti, Tiwari-ji came over as trouble. The South Indian said something in Tamil to his wife who had popped out of the only other room of their dwelling. She scowled at the visitors and muttered something to her husband who, in his accented Hindi, asked Tiwari-ji if he had spoken to the lawyer.

'You're the first. You deserve to be treated a bit differently. We don't want you to become embroiled in a circumstance not of your making, something fraught with uncalled-for consequences. We're here to do you the courtesy of spelling out how serious we're about getting this property vacated—'

'We've lived here for eleven years—'

'Hear me out . . . It'll cause you some difficulty, finding a new place to rent which won't be as cheap as this. But there's one thing in your favour. Since you're from the South, no landlord would see you as a potential nuisance . . . The lawyer, who is a problem here, might need to be exposed to a different medicine. You know what I'm saying? Don't tell him. He'll try to dissuade you. Your cooperation with us would make his position a notch more untenable,' Tiwari-ji paused, 'He needs you more than you him. He'd find it hard to rent a place. People are wary of a lawyer-renter.' The South Indian looked at his wife.

'We'll pay you five thousand as a goodwill gesture. That's the final sum. Take it or leave it. But leave this place you will, willingly or unwillingly. Think it over and be ready with an answer in a day or two.'

Just before leaving, Tiwari-ji told the South Indian, who had walked them to the gate, how they had got their property in Kanpur freed from the unhelpful, stiff-necked tenants and that Dr Ram Mohan wouldn't buy a house if he couldn't use it as he wished.

'What next? Should we approach others?' asked Ram Mohan

'Let's wait for the South Indian's response. If he accepts our offer, then we should go for others, after taking possession of the vacated portion.'

The next evening, Nishant learnt from his friend, the one through whom he had learnt about the property, that the South Indian was asking around to see if he could find a place in the same locality. When they met him again, he sought two weeks to shift, but got a place within a week. The man on the upper storey of the annexe was also willing to take five thousand rupees. The lawyer had let fly at them with a torrent of rudeness, accusing them of treachery. Tiwari-ji asked the South Indian, 'How exactly would you describe his reaction? Is he willing to pit himself against someone of Dr Ram Mohan's stature?'

'He did a lot of fighting talk but looked disturbed, if not scared. He wouldn't be an easy customer like us,' he looked at his fellow tenant sitting by him, the clerk who lived upstairs.

'Fine, it's up to him, then. If he thinks he can take on us, we won't be to blame. He'll have it coming. Plus, he'll have thrown away a chance to be five thousand to the good. What about the PWD man on the ground floor?'

'He stood right behind him when the lawyer launched into a harangue but didn't say a word. I doubt if he can take the heat of the situation!'

Tiwari-ji signalled to Nishant who, unzipping the small Rexine bag he was carrying, took out two bundles of fifty-rupee notes, handing one to the South Indian, the other to his fellow tenant.

No sooner was the South Indian gone than Ram Mohan and Tiwari-ji moved in. The tenant above took a week longer. Ram Mohan's things in the Commission Bungalow were shifted to the ground floor of the annexe with an additional bed for the second room. The day the upper storey came into their possession, Tiwari-ji and Nishant went to see the PWD man, who insisted they speak to the lawyer. They can't be evicted like that. Tenants had rights.

Tiwari-ji was put off. He didn't pursue it further and made for the first floor of the main building and said to Nishant, climbing up the stairs, 'Our going to see this character is just a formality. We know his answer. The scumbag has convinced the PWD fellow that they have the upper hand. If they stay put, nobody can force them out.'

The lawyer had seen them talking to the PWD man from the window upstairs. When they knocked, the door was wrenched open, and the short, slender frame of the lawyer filled the opening. The obstinacy of his posture couldn't be missed. He listened to Tiwari-ji and said no. They left. Just when they reached the staircase, he called out, 'You shouldn't think of using threats. I know how to deal with you guys.' Tiwari-ji stopped Nishant from retorting.

* * *

The lawyer's words fired Ram Mohan with effervescence, vim. That his friend was still game for a fight pleased Tiwari-ji, who knew that unlike those retiring, Ram Mohan wouldn't let the looming void engulf him, leaving him teetering at the edge of nothingness. He would find some undertaking worth his while. Thanks to the lawyer's intransigence, he got something immediately. 'The nature of the task before us is clear. We need to mount a well-thought-out campaign.' To brainstorm in peace, Tiwari-ji and he returned to the Commission Bungalow.

The following morning, Jaan Muhammad dropped in. He would swing by the Commission Bungalow now and then, even after Ram Mohan was no longer his boss. He said if one of the mob bosses of Allahabad could lend a hand, it would help. Tiwari-ji said, 'That we should keep for the last. If nothing else works out. There's always a chance of things getting out of hand when the services of gangsters are sought.' He recounted an incident from a few years ago in Fatehpur. Some people had encroached on a plot of a schoolteacher who, on approaching the police, was told that the police intervention could be politicized by the encroachers who were the supporters of a local politician. The teacher sensed the job would have to be entrusted to outlaws. The father of one of his pupils was a government contractor. He went to him. The contractor sent a Jeep full of goons, and when they set about dismantling the mud structures and beating those resisting, they got surrounded by a local crowd. A melee ensued. One of the goons fired in the air while another stabbed a member of the scattering crowd. 'The poor teacher, as a result, found himself in a soup.'

'I'm not that teacher,' said Ram Mohan, 'who went begging for help to that character who, as a courtesy, sent his men with no plan and with no one to command them. Yet the point you make does hold water. We should start with something else first. Some other way to send the lawyer the right message that should give him some idea of the life he'll have so long as he keeps us knocking on the door of our own house, the message that it's time he battened down the hatches.'

'Yes,' said Tiwari-ji. 'For starters, we can start harassing their visitors, stop the peripatetic vendors from serving them. If they can withstand all that, we'll let them have it. We'll toss them out, using actual force.'

'For that, we should make plans in advance.'

To discuss it, Ram Mohan had Chaturvedi-ji and Sinha Sahab over, and was pleased to know that among Chaturvedi-ji's regular clients was the dreaded duo of Maula–Bhukkal, the brothers, the bosses of the Karvariya gang, one of the three biggest organized criminal outfits in Allahabad region.

'I mostly interact with Maula, the older one. If he's in town, I can have him come meet you tomorrow,' said Chaturvedi-ji.

'Dr Sahab wants to keep it as the last option,' Tiwari-ji said, 'though to discuss the problem with Maula would do no harm.'

'Definitely. It's better to keep him in the loop,' agreed Sinha Sahab. 'At least he'll have some time to think. Given his long innings in the realm of villainy, he'll know what's warranted here.'

'Regardless of the nature of the disease, they know of only one medicine,' Chaturvedi-ji said. 'The measure in which to administer it is determined by the gravity of the problem. They specialize in that.'

'That's exactly what I'm saying,' said Sinha Sahab.

* * *

It was nine in the morning when Chaturvedi-ji called. Not long after, an Ambassador pulled up in the portico of the Commission Bungalow, with two Jeeps right behind in the drive. Ram Mohan was in the porch to receive the visitors. First to climb out of the car was Chaturvedi-ji, thereafter Maula, a man in his early fifties, lean and of medium height, wearing a light brown kurta and white dhoti, with good features and an oblong face made impressive by a walrus moustache going grey. The men in the Jeeps, armed with guns, stayed put, while the two that carried no firearms in sight followed their boss inside.

'I've been familiar with your name, Dr Sahab, ever since you contested your first election,' said Maula as they sat down in the drawing room. 'Our family was hardcore Congress supporter . . . Still is . . . I'm talking about the Lok Sabha polls. Udai Pratap Singh was the Congress candidate who had won those battles, but you put up such a good fight, on both occasions!'

Ram Mohan looked as if he wouldn't mind Maula going on in that vein a bit longer, but Chaturvedi-ji had no stomach for something nothing to do with the task at hand. 'Maula bhai, do something to help extricate Dr Sahab's property from this menace.'

Maula, already briefed, said, 'I know of only one way, a tested and tried way . . . You hold the police back just for a few hours and I'll have the property cleaned out and the garbage dumped outside the city limits.'

It was a sure shot way of producing the desired end. Once the tenant was thrown out along with his belongings, he couldn't claim his tenancy unless he had a legal agreement. Else, whatever he had to say to the authorities, would be his word against the landlord's. If he pursued the matter in court, it would take ages to get a verdict.

'I'll do that when we get to that stage,' said Ram Mohan with a smile that spoke to those who knew him of a change of mind. 'First, we'll try some other means to make these blockheads realize that if they think they can keep us at bay, they're living in a fool's paradise.'

'The method I mentioned should be the last resort,' said Maula.

After Maula took his leave, Ram Mohan said to Chaturvedi-ji, who had stayed back, 'What he offered by way of help, I too can manage. If the lawyer remains adamant, I'll have Gulab Singh send a truck and his men who'd pack it with their stuff and offload it somewhere on their way back.'

'You'll have to be careful that none of them gets out during the operation,' said Chaturvedi-ji. 'If they get the word out or have somebody inform the police, the police will be forced to intervene—'

'We'll take every precaution,' said Tiwari-ji.

'That's settled then,' said Ram Mohan. Tiwari-ji and he moved back to the Annexe.

FIVE

L ife in the post-Commission world wasn't going to be the same for Ram Mohan and his family. They had to cope with their diminished clout made plain by a sudden, in some cases gradual, disappearance of certain people from their circle of friends and acquaintances.

Such defectors were mostly those holding critical positions in their bailiwick. One such group was that of the doctors of the main government hospital, the doctors, specialists of various kinds, whose services were available to them all the time, as the Commission had the authority to clear them for confirmation, promotion, etc. This, the easy availability of medical expertise, the best Allahabad could offer, was one of the benefits the Commission had brought to Ram Mohan.

But he was too astute to bemoan the loss of these associations, too wise to the vanity of such relations, too wise to the futility of even nursing a desire of that nature. Plus, he was confident of finding a new set of adherents, the type who wouldn't have the cultural footing to feel at ease at the Commission Bungalow. Some did drop in. But too infrequently to develop the kind of bonhomie Ram Mohan had with his regular visitors—local politicos, civil servants, officials from the city administration, lawyers, university professors, literary figures, etc.

Not that Ram Mohan had any issue with the members of the hoi-polloi. Thanks to his rural background, he had the resources to enjoy the company of people with a touch of rusticity about them, the type in whose eyes he still had status. As ex-member, Public Service Commission, he could get appointments with important personages, who were too conscious of the possibility of him securing a position of influence again, to ignore his modest requests.

Not an ordinary retiree, Ram Mohan could, by his rhetorical power, style, literary flourishes, by sheer force of his personality, command anybody's attention. His new adherents were fortunate to have easy access to someone like him, the majority of whom were Patels, people of his own caste, hailing from villages on the other side of the Ganges but staying in the city, employed variously. Prominent among them were district court lawyers, teachers in higher secondary schools or degree colleges, junior engineers, along with those unemployed but with political aspirations. There were some young men too, who nursed the ambition of becoming civil servants.

In no time, the Annexe became quite a sought-after place. First came the previously acquainted, then a stream of others. This change in the composition of visitors vis-à-vis his ongoing battle with the two remaining tenants, suited Ram Mohan's book. Some of the callers offered to give the lawyer a hiding, but Tiwari-ji, while appreciating their ardour, pointed out why it wasn't a good idea.

'That will exacerbate things. They can go to the police. But we just won't sit by and let these vermin live in peace. No, we'll keep breathing down their neck.' He spelled out the plan and how they could pitch in with its execution. 'We should pick quarrels with their visitors and those selling or delivering things.'

It was a Sunday mid-afternoon. Some visitors to the Annexe went to the entrance of the main building and began talking loudly. The PWD man came out and said, 'Please don't crowd the gate . . . What are you guys looking for?'

'We're looking for nothing. But you're looking for trouble. Don't worry. Your families will get used to it.' They all exploded with laughter. The PWD man threw a glance towards the Annexe and went back inside. Then Nishant, leading a group of young men, told a peripatetic vegetable vendor to shun the two tenants as his customers. He said this in front of the PWD man's wife, who had come out with a basket. The day following, two guests of the lawyer were abused and manhandled. The day after, the man who came to deliver the cooking gas cylinder to the lawyer, was chased away. The lawyer went to the local police station but couldn't persuade the sub-inspector to visit the locality. 'If we pay mind to these bun fights, we'll be left with little time to tackle real crimes. You sort it out between yourselves.'

Kanti, Deena and Mayank hadn't seen their new house. Ram Mohan asked them to come and have a look. Obviously, they couldn't enter the main building. Even Ram Mohan or Nishant had no idea of its interior. Its grandiose façade was enough to convince them of its worth. In normal circumstances, a property like that would be beyond their means. They knew of people who didn't rank as high in social standing but were head and shoulders above them financially. Conscious of his family's ire of his economic management, Ram Mohan pointed up that taking care of such a large family wasn't easy. Yet he managed to be equal to the challenge. 'I'd paid about thirty thousand for the Kanpur property,' said he after Kanti, Deena and Mayank were done looking around the Annexe and its grounds. 'The same property fetched eleven times that amount, just in a few years! Now look at this huge thing and imagine its value once we get it cleared of the tenants!'

Kanti nodded as Tiwari-ji, who had been strolling outside, returned. 'The lawyer's teenaged son and his friends are chatting out front.'

'Deena should go and object,' said Nishant, 'I'll stay a few paces behind.'

'Be belligerent,' said Tiwari-ji.

Deena went over to them and thundered, 'What's happening here?'

'I'm talking to my friends,' mumbled the lawyer's son.

'This is not the place to entertain your friends!' The son tried to say something. Deena screamed, 'Not a word, just beat it.'

'Who are you to object?' said one of his two friends, trying not to be cowed.

'You must be out of your senses if you don't get it.'

'Don't talk to me like that.'

Deena jabbed him in the stomach with his fist. So bold and sudden that they made a bolt for it, leaving behind their bicycle. Their host retreated into the main building while Deena, under the sway of the effect of his aggression, lifted the bicycle and threw it. Some neighbours surveyed from over their boundary walls. Returning to the Annexe, Nishant drafted, with Tiwari-ji's inputs, a complaint to the police: how the lawyer got goons to create a ruckus outside the Annexe. When one of Ram Mohan's sons questioned their behaviour, not only were they abusive but one of them hit him.

The officer in charge of the police station duly accepted it. Tiwari-ji described how an ex-member of the Public Service Commission was being harassed by the squatters in his property. The inspector promised to give the lawyer a piece of his mind. And lo, just as they were leaving, showed up the lawyer with his version of the incident. He had been beaten to it. Whoever filed their complaint first acquired an edge. Then there was no comparison between the two complainants.

The man in uniform told the lawyer that he should be ashamed of himself for employing these tactics against such a venerable personality. 'If you seek to deal with the dispute through threat and aggression, the police will be forced to take action.' The inspector held out a hand to take the two sheets of paper from the lawyer, his version of the incident.

'It shouldn't be long before these two fellows decamp, bag and baggage,' said Tiwari-ji to Nishant on their way back.

* * *

To disrupt the peace out front, some more incidents were staged with no dearth of pretexts to start an argument with anyone entering or exiting the main building. A few young visitors to the Annexe enjoyed being the scourge of the tenants. 'There must be no let-up in the effort,' said Tiwari-ji to a group of Patel students at a degree college, one of whom, the one most vocal, was contesting for president of the students' union.

'Sir, a nod from you and see what we do. It'll hardly take a week to make them clear off,' said the student leader.

'No need for that. They know that their days of a hassle-free life here are over.'

One day, the PWD man decided to move out. He had had enough. The lawyer argued that if they stayed the course, they could extract from the new landlords a lot more than what the tenants of the Annexe had got. The PWD man didn't think so. Things were past that point. That's what the cleaning woman had heard.

The PWD man came by the Annexe. It was eight thirty or nine in the morning. Ram Mohan had just finished shaving and Tiwari-ji was reading the paper, both waiting for jalebi and yogurt from the nearby sweetmeat shop. Their lunch and dinner too, came from there. Only morning tea was homemade, made by Tiwari-ji, on a small kerosene stove. Tiwari-ji saw the PWD man when the boy from the sweetmeat shop arrived.

'Please come in, take a seat . . . Have some jalebi,' said Tiwari-ji. Ram Mohan looked on.

'I just wanted to inform that I'll be moving out in two days.'

'We wish you hadn't taken so long,' said Tiwari-ji. 'You were in thrall to this obnoxious fellow on the upper floor. You even let slip the chance to be richer by five thousand rupees.' The PWD man responded with a look of regret. Ram Mohan was still willing to give him two thousand rupees.

'The lawyer can't hold out now that the cards are stacked against him,' said Ram Mohan. Tiwari-ji agreed. But the lawyer, according to the PWD man, seemed to have nerved himself to sit it out, the pressure to vacate. His wife was against the continuance of the fight for which they had neither means nor grounds. She also feared for the safety of their children. But the petulant man, her husband, stood his ground. To relinquish their possession of the house at this stage wasn't a good idea. To prove his point, he had some stories to recount, stories of how some people succeeded in wresting ownership of their rented quarters from the landlords left with no option but to sell their properties to the tenants. The lawyer, though, was willing to settle for a much less ambitious outcome. He would vacate if paid thirty thousand.

'The scoundrel has got the wrong end of the stick,' said Ram Mohan. 'He'll pay for his failure to understand who he's dealing with. It's just in time that you woke up to the reality.'

Just as the PWD man was leaving, Ram Mohan gave him twenty hundred-rupee notes. The man recalled something else. The lawyer wanted his mother to come and stay with him till the crisis ended. Her presence might deter the landlords from going overboard in attempts to frighten his family. The mother was living with her younger son, employed in a public sector steel plant in Bhilai, and the idea of her moving all the way to the lawyer's first floor lodgings in Allahabad to allow him extra purchase on the situation, would be hard to sell. Yet it couldn't be brushed off.

Ram Mohan and Tiwari-ji decided to take it to another level. 'Let's give the bastard his first taste of the real thing, a taste of what to expect if he carries on with his dumbness. Shall we bring Umesh in? I can tell Sateesh.'

'Not a bad idea. We can get some students here to stand by him. Or we can request Maula for some goons to make a show of the threat to the lawyer.'

'Why burden ourselves with a debt to him when we can manage it by ourselves? We had better use students. Goons can mess up things. Let's first see what the lawyer has to say now that he's the only one left.'

Nishant went to fetch him. He came but his manner suggested no change in his outlook. One look at his saturnine face, and you knew the man was hard to please. Ram Mohan motioned him to a chair. A momentary silence ensued before Tiwari-ji began, 'Vakeel Sahab, our Dr Sahab needs to vacate his Commission Bungalow soon. We can't let you keep occupying our house. Please understand and move out. Just as others have done.'

'For your cooperation, I'm willing to give you five thousand.'

The lawyer smirked. 'If that's what you had in mind, there was no need for this meeting, and what's keeping you from moving into the ground floor? You've got the Annexe too.'

'You have the audacity to say this to the owner of the house,' bellowed Ram Mohan.

'What did I say to offend you, sir? I'm just being realistic.'

'You're not being realistic. If you were, you would see the problem from my perspective and—'

'Your idea of settling the issue is that I go looking for another place. That's your idea of my cooperation.'

'You're again being impolite,' said Tiwari-ji.

'What is this, sir? If I put my point across, you dub it rude. Please hear me out.'

Ram Mohan fixed his gaze on the lawyer, who said, 'Okay sir, just consider my argument. I'd be very brief . . . Just think . . . If not for my presence, could you have got it this cheap? Okay, there were other tenants too, but I was the main hindrance to this property bringing in the price it deserved . . . If you want this to end, here's my proposal—' his eyes lingered on Ram Mohan and then shifted to Tiwari-ji.

'Go on,' said Ram Mohan.

'You give me two months to move out along with some money for the trouble.'

'Let me first rid you of the notion that it's because of you that I've got the property rather cheap. No. It's because of me, my confidence and the fact that I'm capable of making a lawyer like you see the light. Let me come to the point,' Ram Mohan looked out the window against which the lawyer was sitting, and resumed, 'The time you have is two weeks, maybe three, not beyond that. Tell me how much money you want. I have a sum in mind. Let's see if there can be an agreement between the two.'

'Thirty-five thousand.'

'You can fancy any sum. I don't mind your right to dream . . . Seven thousand. That's the final sum, two thousand more than what the two tenants of the Annexe got and that's because you're occupying a bigger portion. And your former collaborator, the man on the ground floor, wanted nothing but a safe departure! Yet I gave him two thousand . . . See, I'm not unreasonable. I give you two more days to reflect. My offer's final.'

'Very well, and thanks for the two days you've allowed me to think it over. I'd like to request you not to close your mind to my proposal. I'm not rigid. I might drop five thousand.'

Not one jot did his attitude worry Ram Mohan. Tiwari-ji and he had had no illusions about the likely outcome of their meeting. They just wanted to be sure of him being delusional. 'Did you notice the smile on his face?' said Ram Mohan.

* * *

The next day, the lawyer informed Nishant that he couldn't accept his father's offer. He wanted more.

'No use talking to him,' said Ram Mohan.

Tiwari-ji agreed, 'Now's the time for some action.'

'Shall I ask Sateesh to bring Umesh?'

'It was okay to use Umesh in Kanpur,' said Nishant, 'but here, where we've lived for six years . . .! He's young and respectful, but to have him travel to Allahabad to help us again isn't a good idea.'

'Nishant has a point,' said Tiwari-ji. 'I can get some people from my area . . . but they're too rustic to—'

'No, no,' cut in Ram Mohan, 'To request Maula should do fine!'

'I'm friends with Daya Shankar Singh. I can ask him over,' said Nishant.

A formidable name, a veteran in student politics, Daya Shankar Singh was the outgoing president of the university's students' union, a post he had won by a massive margin, beating all earlier records. He had an army of admirers across the social and antisocial spheres. Two of the top mob bosses of the city would travel any distance to carry out his wishes. One of the reasons students voted for him was his pledge that if elected, he would make the campus violence-free. No instance of eve-teasing would pass without the perpetrators being punished. He kept his word. During his time as president, not one incident of stabbing or shooting or bomb-throwing occurred on the campus, and the girls had never felt safer. It was an unusually peaceful period in the recent history of the university where several such incidents a year had been the norm. The absence of violence and the girls being spared some form or the other of harassment was no accident. Doing the rounds was many an anecdote, some apocryphal, some true, about the lessons that those imprudent to ignore Daya Shankar Singh's dictates were taught.

Ram Mohan beamed with pride. Nishant had never mentioned his friendship with Daya Shankar Singh, a fact that Ram Mohan, who had been opposed to his children's involvement in anything that could draw them away from their focus on getting employment after college, could appreciate now that his control over things was diminishing. He was learning to grin and bear the altered reality, though not giving up the effort to stay relevant in his children's lives.

Nishant told them how he had earned a place among Daya Shankar Singh's core supporters in the university. How in the first election-meeting, his speech had drawn notice and he had become one of the main speakers of the campaign. 'I've no doubt of Nishant becoming a lawyer who can powerfully argue his clients' cases,' said Ram Mohan to Tiwari-ji.

In his early thirties, Daya Shankar Singh was short and slim, had a luxuriant beard that mocked his receding hairline. Always escorted by five-six burly men, he evoked awe. It was his swagger that made him stand out. Ram Mohan and Tiwari-ji were impressed by his amiability and confidence. Nishant had briefed him on the problem. Tiwari-ji recapped it and told him of the final solution they had in mind when everything else had failed. 'We've reached that point but want to give the lawyer one more chance to realize the gravity of our intent.'

'Not an issue. I'll have that relayed tomorrow just as it's getting dark,' said Daya Shankar Singh, shooting a glance at one of his men, who got to his feet and a minute later was heard riding off on his motorcycle. 'That's a Bullet,' said Tiwari-ji, recognizing the distinct sound of the celebrated motorcycle identified with tough guys.

Ram Mohan treated them to his favourite sweetmeat, cream laddoos, a box of which he kept handy. When Daya Shankar Singh declined to have more than one, Ram Mohan was surprised that he could be so health conscious.

* * *

Deena didn't want to miss the lawyer being given a glimpse into the depth of his family's resources. With real goons pressed into service. Deena felt oddly awed by men with power to strike terror into those unwilling to do their bidding. He was thrilled that the most feared president of the student union in the history of the Oxford of the East was friends with Nishant.

That day, in the evening, Deena rode his Vijay Super to the Annexe with Mayank on the pillion seat. Ram Mohan had bought these two-wheelers for Nishant and Deena after laying his hands on the proceeds of the Kanpur property. Few could match his generosity when he had ready cash. 'They're working now and deserve to have a means of transport of their own.' That couldn't have been Bajaj, the best, the most desirable, which wasn't freely available and could be bought only on a thriving black market at a price three times higher. The company making Vijay Super was owned by the state and had no limit on its production. When Sinha Sahab had once remarked that most state-run companies depended on public money to survive, it was put down to his grudge against Indira Gandhi.

* * *

Ram Mohan and Tiwari-ji and a couple of Patel guests sat on the veranda of the Annexe when Deena and Mayank arrived. He had hardly killed the engine when Ram Mohan called out, 'Bring the scooter inside the gate,' then led everybody into the room, muttering, 'We don't know how it might unfold when they come.'

When Nishant reached the Annexe, there was someone else with him, a stranger to all but Deena, who breathed to Mayank, 'Ghanshyam', the man who had cooked Nagina's goose, Nagina, the notorious pederast, who once used to prey on young boys at the GIC and other schools. Welcoming Ghanshyam, Ram Mohan said how fond he was of the doughty, of those who had the guts to defy the usual, and Ghanshyam threw light on what great regard his boss, Om-ji, had for Daya bhaiya, and Daya bhaiya wanted Ghanshyam to oversee the event, to see that things didn't go sideways, that none of their men did anything to jeopardize the cause they were to further. Ghanshyam's courteous and shy manner bowled Deena over. Was he the same man who had socked Nagina?

Just as it began to darken, they heard a motorcycle. Ghanshyam darted outside. A minute later he returned. 'The boys have arrived and are lounging around a corner nearby. They'll wait another twenty minutes.' Ghanshyam went out again and began strolling along the street out front. The beam from the incoming Bullet's headlight caught Ghanshyam, who signalled it to stop, and walked up to the men straddling it. Right behind was an open Jeep carrying five people, who could be heard bantering. Ghanshyam came and said to Ram Mohan, 'Sir, don't worry. They know their job.'

A voice boomed out from the street. One of the men on the Bullet had let out a barrage of profanities directed against the lawyer. What he was saying had nothing to do with the purpose at hand. Ram Mohan and Tiwari-ji cast a bewildered look at Ghanshyam, who smiled and said, 'No, we're not here to tell him to vacate the house. We're here to accuse him of hitting the mother of one of the boys in the Jeep with his scooter and riding off, leaving her injured and dazed on the road. Her son and his friends are here to call him to account.'

'There was no such accident!' said Ram Mohan, mystified. Ghanshyam chuckled, 'No, that's just a pretext, a lie. The method's quite effective. If a group of men descends on somebody, charging him with something about which he's clueless, the befuddled man will be frightened like hell. Then, the next day, they'll accost him again somewhere, threatening him to make amends, say, by way of a big sum of money. Or he'll be left to curse himself—'

'The lawyer will know what it's really about?'

'Right away, and he'll be terrified.'

They looked out the window. The men in the Jeep and on the Bullet had become raucous, their language foul and savage. Nishant, who had gone upstairs with Deena and Mayank for a better view, returned with the news that when the lawyer tried to flash a torchlight, a gun and a machete-like thing was waved from the Jeep, then the two riding the Bullet entered the grounds of the main building.

'They'll tell the lawyer what awaits him if he doesn't atone for the accident,' said Ghanshyam. 'I think it's time we wound up.'

A moment later, they heard the Bullet and the Jeep take off.

The day following, Ghanshyam informed Nishant of the plan. Ram Mohan said, 'I hope they don't thrash him too severely.'

'They'll just rough him up a bit, demanding that he compensate their friend's mother for injuries.'

'As you pass by the sweetmeat shop, tell them to send two kilos of fresh cream laddoos,' Ram Mohan asked Nishant, who was leaving.

* * *

Ram Mohan and Tiwari-ji saw the lawyer trying to park his scooter. Something was wrong with its stand. Vexed, the lawyer let the scooter tip over to one side and headed to the Annexe. 'Let's not look towards him,' said Ram Mohan.

'Come on in, Vakeel Sahab,' Tiwari-ji said as the lawyer stepped onto their veranda, his hair rumpled, the faded black jacket crumpled, the thin, lined face looking slapped, and that stock of a neck had purple marks.

'What's the matter? You look out of sorts! Take a seat,' said Ram Mohan. The lawyer kept standing, looking pitiable. He tried to say something but failed, then swallowed hard and blurted, 'I know who is behind all this.'

'You mean behind that ruckus yesterday that kept me from finishing an article? I didn't know you had dealings with such elements. If that happens again, I'll give you a thrashing myself. Your quarrels with these hoodlums, you take elsewhere.'

Tiwari-ji said, 'We ask you one more time to vacate our property—'

'Or you'll be in the shit, real shit,' added Ram Mohan.

The lawyer stood confused. Scared too. Then said, 'Either you give me my due or I stay. I need that money. You think you can dispose of me. Just like that! That can only be over my dead body.' And he left.

'Did you notice that look on his face?' said Ram Mohan. 'I think he's a bit odd in the head. One more dose of Ghanshyam and he might slide into the realm of unpredictability. These tactics work well on normal, sensible people. To use them against insanity can land you in another kind of situation.'

'He's nuts. He isn't even listening to his wife. It's time we stopped beating about the bush.'

Then came Nishant, riding his Vijay Super. Ram Mohan told him about the thrashing of the lawyer. 'Tell Ghanshyam to stop—'

'That's about it. He won't do anything else unless told. That was the plan. To terrorize the lawyer. For any further help from Omji, we'll have to speak to Daya Shankar Singh again.'

'That won't be necessary. They've done their job and done it well. Now's the time to take it to its logical end. Let me discuss it with my lawyer friends.'

* * *

Chaturvedi-ji and Sinha Sahab had been to the Annexe just once. It was Ram Mohan who would drop in on them now and then.

It was getting dark as they drove up to Chaturvedi-ji's. He was in his home office, a chamber filled by a large desk, chairs in front and bookshelves lining the walls. He saw them through the window and sent his clerk to have them seated in the drawing room. Lolling on the veranda outside his chamber was a group of men, two young, the rest grizzled.

'Chaturvedi-ji has built quite a practice,' said Tiwari-ji, as the clerk trotted ahead towards the drawing room.

'You bet,' said Ram Mohan, and continued once they were seated in the plush sofas, 'I've never asked him about his income. It must be around twenty or twenty-five thousand a month!' He looked to Nishant.

'Maybe more,' said the budding lawyer, 'Once a criminal lawyer has earned his spurs, he has more clients knocking at the door than he can handle.'

'What about Sinha Sahab? He doesn't even have a car,' said Tiwari-ji.

'He has a Bajaj,' said Nishant.

'Sometimes he rides his Bajaj here, to Chaturvedi-ji's, and goes to the court in his Fiat,' said Ram Mohan. 'He's good company. His stock of political gossip keeps you regaled.'

Chaturvedi-ji's boy-servant came in with water. 'Sinha Sahab's heart isn't in this profession. He might have done well in politics,' said Tiwari-ji.

'His family's always been a staunch supporter of the Congress. His late father was close to Nehru. Sinha Sahab had long fostered the hope that Indira-ji would reward him with some position, political or non-political, a Rajya Sabha seat or some other sinecure. That wasn't to be. Now he doesn't tire of spewing venom against her, her party, her politics, her policies and suchlike.'

'He was never considered for any such favour in the first place,' said Tiwari-ji, 'unlike you, who came close to being sent to the Rajya Sabha.'

'At least I got the Public Service Commission. After Sinha Sahab's hopes were dashed, he had nothing to fall back on, not

even his career in law. He'd been behaving like a laggard as a
lawyer. I had other things to turn to. The same is true in Tandon-
ji's case. Not many could boast being as close to the Nehru-Gandhi
family as Tandon-ji. I've seen pictures of him giving Indira Gandhi
lessons in bicycle riding. He was a minister in UP. Now he too lies
forgotten, though she responds to his letters . . . Is he bitter about
it, about being forgotten? Far from it. He cherishes his memories
of those good olden days, has been writing about his experiences of
that time. He has no time for whining. Yet when not angry, Sinha
Sahab's fun to be with.'

Chaturvedi-ji entered, greeting them loudly, and going straight
to the door connecting to the rest of the house, he called to his wife,
asking for tea and refreshments. He had a single child, a daughter,
the same age as Sandhya, but unmarried, despite the promise of
a good dowry for any prospective groom's family. She was slim,
of average height and fair skinned, which, according to Indian
outlook, redressed her lack of good features. The problem was her
pock-marked face. No, there was no dearth of families willing to
have her as their daughter-in-law in exchange for a hefty dowry.
Chaturvedi-ji was wary of a deal of that kind. The idea of plastic
surgery seemed a bit farfetched back then, but he was resolved to
rid her face of those pits. To meet a specialist, he was planning a
trip to Bombay. Of that he told Ram Mohan after plopping himself
down on a sofa.

Ram Mohan lauded his friend for the idea of plastic surgery
before mentioning the purpose of his visit and asked could Sinha
Sahab also be had over. No harm in having his opinion too, before
going ahead with his decision to remove the scourge from the main
building.

'Ah, I didn't tell you,' Chaturvedi-ji said. 'Our friend's about
to have a big problem on his hands,' he stopped and called out to
his boy-servant that his friends would have dinner with him. Ram
Mohan said to Nishant, who was still in his advocate's outfit, 'You

must be tired. Why don't you go and leave the Fiat at the Annexe and go to the Commission Bungalow? Chaturvedi-ji will drop us back.'

As Nishant left, Chaturvedi-ji began, 'The other day, when I went to drop him, Sinha Sahab insisted I come in and have tea . . . You know his son who's doing his MD in Pathology in England, who's been Sinha Sahab's pride and joy—'

'Like Mayank's been mine.'

'Exactly . . . He was always admired for his academic excellence. After his MBBS, he won a scholarship to study for a postgraduate medical degree course in pathology in London. Foreign students must clear some test before being admitted to a medical college there. His performance in this test was outstanding . . . As part of this degree course, he's now working in some hospital—'

'What happened?' cut in Ram Mohan.

'Sinha Sahab suspects that he, the jewel in their family's crown, is about to bring unspeakable shame on the family.'

Ram Mohan and Tiwari-ji couldn't bear the suspense! Chaturvedi-ji hurried up.

'That day, Sinha Sahab showed me a bunch of pictures from London, specifically two, and asked what I made of them. Both were taken in some park. One had this tall young girl leaning on a tree with a grin on her face and the other showed his son and this girl both. A decent pose, nothing to suggest other than friendship—'

'Come on Chaturvedi-ji, he can't send his family anything more than that. That he sent the pictures of this girl should be enough to upset our Sinha Sahab. His doctor son wants to prime his family for the shock when he socks them with the news.'

'Yes, or why he'd do this, knowing the pictures would send his father's thoughts flying in a specific direction.'

'What's the problem?' said Ram Mohan. 'Let him marry this girl. I wouldn't mind any of my sons marrying a Briton, an

American, a French . . . Why should he . . .? I can understand Sinha Sahab's anguish, though. The only son he could flaunt to the world, the one with the potential to bring a big dowry, let alone the importance the process, would accord to Sinha Sahab the prospects of all those fathers pleading the cause of their daughters. Of all that he'd be deprived if his doctor son picks a foreigner to be his wife and settles in England, bringing down the curtain on all expectations the parents would have had of him, the brightest of their children,' Ram Mohan stopped on noticing Chaturvedi-ji's knitted brows and a funny smile. 'Is there anything else?'

'There is, but it doesn't take away from what you just said about Sinha Sahab's predicament. That stands. What I'm going to reveal will impart a different dimension to the gravity of his distress, something so monstrous that anyone in Sinha Sahab's shoes would wish he'd been spared the birth of a son like this.'

'What else is there to this girl?' asked Tiwari-ji.

Ram Mohan waited for Chaturvedi-ji to end the suspense.

'To most of us, the word "foreigner" denotes someone white, but this girl isn't just a foreigner but a Hubshi, a Negro. We forget sometimes that in Europe and America, there are Negros too. People from Africa, former slaves.'

'Oh hell,' pronounced Tiwari-ji. 'It's odd that someone from north India could fall for a Hubshi girl.'

'But the girl's surely pretty, very attractive, with chiselled features and all. Looks statuesque,' said Chaturvedi-ji.

Tiwari-ji said, 'In that case, a typical Indian would say you just have it away with them on the sly, enjoy their physical charms but marry them you don't. You don't send their pictures to your parents. I've seen them in photographs in magazines and papers. They're totally black, even darker than the darkest amongst Harijans here—'

'Or the darkest South Indians,' chipped in Chaturvedi-ji.

'Yes, but I'm amazed that someone from UP could do that.'

'Sinha Sahab might persuade himself and his family to agree if she were white, even at the expense of the dowry,' said Chaturvedi-ji, 'but if his suspicion turns out true, he'd feel hard done by. What an act of betrayal, perfidy of the worst sort. This son of a gun.'

'If the boy weren't serious,' said Ram Mohan, 'he wouldn't have sent those photographs. It's not as bizarre as it seems. There're people who rate a girl's features and figure above her complexion,' then to Tiwari-ji, 'You've seen our Mahavir's wife. I hadn't seen a dark skin like that before. Almost bluish.'

'As a matter of fact,' said Chaturvedi-ji, 'there are many men who get smitten by dark-skinned girls, though few would go beyond a secret dalliance. Not because they think these girls unworthy of being their life partner. It's the stigma attached to black complexion. The prospect of living with the taint of being married to someone like that would put any upper or middle caste man to flight. Talking of Mahavir Wilson, he comes from a Harijan-Christian family. He could do it like other Harijan men who have no choice. Fair skin's a rarity amongst them.'

'And he's someone who doesn't give a hoot to what others think,' said Tiwari-ji.

'What does this girl do? Is she also a doctor?' asked Ram Mohan.

'She's a nurse in the hospital where he's doing his internship. He's about to become a pathologist.'

'Sinha Sahab should keep the heat on,' said Ram Mohan. 'He must keep pressuring the boy into giving her the push. He'd resist. Might get mad. That's fine. But the pressure from his family would alter the way he views his relationship with her. He'd start faulting her on this and that, leading to quarrels, and in time he, and she too, would find it a strain to carry on . . . Okay, we'll visit the issue later when we visit Sinha Sahab one of these days. Let's discuss the problem I have on my hands, a full-blown one!'

'What's the latest?' asked Chaturvedi-ji. 'I must say this lawyer fellow's a real pest.'

* * *

A day later, Nishant took the Kanpur bound passenger train to Parsadpur. Chaturvedi-ji had endorsed their decision. He had advised them to hurry. 'If he moves court, he could get a stay order. He hasn't done it because he wants to extract money from you. The second he senses the danger of being evicted by force, he'll do that, leaving you with no choice but to wait out the time the court takes to decide the case. The decision would be in your favour for sure. If you don't want to wait that long, this is the time to throw him out.'

Nishant returned next day after delivering Baabuji's message to Gulab Singh in Ballamgaon. 'The truck carrying four men will reach here the day after tomorrow by ten or eleven at night. Gulab Chacha thought we might also need some armed men. I told him we had people to keep the lawyer on the leash while the truck's loaded up.'

'It should be done about two or three in the morning, the time when the neighbourhood's fast asleep,' Ram Mohan said.

'That'll be the right hour,' said Tiwari-ji.

'You should meet Daya Shankar Singh,' said Ram Mohan to Nishant, who said, 'No need. He told me to contact Om-ji or Ghanshyam for any further action.'

The entire operation was quiet and peaceful. It took barely an hour to empty the lawyer's accommodation out into the truck. No pleading and begging had any effect on the two menacing faces that Ghanshyam had sent. The lawyer and his family and their things, were unloaded on the side of the road outside the city while it was still dark. The truck, then, had carried on along that highway towards Kanpur. Ghanshyam told them how the lawyer's wife had kept cursing her husband between sobs for being so churlish and obdurate.

SIX

Ram Mohan hadn't seen the main building from the inside. Not even the ground floor vacated by the PWD man. 'We won't go inside the building till we have the whole of it.'

Each floor had four rooms, a kitchen, bathrooms, places for storage and an inner courtyard at the back on the ground floor. The first floor had a terrace. What shocked Ram Mohan and Nishant when they entered, was the state of its interior, whose upkeep had been of no concern to the PWD man and the lawyer. Both floors needed much repair work; the wiring and electrical fittings screamed for attention too.

Ram Mohan, who had a little over half the proceeds left from their Kanpur property, got the essential repair work started right away. That gave his sense of purpose another lease of life post-Commission. The Annexe continued to serve as his base, where he, apart from receiving visitors, held meetings with persons hired to fix an assortment of problems in the main building. Anyone failing to come up to his expectations would be turfed out.

'He's the lawmaker and the law enforcer both,' said one of the post-Commission devotees of his. Mishra-ji had a PhD in Sanskrit, a fact noted with interest by Ram Mohan when he was introduced

to him. Married, with two children, Mishra-ji scraped a living by
being temporarily employed at the university library and was looking
for a permanent situation. He had also done BEd, a routine degree
to make one eligible for teaching in higher secondary schools. He
had known no one of Ram Mohan's standing, no one with enough
clout to get him a job in some government school. That was one
big reason Mishra-ji had sought Ram Mohan's proximity. He also
came to be in awe of his other gifts, linguistic, literary, oratorical.

Every day, before going to work, he cycled to the Annexe to
know if there was anything for him to do, and came again in the late
afternoon. Apart from running errands for Ram Mohan, Mishra-ji
was his chief aide in supervising the renovation work in the main
building. Ram Mohan enjoyed the scene that had an element of
gaiety to it. He watched men at work, and laughed and joked with
them, particularly those who seemed rather thick. They were his
favourites. Even if they didn't know how to be courteous with
him, he wouldn't mind. He relished their uncouth way of speaking
and would find something hilarious in their responses. Anyone
sparkly or clever among them, he couldn't stand, suspecting him
of being up to something more than his immediate task and would
sound off about his work. Several of them were booted out before
they could finish what they were hired to do.

While talking to Nishant or Deena, Mishra-ji admitted that
in deference to such idiosyncrasies of Dr Sahab, he accordingly
dressed up his reports on the work and the conduct of the men
involved. Nishant and Deena disapproved of their father's way of
dealing with these men, two or three of whom came close to being
thrashed after being reported for the poor quality of their work or
for being sluggards. Mishra-ji would recount ad nauseam, in Ram
Mohan's absence, these episodes with great relish, the episodes of
the mauling, usually verbal, of some skilled or unskilled labourer
at Dr Sahab's hands, a result mostly of Mishra-ji's feedback. He
jokingly boasted, 'My reports go straight to the ultimate authority

who not only makes rules and ensures their implementation but can mete out punishment to the offender with his own bare hands.'

The last of these episodes involved the electrician who had replaced the one who had failed to conform to Ram Mohan's notion of efficiency. This new guy possessed a cheerful disposition, a trait of which Ram Mohan was suspicious in someone from the uneducated class, a trait he thought indicative of the man feeling horny. If the man happened to be a youth like this new electrician, he just couldn't stand it. He preferred them dour, uncouth, dull-witted, even sullen, would tolerate their impoliteness, rather would have a good laugh about it, about their rude responses.

The new electrician wouldn't forget what he experienced at the hands of Dr Sahab. Making it more bizarre was that he had no idea of what might have occasioned it. Even Mishra-ji, who had nothing to do with it and thought the young man was doing a capital job, was puzzled at Dr Sahab accusing him of being keen on things other than his work, things like being cheery and chatty, laughing and dancing. Dancing? Well, I'm coming to that in a bit. Everybody barring Mishra-ji, everybody in Ram Mohan's family, knew why he was roused to such fury. It was the second time the electrician was caught being cheerful.

At work on electrical fittings on the first floor, he chuckled now and then while talking to Mayank and this lad from the neighbourhood who stood over him, watching how expertly he drilled holes in the wall-switch panels lying loose about him. 'You must enjoy being in other people's houses, getting to interact with their family members,' bawled Ram Mohan. None of them had heard him come upstairs.

'That's how you behave while working, unable to contain your zest for laughter, for a natter? You don't know the value of your own and others' time. I know what the matter is with you.'

After sending Mayank and his friend downstairs, he charged at the electrician and slapped him, hissing through gritted teeth,

'You're intoxicated with your youth, and I know how to make people like you clear-headed.' He ordered him to come down to the Annexe. The electrician stood, pale and trembling, at a loss.

'What's my fault, Sahab? I've been working hard. You can ask Mishra-ji.'

'Move it, now.'

The electrician stirred, then stopped, thinking he was to follow Ram Mohan. When the latter made as if to smack him, he quickly got out of the door. Ram Mohan observed his loose-limbed frame with a narrow waistline and the way he walked! How to put it . . . effete . . . epicene? At least not the kind considered manly or red-blooded.

The worst part of the hot and humid weather was over. Back on his takht in the Annexe, Ram Mohan mopped his brow with his khadi handkerchief as the electrician stood by the door, looking pathetic. Ram Mohan motioned him to the stool near the window. Right then, arrived Deena on his Vijay Super. Horrified at Baabuji's plan to have all the trees in the grounds of their property cut, he came to the Annexe daily, wanting to somehow talk him out of it but had yet to find the right moment.

Five trees in total, including two bottlebrushes standing a few feet apart by the front boundary wall, lending a great charm to the front of the house. The rest were in the big backyard behind the Annexe. I can't recall what trees they were but their presence on the property was a matter of pleasure and pride to Deena, who was so disturbed by the prospect of them being gone. On his prompting, Mayank had spoken to Baabuji, who then expounded to him the kind of garden he wanted to have, something in line with the Mughal Garden at the Rashtrapati Bhavan.

'You have no idea of its beauty, its majesty. Once I have it developed right here, you will realize the folly of your demand,' he had said. Thus, Mayank got co-opted into Baabuji's grand vision. To Deena, anything justifying the felling of those trees was barbarous, vulgar. He resolved to make so bold as to tell Baabuji to his face how heartsick he was at the thought of those trees gone.

Mishra-ji, who commiserated with him, said, a bit tongue in cheek, 'Dr Sahab has little else but time on his hands these days. He's been busy disposing of the property in Kanpur, buying this one here, removing tenants from it. Now he's eager to get this repair work done. To my mind, he, more than anything else, more than his professed wish to have a replica of the Mughal Garden, simply loves the sights and sounds of this ongoing work. The felling of these tress, sending the logs to a sawmill to have some furniture made, is just part of it. I baulked when he told me about this furniture thing the other day. The timber from these trees will make for rough and heavy furniture, but in front of him, I couldn't have agreed more.'

If it was just the sights and sounds kind of thing for Baabuji, then maybe he could be persuaded to revisit his decision. But the figure on the stool cut Deena so that he forswore his resolve to reason with Baabuji. What a sight the electrician looked, a picture of distress and bafflement. Baabuji asked Deena to sit, and yelled, 'Nobody told me this man isn't an electrician but a dancer.' (He said the word *Nachaniya*, the pejorative Hindi term for a dancer, any dancer but in the context of a man it's more offensive.) A minute later, Mishra-ji and Nishant arrived. Something wasn't right. They quietly sat down, throwing quick glances at the electrician, at Deena, at Baabuji, who said, as if disclosing something urgent, 'Did anybody know this man who we thought a mere electrician, specializes in the great art of dancing?'

Nishant knew the electrician was in trouble, but Mishra-ji looked startled at the revelation and said, 'He didn't tell me.' He addressed the man on the stool, 'Is that correct? Do you perform professionally or what?'

'No, I'm an electrician,' the man yelped. 'I don't know what made Sahab so mad.' Ram Mohan leapt to his feet. The electrician recoiled and got up too, shaking and leaning backwards. Ram

Mohan pushed him back onto the stool, ordering him to tell the truth. Was he a dancer or not? Before he could deny, Ram Mohan slapped him. He fell off the stool. As he lay on the floor, cowering and sliding backward, trying to ward off further blows, Ram Mohan kept repeating the question. The electrician kept entreating to let him go. Ram Mohan said not until he had told him about his real profession. When he said yes to what was demanded of him, he was asked to gather his things and hightail it. Mishra-ji paid him whatever money was due to him.

* * *

The cost of improving the interior of the Main Building was set to go past Ram Mohan's estimation. Parsimony was alien to him. He couldn't abide to come off miserly and would sooner spend than save. But the speed with which the repair work ate into his finances, put him off his stroke. Even the cost of having those trees felled, cut into boards, made into trashy articles of furniture, exceeded his guess. Did it make sense? The endeavour to make the inside of the house accord with its majestic exterior.

'At this rate, all our cash will be gone by the time we finish. I've decided to halt the repair work . . . I want to keep some in reserve for Nishant's wedding and other things—'

'It's against your principles,' said Mishra-ji, 'but if you so desire, Nishant's wedding could bring in much cash.'

'I am against making any such demands but won't say no to what the bride's family gives of its own free will. To make marriage conditional upon dowry, upon the size of it, disgusts me. I want to take care of the wedding expenses myself, so it's better to stop this repair work. And we need to vacate the Commission Bungalow.'

Within a week, they all were living in their new house. Ram Mohan kept on living on the ground floor of the Annexe, in the front room; the other room held his bookcases and a heavy takht made of the planks obtained from one of their own trees, for whose demise Deena was still grieving. The upper portion was earmarked for overnight guests.

The corner front room in the main building was given to Nishant, who, after a stint as a junior to that shit-hot lawyer, was on his own. Ram Mohan paid for getting his room fitted up with things needed to make it look like a lawyer's chamber. Of utmost importance were books, big thick volumes dealing with law and cases in the past. No lawyer could make an impression on clients unless his home office sported bookshelves filled with these tomes. Nishant bought just those basic to his being able to set up shop.

Many successful lawyers take it over from their fathers, all of it, the profession, the clientele, a roomful of law books. That wasn't the case with Nishant. If Ram Mohan had money, he would set him up by decking his room with whatever would impart it the air of a successful lawyer's office, for unlike those who got a law degree just so they could avoid the ignominy of being unemployed, it was no vain attempt for Nishant. He had chosen a legal career in preference to other possibilities. A job in the Railways had once been his for asking, but he had resolved to make it in life on his own, unless Baabuji could offer something big, something to help him stand out, and that, given his father's failure to make it big in politics, wouldn't be coming his way.

Ram Mohan knew it and wanted to help in whatever manner possible, along with some hard cash from his falling reserves.

* * *

They were thankful Sandhya was around during the shifting. Taking up the offer of a better position in another company, Varun, her husband, wanted to have some time off before joining the new venture. They were in Allahabad for a week. Deena and Mayank were ecstatic. They could never have enough of the company of their sisters. Soon, Nisha too was due in Allahabad, along with Shivika, their cute little niece. Shekhar, with less than a year left to complete his PhD, needed to be free from distractions, mostly of two kinds: his fondness for Shivika and sporadic fights with her mother, and since smoking helped him focus, they feared an increase in their quarrels.

While in Allahabad, Sandhya helped them shift and arrange things on the ground floor of the Main Building. Other than Nishant's room in the front, his home office, there were two bedrooms in the back. The new drawing-cum-dining room held the dining table and a sofa-set. Two sofas were put in Nishant's room in addition to a big desk and a fancy chair to go with it, both purchased with the money Baabuji had spared, half of which was spent on books that filled two of the several shelves, part of the hideous furniture procured from the butchered trees, mounted on the walls all over the place on the ground floor. The upper floor had been set aside for tenants.

'It can be rented to two small families. Their rentals should be enough for your monthly provisions and other overheads,' Ram Mohan had said. 'My pension's so meagre, it wouldn't be adequate even for my own needs. To pay for Mayank's books and university fee, I'll have to put aside some money from whatever hard cash we have left. Deena's salary should suffice for his expenses. Nishant should start earning from his law practice soon,' then turning to Kanti, 'So long as I'm around, you don't have to worry. Even after my death, you'll be looked after by Mayank.' Kanti objected stridently to the mentioning of death. Ram Mohan laughed.

* * *

Ram Mohan had an advertisement placed in the local papers to let out their upper floor. The rental they quoted for each of the two portions upstairs was nine hundred a month, which would have to be brought down by at least two hundred. Within three days, they found the tenants: first, Mr Sahani, then the Doctor. A probationary officer at the State Bank of India, Mr Sahani had a small family—he, his wife and a seven-year-old daughter—and the portion he chose had the original kitchen while the other had a makeshift one that Ram Mohan had got built in one corner of the terrace. The Doctor came a day later and was happy with what he got. He had no children. Even his wife was barely there. Barring a few occasional glimpses, she would remain invisible. Ram Mohan's family didn't like the thought of such a ghostly presence in their midst.

What a mistake it was, they would learn the hard way, the mistake of taking in a lodger like the Doctor, who had hoodwinked them into believing he was a physician, an allopath, with a successful practice in a locality on the periphery of the city. Successful he was, not as an allopath but as a homeopath, a doctor of a wholly different variety, of which Nishant learnt from a lawyer friend who had once been the Doctor's neighbour.

'What do you mean?' said the Doctor. 'A homeopath isn't a doctor? Come on! Had you asked, I would have told you. I've nothing to hide. So many people have faith in homeopathy, an inexpensive system of medicine that has a cure for everything under the sun. Leave that aside. How does it matter? You should complain if I don't pay the rent on time.' To that, Nishant had no answer. But in a few months, the homeopath started falling behind with the rent. Then no rent for a while. One day, he moved out, promising that a week later, they could collect what he owed. When Nishant and Prakash, a student leader close to Ram Mohan, went to the Doctor's new quarters, they met with a situation that made them beat a quick retreat. I will narrate this episode at an appropriate time.

It was around then that I came to reside with them. I had lived in my rented room till the time I was asked to vacate and

was looking for a new place. Ram Mohan Uncle asked me to
shift to the first floor of the Annexe. Deena came in the Fiat to
help me move. The first week of our togetherness was blithesome.
Ram Mohan Uncle had gone to Parsadpur, where awaiting his
intervention were several disputes, one of which could have boiled
over but for him.

His absence meant we could enjoy ourselves in the best manner
possible. Deena took a few days off. Adding to our joy was Nisha
didi's presence. We spent a great deal of time just chatting. We
would go to the Civil Lines market, to the movies, just the three
of us. Nisha didi couldn't because of Shivika, and what a cute little
thing she was. Deena and Mayank doted on her.

It was a time of such memorability in our lives, a time of great
significance to us, a time to which could be traced the beginnings
of our consciousness of a life by which we were to set great store,
the life of the mind.

* * *

It was during this fun week that Deena was roused to the
'importance' of English, to the importance of a world of whose
existence he had remained in denial. *It was a wilful denial on my
part,* Deena would own later. *I too, like many others of my ilk, would
make catty remarks about the English-knowing, about their showing off.
But my hostility to this foreign language stemmed from my deep envy of
those who knew it. All my arguments against the continuance of English in
India were nothing but an attempt to conceal this envy. Had I had as much
familiarity as Mayank or Sandhya had with the language, I would have
thrown myself into mission English long ago and my fondness for fiction—
popular, pornographic, literary—would have helped me attain proficiency
in it. But the thought of starting it as a complete novice was disconcerting.
First, it would have consumed much of my time that I wanted to devote to
Hindi literature. Second, if it were French or German or Spanish or some*

*other foreign language one wanted to learn as an adult, the effort would
draw applause. The thought of starting English from scratch as an adult
was mortifying. If it had to be done, it had to be done unbeknown to those
who, among our friends and acquaintances, didn't know that English was
to me what Chinese was to them.*

It was the day before Ram Mohan's return, the day when,
in the late afternoon, Deena had a small audience under his spell
as he rendered some Hindi verses and glossed with elan their
complexities—the ideas, imageries, allusions, quivering beneath the
obvious. We stood in the driveway of the main building, latching
on to his words coming in a torrent, and then, just as he paused to
savour our awed looks and get some more poetic gems in position
to launch, the suggestion came, and came like a bolt from the blue.

'Deena, it's high time you learnt some English.'

My friend was struck dumb with disbelief, embarrassment.
So utterly out of context was it, the suggestion, that we couldn't
believe it was made at all. Yet we couldn't help smiling because
of its abruptness or because it seemed so pointless, and the person
who made it couldn't be accused of being mean or spiteful. He
was always affectionate towards Deena. It was Shekhar's nephew
visiting Allahabad. He was known for being forthright. Nothing
else could be read into his apparently brusque remark. It meant
what it said. Deena should acquire some knowledge of English,
whose ignorance didn't become him. My friend, who had no
reason to feel disgraced, admitted with a grim smile that he needed
to be hauled up. He couldn't go on being naïve. He also approved
of the way it was done. Rather it was the manner, the severity of
it, that fired him up about English, the manner that juxtaposed his
literary sensibility and command over Hindi with his innocence of
English. The effect was devastating.

That was the day Deena resolved to embark on a struggle to
tame English. No. That would be too strong a word for what he
had in mind. Not tame it. He only aspired to the ability to read and

follow it. That sounded quite modest at first. But no. Deena wanted
to be able to enjoy English writings that were literary and serious
and thoughtful, writings by which he could profit emotionally
and intellectually.

* * *

'It feels great. It feels like half the battle,' said Deena, having
made the resolve after getting the shocker of a suggestion from
Shekhar's nephew, though he had yet to absorb the magnitude of
the challenge.

With English on his mind, Deena recalled from their days at the
Commission Bungalow, a house in a street he took while cycling
to and from work. He remembered because standing near its gate
on the inside of a low boundary wall was a signboard advertising
that they gave English lessons.

On his way back that day, Deena visited the place. Physically
disabled and confined to a wheelchair, the man in charge of the
said lessons was an alumnus of the city's elite St Joseph School and
a big reader of books. 'That's one big advantage of my condition,'
he laughed. Polite and soft-spoken, he wasn't surprised by Deena's
condition, his English handicap.

Mayank and I were to keep it quiet, his joining these lessons. He
wanted to surprise everybody with a sudden display of his prowess
in English. What a reality check it was, his very first day at the
English teacher's, when he discovered something so heartbreaking,
he despaired of his goal. He had assumed his fellow seekers after
English to be in the same boat as he.

Besides Deena, there were three more students in the room
that had some chairs and an upholstered bench placed against
the wall and a desk sitting in the middle, waiting for the English
teacher. Two of them were reading for their MA while the third
one was in BA final. They were impressed that Deena was a bank

employee. My friend held his breath, dreading the next question, 'Which bank?' But they began discussing the merits of the job, casting envious glances at Deena who thought how long he could avoid the embarrassment that he was a clerk-cum-cashier at the District Cooperative Bank. Right then, the English teacher rolled in through the internal door.

He greeted them, as they rose and watched him manoeuvre the wheelchair into position behind the desk. He complimented Deena on his decision to take English lessons and recapped what would have been expounded to others who had joined a week earlier, the growing relevance of English. He spoke in Hindi with a sentence of English here and a sentence there, making stronger Deena's resolve to bend his efforts to its acquisition. The prospect of no longer having to harbour resentment towards English filled my friend with ineffable delight, the prospect of freedom from a certain constriction, the prospect of breaking ranks with those bewailing the insidious growth of English.

Yet the notion that real writing, the expression of the self, wasn't possible in a language not one's own, would hold him in a vice-like grip for so long that when he realized that this notion was probably overstated, it was too late, he thought, to succeed in the crossover and his refrain before arriving at this realization had been: 'To have access to great writings of the world has been the chief motive in my dogged quest for English. Also, I couldn't stomach the thought of the English-knowing looking down their nose at me. These two reasons have kept me buoyed up during my exertions. But I have had no illusions that if I want to discuss in writing something close to my heart or do some creative work, it would be in Hindi.'

'Before we begin,' the English teacher was saying, 'I'd like to know the extent to which you're conversant with the language, each of you.' Deena felt a tightening in his chest and his face clouded over with shame. 'By the time you're done here, you'll have advanced some way towards your goal of proficiency in English that includes listening and reading comprehension, writing and speaking . . . Everybody wants to master spoken English first and fast, but for people long past their formative years, learning a new language is an onerous task, demanding perseverance, a great deal of it. Thankfully, English isn't an alien language, at least to a good chunk of the urban population. It's not like Japanese or Chinese. Those with some schooling in towns and cities, and even in villages, are bound to have had some exposure, but what really matters is that there's a huge motivational factor for its acquisition, which keeps one upbeat about making it one's own. Though it also has a demoralizing aspect to it. Being a prestige language, English tends to thwart some of us in our attempt to practise it freely, for fear of making mistakes . . . But you must be bold. To hone any skill, let alone linguistic, demands constant practice. I'll help you overcome your inhibitions about writing and speaking. You'll make mistakes, I know. You try to form a sentence but can't. No problem. You grope for the word you need but fail. Not to worry. You stutter, you stumble. You make terrible grammatical blunders. No issues. So long as you don't quit, nothing else matters. I'll keep correcting your errors till you get it right. We'll talk about syntax, figures of speech . . . Now I'd like you to introduce yourself again, in English, one by one.'

The one most vocal among them jumped at it and did well. Or so it seemed to Deena, who had no means to spot mistakes. The next wasn't as good and could finish only after some hiccups. The third couldn't go beyond his name, while a highly strung up Deena just sat there in dumb silence, sweating, and after the prompting of the teacher, he stammered out, 'My name is Dinkar.' That's exactly what the one before him had said. Only the name was different.

The teacher praised the one who had spoken confidently and said, 'Hesitation is the enemy number one of those interested in spoken English. It keeps you corked up. You must get this monkey off your back, this nasty creature called hesitation. If you don't know how to say what you want to say, just say it in Hindi. I'll tell you how it can be done in English.' After elaborating a bit more, he said, 'You should try and compose something in English at home, without hesitation. It can be about anything, any subject, in any form, so you know of the state of your grammatical grasp.' That was their homework.

Deena felt like screaming. It was to no purpose. He cursed himself for being so purblind as to have no idea of the kind of English lessons were on offer here. He didn't see fit to try and get his condition across to the English teacher. That wouldn't make sense. It was clear the teacher presupposed some elementary knowledge of English by his students, the kind even students at Hindi-medium schools would have. Deena decided against continuing.

'Now that you've paid the fee, you should attend a few more lessons,' argued Mayank.

'If I've wasted some money, it doesn't mean I've to waste some time too. I need to learn the rudiments of English grammar by myself . . . with the help of *New Light General English*.'

'That's a good idea. We all have used it,' said I.

SEVEN

Meanwhile, a bitter exchange between Nisha and Shampa resulted in something none of us could have imagined: the end of their bond, their friendship, Nisha and Moon Auntie, a friendship that had seemed for keeps.

After her MA in Hindi literature, Nisha had enrolled in PhD. Dr Moon Agarwal was her supervisor, and the topic was such that a rehash of Dr Moon's old research work could spawn a new thesis. Even that had sounded like much work to Nisha, whose mind and energies were divided between various other things: her trips to Delhi and Shekhar's to Allahabad, her final move there, their fights and patch-ups, the fun she had visiting and hosting Shekhar's friends, her sense of pride in living in Delhi, her getting pregnant with Shivika, later her birth.

To top it all was Shekhar and Baabuji's questioning of the need for a PhD now that she was in Delhi, where she could find something better to do, something more suitable to her dash and confidence. Then, being saved from the labour of reworking Moon Auntie's thesis into her own would have had no less appeal, not to mention that the idea of a PhD in Hindi was dull and drab against something like, say, the job of a newsreader on Doordarshan that could make you a star overnight. To make it to the screen of the national TV, however, was as unrealistic as a pipe dream. Even the deserving had to have some bigwig in New Delhi to pull strings.

Then there was this other option if nothing else worked out. She could obtain a BEd through correspondence and try for a Hindi teacher's job at one of South Delhi's English-medium schools, where she could improve on what little spoken English she had picked up. She couldn't sustain a conversation in English but whatever sentences she could manage in between, she delivered with such panache that few would suspect her of being from a typical Hindi background.

The cooling of Nisha's interest in her PhD hadn't escaped Moon Auntie. She was waiting for the right moment to bring it up. She didn't want to spoil the mood of the occasions of Nisha's visits, during which Nisha wouldn't tire of singing praises of New Delhi. Not only was the thought of settling down in the national capital exciting but she was also getting along well with Shekhar. The interludes between their fights had got longer after she relaxed her outlook on Shekhar's smoking. So long as he didn't smoke at home, she wouldn't get fractious.

But Moon Auntie was upset. She couldn't bear Nisha throwing away a chance of getting an easy doctorate, easy as a pie, a cinch, compared to what it normally meant, real hard work, a lot of doing. She couldn't keep her disquiet from her husband and daughter. Mr Aggarwal, though commiserative, didn't think it something to be tormented by. Nisha wasn't a child. It had to be her decision. But Shampa, now a mature young lady, appreciated her mother's disappointment. She herself was looking to earn a PhD after her MA in English and had no illusions about what it took to accomplish that, and that explained its worth and value. Nisha just had to change the title of her mother's thesis, rename its chapters, reword the text and revise its bibliography. That was all.

'It'll take some time and effort,' Shampa had said to Nisha, 'but that's nothing if you measure it against what you get in return, a PhD, a high return on a meagre investment.'

'I should pursue something that'll serve me better in Delhi,' she mouthed Ram Mohan's words. 'A PhD from here might be of no use when it comes to teaching positions in Delhi. Preference is given to those who have a PhD from one of the universities there. How can one compete with persons who have academic mentors in these universities?'

'A PhD is a PhD, regardless of from where you do it, a highly valued degree that distinguishes you in whatever profession you are . . . And it'll be a big let-down for mummy if you abandon it. She went out of her way to ensure you get enough marks in MA to become eligible for it.'

That had got Nisha's back up.

'How old are you? How can you take it upon yourself to meddle in what Moon Auntie and I can discuss, and decide what's good for me now that Shekhar and I are certain to make Delhi our home—'

'I'm her daughter. I've every right to intervene in anything that concerns her emotionally. She's been anxious for you to lead a good, secure life, to have some independence . . . Whatever she's done is irrelevant now that you're going to settle in Delhi—'

'How dare you take that tone with me! I won't engage you in an argument like this. It's beneath me.'

It was a Sunday. Mr Aggarwal and Moon Auntie, who were outside, taking stock of the state of their garden, rushed back in after hearing loud voices. Shampa was sobbing. Nisha too was close to tears. Too shocked to think of a way to salvage the situation, they couldn't stop Nisha, who had darted out. That was the end of it.

* * *

Told of Deena's mission English, Ram Mohan called us to the Annexe after dinner.

'Any language that you want to learn as a grownup, you do it through your mother tongue. Learn the basics first, the elementary rules of grammar, of its tenses, going on to direct and indirect narration, active and passive voice. Master their simpler versions first. Don't get intimidated. That's the key. Get a grammar book that explains the rules in Hindi.'

'There's this book for Hindi-medium students, *New Light General English*. I have it,' said I.

'That's the one,' then to Deena, 'Go straight to the section that deals with tense. Stay with it till you've got the hang of the rules clarified there. Go over and over them. When it's something as time-taking and complex as a new language, the only precondition for success is your capacity for revision and practice.'

Ram Mohan's advice had a decisive impact on Deena. The way he held *New Light General English* in his hand after I handed it! His resolution showed through. From then on, much of his time at home would be spent in the company of this grammar book.

His sense of purpose got a big fillip from a visit by Mahavir Wilson and his wife, Malti. We were lucky to have them to ourselves for a while, as minutes after their arrival, Chaturvedi-ji called with the shocking news of Sinha Sahab suffering a heart attack. He was going to pick up Ram Mohan on his way to the hospital. That delayed Wilson sharing the good news—the reason for his visit—with Ram Mohan, the news about his selection as Reader in the History department of Delhi's St Stephen's College. (Sinha Sahab's heart attack and his subsequent death, I would discuss later).

Delighted that Mahavir bhaiya would be living in Delhi, Nisha chatted chirpily with Malti who, though wanting the loquacity of her interlocutor, made a great impression on them all. She had grown lovelier, more prepossessing, than when they had last seen her. She was as inky black as before, but such was the power of her face and figure that her complexion added to her allure, imparted to which now was something else, some special quality that had to do with her demeanour, her poise, the way she carried herself. All that spoke of elegance. She looked chic.

This transfiguration, the singular change in her personality, now complete, had been in the making ever since she had come to live with Mahavir Wilson's family in Kanpur. Deena couldn't but marvel at her ability to produce English sentences every so often, easily and stylishly. Even Nishant was awestruck.

Malti's knowledge of English and her stylish pronunciation was what formed the basis of this turnaround in her persona. A frisson of optimism swept through Deena. 'I won't rest till I not only understand but write and speak in English.' Earlier he used to insist that since he could be creative only in Hindi, he would limit his efforts to reading comprehension of English texts.

Mahavir Wilson was holding forth about his move from Christ Church College in Kanpur to St Stephen's in Delhi. When tea arrived, he paused. Nisha nudged Deena. Then blurted herself, 'Deena wants to learn English.' Mahavir bhaiya reached out his hand to pat him on the back and heard him out.

'Dr Sahab's right. No one of your age can learn a new language the way a child does. You must first become familiar with its basic grammar, the broad rules that underpin its sentences, for which *New Light General English* is the book you need.'

Deena would go all out to acquaint himself with some elementary rules of English grammar, and experience the ordeal of the challenge. The more he tried to forge ahead, the more arduous the journey seemed. Not to lose interest and focus, he reminded himself of his resolve every day.

* * *

Things looked settled for Ram Mohan's family except that their big house and its grounds gave the lie to their finances. Their neighbours, though living in smaller houses, were much better off than they. With no income other than his skimpy pension, Ram Mohan had to fall back sometimes on the money he had left after getting the interior of the main building in order. Even that, this reserve, was in danger of dwindling fast if not for the rent from the first floor. Ram Mohan was thankful for having bought this house, undaunted by it being overrun with squatters. The rent that the two new tenants paid came in so very handy, just about enough for their monthly provisions and other expenses.

He was hopeful that Nishant would start doing well as a lawyer soon. Deena had become a regular employee of the District Cooperative Bank with a monthly salary of three hundred and seventy rupees, and after his BA, would become due for promotion. It was only Mayank that Ram Mohan had to support. He had his hopes up about him making it big in life. When Kanti fretted about who would look after them in their advanced age, Ram Mohan admonished her, 'How can you be anxious about problems, economic or health-related, any problems, when you're so fortunate as to have a son like Mayank? Can there be any doubt that he'll take care of us? Can you ever imagine him leaving us to shift for ourselves in the winter of our life when we'll have little to offer but need all the care and warmth? It's inconceivable.'

'I know he'll be there for us, but is it right to burden him with our old age?'

'Nonsense. He's the only one who'll have means to carry this burden if you call it that. Mayank! My gosh! He's in a league of his own when it comes to be tender, solicitous and caring towards his dear ones. He'll be there for Deena too, who, without him, will have a rough ride in life. Let me tell you, I haven't given up on myself. I may become politically relevant again.'

'Has Saansad-ji offered something?'

'No, it's not like that. It's not for immediate gain. For that, I'll need some well-wisher in the Congress, the ruling party . . . I'm no longer friends with Shukla-ji . . .'

Nisha, who was giving Shivika a bath, stuck her head out of the
bathroom, 'Is there any good news? Wait, let me also hear it.' Ram
Mohan laughed, 'No good news yet. But I do have something
in mind. I'll discuss in the evening when everybody's here.' He
went back to the Annexe. Jaan Muhammad was coming. He had
become a regular visitor to the Annexe.

* * *

When we gathered at the Annexe later, Nisha echoed Kanti, 'I
guess it's Saansad-ji who—'

'He's nowhere near recovering his lost ground. When Sanjay
died, Indira-ji was lost but now that she's got Rajiv to take his
place, she's firmly in control . . . I don't know about Saansad-ji,
but I'm not looking for an overnight political yield,' Ram Mohan
surveyed us and asked, 'Have you heard of the man called Kanshi
Ram, any of you? He's Harijan. Now they prefer to be known
as Dalits. The term Harijan, bestowed by Gandhi-ji, is viewed as
euphemistic and patronizing. If you've heard of Kanshi Ram, you
must also know of his political mission.'

Kanshi Ram had emerged as a political pariah and was treated
as such by the press too. No stickler for political correctness,
he pulled no punches when giving vent to what he thought of
upper castes and their leaders who wouldn't allow Dalits, unless
obliged, the opportunity to rise in life. Nobody could help Dalits
if they wouldn't help themselves. They had to have their own
representatives in the corridors of power. They had to have a say in
the business of governance.

'He's regarded as a weirdo, a clown with zany ideas,' said
Nishant. 'Few take him seriously. It's only to scorn and ridicule
that people mention him. His in-your-face utterances against upper
castes are dismissed as nonsense, sired by a nutty mind.'

'Because he seems a political cipher, a nonentity,' said Ram Mohan. 'To mainstream politicians, he comes across as naïve, a simpleton, or like you said, a clown ludicrously engaged in putting together a flock of goats in the hope they could challenge the pack of wolves ruling the country.'

'But how daring he is! Daring in that some of the slogans his supporters use, are offensive to higher castes. No less than name-calling.'

'The reason he gets away with it is that these slogans single out no specific upper caste but are directed against the whole lot of them, Brahman, Thakur, Baniya. Being lumped together helps these castes not to take offence and laugh it all off. But through these resonant slogans and catchphrases, along with his informed speeches, Kanshi Ram is stirring Dalits up. He's making progress in his endeavour to help them unite against their traditional exploiters, most of whom support the Congress, the party that Dalits have served as a reliable vote bank for all these decades. With the advent of Kanshi Ram, it's the Congress that should be worried. As far as I can see, he'll wean all Dalits from it, at least in UP, to begin with.'

'The trend's pretty visible,' said Nishant. 'One can't but notice his outfit's flags, those tiny blue things, sticking out of so many low-roofed houses in Dalit localities. Congress wouldn't so much as admit to his existence and might go on treating him as a figure of ridicule, but Kanshi Ram has surely gained a foothold in its formidable vote bank.'

'A lot more than a foothold. His support amongst Dalits in UP is everywhere, thanks to his years of sustained campaign—'

'He might succeed in freeing Dalits from the sinister grasp of the Congress. Even then, even if he's able to secure all Dalit votes, how is it going to help his people's cause? It won't lead to electoral wins. Who knows this anomaly better than us, the cruel oddity that it is . . .? Our entire caste was behind us in Fatehpur, in all the three elections we fought, but all those votes, however substantial in number, failed to hand us a win and—'

Ram Mohan raised his hand as if to correct him. Nishant understood, 'Yes, the assembly was close, but the fact remains that even with all this support among Dalits, Kanshi Ram would win few seats. That too mostly in the assembly.'

'You think he's so dumb as not to be aware of this phenomenon?'

'He has a long-term objective. I know. He wants to weld all of them together, Dalits, OBCs and Muslims—'

'Weld them into an electoral behemoth to crush the Congress that symbolizes the dominant worldview of our polity . . . These three sections make up around seventy–eighty per cent of the Indian populace. One can only wonder about the look and shape of our Parliament and state assemblies if Kanshi Ram succeeds in his mission. If the majority of these three sections throw in their lot with him.'

'That's an epic task, given the political affiliations on the ground . . . In north India, the majority in the backward castes supports Baran Singh, while Muslims are with the Congress. Any shift in their loyalties is unlikely to come about soon.'

We all, Kanti, Nisha, Deena, Mayank, and I, were enjoying the spirited dialogue, enjoying the way Ram Mohan listened to Nishant's arguments and nodding at his understanding of politics.

'That's why Kanshi Ram calls it a mission,' said Ram Mohan. 'He has no doubt about it being a tough challenge. It's going to be hard and time-taking. We all know that . . . But then, the headway he's made with getting Dalits out of the Congress would have seemed implausible a while ago.'

'Quite an achievement, no two ways about that. But his mission is identified with Dalits. He himself is a Dalit. His supporters say Jai Bhim to greet each other, victory to Bhim, Bhim Rao Ambedkar, their icon in chief. So, getting Dalits on board is a pushover compared to bringing backward castes and Muslims around to the reality that Congress, the successor to the British rule, has only shored up a supremacist high-caste outlook by giving it political legitimacy . . . But Kanshi Ram's idea doesn't jibe with the idea these backward castes have of themselves. They wouldn't approve of being bracketed together with Dalits, who are no less outcaste to them than they are to the traditional upper castes.'

'You have a point,' said Ram Mohan, 'but political affiliations aren't written in stone. The way I see it, Kanshi Ram might succeed in convincing some of the backward castes that they stand to gain from aligning with his party. That their leader Baran Singh is at the fag-end of his career, and as for his foreign-returned son who is being groomed to fill his shoes, I don't think he would go far. How can he measure up to his father's stature? Then there would be others, more grounded in realpolitik, battling for the farmer leader's mantle. Kanshi Ram might have an opening here, to expand his support base. He's already got aboard some Patels in the Allahabad region. One of them approached me a week ago, and I'm going to meet Kanshi Ram when he comes touring this region shortly. He'll be intimated about my desire to put my shoulder to the wheel of his great mission.'

The revelation left our mouths agape. None of us could help feeling a thrill of excitement.

'I thought you were done with active politics,' Kanti said.

'No, it's not just politics, it's a mission. I want to be part of it.'

Later, Mishra-ji said he knew Dr Sahab would find something, some purpose, some challenge to suit his personality. 'A man of his calibre and charisma can't sit quiet for long. He's not the one to watch the show from the sidelines for long.'

* * *

Meanwhile, all three of us, Deena, Mayank and I, were trying to make the most of our being together. We were into reading books, chiefly the books on philosophy and history, two of the three subjects that Mayank and I had in BA. It was only the third subject that we didn't have in common. Mayank had opted for economics, while I had picked Urdu literature, still my passion.

Deena, too, was fond of history and philosophy, and had some basic books in Hindi. No outsider could suspect that far from being a university student—his repertoire included copious references to Hindi literary texts that would widen the context of our discussions, allowing me to show off my arsenal of Urdu couplets—he was a lowly employee at a lowly bank.

Catching on to English grammar, Deena now wrestled with the prose of the *Northern India Patrika*, the local English daily. Occasionally, he had to seek our help, Mayank's, or mine, and when he could make sense of some complex sentence by himself, his morale soared, reinforcing his tenacity to strive on. To build on his nearly non-existent English vocabulary was his biggest challenge. The frequency with which he had to consult a dictionary, English to Hindi, would be exasperating to anyone. He would recall later: *Having to look up three-four words in just a moderately long sentence was akin to tedious manual labour. So terribly frustrating was my snail-like progress, I sometimes wished I hadn't taken up the challenge.* It was around this time, at some point during this phase, that *Northern India Patrika*, the paper that made Deena see stars those days, published Mayank's letter in response to a piece on Indian classical music it had published.

We all gasped. What an achievement! An ecstatic Ram Mohan held a small get-together the same evening. That Mayank could think of composing that letter and send it to the paper, hoping it would find its way into its Letters to the Editor column, was something I lacked. Deena too. That something was Mayank's courage and confidence. Ram Mohan had long voiced his belief in his dearest child, in the certainty of his attaining great success, of becoming a great man one day.

That day when the letter was being discussed—the beauty of its construction and the way Mayank had employed the word 'cascade' to evoke the grandeur of Indian classical music—that day, Deena found staring him in the face the sad reality of the distance he had to cover to get to the level of even Mayank's English at that point. It wasn't that his brother had been to St Joseph or any other English-medium school. Deena had, for a moment, despaired of being able to continue with his endeavour. 'I'm not sure if I should have taken up this business of learning English, so taxing, and I'm doing it at the expense of my love for Hindi literature. Rather than engaging with literary texts in Hindi, I'm devoting whatever time I've left after my job, to learning a language that was alien to me just yesterday.' Deena's anguish and dilemma were profound. So was the fact that he had moved ahead and couldn't go back to being blithely blind to what English had to offer. I told him whatever knowledge of the language Mayank and I had would come in handy for him. Presently, he was to be given a further lift by Baabuji.

* * *

Often, Deena and Mayank would stay the night with me on the first floor of the Annexe. That day, being a Saturday, we had planned to have a late night and do some serious studying. I was on my takht, reading about the history of the French Revolution while Mayank half lay on the mattress on the floor with his knees drawn up, the head and shoulders leaning on the wall as he held one of his philosophy books before him, poring over a chapter on the Idealism of Hegel, the points on which he agreed with Kant and how and where his theory diverged from that of his celebrated forerunner.

To any chance observer, the one who would appear the most studious and diligent was Deena. Sitting at my desk, he was immersed in an Enid Blyton. Constantly consulting the dictionary, filling up the margins of the book with the Hindi definitions of words that eluded him. There were so many. No wonder he had been on the second page of the book for over an hour, sparing no effort to make the most of *The Castle of Adventure*. It was then that Ram Mohan padded up the stairs and into the room. He looked gleeful. He had just had a visitor, a Patel fellow, who was close to Kanshi Ram and had come to inform him of the Dalit leader's three-day visit to Allahabad. He had fixed up for Ram Mohan to meet him. He then turned his attention to our apparent devotion to studying. 'Way to go! This's what lays the foundations of a great life ahead, of a stature many crave but only a few can achieve, for to turn your dreams into reality entails much sweat and industry, patience and commitment, without which nothing's possible, no matter how talented you are.'

He stepped up and took the Enid Blyton from Deena and read a few lines before flicking through it and said, 'This is called English. I always knew about my Deena's potential. The only cause for concern was his utter neglect of his own abilities, his unwillingness to pass his exams, but then he went all out to acquire a good grasp of Hindi language and literature. Some hard work that was. Look at his own verses in Hindi! His choice of words, over and above his sensibility, and now that he's woken to the significance of English, to its clout and power, nothing can stand in the way of his getting a handle on it.'

When Baabuji left, Deena said, 'Let's go to the university library on Monday. I want to pick up a few English books before Mishra-ji bids adieu to the place, some good literary ones whose presence on my bookshelf would keep me motivated, as a reminder that I've to develop the ability to appreciate and enjoy them one day.'

Mishra-ji's association with Ram Mohan had finally born fruit. He would be appointed Sanskrit teacher to a senior secondary school. It was the chairman of the body that recruited teachers for state-run schools who had informed Ram Mohan of Mishra-ji's

selection the very day the interview took place. Ram Mohan had
pursued the matter with the utmost sincerity and concern. He had
called the chairman when it was still early days and went to meet him
when the day of the interview neared.

With this teaching job in the bag, Mishra-ji was about to quit his
temporary library job. It was now or never if we wanted to grab some
good books for free. We agreed to visit him at work on Monday,
something we had been putting off, despite Mishra-ji's reminders
that by delaying it, we were limiting our choice, for not a day passed
when a few good books wouldn't leave the library for good.

The next day, when Ram Mohan was off to his meeting
with Kanshi Ram, Mishra-ji arrived. The man was never short
on humour. One of the reasons for Ram Mohan's fondness for
him was his ability to produce funny comments at will, though it
was only in his absence that we found Mishra-ji at his best, when
he could even jest about some behavioural aspects of Dr Sahab
himself. We looked forward to such occasions. That day, he wasn't
his usually jocular self. Which was strange. The more so, because
we had expected him to be in his element as his long-nurtured
hope stood fulfilled. He had clinched a government job, the job of
teaching Sanskrit to senior secondary students.

We had hardly sat down in Ram Mohan's room when Nishant
too joined us and fixed Mishra-ji with an enquiring gaze. Why he
looked so down! Then, to our disbelief, the corners of Mishra-ji's
mouth and chin quivered, and tears sprang to his eyes. Nishant
got up, stepped across, planted himself beside him on the sofa and
put his arm around his shoulders. Mishra-ji began to whimper.
We exchanged glances. Nishant waited. Mishra-ji took out a
handkerchief and did the needful, and said, clearing his throat, 'If I
hadn't been so fortunate as to meet Dr Sahab, the possibility of my
getting this job would have been very slim, maybe nil.'

'You deserved it,' said Nishant. 'That's what Baabuji told me
when he was going to meet the chairman. Given his fondness for

Sanskrit, it's a big compliment. You must be good at your subject!'
Overwhelmed, Mishra-ji caught hold of Nishant's hands. 'That's
the truth,' Nishant pressed on. 'Then, the way you looked after
things during all that repair work as if it was your own house—'

'It is my own house and Dr Sahab my benefactor. That will
never change. My uncertain future is history. I've no words to
express my gratitude.'

To convince Mishra-ji of his being worthy of his father's help,
Nishant mentioned how, in the past, some disagreeable creatures
had inveigled themselves into Baabuji's confidence, obtaining
positions for which they were as undeserving as Mishra-ji was
deserving for a Sanskrit teacher's job. The prime example was
K. Dwivedi. 'Had it not been for Baabuji, this man would still
be making do with piffling bribes as a booking clerk at Kanpur
station. Look how fast he's making good now! I haven't seen such a
turnaround in the fortune of anyone known to us. A petty railway
clerk, who, not so long ago, lived just a notch above the level of
subsistence, that very fellow is an important official in the state's
labour department, whom not many business-owners would dare
annoy. He's well on his way to becoming wealthy and propertied.
He had just had to butter up Baabuji.'

'And Dr Sahab doesn't mind it in the least bit. In fact, he's all
for it and unlike others, he bluntly admits to his desire for being
soft-soaped.' Mishra-ji giggled as he recalled something, then
continued, 'The other day he took me along to see Tandon-ji . . .
And when Tandon-ji grumbled about Indira Gandhi promoting
a culture of sycophancy in the Congress, Dr Sahab pointed out
that this culture had well been established during Nehru-ji's time.
Tandon-ji said there was a difference between genuine praise and
flattery. "I know," said Dr Sahab. "You can praise anybody, even
your servants for their good work, but flattery is reserved for those
you think important . . ." Tandon-ji gave his rictus of disgust and
said flattery was dangerous for one's ability to stay clear-sighted,

let alone that flatterers keep one away from one's genuine well-wishers—'

'Tandon Uncle's right. It was K. Dwivedi who had manipulated Baabuji into deciding against fighting that election, which he was certain to win—'

Mishra-ji cried out, ignoring Nishant's keenness to continue with his excoriation of K. Dwivedi, 'Please hear this . . . What Dr Sahab said next stumped Tandon-ji, "Flattery that you receive or don't receive is an authentic barometer of your standing in your field. Hence it's meaningful." Then he took out his tiny notebook from his shirt pocket and read out this quote in English. I don't remember it, but Dr Sahab explained to me in Hindi, which is something like—'

'That's from one of GB Shaw's plays, "What really flatters a man is that you think him worth flattering."' It would have been a recent addition to Ram Mohan's armoury of quotes as none of us had heard it from him, barring Nishant, of course.

'Yes, that's the quote.'

The mention of the great playwright reminded Deena of their plan to visit the university library. 'Mishra-ji, we're thinking of coming to the library tomorrow.'

'Oh, it's good you remembered. I'm only there till the end of the week. I've to go visit my village before the new job takes me away . . . Come any time after two, when the crowds of students start thinning out.'

The next day, Deena took a half day off from work and met us at the university. We walked in through the impressive portal of the British-era library building. At the far end of the entrance hall, behind a big counter, stood Mishra-ji, talking to one of his colleagues. As we began to wend our way towards him, he signalled us to wait. He had seen us. We stepped across to the right side of the hall, close to the wall. Shortly, he motioned us to follow, as he left the counter and made for the threshold of the passage that took you inside the library. 'Whatever books you gather, just put them on some empty shelf,' he whispered, 'at least three books, slim ones, you can tuck, one each of you, in the waistband of your trousers under the shirt and walk off. The rest I'll get you later. Don't be nervous. Students do this all the time. Some professors too.'

Mishra-ji returned to his place behind the counter as we went in. That books were pilfered regularly was obvious from many half-empty shelves, a fact Mayank and I knew from our earlier visits. However, the tall steel bookcases, rows, and rows of them, still held many good titles. Eager to get my hands on something on Ghalib, I went to the Urdu section, leaving Mayank with the task of finding books of philosophy and history, our common subjects in the university. Deena went looking for the section on English literature.

Only four or five people were in the library at this hour. We had identified, for the purpose of keeping our picks, a desolate shelf in a bookcase that stood in a gloomy corner. Between the three of us, we harvested seven books. There were many more we would have liked to take. Mayank got two: *An Introduction to Philosophical Analysis* by John Hospers and *A Hundred Years of Philosophy* by John Passmore. He couldn't find the book he was most keen to grab, *A History of Western Philosophy* by Bertrand Russell. Deena picked the seventh volume of *The Pelican Guide to English Literature: From James to Elliot* and both volumes of *Mortals and Others, American Essays 1931–1935* by Russell, containing short pieces the author wrote for the Hearst Press in America, so trenchant and wise, they could result only from a penetrating understanding of human affairs. That much Deena could discern, despite his yet very limited grasp of the language. Discern, he could also, the beauty of the prose of these pithy essays. In time, Deena would become a rank admirer of Russell, a devotee of his relatively popular writings, the kind not dealing in academic abstractions and theoretical fine points.

The books I managed to obtain were exactly the kind I was looking for. A biography of Ghalib and a selection of his letters that he wrote to his friends and disciples, letters that, written in a conversational tone, brought out a great stylist in Ghalib. The third book I got was a book of verse, ghazals to be precise, by Firaq, who had died a few months before. That he had taught English literature at Allahabad University, raised his literary stature in my eyes. A peerless wit, he was known to pull no punches, saying whatever he thought fit, mostly to his audience's amusement or disbelief, and when it came to being boastful of one's own talents, few could rival him. A great many jokes and stories involving Firaq were always in circulation, some spoke of his sharp intellect while others alluded to his congenital yearning for good-looking boys.

While Mayank went to inform Mishra ji that we were done, I wandered to where history books were and when my eyes lit upon *The Wonder That Was India*, I took it out and added to the pile.

* * *

Dressed in loose-fitting light grey trousers and a brown and white check short-sleeve shirt, Kanshi Ram struck Ram Mohan as a plain, simple man, nondescript, with little to tell him apart from a lower-middle-class townie. What brought out his 'extraordinary ordinariness'—Ram Mohan's words—was his toneless voice and want of style, something at odds with his ambition, the scale of it. Yet there was no gainsaying that he was making strides in what he had set out to attain. It was only when, after a bit of small talk, they came to the point, the purpose of the meeting, that Ram Mohan began to have some idea of what it was wherein lay his appeal. What was it that marked him off from other Dalit leaders, mostly in the Congress, all of whom, according to Jaan Muhammad, had long been co-opted, beginning with Jagjivan Ram?

To Ram Mohan, it was his sincerity, his commitment to the cause, so evident in the magnitude of the task he had taken up, a task that asked for a long, gruelling struggle, promising no short-term reward. He was there for the long haul, looking for no less than a paradigm shift in electoral politics. 'Until you take things into your own hands, until you have a go at the reins of political power, until you refuse to be content with the crumbs the Congress has thrown since Independence, your condition won't change. Until you alter the way you've been voting, you can't alter the prevailing situation.'

The rhetoric apart, what made up for the absence of tonal fervour and frenzy in his speeches was his calm logic braced by all the relevant facts he had at his fingertips, added to which, was his clearheaded, realistic take on the political agenda of their movement, making his fellow Dalits believe he wasn't the one to sell them down the river.

Kanshi Ram gave Ram Mohan a short account of his life and journey. 'I come from Punjab and am Sikh by birth. It's not that there's no caste hierarchy in the Sikh community. But it's nothing like what Dalits have to contend with outside Punjab, the kind of humiliation, intolerance, prejudice, of which I had had no inkling till after moving to Maharashtra. I can't recall even one instance from my school and college days in Punjab when I had to suffer or feel humiliated on account of my being a Dalit Sikh. That's not the case in the land of the Sikh gurus whose teachings put stress on equality and compassion, where even Dalit Sikhs can get ahead in what they choose to do in life.

'It was only after getting into the central government service through the scheduled caste quota that I realized what it meant to be Dalit. The real shock came a bit later when I went to work as a lab assistant in this military weapons factory under DRDO, the Defence Research and Development Organisation in Maharashtra, where I came face to face with what a raw deal scheduled caste employees got at the hands of their high caste superiors and fellow workers. Leaving me further stunned was the fact that victimization and ill-treatment of Dalits at large was so common in Maharashtra. Not that I had ever been forgetful of my Dalit roots, of the fact that my family had converted to Sikhism, but growing up in Punjab, I couldn't have known the grim reality of what they had to face in other parts of the country.

'It was in Maharashtra that I was hit right in the eye by the reality of being a Dalit. Then this colleague of mine, with whom I had become friends, a Dalit hailing from Nagpur, it was he who put me in touch with Babasaheb Ambedkar's writings and—'

'Mr Khaparde,' said the host, the Patel who had arranged for Kanshi Ram and Ram Mohan to meet at his tawdrily furnished house he had built in a new but rundown or 'half-made' locality, where the walls of most houses were without plaster, the streets and lanes without asphalt and where hungry pigs scavenged through dumps of refuse.

'Yes, D.K. Khaparde . . . I was gripped by Babasaheb's writings, in total awe of his razor-sharp intellect and wisdom, the depth of his understanding of India's problematics, his *Annihilation of Caste* and other tracts. Be it about untouchability, caste and class, religion, Buddhism, democracy, about Gandhi and Gandhism or his thoughts on Pakistan, he writes with such acuity I found it hard to believe his writings were hardly available outside his home state . . . and later realized that that was the very reason for this conscious neglect of his perspective and thought, this criminal indifference to his voice. That's the reason for him to be a pariah to the Nehru-Gandhi's Congress and mainstream Indian publishing.

'Thus, the origin of my present endeavour can be traced back to my exposure, real exposure, to being a Dalit and to Babasaheb's writings. What cranked it up was the clash that Dalit employees had with the DRDO administration over our desire to be granted special leave to celebrate Babasaheb's birthday and of a couple of other historical figures identified with the cause of the downtrodden, the persecuted. After that, Khaparde-ji and I, along with some other colleagues, founded an outfit to safeguard the interests of Dalit and other backward class employees in government organizations . . .'

'BAMCEF,' said the host.

'All India Backward and Minority Communities Employees Federation,' said Kanshi Ram, giving Ram Mohan the full form of the acronym. 'There was one before that too, its earlier version. It's a long story, Dr Sahab. But now that we're on the same page as regards this mission . . . to bring Dalits, backwards and minorities together to effect a real change in the way the Indian system works, let's talk about that.'

'Patel-ji has explained everything,' Ram Mohan waved towards the host. 'I fully agree with the purpose of this great undertaking. Please tell me how I can be of help. I'm at your disposal.'

'That's very kind of you. I've heard a lot from Patel-ji and others about your attainments in the fields of literary scholarship, education, and social work.'

'Dr Sahab's stint at the Public Service Commission is talked about in glowing terms,' added Patel.

'What interests me most is the story of your electoral battles in Fatehpur,' said Kanshi Ram, 'the way people of your community had voted for you.'

'Yes, but that wasn't enough. If not for those defeats, I would have fought again on a People's Party ticket. That was a miss. A critical one.'

'It was a landmark election. The whole north India had turned hostile to Indira Gandhi and Sanjay. People were seething at their regime. It was a vote against the Congress, not for the opposition. All castes and communities came together to punish them, the mother and the son, for the atrocities let loose on people during Emergency.'

'That was an outcome of extraordinary circumstances,' said Ram Mohan.

'Now politics is back to the old and tested caste and communal equations,' chimed in Patel.

'Dr Sahab, let me have your frank opinion . . . What do you think of the idea of the political coalition I'm looking to build?'

'If I had reservations about it, I wouldn't be so keen to meet you. No single caste or community can ever be enough to help you win elections, no matter how enthusiastically it votes for you. One must find ways to broaden one's appeal, to add some other sections to one's core support base, which isn't easy, given the depth of caste and communal divisions defining our polity. When the popular rage against Emergency had papered over these divisions, the result was astonishing. But papering over is papering over, occasioned by an extraordinary situation. It's never durable. To build a case for a serious political coalition of non-upper castes, it's imperative to find some genuine logic to bind our target constituencies together. That's what you're trying to do and I'm here to lend a hand.'

'That's clearly and neatly put, Dr Sahab. Our tireless endeavour has indeed resulted in great gains in UP where most Dalits are swearing by our organization. Just out of habit it is that some still look up to the Congress. We'll have them on board before long. Now we need to win other backward castes over, to convince them of our objectives. That's where lies the need for us to have on board some articulate OBC leaders. People like you, Dr Sahab.'

'Here I am. Just let me know how to go about it.'

'As of now, my idea of a grand alliance of Dalits, OBCs and Muslims has hardly moved past being just an idea. Muslims remain enamoured with the Congress, except in some parts of western UP, where they also support Baran Singh. The only people amongst OBCs, with whom this idea seems to resonate, are those of your caste, Kurmis. Yadavs have been Baran Singh's dyed-in-the-wool supporters. To reason with them would be a wasteful expenditure of time and energy. After Baran Singh, they might go wholesale to his protégé, Komal Singh Yadav, the thug.'

'But farmers, people of our caste,' Ram Mohan looked at Patel, 'also support Baran Singh. Not all, but a sizeable chunk of them.'

'Correct. Yet the kind of response we're getting from among them in Allahabad, if that's anything to go by, I can say with a fair

amount of confidence that this is the one backward group, second
only to Yadavs in numbers, to whom this idea of coalition can well
be sold. We need to work on them, doggedly, without looking for
an instant outcome.'

'Yes, I'm of the same mind. Kurmis have of late been
grumbling about being kept under the shadow of the Yadavs in
Baran Singh's party. They can be persuaded to move on to new
political pastures.'

'Still, we shouldn't give up on others, I mean OBCs other
than Kurmis. Baran Singh's an old man. Who knows, we might be
able to woo his diehard support groups too, not even Yadavs do I
rule out. I think there's a better way to employ the abilities of an
intellectual like you, better than just to have you campaign among
the masses. Have you heard of Jotirao Phule?'

'The name sounds distantly familiar. I can't place it. I may have
come across it somewhere, in the newspaper or in some book.'

'He's one of the real great men our country should be proud
of, one of the great social reformers, whose struggles should be
cherished and taken forward. I consider him to be the tallest among
all the social reformers of his time, people who fought against the
caste system and other societal evils.

'For Phule's unshakable stance on the question of women's
education and that of Dalits and other lower castes, no words of
admiration can suffice. The odds were stacked so heavily against
him and others of his mind, figures as luminous as Ranade,
Lokahitawadi, Pandita Ramabai, Chandavarkar, Karve, and
others, figures truly audacious in the ambition of their struggle,
in the immensity of its aims and objectives. What they had
been striving to achieve was infinitely more profound, more
compassionate and humane than the supposed Independence,
for which all those Congress luminaries, Gandhi, Patel, Nehru,
and others, were fighting. Not only that. It was infinitely more
intrepid of the reformers. Babasaheb Ambedkar has observed

somewhere . . . I don't recall his exact words but it's something to the effect—and it was in the context of India in those times—that there can be no comparison between the two: the kind of challenges a patriot struggling against a particular government faces and the kind which a social reformer is up against. A political crusader or nationalist has the entire society behind him, but a social reformer is condemned to be an outcast in his own society. He's hated, jeered, called names and avoided. The severity of his situation can't bear comparison to what a patriot confronts while confronting a government like that of the English . . . His exact words to describe the situation of a social reformer are, "There's nobody to hail him a martyr, there's nobody even to befriend him. He's loathed and shunned."'

Just as Ram Mohan was about to say something, Kanshi Ram spoke again, 'I was saying that our movement can benefit from you as a scholar, an author, more than if you just go around canvassing support among OBCs. Phule belonged to a backward caste, the gardener caste. He, along with Buddha, Ambedkar and some others, is a great iconic figure in the realm of our cause. It's deplorable that few in the Hindi belt have any idea of who he was, what he stood for, of his lifelong crusade against social injustice and the inhumanity of the caste system, of his howling rage at the savagery of ten-eleven-year-old girls being forced into marriage and raped by their husbands; of his campaign to educate and empower the weakest in our society, women and Dalits and other lower castes. It was he who suggested that all non-upper castes come together to fight for social justice. He had called them Bahujan Samaj. I'd like you to write a book on him. His life and work thus propagated can go a long way to—'

'What about Ambedkar, we can start with him!'

'Babasaheb is identified with Dalits. He himself was one. But Phule was of gardener caste, a backward caste. It would be better if we have him argue our case before the OBCs in UP, especially

Kurmis. You can author a book dealing with Babasaheb's life and thought later, after Phule.'

'I'll speak to my son-in-law in Delhi . . . if he can get me something on Phule there. Delhi has some good libraries—'

'Don't bother about that. There's this book in English, titled *Mahatma Jotirao Phule: Father of the Indian Social Revolution*, which I'll have delivered to you soon. Its author, by the name of Dhananjay Keer, he specialized in the genre of biography and has to his name books on Ambedkar and others. Later, if you decide to do a book on Babasaheb in Hindi, Keer's biography of him would furnish you with sufficient material.'

* * *

Kanshi Ram invited Ram Mohan to speak at his party rally to be held in the city at the close of his tour of Allahabad region. 'Dr Sahab is a powerful speaker,' said Patel ji as they all rose and walked out and into the tiny front yard.

'I've heard a lot about your oratory. That's going to be an asset to our cause.'

'I look forward to this rally,' said Ram Mohan and then, after a slight pause, 'Kanshi Ram-ji, I have this Muslim friend who was my PA at the Commission and is now retired. He's brilliant, clear-headed and well-read. The way his mind works, he can come up with solid arguments that why Muslims should join this movement.' Kanshi Ram said he would like him to speak at this rally.

For anything to be conveyed to Jaan Muhammad, Ram Mohan called one of his neighbours. He couldn't get through that day. The neighbour's telephone wasn't working. His former PA's house was in old Allahabad, in a Muslim locality, a web of cramped, constricted alleys, not far from where lived my Persian tutor, the Maulvi, recommended by one of my Urdu teachers at the university, whom I would visit two-three days a week. Kanshi

Ram's public meeting was two days later. Jaan Muhammad had to be notified.

'Baabuji's calling you downstairs, Kartik bhaiya,' announced their new boy servant as we, Deena, Mayank and I, were engrossed in thumbing the pages of the books we had sneaked out of the university library and couldn't wait to get hold of the remaining ones that Mishra-ji would bring.

'He should have been informed before being pledged to addressing the rally,' I heard Nishant when I entered the room downstairs.

Asking me to sit, Ram Mohan said, 'That's fine, he won't mind. Far from being a votary of the Nehru–Gandhi family, he holds them exclusively responsible for the wretched state of the country, for its endemic poverty. He detests them. They've done great injustice to India's economic and social potential through their reckless disregard of what needed to be done, through their self-assuring hubris. He'd love to speak his mind at the rally. He only needs some time to prepare,' then turning to me, 'Kartik, I understand your Maulvi lives in the same neighbourhood as Jaan Muhammad!' I nodded. 'When you go there in the morning, just ask him to come here tomorrow. It's urgent. He should make it around noon or early afternoon.'

'I'll give you the address,' said Nishant.

I had no plan to go for my Persian lesson that Tuesday. Now I had to. I went back to the room upstairs and asked Deena to come along. The days when I cycled to the Maulvi's at seven in the morning, were always a bit hectic, because after returning, I had to rush to the university. That morning, when I had this additional task, was going to be frantic unless Deena gave me a ride on his Vijay Super. Deena was grinning. Why? I knew. It was the Maulvi's granddaughter, petite and pretty and dusky, a girl of fifteen, about whom I had told him. Now he had a chance to clap eyes on her.

* * *

After delivering the message to Jaan Muhammad, Deena had to go agonizingly slow as the Maulvi lived in a more congested part, in the innards of the locality; the alleys and passages leading to his house were narrower, noisier, dirtier. There were odours, a medley of them. The Maulvi's poky little two-room quarters looked squashed up against the press of activity and noise out front, the chief source of which was this knot of raucous women, out to collect water from the community water tap on the other side of the alley. Then there were pedestrians, and cyclists, and peripatetic vendors and children hurrying off to school. In this thoroughfare, there seemed to exist no room to park the Vijay Super.

'Don't forget to pick up salt on your way back.' I turned my head to the left and saw standing in his doorway the Maulvi who had called out, cutting through the ongoing cacophony outside, to his granddaughter, as she and her two little brothers were about to round the curve on the far side of the alley and pass from sight. I poked Deena with my elbow, who was trying to squeeze the scooter into a narrow space by the open fetid drain running along the outer side of the rows of contiguous houses. His face fell. 'Don't worry,' I said. 'She's walking her brothers to a nearby seminary, where local Muslim boys go to memorize the Quran. She won't be long.' Once Deena parked the Vijay Super, he wasn't sure it wouldn't fall into the open drain.

'Kartik, what's the problem?' shouted out the Maulvi whose eyes happened to fall on me. I pointed to the scooter. 'Bring it here.' I couldn't see any room, but we wheeled it down to where he stood. He pointed to a place at the edge of the passage close to the threshold of his house. Deena wavered. 'It would slow the traffic down.'

'Don't bother. People here are used to these temporary bottlenecks,' said the Maulvi while eying Deena.

No sooner did I tell him of my friend's pedigree than his face assumed a look of geniality. 'I'll go get some tea,' said he and left, ignoring our polite protests. We sat in his small, square-shaped front room, messy and a bit smelly. Deena wrinkled his nose. 'Don't do that,' I said. He looked about, taking in the room and its contents. For furniture, it had two grime-encrusted plastic chairs that we occupied, an iron table and a narrow, sagging charpoy pressed to the wall that had a niche wherein rested an old copy of the Quran and other books, also to do with Islam, dog-eared, shabby, fraying at the seams. In one corner, stood a rolled-up prayer mat by which sat a copper jug with a long-curved spout. The wall to our right had a three-year old calendar with a picture of Kaaba, a gigantic block of a square building, soaring over the milling crowds of Muslim pilgrims, while hung on another wall was the declaration in Arabic, embroidered on a piece of cloth, *la ilaaha illallaah, muhamadun rasulallaah.*

'She's back,' I breathed to Deena. He jerked up straight as she came in, making her self-conscious. She even ignored my smile. I always smiled at her if her grandfather wasn't looking, and she would respond by shyly curling her lips inward and adjusting her dupatta on the head. That day she just walked past. Before Deena could say something, the Maulvi returned, holding two small glasses of tea that he handed to us before parking himself on the charpoy.

The Maulvi was now trying to explain the importance of compound verbs in Persian. His heart wasn't in it. He stopped. I closed my notebook. He began to tell Deena about the tragedy that had struck his family, something he had told me twice before.

He had fathered three sons and five daughters, of whom two sons and one daughter had survived. The rest had died either at birth or soon afterwards. The only daughter, the youngest of his three remaining children, was long married and busy giving birth to her own offspring. The two sons, while still in their teens, had demonstrated through their behaviour that they wouldn't give in to scraping a living from drudgery, the fate of most of their station. They won their spurs in thuggery, graduating quickly from small-time offenders to extortionists and killers. At the time of their deaths, they were accused of five murders and other felonies.

'I had got them married when they were eighteen and nineteen, hoping family responsibility would make them change course. Then one day, the new police inspector of our area killed them in a staged encounter.' The Maulvi had teared up. 'Now I've these three grandchildren on my old hands, but God is merciful, and Him willing, I'd soon be able to marry off this girl, the daughter of my elder son—'

'You have someone in mind?' asked Deena. His curiosity startled me. Why did he have to be so nosy? I also discerned a hint of anguish in his voice. Later, when I would confront Deena with what I thought so utterly nonsensical on his part, his answer was, 'It would have sounded absurd, especially when I'd hardly laid eyes on her, not beyond a glimpse, but the truth is that the day you'd told me about her, the day your description had made her come alive in my mind was the day I became besotted with her. How frequently I thought of her, taking her clothes off, relishing her dusky nakedness, kissing her all over, making love to her!'

Deena couldn't endure the thought of her being not far from the day when someone would have her reveal to his feverish gallivanting gaze, that breathtaking feast of her delicate curves and moulds. 'First, it was pure jealousy. Then when the Maulvi told us about the groom he had in mind for this slip of a girl, I was assailed by an overwhelming sense of pity for her, for this petite innocent beauty. It was a double whammy for me.'

In answer to Deena's question, the Maulvi said he didn't have much choice and had accepted the offer from the family of this cleric connected with the same seminary to which his grandsons went. In his early forties, this man, the cleric, had lost his first wife in childbirth and was looking to marry again, professedly for the sake of his two small children and old parents. A dismayed Deena turned his head to the right and what he caught through the open door horrified him and tore at his heart. He forgot the Maulvi and his granddaughter, as boiled up inside him his deeply held hatred of the two-facedness of mankind, its inexhaustible capacity for cruelty and violence on one hand and infinite potential for compassion and tenderness on the other.

I had told him about this, about the abattoir near the Maulvi's house, and the procession every morning of blood-dripping carcasses of water buffalos, male and female, of varying sizes, some very young, freshly slaughtered in line with Islamic rituals, meaning a slow agonizing death, and skinned but not yet gutted, carried away on handcarts filing past his house, something I was used to witnessing as the Maulvi explained the beauty of some Persian verse. I had told Deena about this. But no telling can match the actual when it has to do with such blood and gore, a sight as gruesome as that from a savage killing of the living.

Unlike others, Deena couldn't separate the killing of human mammals from that of non-human ones, who, endowed with the central nervous system, are no less sentient and go through the same mortal, insufferable pain as human mammals if subjected to such brutality. '*I've seen their response to any such violence near them,*' wrote Deena, '*and gosh, how terrified they look!*'

Deena did make a distinction between atrocities that humans deal out to fellow humans and the barbarity they inflict on other animals. *In the first instance, it's mostly because of some sort of rage or loathing occasioned by a variety of reasons*, says one of Deena's notes. *It can be to seek vengeance or to ward off imaginary or real threat and danger. It can be to subjugate or seek dominance. It can result from a clash of ideologies, communists destroying class enemies or believers finishing off non-believers. Yet no large-scale violence perpetrated by one set of people or a country on another can go now without raising a global outcry. When it comes to other animals, all our compassion, all our feelings about fairness, justice are put out to pasture, as all of us, people cruel and kind, all societies, all countries, we all come together and concur in coolly and mechanically wreaking terrible pain and suffering, day in, day out, on animals who are not only so very innocent but capable of responding to our care and love, our compassion. "The horror, the horror!"*

This aspect of Deena's emotional makeup, I have brought up before—his visceral antipathy to humans' inhuman treatment of animals—in *The Politician*, but the note I have quoted above, he wrote while describing the episode of his visit to the Maulvi's house. He wanted to include it in the book he couldn't write. It would have been the time when he was reading or had just finished *The Unbearable Lightness of Being* because right under his note, he copied these lines from this very book:

True human goodness, in all its purity and freedom, can come to the fore only when its recipient has no power. Mankind's true moral test, its fundamental test (which lies deeply buried from view), consists of its attitude towards those who are at its mercy: animals. And in this respect, mankind has suffered a fundamental debacle, a debacle so fundamental that all others stem from it.

* * *

By the time we got back from the Maulvi's, Jaan Muhammad had arrived. The Annexe was ringing with spirited conversation. I felt tempted to be part of the audience comprising Kanti, Nishant and Mayank, but on seeing me, Mayank came out, 'Come on, let's go. We'll be late for our history class.'

Nishant, Deena and Mayank were excited that their father was trying to pick up the threads of his political life, though the thought of being identified with Kanshi Ram was somewhat unsettling. It would draw sneers from their friends. Their unease proved unfounded. None of their friends would learn of their father being part of a Dalit rally. With the press holding firm to its policy of laughing off Kanshi Ram, not a word about this well-attended rally in the city's famous P. D. Park was in the papers.

Ninety-nine per cent of the crowd was composed of Dalits. Kanshi Ram's attempt at hammering together a big political coalition, by adding backwards and Muslims to his core constituency of Dalits, showed little sign of success. He needed forceful communicators from these communities. In Ram Mohan he had found one, but Jaan Muhammad wasn't in the same league when it came to verbal firepower. He would be more compelling in a small group than in a political rally. 'Your offbeat way of looking at things is stimulating, thought-provoking,' said Kanshi Ram to him. To Ram Mohan, 'Your speech surpassed what I heard of your eloquence. It's as if all the words and phrases you need, queue up before you in advance. It won't take you long to finish this book on Jotirao Phule—'

'You just provide me with this biography, the one you mentioned.'

'Give me a week.'

Kanshi Ram had the book delivered in five days, and Ram Mohan, before being halfway through it, formed a broad idea of the shape and tone of his own book in Hindi. To induce the other backward castes to team up with Dalits, he had to fashion his argument around Phule, an OBC himself, but whose fight was to serve a larger social cause; that of Dalits and women, the girl-child, and the OBCs.

Later when Jaan Muhammad argued that the OBCs treat Dalits the same way as the upper castes, Ram Mohan said, 'That's right. But if you're aiming at a specific end, you need to be careful about what to emphasize and where to stay quiet. You need to identify something that can draw the desired support for your objective, something about which you must be loud and clear, so loud as to drown out facts that clash with your contention.'

'Yes, things that could dash the claims of your grasp of a given phenomenon, of your theory about it, are ignored. So is the case with Kanshi Ram's idea of a political coalition of Dalits, Backwards and Muslims. As an idea, a theory, it's very attractive. But as to its defeat, there's little doubt, defeat at the hands of the realities on the ground.'

Ram Mohan laughed, 'When it comes to dealing with the human case, there's an unbridgeable divide between theory and reality. Still, I don't think it's going to be an entirely futile or wasteful effort. Some good can still come out of it!'

'You've hinted at something important, subtle. Yes, there's no harm in making such an effort because it might result in something good for Kanshi Ram's overall objective in the long run. It's a positive thought on his part, appealing to the better sense of all non-upper castes and Muslims. Who knows, it might lead to something entirely different, something that nobody can foresee now. Things can't stay static for long. There's bound to begin some stirring in not too distant a future, something of fundamental nature that would change the way we view our politics, our society . . . The book you're going to write on Phule is worthy of your effort.'

It would be another three months before Ram Mohan could make a start on his book.

* * *

Not that the question of Nishant's wedding was ever absent from Ram Mohan's mind. It surely had got nudged aside by his recently revived enthusiasm for active politics. One day, while busy finalizing the structure of his book with the help of the notes from Keer's biography of Phule, he got a letter from someone from Barabanki near Lucknow, who had been a friend of Chaudhary Baran Singh, propounding his granddaughter's marriage with Nishant. 'I hear the boy's well on his way to becoming a successful High Court advocate.'

Ram Mohan called Nishant to his room in the evening, along with Kanti.

'Am I in a position to marry?'

Nishant's law practice had barely moved from when he had started out. But Ram Mohan thought that to delay the marriage on this account wouldn't be a good idea. Joining hands with another family through marriage added strength to one's will to succeed in life. 'You can't find people more genuinely concerned about your career than your wife's side of the family.'

Kanti agreed. But Nishant, who suffered from a sense of high self-esteem, said, 'To get married before financial independence isn't advisable either.'

'Your wife isn't there just to enjoy a life of ease in your house. She's also there to lighten your burdens, share your problems, help tide you over.' Ram Mohan looked at Kanti, then at Nishant, 'You know how your mother's presence in my life gave me freedom to pursue my interests and goals. Sometimes successfully, sometimes not so successfully. She never complained and took care of so much without so much as a sigh.'

Kanti wiped her eyes as Ram Mohan pressed ahead, 'My point is that instead of a liability, married life can be an asset, allowing you to focus on your career better, free from distractions. And you'd get enough by way of furniture and other household items to help set up a functional home. There should be some cash too!'

'Where's the room to accommodate all these things?' said Kanti. 'And you seem to have accepted this proposal even when we know nothing about the girl.'

'Whether we accept or decline, the call will be of Nishant. To the question of the space for the bride and the things she'd bring, I know the answer.' Kanti and Nishant gave him a curious look.

'After Nishant's marriage, I'd move to the Main Building, into his present room-cum-home office, and he can have this entire Annexe to himself. This room in which we're sitting can be converted into his home office, and the other room he can use to put up his clients from out of town. These two rooms downstairs and those above should be enough for whatever furniture his bride brings in. As for Kartik, I don't know what his plan is. He might move out. If he wants to stay, he's most welcome. He can stay in the Main Building with Mayank and Deena.'

Nishant looked far from convinced. Ram Mohan looked at Kanti, then in a manner suggesting he had no choice but to say what he had to say, 'How long do you think your law practice will take to get off the ground?'

Nishant had no answer. Ram Mohan pushed on, 'Listen carefully, nobody knows that you're still treading water. People think you're going to be a successful lawyer. That allows you to appear worthy of any girl . . . So many people are eager to form a relationship with our family. They see potential in you. In time, you can have a flourishing practice and an impressive social life. You can also be appointed High Court judge one day . . . All that and much more. I think this is the best time for you to get married. You don't know how long before you start making headway as a lawyer. Your career's being closely followed by all these families with marriageable girls. If they sense you're floundering, they'd lose interest and look elsewhere. A girl's family can't wait when the wait is no guarantee that things will work out fine. Let's assume you take a few more years to start drawing clients, just assuming because I'm positive about your doing well sooner than that, let's assume that situation for a minute. Would there be enough good-looking girls left to choose from? Hardly. All these overtures will have dried up by then, leaving us with a limited choice. But if you decide now, you can have the pick of the bunch.'

As Nishant seemed to reflect on this, Kanti said, 'Even these many years later good girls will be available. Nishant for a son-in-law will take longer than that to lose its appeal. The delay would only mean a bigger age difference between him and his bride. Instead of four or five, it would be ten or twelve years. So what?'

'Not that simple. I know what you're saying. Which makes sense if we're certain that in four-five years, Nishant will triumph as a lawyer. Then, yes, it'll nullify the adverse effects of the perception that his practice is failing to take off. Suppose it takes longer than four-five years. Suppose it takes ten years or more. Then what? On what grounds can we evade the question beyond a point? Or we simply declare that so long as his law practice remains in the doldrums, our Nishant will remain single. Let me spell out the consequence of that: his prospects in the marriage market, if not finished, will diminish drastically.'

With no hint of his former resistance, Nishant said, 'I just want a little time. Not four or five years. That's out of the question. All I need is three–four months. I want to devote this time to finding some local advocates in Fatehpur and Kanpur, willing to let me handle their clients in the High Court.'

'First, we need to see the girl,' said Kanti.

'Of course. I'm going to write back to the girl's grandfather.'

A few days later, the grandfather was driven down to Allahabad. He had brought a picture of his granddaughter, who looked so pretty that Nishant agreed to a pre-wedding ceremony.

* * *

Meanwhile, the Union Public Service Commission had announced some job vacancies at Doordarshan (DD). Nisha had applied. MA in Hindi with a second class was a prerequisite that Nisha, with her first class, met amply. Short-listed candidates were invited for an interview and Nisha's had gone fantastically well. The chairman of the interview board was impressed by her extracurricular activities in school and college and later her broadcasting on women's issues on AIR in Allahabad. The chairman had lamented that the job in question had nothing to do with broadcasting, for which she was perfectly suited. 'Maybe at some time in the future, you'd get

the opportunity.' He also suggested that she keep an eye out for
vacancies for newsreaders or announcers on DD. Nisha had written
to Kanti that she might get this job.

The result of her interview wasn't expected until after a month.
She could visit Allahabad for a couple of weeks. It was easier for her
to come from Delhi than for Sandhya from that far-off town where
Varun's employment was. A telegram was sent to Nisha. Kanti
wrote to Sandhya about Nishant's wedding being in the works.

'If I'm selected, I won't have much time to myself,' said Nisha.
We all sat in Ram Mohan's room at the Annexe. He said, 'There'll
be a time-limit to join. Maybe a fortnight from the day you receive
the intimation. One mustn't put it off. Even a slight delay in joining
can make you regret later. One can lose out on promotion because
somebody, by dint of a day's seniority, beat one to it.'

'Exactly. Assuming I get this job, I suggest Nishant's wedding
be held in a month's time if the girl's family consents.'

Two days later, when the girl's father and brother came to
Allahabad to discuss the date of the wedding, Ram Mohan asked
if the wedding could be held in a month's time. He didn't believe
in auspicious days. Any day that suited him was auspicious. If they
desired, they could consult some pundit. Nishant's soon-to-be
father-in-law said, 'That shouldn't be a bother. Any pundit with
his palms greased will dig up sufficient grounds for any day to be
propitious, interpreting the relevant scriptural dictates to accord
with your needs.'

'If the day of your choice is singularly inauspicious,' added
Ram Mohan, 'they'll have some ritual up their sleeve to nullify its
bad effects.'

* * *

Putting the Phule project off till after the wedding, Ram Mohan
took command of the preparations. They had less than three weeks.

But in dealing with rushed situations, Ram Mohan couldn't be found wanting. Nishant and Deena were tasked with drawing up a list of guests to know how many invitation cards were needed. Nisha and Kanti got busy making the rounds of various markets to pick assorted items traditionally sent to the bride. The question weighing on Ram Mohan's mind was how to arrange the jewellery to be gifted to the bride. He refrained from sharing it with Kanti or anybody else.

Kanti had come into a fortune in gold ornaments and gold coins when her mother-in-law had died. Most of it had later been taken away by Ram Mohan, with the exclusive purpose of funding his congenital need for cash. To her reluctance to part with the family jewellery she wanted to save for their children, he would say, 'You impugn my ability to marshal funds to buy ornaments when needed? Our material condition is going to improve decidedly before long. It saddens me that you're unable to see the kind of future I see for my family, a future with economic freedom.'

Their move to Allahabad had indeed been a great leap in their lifestyle. But the future Ram Mohan had envisioned for his family remained a wilderness of desire and hope. After the failure of his UPSC project and now with no powerful politician behind him, Ram Mohan was hardly the man who could talk big. Yet he did. Especially when talking of his achievements: Sandhya's marriage and Deena's bank job—though lowly, it was an achievement, considering Deena's unemployability—and Nishant being a High Court advocate and Mayank showing great promise. Not least that they had a big house in Allahabad.

* * *

If forced to draw from the remainder of the proceeds of their Kanpur property, and if the girl's family—given his reputation for being against the dowry system—held back from giving some cash, Ram Mohan would be facing rough waters. But before the situation could turn up the heat, his optimism kicked in. He was confident of his friend Gulab Singh bailing him out like he had done on Sandhya's marriage. 'All functions related to the wedding will be in accordance with our social status,' declared Ram Mohan, before leaving for Ballamgaon.

He knew that all hadn't been well in Gulab Singh's household. What surprised him was Gulab Singh's acquiescence to what his two sons decided, making him withdraw from the fuss of active life, the life of a gang boss, reducing him to being a figurehead. 'It's not that they respect me any less,' said Gulab Singh. 'If anything, they're more respectful while seeking my counsel. But yes, for all practical purposes, things aren't the same as before. They're trying as best they can to weather this unexpected downturn in our situation.'

His sons wouldn't agree that this downturn had been unexpected. It was only their father's refusal to see what had become so apparent on the horizon when Indira Gandhi had, in less than two years into the Emergency, decided to hold general election, a lethal misreading of the situation on her part. Despite his sons' exhortations, Gulab Singh, instead of climbing on the People's Party's bandwagon, had stuck by Liyaqat Argali, had even organized an election rally in his area for Shukla-ji, the then Chief Minister.

'It was on your account,' he said, 'that I couldn't bring myself to leave the side of Argali. Had you taken Saansad-ji's offer to contest from Fatehpur, I'd have joined your campaign, quitting the Congress.'

Later when all those close to the Congress had become the target of the People's Party regime, Gulab Singh had suffered massive losses in his contractual ventures. Not only were his contracts revoked but he had had to pay bigger bribes than before to the concerned ministers and officials of the new regime, to get the money owed to him released. It was then that his sons prevailed on him, stressing that the baggage of his past associations

was impeding their way, to take a backseat and let them deal
with the problems arising out of the changed political landscape.
They got down to forging new alliances in the state government.
That wasn't easy. All the ministers were already surrounded by
their loyalists to whom the idea of new claimants to their leader's
attention was an anathema. They would do their best to keep these
'interlopers' and 'opportunists' from succeeding. What finally had
helped Gulab Singh's sons break through these barriers was hard
cash, big amounts of it, something that they were in no position to
dispense without risking bankruptcy.

'Some people here read my troubles as the setting of the sun.
What shocked me was that two of them, whom I had mentored,
even they—I don't know how they got ideas put into their heads—
even they began to raise their game, thinking the boot was on the
other foot now,' Gulab Singh laughed. 'They all, then, set about
having it out with each other first, including these two, taking the
imminence of my departure from the scene as a given. Three or
four of them got butchered in the process. Not these two. They
had joined hands and had worked out everything—'

'They would have learnt a lot working under you!'

Gulab Singh gave a wry face, 'They were focused on doing away
with all serious threat to their wished-for supremacy, believing that
my family had acceded to the inevitable. That we were willing to
look up to them and support them for old time's sake . . . My sons
were straining at the leash to stamp out this blazing indifference to
our hitherto unquestioned authority. I reined them in. These two
and others were saving us much trouble by going after one another.
There was this one thing that had me worried at first. Some of the
hoodlums had the backing of the local MLA, the ruling People's
Party's MLA, so I reckoned that before we could regain the lost
ground, we would have to befriend the new political regime.
Then it occurred to me that every politician would view backing
someone with waning influence as more trouble than it was worth.

You don't deserve political patronage unless you have unshakable credentials.'

'You kept this from me.'

'Congress was out of power. It was something for me to handle, at my level . . . It was a month before your falling out with Argali and Shukla-ji—'

'That was unforeseen. That's a long story. You were saying—'

'Yes, I knew what needed to be done. My sons were thrilled—'

'I heard of some murders. I knew you would have had your reasons. It was the time when I was busy with my association with Argali and Shukla-ji. The People's Party regime was wabbling on the brink of collapse. Indira Gandhi had launched her mass contact programme. Congress was on a comeback trail, and I was certain of my appointment to the UPSC in Delhi. That it was a matter of time. If you'd needed my help, you'd have come to me, so I had shrugged those murders aside. Now I know what it would have been like. A do or die situation. You had to do something decisive to stay on the top of the pile!'

'They were taken unawares. None of them could have imagined that I, who had no friends in the new regime, would go berserk the way I did, killing those close to the local MLA. They were no ordinary killings! Their heads and limbs were chopped off without much fuss. I needed to make an example. A no-nonsense message had to be sent across, a cut and dried message,' Gulab Singh guffawed. 'Even the MLA, a newbie, even he had peed in his khadi dhoti.

'It worked. About a week later, I met this local leader of the People's Party, who came bounding when told of my wish to see him. He had this ongoing rivalry with this local MLA of his party, who had hijacked the party ticket that should have been his. He took us to meet his political master Komal Singh Yadav, who was minister of state in the state government—'

'He was minister for cooperatives and had made lots of money.'

'Komal Singh welcomed us. "I've great regard for the brave and undaunted, people who know where they want to go." These were his words. He had been told of the murders.'

'He's extremely ambitious. He's around forty?'

'Yes, he was thirty-seven or thirty-eight when he had become state minister, and ever since Congress's return to power, Komal Singh has kept his nose to the grindstone, tirelessly visiting and revisiting areas that hold the key to fulfilling his ambition to become Chief Minister one day. He's striving to rally the support of all backward castes, particularly his own, Yadavs. And Muslims.'

'These are the vote banks the claimants to the legacy of Lohia and Baran Singh could hope to win over.'

'But Baran Singh has been known for personal honesty in public life, despite his inclination to make compromises to get what he wants—'

'So was Lohia, upright and honest,' said Ram Mohan, 'but we don't know how he would have behaved in power, to which he never came.'

'Komal Singh Yadav is the opposite of the concept of honesty. His gaze is so rigidly fixed on his goal, he'd do anything to realize it. I tell my sons to keep strengthening their ties with him while he's out of power.'

Ram Mohan then explained the reason for his sudden arrival in Ballamgaon. Nobody in Parsadpur knew about it.

'Like I've said, we're pressed for hard cash these days, and over and above that, my sons are managing the show now. The cash we have left must be used judiciously until things are on the up. If things were as before, I wouldn't let you spend a rupee of your own on such occasions. Yet I'll do what I can on my own, from my personal funds.' Gulab Singh left and returned with a small cloth bag, a satchel, and said, handing it to Ram Mohan, 'Put it in your briefcase. My wife's coming to meet you. It's not much but that's what I can do for now.'

* * *

The contents of the satchel surprised Ram Mohan. It was more than what he had expected after learning of Gulab Singh's finances. Twenty thousand rupees and five gold coins, one hundred and forty-two years old, with East India Company and a figure of a lion embossed on them.

EIGHT

'How is it going?' Chaturvedi-ji asked Nishant, who had driven Ram Mohan to his place.

'He's trying hard but real work has yet to come his way,' said Ram Mohan.

'Uncle, I need to visit district courts in Kanpur and Fatehpur more often and meet local advocates—'

'And offer them bigger cuts than what they get from other High Court lawyers. Once you get some of their jailed clients out on bail, more business will start coming in. Just don't lose heart.'

Chaturvedi-ji glanced at Nishant and then changed the topic, 'I miss Sinha Sahab.'

'I thought he was saved after he survived the first heart attack,' said Ram Mohan

'It was Anoop's insistence on marrying that Negress! He had no idea how distressed his father was.'

'He finally broke up with her!'

'Yes.'

* * *

Sinha Sahab's first heart attack was put down to the letter he had got from his son, who was pleading with his family to accept his girlfriend as their daughter-in-law and wanted the wedding in India, in Allahabad, according to Hindu ritual. That was his way of assuring his parents that he cared for his cultural roots. The letter had borne out Sinha Sahab's worst fears.

'What solace is there in it for me?' Sinha Sahab had said to Chaturvedi-ji. 'We'll be the ones to suffer the brunt of his folly, be the butt of uncharitable jokes. Do I care whether his marriage ceremony is performed the Hindu way or not? I would much prefer that he had a civil wedding and settled here, married to some Indian girl rather than going through the whole rigmarole of a Hindu wedding with this Black girl as his bride and return to England, deserting his family, deserting me, deserting his mother.'

As it turned out, the problem was to be resolved the way Sinha Sahab had wanted. If he could have just hung in there! Even at the time of Anoop's letter, all wasn't well between him and his girlfriend. Just as Ram Mohan had said—after Anoop had sent the pictures to test the waters—that if they kept up their opposition, things couldn't stay the same between the two in London. His perspective on her person was bound to change. He would start finding fault with her behaviour, her way of doing things, with the way she looked, the colour of her skin and all, and being an independent London girl, she would refuse to take it lying down.

That's what happened. After his father's first heart attack, their relationship worsened. Later they would break up. The second heart attack, the fatal one, had left Anoop mortified, which along with his sense of guilt, made him decide to return to India. The task of finding him a wife, he entrusted to his family. He would marry any girl they thought suitable.

* * *

The wedding function in Barabanki went swimmingly. The arrangements were in keeping with the social station of both the families. Gulab Singh, with a posse of armed men, along with several old friends of Ram Mohan's from Parsadpur, had joined them in Barabanki, travelling in two Jeeps, making quite a splash at the venue.

Ram Mohan was now keen that the reception in Allahabad wasn't found wanting. Getting back the next day, he sent for the people signed up for taking care of the arrangements for the event. The venue for the reception was the vacant lot right opposite the Main Building across the street. The guests, in addition to relations, friends and acquaintances, included some local VIPs, prominent among whom were the DM and the police chief. As for his political associations, there wasn't much to show off. Saansad-ji was in Delhi, sparing no effort to stay afloat politically. His wife and son came. Kanshi Ram, busy campaigning in the western part of the state, sent two of his lieutenants. Patels of all political stripes were there, some belonging to Baran Singh's party, a few to Kanshi Ram's outfit and two to the Congress. Overall, the event went as planned and was becoming for Ram Mohan's social stature.

Tiwari-ji thought it should have been a modest affair. His friend didn't have to go to this expense. Nobody associated him with material riches. He was known for more prestigious attributes. He was known for his erudition, his mastery of Hindi language, his literary abilities, his oratory, for the development he had brought to his village and above all, for being Ex-Member, Public Service Commission. Ram Mohan listened. He had become mellower, not with age but with being in no position to dictate terms. He could now abide views not in accord with his own, and if logical, he would assimilate them into his way of thinking.

* * *

A month later, the crunch came. One of their two tenants, the homeopath, began to fall behind with the rent. If not for Sahani Sahab, who paid on time, Ram Mohan would be obliged to contribute the entire amount needed towards the monthly household budget. He saw it as a sign of a bigger problem ahead, the problem they might have with the homeopath, whose behaviour of late wasn't the same as before. He had become irritable. Didn't like to be reminded of the rent. Nishant, who dealt with him, needed to play it cool. Getting angry could make matters worse. They might have to ask him to go and then he could become a real problem, the same as the lawyer before him. Ram Mohan knew they were going to have another hostile tenant on their hands. Tiwari-ji thought so too.

Within days of Nishant's wedding, Ram Mohan shifted to the Main Building. Nishant moved his things to the Annexe. His home office was set up in the two rooms on its ground floor. Things that had come from Barabanki found their way to the rooms upstairs that had been my abode until then. I wanted to look for a room to rent, but Ram Mohan Uncle insisted there was no hurry. He suggested the garage in the Main Building be turned into a makeshift study.

* * *

Nisha got the job at Doordarshan. Shekhar had begun teaching at the IIT after his PhD. Who would look after Shivika while they were away at work? Fortunately, there was a crèche-cum-pre-nursery school not far from the IIT campus. But what when Shivika started going to nursery school? Somebody had to pick her up at the school bus-stop and mind her till her parents were back. That somebody was Kanti. Nishant's wife could take care of things in Allahabad. The boy servant was there too. Kanti was put on a train to New Delhi, and soon after, the situation in Allahabad took a turn for the worse.

* * *

The rent from the homeopath was long overdue. One late evening, Nishant went upstairs and found the renter turned rent-dodger as tetchy as ever, 'Have a little patience. I'm not running away.' Just as Nishant began to descend the stairs, Sahani Sahab caught him up.

'I just wanted to let you know we'd be moving out next month.'

'Why . . .? Is there any problem here?'

'Nothing in particular—'

'Please speak your mind.'

'We don't feel comfortable living next door to this man.'

Nishant wrinkled his brow.

'Whenever we come across, we hardly go beyond a nod. He keeps to himself, and the way his wife stays indoors! I can't describe the feeling . . . Puzzling, weird. Once when my wife ran into her, she reacted as if caught stealing and dashed back inside. Then, about a week ago—'

'They don't trouble your family, do they? They prefer to keep to themselves! So let them be. Why should that be of any concern? They're better than rackety neighbours.'

'It's not the kind of quiet one would prefer. It seems forged, ominous. Not peaceful. Kind of creepy. And from what we hear through the closed door that separates our portions, they always talk in undertones. It's the homeopath who does the talking. We've never heard her voice. A while ago, my daughter heard loud whispers. She was going to the bathroom but ran back, scared. When my wife got to the closed door, it had become louder. Other sounds were added to his ferocious whispering. He was beating her. The way she bore everything, not a sound from her, no sobbing or wailing, it was scary. We don't want our daughter to be in the vicinity of such people.'

'Okay, I'll tell my father.'

'I'll meet him tomorrow.'

Ram Mohan was at a neighbour's place for a post-dinner chat. When he returned, Nishant told him. He was quiet, taking in the situation, then, 'We'll have to do something about this homeopath. He not only doesn't pay rent on time, but is also the cause of the departure of the one who does. I won't be surprised if the last payment stays the last forever. Let's ask him to clear the dues and leave. One more thing . . . You and your mother might not approve but I'd like you to weigh it up, the suggestion I'm going to make. I'll discuss it with Deena and Mayank too.'

Nishant looked at his father, his curiosity roused.

'After the homeopath, let's not take in any new tenants.'

'If no rent, we can't even feed ourselves.'

'I've been turning it over in my head. How long can things go on this way? The rent from the upper floor will barely suffice for the monthly ration and other expenses. What about the upkeep of the place? How do you pay for that? I say, let's put it up for sale before things get thornier,' ignoring Nishant's incredulous look, he went on, 'Why have a house like this when you have no money for your needs—'

'But—'

'Let me first give you my entire outlook, the way I view our situation . . . People in their prime overlook the truth of human mortality when making choices. To take the long view of things is admirable only if one can keep it in proportion. To me, it's foolish not to use what one already has . . . for a better today, for a better life. One must weigh the worth of what one wants against one's lifespan, against the brutal rush of time. Hence the question: What's the point in having a property like this if you're going to struggle to make ends meet?

'Assuming you start doing better as a lawyer, will you be able to look after the entire household plus the maintenance of the two buildings? Even if you want to do that, is that realistic? Soon, things would begin to unravel. Let's take a sensible view of the situation.

'You're now married. In a few years, Deena too would like to marry! And you can't expect him to contribute towards the monthly budget here. We all know what his salary is!

'As for Mayank's needs, I'll take care of them. He's so thoughtful. Seldom asks for anything unless necessary. I don't know what career he—'

'There's not much choice in the job arena,' said Nishant. 'For anyone good at studies, the only thing worth pursuing is a place in the IAS. The kind of power and comforts an IAS or IPS officer enjoys is—'

'Whatever Mayank decides, he'll have my support . . . The question that needs to be addressed now is: How wise is it to cling to this property while your hands and feet are tied with the rope of financial stringency? Does it make sense? And after you have children and Deena too, after his marriage, and Mayank . . . Then this very property will become the cause of a quarrel among you all, a real mess, generating bad blood.

'After I'm gone, the problem will become intractable. I know this from experience. Have seen many such disputes. Not just do they distance brothers from brothers but turn them into enemies. Plus, this property can't be divided equally without selling it. Other than that, each of you would like to lead your life the way you see fit, according to your own taste, with nobody interfering, with some freedom. In a joint family, lives are cramped, to say nothing of the smouldering tension underneath, which keeps things on the edge,' Ram Mohan paused as Nishant seemed cogitating. 'Think hard. I'll speak to Deena and Mayank too.'

* * *

The next day, Ram Mohan called everybody to his room, including me. Kanti was in Delhi. He recapped what he had told Nishant, which made sense to Deena and Mayank. They decided not to let out the upper floor. Ram Mohan then changed the topic, 'Now I'd like to read out a little from the book I'm writing. The book on Mahatma Phule.' He lifted his writing pad off the books and papers stacked against the wall along the edge of his takht, but catching Nishant looking at him, asked, 'Is there anything else?'

'The Annexe and the land behind it are separate from the Main Building. A fence or a wall can be put between the two, to set them officially apart—'

'To what purpose? You think it'll get us a better deal if sold as two properties?'

'No, what I suggest is that we put on sale only the Main Building. The Annexe should be transferred to my name. I can go on living in it. I'm struggling to put in motion my floundering practice, and can do without the strain of looking for a place to rent and set up everything afresh.' Ram Mohan put the writing pad aside and said he needed some time to think. We all left. After the evening meal, when Nishant and his wife retired to the Annexe, Ram Mohan sent for Deena and Mayank.

'I know what it entails. It'll be an unfair division. What Nishant wants is worth two and a half times more than what you would get from the proceeds of the Main Building, your mother, and you two . . . What's the alternative? You can decline and keep living here for the rest of your lives . . . What a waste of life that would be. A big old house to live in but nothing else. No money to help you pursue what you like. And who would pay for its upkeep? It can never be sold unless you all agree. It's better to defer to Nishant's request. If you refuse, this house will be a place where you just stay . . . How can you claim to own something you can never sell? Just give it a thought and you'll have no reason to feel hard done by.'

Deena and Mayank gave their consent. When Nishant was leaving for the High Court in the morning, Ram Mohan told him that everybody was fine with his suggestion. Now they should speak to the homeopath about the pending rent and at an opportune moment, he should be asked to leave.

* * *

It had been three months since Sahani Sahab's departure. The homeopath was staying put without paying rent. Nishant didn't want him to go till he had coughed up the rent he owed, because then the money would be as good as lost. But how long could they afford to wait? The cash that Ram Mohan had was running out. 'Enough is enough. We can't just sit around and encourage the louse to think he's in control . . . Tell him he must settle what's due and clear out. Give him a hint of what to expect if he demurs.'

Later, Nishant went upstairs and knocked. He could hear the homeopath's wife behind the closed door, who, without opening it, said her husband wasn't home. Nishant decided to wait downstairs, sitting on the front veranda of the Main Building, reading one of his law books. Ram Mohan was out visiting one of the Patels.

It was eight in the evening when the homeopath was heard opening the big main gate. Just as he parked his scooter at the edge of the driveway, Nishant called out, 'Dr Sahab, one moment please.' They stood near the entrance to the upper floor. 'We can wait no longer. You must pay five months' rent that's due and vacate the place.' The homeopath nodded and said, 'I've been thinking of shifting somewhere close to my clinic and have found one such place. Now that you've asked, I'll vacate soon, sooner than my earlier plan, in less than two weeks!'

'After clearing the remaining rent!'

'The delay in payment won't mean non-payment. I'll meet your father tomorrow.'

* * *

The homeopath told Ram Mohan of his financial difficulties and that he would soon receive some money from the sale of his agricultural land in the village. But he couldn't wait to shift to his new quarters. 'I'll stay in contact,' he said before leaving. Ram Mohan had to take his word for it. Anyway, to be rid of such a dubious character, that too so easily, was itself an achievement. 'We know where his clinic is. If he doesn't make good on his word, we can always send someone to lean on him. He can't get away with bilking us out of an amount like this.'

Three weeks passed. No word from the homeopath. 'Pay him a visit, and don't go alone. Take someone who can talk tough,' said Ram Mohan to Nishant. There were several such young men to choose from. The one Nishant settled on was a student leader, a rising one, Prakash, who came from Fatehpur and was one of the young men who would drop by daily during their campaign against the lawyer and the PWD man.

Prakash offered to bring some of his rowdy supporters along. Nishant said no. He just wanted to remind the homeopath of his promise to pay up. It was a Saturday afternoon when they went to pay him a visit. His clinic and dwelling were in an old settlement situated on both sides of the main highway, just outside the city. The clinic was closed. Hovering in the vicinity were knots of people, whispering and throwing glances towards the padlocked clinic, so squeezed in the commercial thoroughfare that, without the big signboard announcing the homeopath's name and qualifications it would be hardly noticeable. Two armed police constables stood nearby. Prakash went to find out. Nishant waited by the Vijay Super, at the edge of the road. He saw Prakash talking to a shopkeeper.

'Let's get out of here,' said Prakash on returning. They rode back towards the city and about a furlong later, Nishant pulled over on the side of the highway to hear what Prakash had to say.

In the morning that day was found the headless body of a young woman stuffed in a gunnysack, propped against an electric pole across the road from the homeopath's clinic. There was nothing on the body, not a stitch, other than some injury marks. The killer or killers had taken care to render her unidentifiable.

As the police began making enquiries, an old man told them that at about two, in the still of the night, he had heard a dog barking before somebody hit it, making it skitter away yelping. The old man lived in the same lane as the homeopath. The police went to his clinic to ask if he had noticed anything unusual the previous night. The homeopath looked tired and was fumbling for answers. When the police inspector said they would like to have a look inside his house, the homeopath's reaction, the look on his face, left the police in little doubt that they were about to solve the case.

He knew nothing about it, squealed the homeopath. He lived alone. His landlord and neighbours confirmed it. But the police forced him to take them inside his house, where, in the bathroom, they found the severed head wrapped in a cotton mattress. A further search resulted in the discovery of a gold chain and a couple of rings. What couldn't be traced in the dingy, sepulchral quarters was the murder weapon. But a few lathi blows on the homeopath's behind and legs led the police to the ditch a kilometre up the highway towards Fatehpur, into which the knife was thrown.

'Our three thousand five hundred rupees are gone,' Nishant said.

'Forget about that,' said Ram Mohan. 'Imagine what could have happened if he hadn't moved out. He might have killed her here, in our house, and then how hard it would be to find a good buyer . . .! Let's take out an ad in both Hindi and English papers, and dispose of it. I'm getting cleaned out of cash.'

* * *

The ad had a tremendous response. Many interested parties came calling and were impressed by what was on offer, but the asking price seemed beyond the means of most of them, one of whom even remarked that the property wasn't overpriced. Rather it was worth more than what was quoted—seven lakh rupees. Two businessmen also came but thought an investment like that in a big plot of land, or several small ones, promised greater returns. Even if they wanted a house this big, they would construct it in line with their needs and taste rather than have something thrust on them.

Weeks passed. None of the offers went past four lakh rupees. Ram Mohan called everybody to his room and set forth his suggestion, 'We should bring the asking price a trifle down.' Deena and Mayank looked at Nishant, whose views on such hard practical matters were valued. He differed. He was sure of someone coming along, someone who would settle for no less than six lakh, and that someone would be some government officer, the creature that could make lots of money in no time.

'Hard cash keeps pouring into their pockets till they retire,' said Nishant. 'You work hard to get into the bureaucracy but once there, you become part of a system that gives you access to endless ways of getting rich. It's up to you how you plan to do it or what suits your temperament. You can be rapacious, or moderate, in your devotion to the pursuit of easy money!' Nishant glanced at us, Mayank and me. He had been enjoining us to aim for IAS.

Mayank said, 'If I become a civil servant, I can't bring myself to be on the take.' Earlier, Ram Mohan would have been proud of him. Now, he wasn't so sure. He kept quiet as Nishant said, 'Honest bureaucrats are melting away . . . Even if you refuse to join the money-making crowd, this job, by some distance, is the best in the land because of the kind of power and perks it bestows. And the toiling masses,' Nishant chuckled, 'people in other professions, when you survey them from your hierarchical perch, they look so small. Boy, the power the bureaucracy enjoys!'

'Even the jobs that some people claim to view as not merely jobs but their calling,' said Ram Mohan, 'even those, and even those that from time to time are mentioned in exalted terms, lavished with such esteem, identified with a noble cause, jobs of teachers, doctors, etc., whatever lofty things are said about them on certain occasions, only a fool would see them as anything other than pure rhetoric. There are few, if any, domains that bureaucrats don't lord it over.

'I loved teaching, loved to compete with my colleagues at DAV College, loved to flaunt my linguistic and literary knowledge. And then I realized how humble, kind of low-born, a teacher looked beside an IAS officer . . . How I was made to feel small in Kanpur when the organizers of literary or social functions, of which I'd be part as a speaker, when they approached the DM or the SSP or a local MP or MLA, for inaugurating the event or gracing it as chief guest, and whomever of these personages was there, others and I, on the stage, would acknowledge his presence in glowing phrases. If it were a poetic assembly, some poets would recite a verse for him, a tribute to the fact that he was the most important person amongst us. It was around this time that I'd made a resolution not to stay content with being a literary scholar.'

Ram Mohan went on to describe how he resented having to flatter these people. Nishant eyed Deena with a look of surprise. He was expecting him to challenge what he had said about the importance of being a bureaucrat, which Baabuji, too, endorsed. Deena was silent. We all took note. He, too, had accepted that reality. He, who had always placed writers at the top on his list of the big guns of humanity.

Not that Deena hadn't been aware of the power government officials had over ordinary people who could be held to ransom by even a police constable on the beat or a petty clerk sitting in a rundown government office. He was aware. But thanks to the protection Ram Mohan provided his family against the depredations of the world outside, none of them had had to experience the tyranny of this nature.

Deena acquiesced that in terms of power and prestige, no other occupation worth its salt could come near that of a government bureaucrat. What made Deena agree was a big development at the District Cooperative Bank. The removal of Bachchu Pathak as chairman by the DM, an IAS officer. Pathak had allegedly been abusing his position, and the person given charge of the bank was one of the Additional DMs in Allahabad, who had previously served as Deputy Secretary at the Commission when Ram Mohan was a member.

That he knew Deena became known at the bank. Deena was always treated politely at work and that he was into Hindi literature and wrote poetry, was viewed with admiration. Yet the kind of indulgence he was shown now wouldn't have been possible earlier. The advent of this new administrator, the ADM, had imparted so much informal heft to Deena's otherwise lowly position, making him kind of VIP among his colleagues.

The first task that the new chief of the state-funded bank had taken up was to clean up the mess left by Bachchu Pathak, who had been on a recruitment spree that was rumoured to have made him much money. His point man on the scam, going by the gossip, was his eldest son. Some of these jobs had, no doubt, been given for free, but only to those who had influential patrons or relations.

After the ADM taking charge, word got out about a comprehensive list of the staff in the works, causing angst among those hired during the Bachchu Pathak regime. No wonder the existing workforce exceeded the required strength of this bank. Anon, the new boss, the ADM, was presented with this list that had a marker to separate the people recruited by Bachchu Pathak from the rest. Deena was among those facing the axe.

Ram Mohan had had no doubt that the ADM would find a way to save Deena. He was proven right. The ADM redrew the line on the list, saving not only Deena but eighteen more in the bargain. All those coming after him had got the boot.

What a luminous moment it was for Deena! Hailed as the saviour of those poor men's jobs, he couldn't help feeling a glow of gratitude to the ADM. It was the day he had bowed down to the power of bureaucrats, the power they enjoyed over peoples' destinies. No other talent could match this power.

No wonder Deena would become the keenest votary of the idea of Mayank and me taking the UPSC exam and that Mayank should have the right kind of atmosphere and space to study, which was not possible in the Main Building. Still, the chief impetus to accede to Baabuji's suggestion that they should dispose of the Main Building, was the menacing maw of economic hardship.

Seconding Nishant's take on the importance of being a bureaucrat, Ram Mohan said, 'We should repeat the ad.'

* * *

Their morale soared when a party made an offer of five lakh for the Main Building, one lakh more than the highest bid earlier. In no position to push the envelope, Ram Mohan brought the asking price down from seven lakh to six lakh thirty thousand, prepared to settle for six. Finally, they were left with one serious contender, an officer in the Indian Forest Service, represented by his uncle, who, just for the sake of it, insisted on paying a bit less than six lakh, though for a divisional forest officer money was no problem. Anxious to conclude the deal, Ram Mohan agreed to a sum of five lakh and ninety thousand.

Once the Main Building legally changed hands, they had one month to vacate. Deena was incredibly happy. Mayank and Kanti and he would live together in a rented house till they found a suitable place to buy, suitable to their pocket.

'Start looking for a decent place to rent. It shouldn't be left to the last moment,' said Ram Mohan.

* * *

They got a place well in time, and in a nearby and upscale locality, Sangam Colony. The landlord, a Sikh family, had a big house and supplemented their income by letting three small rooms at the back, with an approach passage along the boundary wall. Quite a neat affair. To make it rentable, they had built a small kitchen outside the third room, next to a small garden. The rent was eight hundred rupees a month.

That their father was former member, Public Service Commission and Deena a bank employee made Sardar-ji happy. He didn't bother to ask which bank. All the banks in general were well thought of. A bank as dreary and low-ranking as Deena's would escape the consciousness of people of means, people like their Sikh landlord, people that had nice houses in nice neighbourhoods.

In two days, they moved with their things into this new place. The room that opened into the passage leading to the front gate became their drawing room, and the one, the biggest of the three, with a built-in cupboard and attached bathroom, was taken by Deena and Mayank, while Kanti plumped for the room, which, apart from being closest to the kitchen, had a nice, secluded place for her Godrej steel almirah to which she was devoted.

* * *

Kanti had come back from Delhi to sign the papers of the sale of the Main Building. Also, she was no longer needed there. Nisha was going to quit her job. After a few months in the commercial division of Doordarshan, handling ads, scheduling, etc., she decided she had had enough. Unlike her colleagues, who wouldn't forget they were government employees, that they could get away with non-performance, unlike them, she had loads of work to do.

'Take it easy, Nisha. You don't need to work this hard. It won't pay. You'd end up the same way as the next person here.' This was the only other female employee in Nisha's department. She felt sorry for Nisha, whose sincerity would get her entrusted with more work. Some she had to bring home, where Shekhar helped her.

'It's harassment,' said her senior woman colleague one day. Nisha muttered she would complain to the head of the commercial division, about how she was being rewarded for her hard work. The woman told her about him, how till a few years ago, he would try to chat her up. 'I've caught him giving you the eye, but with all those files on your table, you don't have time to look up and see.'

'I'm not comfortable with things held over.'

'That's what I felt when I'd joined. Then the light dawned on me. I hope you realize the folly of being diligent before you get yourself in a hole, deeper and messier.'

Two days after this conversation, Nisha was asked to also manage a neighbouring desk for a week. The guy who manned it was going on leave. 'Am I being punished for slaving away at all the work piled on me?' Fighting back tears, she strode out and into the corridor, at the end of which was the room of their boss. She didn't knock, just entered. He was signing files placed one by one before him by his PA standing at his elbow.

Before the PA could admonish her for barging in, his boss stopped him with a gesture of his hand and clocked her distress. He motioned to one of the chairs arranged from across his big table.

'What's the matter?'

Nisha gave a plaintive sob.

He asked the PA to come back later. When Nisha finished, he said, donning a sympathetic look, 'I'm aware of your hard work and wanted to convey my appreciation.' That put her at ease. 'Somebody told me about your amazing diction and voice, and that your ambition is to become a Hindi newsreader or announcer.' Nisha nodded, dabbing her eyes.

'Director, News and Chief Producer of News, are my friends. I can put in a word.' He smiled and shuffled in his chair. Was silent for a bit, then bending over the table, began to drum his fingers on it. Nisha waited. When he raised his head and looked at her, she knew it, the look on his face, enigmatic, hard to describe but unmistakable. 'It'll take some time, but till then, I'll have something else assigned to you, something less demanding than what you're currently saddled with. By the way, I know what they look for in a prospective newsreader or announcer, and since I'm going to vouch that you deserve it, I must know first-hand how good your Hindi is and how good you're at the way it should be spoken on Doordarshan.'

Nisha kept her eyes on him, absorbing everything, every word, every change of expression in his face. 'We must keep this to ourselves,' he pressed on. 'You know how petty-minded people are here. A hint, a word about it, about the fact that I'm trying to help you, would lead to tasteless gossip.' He rose from his chair, walked around the table, and stood next to her. She tried to get up. He placed his hand on her shoulder, asking her to remain seated.

'I'll get you some old news scripts that you can read aloud like a newsreader. I'll be your audience.' By the time he proceeded to explain his plan to meet somewhere for the purpose, that he was struck by her striking features when he had first seen her, that it wouldn't be long before the world saw her on Doordarshan, she had stopped listening. Her face had a set look.

Though supportive of her decision to quit, Shekhar didn't want her to become a typical housewife. His chief concern, more than anything else, was some extra money coming home. They discussed and decided that she should pursue BEd through correspondence to qualify her for a teaching job in schools.

* * *

Ram Mohan's biography of Phule was in the press. Kanshi Ram's outfit was getting it published. Though still approving of the idea of a grand political coalition of non-upper castes, Ram Mohan was sceptical about its workability. Jaan Muhammad's logic seemed right. How could the OBCs let go of their position of power and privilege they enjoyed vis-à-vis Dalits? Ram Mohan was losing interest in Kanshi Ram's fledgling party, which demanded patience and time that he, at his age, did not have.

'It's better I devote myself to writing. Let's get my little dwelling in place first.' It was Nishant's suggestion that, using part of the money Baabuji had got from their mother's share of the Main Building, they should have a room built behind the Annexe.

This was all but decided, when Ram Mohan had a visit from an old acquaintance of his own caste, who requested something he couldn't decline. It presented Ram Mohan with an opportunity to make use of his talent for leadership—his powers of oratory, persuasion, initiative, taking on challenges and so forth—something he enjoyed and couldn't do without. The plan to build a room anytime soon was dropped.

This old acquaintance was Mr Singh, a big farmer, whose third son had served Deena with that heavenly night, a night of the ultimate coital bliss, the night with that Dalit girl, the memory of which still afforded Deena the best, the most pulsating moments of masturbation, even though he had been taken to Mirganj three times by the friend-cum-philosopher. It's not as if a 'good time' couldn't be had in this famous sex bazaar of the city. It could. But that would be expensive, beyond Deena's means, which he had learnt when the friend-cum-philosopher and he had wandered into one of those quarters upstairs that had a much better breed of women of pleasure or traditional courtesans, but in terms of manner, style and verbal charm, the fare on offer was said to be a shoddy version of that associated with their fabled forebears, to whose legacy this dwindling lot seemed a mere pretender. A show of song and dance they still put up, these nautch girls, in their quarters, and their presence at weddings and other celebratory events was still coveted, especially in the countryside, but their dancing and singing came over as an exercise more in sweat and labour than in talent and skill. That said, the promise of a dizzying experience of copulation was still there for those who could afford it. That's what Deena had learnt when a session of song and dance was thrust on the friend-cum-philosopher and him when they had wandered into one of those places in Mirganj.

The woman in charge had sent for their musician duo that played tabla and sarangi. The house had three girls who could dance and sing, and later, if the visitor wished, he could sleep with any one of them. No, only two of them were thus available. The third, a mistress of a relation of a famous mob boss of the city, was not. The one who danced for them that day was the youngest of the three, not more than sixteen, with a statuesque figure, delectably fetching, and the glances she kept shooting Deena weren't blatant but shy, soaked in the knowledge of what could follow. That brief session of song and dance had already cost Deena two hundred rupees. Making love to her would cost another five hundred, more than his one-month salary. Yet, if he had had that kind of money on him that evening, he wouldn't have wavered. 'I'll come later,' he said before leaving. When queried by the friend-cum-philosopher, his answer was, 'What else could I have said? Can people like us afford such pleasure?'

'Let's visit that alley then,' the FCP said, 'I'm so massively horny.' Twice they had been there, to the alley in question, one of several in that bazaar, all narrow and dingy, where crowding the doorways would be girls of varying ages, some incredibly young, their rates ranging from twenty-five to fifty rupees. Both the previous visits had been frustrating for Deena. First, hardly any privacy inside those holes, crammed into which were two charpoys screened from each other with thin, low-hanging curtains, making it impossible for the client in one charpoy to ignore the goings-on in the other. Second, the girl would be so distant, her manner so brusque and matter of fact, that one had to come to the point right away. No preliminaries. She wouldn't let you properly kiss, caress, or savour her nakedness. You were to get in and spit it out.

'I'm not in the mood,' said Deena and handed the FCP the requisite amount, while himself waiting outside the alley, thinking of the beautiful teen, the nautch girl, her abashed demeanour, her glances, determined to have her after being paid his yearly bonus.

Let me mention right here that Deena would succeed in fulfilling his desire, and was to later describe the experience in writing and in detail, from which I would quote just this much, leaving out the graphic parts: *It didn't seem like paid sex. She was so warm and friendly, behaved like a sweetheart, thoughtful of my passion, my hunger, enabling me to luxuriate in her achingly lovely assets, taking my own time. That's right. It wasn't a rush job. It became another benchmark for me, against which to measure the quality of other such trysts, though I would place it a touch below the one I had had with that Dalit girl, courtesy of the third son* (whose father Mr Singh is still waiting for me to let him put his proposal across to Ram Mohan. I would do that in a bit). *And that's because this being a single-orgasm affair had me craving for more, while the previous one was a whole-night jaunt leaving me suffused with an enchanting sense of accomplishment.*

* * *

It was the kind of challenge Ram Mohan was always game for. He said to Mr Singh, who had come with the request, 'What does Patel-ji think about my heading this outfit?'

A former Congress MP, Patel-ji was the man behind the concept of setting up something like that. In the run up to the last Lok Sabha poll, Indira Gandhi had addressed two rallies in his constituency. Forming part of her motorcade was also the Fiat carrying Tandon-ji, Nishant and Deena. It was there that the Fiat had conked out and Deena had had to stay the night in Mr Singh's village. What a godsent occasion it had been for him!

One of the few seats that the Congress had lost in that election was that of Patel-ji's. His losing that seat didn't mean losing Indira Gandhi's trust. He was about to be sent to the Rajya Sabha. Meanwhile, he had conceived the plan to establish this institution, Sardar Seva Sansthan—named after the biggest Kurmi icon— whose sole aim would be to serve the cause of their caste.

'It was Patel-ji who suggested your name,' said Mr Singh, answering Ram Mohan. 'He's a full-time politician and this Sansthan is no part-time thing. He's of the view that to head it we need someone well-educated and experienced, who has stature and personality to command the respect of people involved in the effort.'

'If Patel-ji thinks I can be of service, what choice do I have?'

'Thank you, Dr Sahab. As its chairman, you'll lend an aura of integrity and gravitas to the Sansthan.'

Mr Singh took Ram Mohan to see the site of the proposed Sansthan. Located on the periphery of the city, close to the new bridge over the Ganges, it was a large tract of land, fenced with barbed wire. Just inside the entrance stood a brick structure, consisting of three rooms and a kitchen, a bathroom, a toilet, all roofed with asbestos cement sheet. Ram Mohan took in the impressive expanse of the plot before following Mr Singh in, who ordered the man who, along with a guard, looked after the property, to make tea. 'This is our makeshift office.'

'I won't mind even living here.'

Mr Singh was startled, unaware how austere in his lifestyle Ram Mohan was. Just a glance at his personal corner in their previous houses and it would have been obvious he didn't care a hang about the aesthetic of his surroundings. A takht with books and a confusion of sheets of paper piled on one side, a writing board, a table, two bookcases and some chairs and a telephone, that's all his room would have.

'I wouldn't have thought you could ever wish to live in this place,' Mr Singh waved his arm at the asbestos ceiling, bare brick walls, iron doors and the mud floor.

Mr Singh then handed Ram Mohan the binder that held the documents related to the proposed Sardar Seva Sansthan. 'You'll find in it the entire plan and a provisional map of the complex.' He went on to narrate how Patel-ji had raised the money to pay for this land, which he got from the government on subsidized rates, and the complex to be developed on it would have a medical college, a youth hostel, a library, a guest house, a coaching centre to prepare Kurmi youngsters for various competitive exams and some sports facilities.

'Once you've gone through this,' said Mr Singh, pointing to the folder on Ram Mohan's lap, 'you'll know everything there's to know about the project. Patel-ji will soon call a meeting of those concerned to announce that you've kindly agreed to be its chairman.'

Ram Mohan had his things moved to the brick structure and went to live there after his return from a long-pending visit to Kanpur.

NINE

It's time to bring the reader up to speed on the goings-on in Deena's life, his intellectual growth, personal affairs and all. As for the best part of his day, it was still a matter of routine, his job in the bank, but yes, the change, a big change, was there in the way he viewed this job now. Unlike before, when he saw himself as a gainfully employed young man, who, in his spare time, could indulge his interest in Hindi literature, he had come to resent having to fill so many hours at work—entering sums and other particulars in ledgers and doing additions–subtractions—the hours he now had a yen to spend trying to get to grips with English.

He had been enjoying James Hadley Chase, and after stumbling across *The Naked Face* while grubbing about a pile of Nishant's discarded books, he got addicted to Sidney Sheldon's potboilers and would finish quite a few. He loved Sheldon's female protagonists who not only were intelligent, ambitious but also seductive. Then he chanced upon *Jaws* and *Godfather*.

'The past always seems better when you look back on it than it did at the time,' this line by Peter Benchley in *Jaws*, and 'Revenge is a dish that tastes best when it's cold,' from *Godfather*, Deena memorized and rendered them to impress his interlocutors, especially the second one. It was I who would tell him, years later, that Mario Puzo had rephrased the famous proverb, 'Revenge is a dish best served cold,' but as to its original author, nobody knew.

He also liked *The Fan Club* by Irving Wallace, mostly for its erotic content. For the same reason, he read Harold Robbins' *Goodbye, Janette*, recommended by one of his neighbours with whom Deena shared common prurient yearnings. He didn't find it engaging, *Goodbye, Janette*. He just dipped into it, reading only where it was sexually explicit, but these two bestsellers helped him get at the real thing. This bookstall in Civil Lines market, from where he rented volumes of popular fiction in English, had a supply of books dealing in erotica. The man running it had no inkling of Deena's interest. Only after he had rented these two novels—*The Fan Club* and *Goodbye, Janette*—did the stall-owner sense what the young man was after. He let him have a look at those anonymously written slim volumes kept on a hidden shelf.

No holding Deena back after that. He read them feverishly, one after another. I have known people in love with erotica, me included, but the way Deena devoured that literature, few could. He justified this crazed behaviour by asserting it wasn't a waste of time, because the best way to learn English was to read the writings to which one could stay glued.

Still, the mainstay of his reading habit remained English thrillers. On learning that the late Firaq Sahab recommended Sherlock Holmes to all those looking to improve their English, Deena bought *The Complete Sherlock Holmes* at Wheeler Book Shop in Civil Lines, which had a rich stock of books on a variety of subjects and was frequented by the city gentry. Many a title that could be found in this elegant bookstore couldn't be found anywhere else in the city. Deena and Mayank would end up buying quite a few books at this bookstore.

Coming back to Holmes, Deena was swept off his feet by this famous resident of 221B, Baker Street, in London. He wouldn't

stop till he had finished all the four novels and fifty-six short stories
the tome contained. Then he decided to cut down on thrillers, to
devote more time to some so-called serious texts in English, fictional
and non-fictional. He bought *Stories by Oscar Wilde* and *The Picture
of Dorian Gray*, Wilde's only novel, so rich in quotable lines.

As for non-fiction, he would pick this or that book of history or
philosophy that Mayank and I had—I was now renting lodging in
my former neighbourhood—because these had been our common
subjects in BA. For MA, I had preferred history and Mayank
philosophy. *The Wonder That Was India*, one of the books we had
filched from the university library, Deena liked to browse through;
in philosophy it was Will Durant's *The Story of Philosophy* bought
by Mayank at the start of his MA previous classes.

Mayank had Deena read its 'INTRODUCTION On the
Uses of Philosophy', which was singularly stirring, chiefly the first
paragraph which they read so many times it became impressed on
their memory. They declaimed it at will in front of anyone they
thought worthy. A more poignant portrayal of the sad conflict
between the life of the mind—the kind we had in mind—and the
world out there, was hard to imagine.

Later, much later, Deena would come to regard as truer what
Cicero thought of philosophy, mentioned in the next paragraph of
the same Introduction—'There is nothing so absurd but that it may
be found in the books of the philosophers,'—truer than the picture
Durant was trying to paint of the subject, though he concedes
that Cicero mightn't be entirely off the mark, for after quoting his
brutal observation, Durant admits, 'Doubtless some philosophers
have had all sorts of wisdom except common sense; and many a
philosophic flight has been due to the elevating power of thin air.'
After that, Durant returns to what appears to be the chief aim of his
introduction: the glorification of philosophy.

Like many in those days, Deena, Mayank and I had developed
a fascination for Marxian gospel, due partially because India, under

the Congress, had long been allied to the Soviet Union, and the propaganda indulged in by various outfits and individuals— journalists, academics—had led many to think highly of the life in the Soviet Union.

After reading the *Communist Manifesto*, we had become convinced of the great emancipatory power of Marxist socialism. Unlike Mayank and me, Deena's romance with Communism wouldn't last, as he, after Mayank and I had moved to Delhi, would be made wiser by a chat with Mahavir Wilson, who had gone to attend a seminar at Allahabad University. The said chat had occurred at Sardar Seva Sansthan, where Wilson had spent some time with Ram Mohan. He told Deena about the kind of life people in the communist bloc were forced to lead.

'Communism has its charm, but only in theory, only if you're living in a liberal democracy,' he had said. Referring to his interactions with some Russian exiles in London, he contended that given a choice, the majority in the communist bloc would flee to North America, England, Western Europe. What exploded Deena's now-much-diminished love for Marxism was a brief discourse by Jaan Muhammad, who visited the Sansthan at least twice a week. On learning that Bertrand Russell was Deena's most favourite non-fiction author, he recommended his autobiography. 'It's a big book and before beginning from the beginning, you should read the chapter about his visit to Russia. What a stimulating read this autobiography is, like most of his other work that lies outside the domain of technical and mathematical philosophy. No, before going to the said chapter, you read the prologue, barely a page long, but it sums up the man for you in as succinct a manner as can be imagined.'

The next day, Deena visited Wheeler Book Shop. I strung along sometimes, mostly for the pleasure of being amidst neatly arranged books in bookcases and to soak up the elegant ambience of the place. Deena remembered to have seen it, the *Autobiography*, on the shelf dedicated to Russell, but hadn't procured it. Nothing could stop him now.

Deena was struck by the beauty and pathos of the very first paragraph of the prologue: *Three passions, simple but overwhelmingly strong, have governed my life: the longing for love, the search for knowledge and unbearable pity for the suffering of mankind. These passions, like great winds, have blown me hither and thither, in a wayward course, over a deep ocean of anguish, reaching to the very verge of despair.*

After the prologue, Deena went straight to the chapter titled 'Russia' and read about the great mind's experience. How was he disenchanted with Communism when he saw it in action, he who had gone there as someone passionate about socialist ideology? He writes: *The time I spent in Russia was one of continually increasing nightmare. I have said in print what, on reflection, appeared to me to be the truth, but I have not expressed the sense of utter horror which overwhelmed me while I was there. Cruelty, poverty, suspicion, persecution, formed the very air we breathed.*

Cured of his love of communism, Deena felt a sense of calm rather than emptiness as he embarked upon reading *The Autobiography of Bertrand Russell*.

* * *

Rajvansh, Deena's favourite cousin, a great devourer of Hindi pulp fiction—who wouldn't show up if Ram Mohan was in town—landed in Allahabad, when he learnt of the latter taking up residence at Sardar Seva Sansthan. Most of his time, during the day, would be spent with Kanti, his *bua*, and Deena and Mayank—Deena had taken three days off to enjoy his company—and in the evening, they all went to the Annexe to be with Nishant and his wife, who was pregnant.

No point in bringing up Rajvansh's visit if not for Deena's sudden madness about a girl. Rajvansh was friends with her family. She, along with her two brothers, was studying in Allahabad. Their mother was with them. They had recently moved here from their village. The father, a farmer, wanted his offspring educated, though the eldest son, now married, had dropped out of school and was helping with the family's agricultural land. His wife managed the village-home while their mother took care of their three younger children in the city. A close relation of theirs also lived in Allahabad.

When Rajvansh told him about her family and asked him along, Deena agreed. Rajvansh's wife was related to the family, but that wasn't the reason for his closeness to them. It was the father's nature, affable and warm, that had made Rajvansh take to him, to the whole family. They, the daughter, her two brothers and their mother, rented a place in a humble locality. The one where Ram Mohan had met Kanshi Ram, at the house of a Patel. That association lasted till the publication of his book on Phule and then he would lose patience with the Dalit leader's long-term political goal.

Deena couldn't take his eyes off Rashmi—that was her name—when she came to serve water. Rajvansh cast an eloquent glance at her mother, who smiled, then he looked at Deena, who sat beside him and was perturbed by what he saw. Rashmi's mother, too, looked puzzled. It was hard to miss, the look on Deena's face, despondent and woebegone. They had tea and the mother wanted them to stay on for dinner. 'We'll come again, some other day.' She didn't press.

On getting back, Rajvansh and Deena went to the drawing room to talk. Kanti was in the kitchen while Mayank was out visiting a friend. Hardly did they sit down across the centre table in the drawing room when Deena blurted, 'I want to marry her.'

'You want to marry Rashmi!' said Rajvansh, without hum and haw. Deena nodded. Rajvansh fell quiet, letting it sink in. Did Deena know what he was saying? Rajvansh knew he could swing it. Few, if any, in their caste, would turn down a marriage offer from Ram Mohan's family, few of the socially better off, let alone Rashmi's family that was from among those of relatively meek stock.

'Think it over and tell me if you're serious,' Rajvansh said. 'Once I get into it you can't have second thoughts! Unless you want my friendship with her family ruined,' said Rajvansh and asked Deena to speak to his Baabuji.

'I know my Baabuji . . . He'll have no problem. You talk to her father, then I'll talk to Baabuji.'

'Her father will agree, and then your Baabuji will have to speak to him.'

'He'll love to meet him.'

Mayank thought Deena was behaving like a child, who, on seeing a toy, refuses to budge. 'It's too early for him to be married,' he said to me. 'This girl Rashmi, I haven't seen her, but Deena's gone off his trolley.'

'He's been in a situation like this before, but he was still a boy then. Our romantic impulses during this mad phase are so intense we don't bother about the demands of the world. Now that he has this job he technically fulfils the criterion for marriage—'

'He knows he might not get a beautiful wife without the active presence of Baabuji in his life, a presence that makes up for what he lacks. It makes up for the lowly stature of his job, and Baabuji is getting old. His name has begun to lose its traction, its shine!'

Yet Mayank and I thought Deena was being impetuous. We wished he would deliberate whether he should rush into it. It was odd, to imagine him to be married so soon. It was odd to think of him as somebody's husband. But his passion for this girl was all but obvious, and Mayank didn't have the heart to be a wet blanket!

* * *

Certain that Rajvansh was being waggish, Rashmi's father made light of it. When told the matter was serious, he said, 'What an honour it'll be . . .!'

Without going into all the nitty-gritty, I would just say it all worked out well, just the way Deena had thought. Ram Mohan was elated and on his next visit to Parsadpur/Ballamgaon, he met the father who was left speechless by the former's warmth.

Deena wanted the wedding to take place as soon as possible and was opposed to waiting another year and a half for her to finish school. He wanted Rashmi to learn English and was dead serious about it. His logic, which made sense to Mayank also, was why lose such crucial time when she could take the twelfth board after marriage, as a private student? Always one for speeding up things, Ram Mohan agreed. No scope for Rashmi's father to demur.

Within two months, a busload of Deena's marriage party arrived in Rashmi's village and the following evening they returned to Allahabad. Everything went as planned.

* * *

Barely had Rashmi settled down in her new home when Deena embarked on explaining the importance of English. She looked no less eager. That made Deena's job easier, almost half as easier. He knew that learning English would become doubly challenging if she wasn't sufficiently motivated. She was spurred on by what her younger brother had said. 'We'll soon have someone in our family who knows English.' It was thanks to Rajvansh, who had been talking about how Deena had taught himself the language, about his Herculean effort, embellishing the story to make it something out of this world.

Deena got English textbooks for her from grade one to five. 'This is the best way to learn basic vocabulary and grammar, in a gradual, steady manner, without feeling daunted. You will progress through them faster than small children.' She surpassed his expectations. He couldn't have asked for more. Kanti, too, contributed to the effort by helping her to read and understand those books.

In a year, Rashmi began reading The *Northern India Patrika*. Oxford Advanced Learner's Dictionary had become her best friend. Soon she could enjoy Ruskin Bond's stories for children. Mayank had Rashmi read something to him regularly to help her with pronunciation.

It was a phase when they were a happy family. Quarrels were rare in their house. Their love for each other was for keeps. At least, it looked that way at the time. Ram Mohan wanted them not to delay buying a house. 'In rented quarters, you don't feel at home after a while. That you'll have to move out one day assaults your sense of security off and on!'

They began scouring the papers. The properties they liked were beyond their means, and those within were either too small or their location violated their taste. One day, Vinod, their businessman friend, took them to see a flat in a residential colony that suited their pocket as well as their taste, somewhat. It was tiny. But anything better and bigger was beyond them. Kanti liked it, as a kilometre further away was the Ganges.

Ram Mohan frowned at its size but knew it was the best they could do. 'In a year, its price will go up,' said Vinod. Everybody agreed. But two days later, Ram Mohan arrived and asked everybody into the drawing room. 'Call it off. No need to buy a house here. In a little over a year, we're going to move to Delhi,' he paused 'You know who dropped me off here just now . . . ! Saansad-ji's son.'

They all, all but Rashmi, knew it was to do something with politics. That it was. Within hours of his arrival in the city, Saansad-ji had sent for Ram Mohan and some other loyalists, and after talking about how people were getting disillusioned with Indira Gandhi, the way she had mishandled the Punjab situation, ordering the army to storm the holiest worshipping place in Sikhism to eliminate Bhindranwale who had made the Golden Temple complex his base. After talking about Operation Blue Star, the way it was fucked up, along with some other issues, Saansad-ji said, 'When the next general election is held, she'll have lost much of public goodwill, and the opposition can drastically improve on its tally in Parliament.'

Somebody said Operation Blue Star might in fact help consolidate her image as a strong leader. Some others murmured their agreement.

'Yes, that could be the case if elections were due soon. They're over a year off and by then the truth of the supposed success of Operation Blue Star will have come out. Few in the country, at this point, know how inefficiently the thing was conducted. Slapdash approach, out and out, hundreds of unnecessary deaths. I'm not counting militants who were meant to be killed. I'm talking about massive loss of life on the army side and deaths of civilians caught in the crossfire. That could have been avoided if she hadn't failed to provide the army with intelligence on the real strength of the militants in the temple complex, their numbers and the kind of weaponry they had. None of you have any idea about what happened during that operation. How much bloodier and more ruinous did it turn out than it should otherwise have. The military was forced to use tanks. Can you imagine? To break through the resistance the militants had mounted. That led to the razing of the Akal Takht Sahib, the holiest Sikh Gurudwara. This I learnt from one of the two or three intrepid young journalists who had managed to hide in the vicinity of the military action while the city of Amritsar was shut off from the world, the whole of Punjab, during the operation . . . When elections are here, we'll tell people. Will spotlight how the Indira regime had first brought creatures like Bhindranwale into being and when things got out of hand, she had so many of our soldiers butchered to destroy her own creation. This will resonate with the public.'

Saansad-ji then disclosed the chief purpose of that meeting. Baran Singh and he had decided to fight the next general election together. A masterstroke. Those to be fielded as his candidates, Saansad-ji met individually. 'We're still a few months from seat-sharing talks,' said Saansad-ji to Ram Mohan, 'but I've got Chaudhary Sahab to agree to your candidacy from Fatehpur. If you add fifty per cent of Muslims to your core support base, plus the fact that Congress is fast losing its support among Dalits to Kanshi Ram, it all amounts to a sure victory.'

* * *

'There's no need to buy any property here,' said Ram Mohan. 'It's a matter of thirteen–fourteen months. You can stay on in this place before we move to Delhi, into the flat allotted to me as MP. Then you can buy something there, in areas not yet expensive. And I'll have enough resources to get Deena a good job in Delhi.'

They gazed at him in wonderment. Ram Mohan spoke up again, addressing Rashmi this time, 'You must pass the twelfth board with a second division so you can do your BA from one of the colleges in Delhi.' She was all smiles. Deena said, 'We must let Vinod know. He'll have to intimate the owner . . . It's not too late. He would have just closed his shop.'

Vinod was still at his shop, calculating the day's take. Their sudden appearance took him by surprise. Deena told him of the development. Ram Mohan expressed regret that Vinod was caused unnecessary trouble. 'It's fine, Uncle. I'll tell the owner. Though I must tell you that if you buy this house now, it'll get you a few thousand more in a year's time.'

But Ram Mohan was against going through all the fuss and bother of buying and selling for a few thousand more.

* * *

A few months later, the shocker came. Indira Gandhi was shot dead. No, first the news came not of her death but of the attempt made on her life. The enormity of the affair brought things to a standstill. The whole city became abuzz with what if she was dead. Who could be behind it? It might be the CIA. Or was it an inside job? Speculations were running riot.

Things came to a halt at Deena's bank. He left early. Riding his Vijay Super through the roads, he could feel a certain awkwardness in the air. As he turned off the main road and into Sangam Colony, there were people, huddles of them, talking quietly. Mayank, Kanti and Rashmi were with their Sikh landlord and his wife in their paved front yard. Deena joined them. Sardar-ji was saying if she was dead, they wouldn't make it public till the question of her successor was settled.

It might just be the case of superficial injuries, said Mayank. Sardar-ji doubted that. 'If that were the case, they would have said so . . . The attempt was serious. She's seriously wounded if not already dead.'

'Whose handiwork could it be?' said Deena. 'A lone wolf, some mentally deranged person?' Sardar-ji shook his head. 'I won't be surprised if they were Sikh militants from Punjab.' Gesturing to the framed picture of Harmandir Sahib above their door in the porch, he said, 'She got army tanks to shell the holiest Sikh place,' Sardar-ji's eyes had moistened. His wife, too, dabbed her eyes.

Just then, there was a commotion out front. Deena flew to the gate. She was dead. Somebody had heard on the BBC. The assassins were her own security guards, probably Sikh, 'acting in retaliation for the storming of the Sikh holy shrine of the Golden Temple.' The AIR would broadcast the news hours later. They decided to go to Nishant's, Deena and Mayank on the scooter, Kanti and Rashmi in a rickshaw. Tension and a sense of foreboding could be felt all over.

In their former neighbourhood, like in Sangam Colony, groups of people were chatting. Nishant was part of a group outside his gate. He disentangled himself and they all went inside. Prakash, the student leader who had gone with Nishant to meet the homeopath who had killed his wife, arrived too. Kanti and Rashmi were upstairs while they all sat in Nishant's home-office on the ground floor. None of them had a clue to what it meant for the country and the Congress, this sudden departure of Indira Gandhi. What did it mean for the opposition parties? 'Let's go to the Sansthan,' Deena said.

All India Sardar Seva Sansthan had made no headway with its professed aims, despite Ram Mohan's effort to set things in motion. He tried to raise the issue with Patel-ji and Singh Sahab, but they were too preoccupied with their own political goals.

What Ram Mohan liked about the Sansthan, was that it drew people from everywhere and from across political parties. He loved this plurality and enjoyed their leg-pulling and making jokes about each other's politics. Now that he was going to be fielded from Fatehpur by the Baran Singh–Saansad-ji alliance, he had gone to the side of those from the farmer leader's party, lending zest to the discussions at the Sansthan. But the assassination had pushed the opposition into an area of insignificance. Its list of complaints and allegations against Indira Gandhi was blown to smithereens.

When Nishant and the party reached the Sansthan, all those assembled were struggling to come to grips with the out-of-nowhere emergence of this giant monster, the monster of Indira Gandhi's vanishment. What impact it would have on politics and on the future of the Congress! Many murmured their dread of the opposition's annihilation in the next polls.

'More than for any other party, it's a rude awakening for the Congress,' said Nishant. 'It's the Congress that's become headless in a matter of seconds, with no one, not a single leader in sight, who looks good to take her place, nobody to match the stature of the likes of Baran Singh, Saansad-ji and other opposition leaders.'

'Rajiv Gandhi might ascend the throne,' said a man loyal to
Patel-ji. 'That's why he was brought into politics. She was left with
no option after Sanjay's death, no option because the Congress is a
family-owned enterprise.'

'Is he up to it?' asked Ram Mohan. 'He's still in the process
of being primed. Even after the next election, it had to be Indira
Gandhi. Rajiv might have been made a minister. So far he's been
involved in the party organization. He's still callow and would take
time to attain the stature of Prime Minister.'

'Now leaders like Baran Singh and Saansad-ji would grow in
importance,' said Prakash.

'I agree,' Nishant said. Others also liked the logic. Ram Mohan
grinned and said, 'Let's first see who they pick to be PM for the
remaining months before the elections.'

Deena and Mayank relished the argument advanced by Nishant,
Baabuji and Prakash. They returned home gaily. The picture of
their Delhi dream that had looked smudged after the news of the
killing, was sparklingly restored.

* * *

The talk that some senior minister would be asked to serve
as stopgap PM till the time the heir to the throne was ready,
emotionally and otherwise, was laid to rest that very day. The logic
of Rajiv Gandhi's novitiate didn't work. Giving someone else the
top job even for the time being was too much of a risk and had
to be avoided at all events by those whose only source of power
was their closeness to the family. They had Rajiv take the oath of
office in a hurriedly held swearing-in ceremony so that he could
receive heads of state coming to attend the obsequies, not only as
the grieving son but also as the prime minister of the country.

Just as the new PM settled to discussing the arrangements for
the presence of so many world leaders, those in his close political

circle got down to the business of settling a score with the Sikh community. Several Congress leaders were deputed to inflame anti-Sikh passions and organize murderous mobs for the destruction of Sikhs and their properties. A renowned public figure, in full public glare, as shown on Doordarshan, gave a call for revenge, raising his arm, 'blood for blood' being his exact words.

Blood for blood it would be. Given Indira Gandhi's stature, nothing short of butchering thousands of Sikhs could supply the amount of blood needed to square with the worth of hers. The first such killing in Delhi took place the following morning—the morning after the killing and the son becoming PM—which, in no time, became a tidal wave of butchery with the active hand of Congress leaders like H.K.L. Bhagat, Dharam Dass Shastri, Sajjan Kumar, Kamal Nath, Jagdish Tytler and others, who not only mobilized bloodthirsty mobs and furnished them with weapons but also led them from the front.

The scene in poor Sikh localities in the capital was inenarrable. The scale and intensity of barbarity was second only to Hindu–Muslim riots during Partition. But then this was no riot. It was a pogrom. A well-organized one and with the nod from powers that be, because when some influential Sikhs contacted the home minister and the country's president, himself a Sikh, imploring to intervene, to do something, they learnt that the president and the home minister were helpless.

Whatever was happening was happening at the behest of people close to the PM, the son of the slain one. The absurdity of these pleadings was obvious from the fact that all senior and junior police officials were collaborating in the carnage. That explained why no one else, neither a single non-Sikh nor a single policeman, was killed or even injured during the mayhem of this proportion, a first in India, in a country otherwise known for its periodic bloodletting between Hindus and Muslims.

Among many harrowing scenes during the massacre in Delhi and elsewhere was the one of which a graphic account would be given to us years later, to Deena and me in Delhi, by someone who had seen it with his own eyes. It had occurred in one of the Sikh neighbourhoods of Delhi when a mob brandishing blood-drenched weapons, led by local Congress leaders, closed in on a terrified teenaged Sikh boy who had taken shelter behind his widowed mother who, with her palms joined, kept begging for mercy, and on seeing some policemen at a distance, she beseeched them, in a voice hoarse, pathetic and desperate, to rescue her son, to which they responded by asking the onrushing mob to hurry up and finish the job. A moment later, the Sikh youth was yanked from his mother's arms and in the merest fraction of a second, one of his arms was lying on the ground, his mother screeching hysterically. 'Beyond that,' said our raconteur, 'I just couldn't see and ran away with my entrails in turmoil.'

It was but a small instance of the uninhibited brutality that, in the aftermath of the assassination, reigned over Delhi and other parts in northern India, says Deena's note. *In Allahabad, no massacre could occur because of timely deployment of the army at localities that had Sikh residents. Sangam Colony was one of them. It had two army trucks stationed on the main road. Though no mob would dare go anywhere near the army's presence, Sikhs in our locality remained wary of anybody in their families leaving home. So was the case with our landlord.*

Deena and Mayank would get them their daily provisions from the local shops for about a week. Thwarted in their bloodlust, the city Congress leaders and workers railed at the situation. It's not that they couldn't do anything. They did get all Sikh shops and outlets set ablaze across the city. The workshop at which Deena was used to having his scooter serviced was also torched along with a few others in the vicinity. They all, located on the road behind the Civil Lines market, had Sikh proprietors.

In Kanpur the situation was conducive to the design of those
thirsting for the blood of Sikhs. Many met a brutal death there.
Rashmi's elder brother, who visited Allahabad a fortnight later,
told them about the barbarity that had gripped that city and its
outskirts. A few Sikh truck drivers were burnt alive or beaten to
death along the Grand Trunk Road on their way to, or coming
from, Calcutta. Several such brutalities had taken place near their
village less than a furlong from this highway.

After all this, Deena's hatred for the Congress would deepen
and deepen further after Rajiv Gandhi, the PM, would rationalize
the holocaust: 'When a big tree falls, the earth shakes.' *That wasn't
enough*, wrote Deena. *To rub it in, all those behind this shaking of the
earth would be rewarded variously. One of its chief protagonists, Bhagat,
would be made cabinet minister.*

* * *

Hardly a month into being PM, Rajiv Gandhi decided to hold
India's eighth general election, a little earlier than scheduled, to
take advantage of his mother's 'martyrdom' still fresh in public
memory. Saansad-ji was in Delhi, holding regular talks with
Baran Singh, about issues relating to their alliance. The day after
the Lok Sabha was dissolved, Ram Mohan went to see Saansad-
ji's wife.

Just the start of winter, but it was cold that day, cold for the
hour. It was almost noon. 'The sun's so torpid,' muttered Ram
Mohan as Nishant and he neared the clutch of people gathered on
the front lawn of Saansad-ji's house, talking nonstop, some louder
than others. 'They're feeling the heat of the coming campaign,'
said Ram Mohan, just as they joined in with them.

Could people be so dumb as to gift Rajiv Gandhi a victory
just because his mother was killed, shutting their eyes to her
bad administration, to the fact that her son had no experience in

anything other than flying aircraft? That was the chief topic of the conversation.

'That he, of all the professions, chose to become a pilot says a lot about the man, about his upbringing, about his narrow outlook on life,' said one, and then adding, 'his Italian wife, I hear, is barely educated!'

'She's illiterate,' barked someone else. Adding grist to the mill of the prevailing mood, Ram Mohan said, 'One thing that never ceases to confound me is that how Indira Gandhi and both her sons focused on only one aspect of Nehru-ji's legacy, that of political power, and how to retain it at any cost. They've had nothing to do with his other aspects, the aspects that were more estimable. Nehru and his father were well-educated, and well-read. And look at their descendants!'

All nodded. One of them called attention to the fact that Maneka Gandhi, on the other hand, was a book lover. 'She was just twenty-three when Sanjay died, and she's very compassionate, somebody close to the family told me once.' Before the discussion could be taken further along those lines, emerged on the front veranda Saansad-ji's wife.

All went trotting towards her. She talked about how important these polls were for their party. They should make ready for a gruelling campaign. In alliance with Baran Singh, they stood a good chance of winning many parliamentary seats. She ended by informing them of Saansad-ji's arrival four days later, when he would meet them all. Just as they began to disperse, she drew Ram Mohan aside, 'You should gird for the battle in Fatehpur.'

He intimated to Patel-ji and Singh Sahab his decision to stand for Parliament from Fatehpur, offering to quit his position at the Sansthan. 'No, Doctor Sahab, your association with the project accords it certain prestige,' said Patel-ji. 'You don't have to be present in person all the time. Your name's enough.' About the opposition's chances in the coming election, Patel-ji and Singh

Sahab aired serious doubt. It wasn't a bad idea if Ram Mohan could revisit his decision. 'Indira Gandhi's murder has altered the electoral scenario. The Congress is going to win by a landslide,' said Singh Sahab, to which Patel-ji added, 'All the more so because it's her own son that people would be voting for. We all know how mawkish the public can be at times.'

Ram Mohan dismissed the prognosis. What else could one expect from a Congress loyalist like Patel-ji!

* * *

Prior to Saansad-ji's visit to Allahabad, Ram Mohan made a trip to Parsadpur/Ballamgaon. A Jeep for the purpose was provided by an admirer who was a regular visitor to the Sansthan and a votary of its objective of helping Kurmi youths compete with their upper caste counterparts in various fields. In his early forties, he was a Junior Engineer in the Public Works Department and, till a year ago, his personal mode of transport was a bicycle; now he owned two motor vehicles, including the Jeep he lent to Ram Mohan for his travels. He was about to move house too. Goodbye to the small dingy thing that had long been his family's abode.

Earlier, he had tried to stick by the vow he had made, while still a high-minded youth, that he wouldn't stoop so low as to be on the take. People like him in his office or in any government department were few. It was Ram Mohan who had disabused him of this folly. Referring to the ways of K. Dwivedi, whom he had, while at the Commission, given a solid job in the labour department, Ram Mohan said that the Junior Engineer didn't have to become as unscrupulous as Dwivedi. He didn't have to loot people. He could be moderate in his pursuit of riches and take whatever bribes he was offered without making demands, a suggestion once advanced by Argali to help Ram Mohan temper his rigid stance on the matter with an entrenched reality.

Ram Mohan hadn't followed the advice himself. But he no longer considered bribe-taking an abomination if one wouldn't become predatory. The Junior Engineer didn't tire of telling others about how Dr Sahab had opened his eyes as to how one could make some money on the side through ways available to government servants, and remain a good person. Not surprising that the Junior Engineer would be one of the chief contributors to Ram Mohan's election fund.

In Parsadpur/Ballamgaon, many were willing to move to Fatehpur to help with the logistics of running Ram Mohan's campaign. Gulab Singh wanted to visit Fatehpur during the election, but his sons put their foot down. Being friends with some Congress leaders in the state, they couldn't let their father champion an opposition candidate. When Gulab Singh said how could they then be friends with Komal Singh Yadav, who too was in the opposition, the elder son said, 'That's because Komal Singh is a real scumbag and pragmatic to the core. He knows that even his friends and well-wishers need to pay court to the people in power, and it's the Congress that's in power.'

Ram Mohan said to Gulab Singh, 'Why displease your friends in the ruling party when doing so wouldn't even help me?'

'But I'll bear the cost of the hire of at least three Jeeps all through the campaign,' Gulab Singh shot a glance at his sons and added, 'We haven't yet fully recovered, but this much I can do for my friend.'

On the way back, Ram Mohan made a detour to see Tiwari-ji, who seldom stirred out of his village now. The next afternoon, they were in Allahabad, the day before Saansad-ji was due in the city. He called Saansad-ji's wife, who asked him to drop in any time after lunch. Saansad-ji would be at home the entire day, meeting his party men.

'It's the real thing this time,' said Tiwari-ji. They were all gathered at the Annexe. 'The Saansad-ji–Baran Singh alliance would get us the support of all backward castes and many Muslims.'

'With the Congress ceding much of its Dalit vote to Kanshi Ram,' said Ram Mohan, 'we stand a good chance of making it to Parliament.'

The next day, Ram Mohan, Tiwari-ji and Nishant went to Saansad-ji's place and were there for over two hours. Those certain to be fielded by the Alliance, Saansad-ji was meeting first. That's what his wife told them. Once done with that, Saansad-ji took them into a separate room away from the noise and press of people in his drawing room. 'Your name for Fatehpur is almost final. It's just that Chaudhary Sahab thinks it shouldn't be made public till we know about the Congress candidate.'

'Dr Sahab's ticket is subject to whom Congress fields from Fatehpur!' said Tiwari-ji.

'What do you think? I'll just say yes if he wants to pick someone else. He knows how keen I'm on Ram Mohan as the alliance candidate from his old constituency.'

Nishant was dismayed. As they came out of Saansad-ji's house and got into the Jeep, Ram Mohan said, 'If I were Saansad-ji, I too would avoid forcing the issue at this moment. To show a little deference to the opinion of the more powerful Alliance partner would help Saansad-ji to fight in my corner later, if things come to such a pass.' The logic palliated Nishant's fear.

Saansad-ji went back to Delhi, and Ram Mohan, his mind fixed on joining the electoral fray, phoned his wife who told him his ticket was all but confirmed. 'We can't just sit around and wait for a green signal,' said Tiwari-ji. 'We must launch into building up to the polling day.' The next day, Ram Mohan and Tiwari-ji left in the Junior Engineer's Jeep for Fatehpur to meet friends and sympathizers there. They must also find a suitable place for their election office.

Nishant and Deena would hang on to the idea of Baabuji's victory. It could transform their lives. Nishant's law practice was still in dire straits. He could use Baabuji's help to become a government advocate. Deena was dreaming of a job in Delhi. Maybe in one of the public sector companies. They knew of a good-for-nothing guy in Allahabad, whose uncle, a bigtime journalist in Delhi, had got him a good position in Coal India, a big state-owned company.

* * *

In Fatehpur, an old supporter of Ram Mohan got him a place for his election office near the highway passing through the town. They met as many people as they could and stayed the night at Dr Om Sharma's house, Tiwari-ji's old doctor. The next day, they travelled to a couple of villages not far from the city to meet some acquaintances from olden times, most of whom were happy that, after a gap of thirteen years, Ram Mohan was going to contest again. Only two spoke their mind. 'If Indira-ji hadn't been killed,' said the more vocal one, 'you would have good prospects of winning. But now with this raging public sympathy for her son, a non-Congress person would only have an outside chance, if at all.' Ram Mohan shrugged it off.

'Some people can't do without some negativity in life,' said he later.

They returned to Allahabad only to move to Fatehpur the following day. Nishant was to keep in touch with Saansad-ji's wife. Any news from Delhi and he had to rush to Fatehpur. Saansad-ji's house wasn't far from the High Court, and every day at lunch break, Nishant rode his Vijay Super there. It was four days later that the unthinkable raised its head.

Saansad-ji's wife had gone to Delhi. 'Papa called,' said their younger son. 'Liyaqat Argali is the Congress candidate from Fatehpur. He's a cabinet minister in UP. Dr Sahab knows him.' A sense of despair and disbelief washed over Nishant as the younger son soldiered on with the terrible news, 'According to Baran Singh, a Muslim candidate from Congress will nullify the goodwill my

father and he enjoy among Muslims. Now they've no choice but
to put up a Muslim candidate of their own. It's not that papa didn't
fight, but the strength of Chaudhary Sahab's logic is obvious. They
want Dr Sahab to align himself with their campaign in Fatehpur.
His sacrifice will be rewarded later. Papa also hinted at the Rajya
Sabha. He'll speak to Dr Sahab.'

Nishant went back to the court to collect his files and rode
to Deena's office. That's what they had feared, when Saansad-ji
had said they were waiting for the Congress to announce their
candidate. He asked Deena to send their mother to the Annexe.
He didn't want his wife and daughter alone during the night.

Four hours later, Nishant stood in front of their father's election
office in Fatehpur. It had got dark. The clamour emanating from
the dimly lit interior got louder as he stepped close to an open
window. Baabuji, Tiwari-ji and others were sitting cross-legged
on the floor covered with cotton mattresses and sheets. A lively
discussion was on. Nishant got hold of a boy from a nearby tea stall
and sent him in, after pointing Tiwari-ji out through the window.
He walked down the road and planted himself at a little remove
from the entrance and called out when Tiwari-ji emerged from
the office.

He recounted his meeting with the younger son and was
surprised that Tiwari-ji wasn't shocked. That's what he had been
dreading all along, he said. 'We should break it to Dr Sahab.' They
went in. Ram Mohan welcomed Nishant and introduced him to
the gathering. Then a glance at Tiwari-ji and he became sombre.
He got up. 'I'm going to the bathroom.'

On the way to the bathroom, there was a storage space at the
back. Ram Mohan said, 'This is a good place to keep our campaign
material.'

'It has a door too, so things can be put under lock and key,'
said Tiwari-ji, just for the sake of saying something before dropping
the hammer. Known for his sangfroid even in the teeth of the

most trying moments, Ram Mohan took a minute to reflect on the news, then asked what they should do.

Nishant said, 'They'd recompense for our sacrifice. Rajya Sabha or something else.' Ram Mohan looked at Tiwari-ji, who said he would like to hear how his friend viewed it.

'When they withheld their decision on Fatehpur, I knew something was amiss. I knew my candidacy was contingent upon Congress not fielding a Muslim . . . I might still consider running as an independent—' Some footsteps. They moved into the courtyard out back. It was dark and cold. Nishant said, 'To defeat both the Congress and the Alliance in Fatehpur is a tall order.'

Tiwari-ji said, 'They might send you to the Rajya Sabha—'

'If there was fifty percent chance of it being true, I wouldn't think twice about not taking the plunge. If Saansad-ji had autonomy to decide about how I was to be accommodated, I'd fall in with his wish without a moment's thought . . . He himself is dependent on Baran Singh's support base of backward castes. Yes, Saansad-ji is popular among Muslims. So is Chaudhary Sahab, and so long as Saansad-ji needs him, the big brother of the alliance, I can't be sure of anything . . . Given their pitiable presence in state assemblies, only a minuscule number they could send to the Rajya Sabha. If the non-Congress parties formed a coalition government, they could nominate some to the Rajya Sabha, but vying for these nominations would be so many others in the coalition.'

'You're thinking of standing as an independent? How will that help if we don't win? We'll be left counting the cost of the loss,' said Nishant.

'That's not correct,' said Tiwari-ji. 'We won't fight just to lose. There's fifty percent chance of our pulling it off . . . We'd tell Kurmi voters about this act of perfidy by the Alliance, the way Dr Sahab was denied the ticket.'

'If we get the support of Kurmis and of some others, we do stand a chance,' said Ram Mohan, 'not only because we possess one major vote bank but also because the Muslim vote will be divided between the Congress and the Alliance. A considerable number of upper caste votes will go to the BJP while ninety percent of Dalits will be allied with Kanshi Ram. With this loss of its traditional vote, the Congress will be left wobbling, and the Kurmis supporting me will leave the Alliance in the lurch. I'll be a major beneficiary of this changed equation.'

'What if we lose?' asked Nishant.

'If we lose, I'll have got enough votes to affect the outcome in favour of the Congress.'

'Argali and Congress will be thankful, occasioning a rapprochement with Shukla-ji,' said Tiwari-ji.

'And the defeat of the Alliance would teach Chaudhary Sahab and Saansad-ji a lesson.'

Nishant was at a loss how to counter this prognosis, which he didn't mind. It renewed his former hope.

* * *

A hush descended in the election office as the import of Ram Mohan's words sank in. Right then, his loud chuckle killed the moment of discomfiture, and when he explained the scenario, the previous mood returned. Many of those present, their chief concern was that Ram Mohan would stick it out. They didn't want to miss out on the fun of electioneering.

'All kinds of people are drawn to an election campaign,' Nishant told Deena and Mayank later. 'Election time is a kind of carnival which, given an inordinate number of jobless people, is eagerly awaited. All established parties have workers known to their local-level leaders, so it's hard for any Tom, Dick, or Harry to attach himself to these campaigns in a capacity beneficial to him. Many such people look to latch on to the campaigns of either independent candidates or smaller outfits, where their offer for help would be welcomed. Aside from meals and refreshments, they get to enjoy free rides in Jeeps into the interiors of the constituency. Where else can they have such fun for free? They're freeloaders. In our election office, they're the majority.'

After Ram Mohan filed his nomination papers, he was contacted by the local chief of Sanjay Vichar Manch, a political outfit launched by Maneka Gandhi, who, after her husband's death, had found herself out in the cold. Her mother-in-law had preferred her elder son to be crowned the successor. Left high and dry, Maneka was trying to lay claim to Sanjay Gandhi's legacy, whatever that was! Ram Mohan had no issues with being backed by or viewed as the candidate of Sanjay Vichar Manch, which, apart from this local chief and four–five of his flunkies, had few supporters in Fatehpur. The local chief got quick approval for his choice from Maneka Gandhi's second-in-command, Akbar Ahmad Dumpy, her late husband's friend and a proven loyalist.

They couldn't have hoped for a better face than Ram Mohan to represent their outfit. The latter thought that allying with them would somewhat swell his poll coffers and allow him a few extra hands to shoulder the burden of the campaign. On the money front, he was to be disappointed. A new kid on the block, Sanjay Vichar Manch was short on resources. The local chief made it clear. 'In this election, our chief focus is on the constituencies of Maneka-ji and Dumpy-ji, so a good chunk of the party's campaign funds is going to be used up there. But I'll hold an election rally addressed by them in Fatehpur.'

About this local chief of Sanjay Vichar Manch, Nishant said, 'He'll squeeze as much money as he can from the party, using Baabuji's name. People like him are adept at making the best of a bad job. This's an opportunity for him to feather his own nest.'

Meanwhile, Ram Mohan had to run to Allahabad to meet at the Sansthan, the potential contributors to his election chest. The Junior Engineer was the brains behind it. He also turned out to be

Ram Mohan's largest donor. In addition to a Jeep, he gave him fifty thousand cash. Before rushing back to Fatehpur, where Tiwari-ji was left holding the fort, Ram Mohan, along with Nishant, visited Sangam Colony. His high-spiritedness prompted Kanti to remark, 'You sound as though your victory is a sure thing.'

'Even my defeat will lead to a kind of victory. I need to poll enough votes to ensure a resounding defeat for the Alliance; that would revive my friendship with Argali and Shukla-ji. It's not that my loss is certain. I've grounds for optimism but can afford to lose if I get close to a tally of one lakh votes. What we can't afford is a sloppy approach to this battle.' He smiled at Rashmi, who looked avid for more of the optimism he was ladling out, then to Deena and Mayank, 'Nishant is in no position to financially contribute to the effort, but Deena, Mayank and Kanti can give twenty thousand, at least.'

Kanti didn't say anything but couldn't hide her look of disapproval. Ram Mohan told her off for being innocent of the reality of the world, the reality that wouldn't alter according to their convenience. They had to find a way to grapple with it. 'I didn't say anything. So why this lecture?' That made Ram Mohan rather happy. He had probably misread her face. Nishant could empathize with the fact that all they had was their share of the proceeds of the Main Building. They had no house, and no regular income. A pittance, Deena's salary didn't count.

'How many Jeeps are we going to have for the campaign?' asked Nishant.

'Not more than six. Not enough to cover a parliamentary constituency. Gulab Singh is sending two . . . And . . . Maybe one more later. But if it can't be helped, it can't be helped. We must use our resources sensibly.'

'Deena and Mayank should buy a second-hand Jeep instead of giving cash. After all, they'll need a vehicle when they join the campaign.'

'That's right,' Ram Mohan beamed at Nishant. 'Buy one. The tempo of electioneering is about to jump to another level.'

Later, Nishant said, 'It's much better, because the Jeep can be sold after the election but the cash you hand to Baabuji won't come back.'

* * *

It was Vinod who helped them find the kind of Jeep they needed. An old model, it was owned by a car mechanic who had had it overhauled. 'Now it's fit like a fiddle and can tough it out during the canvassing.' The mechanic was asking twenty-five thousand but agreed to three thousand less.

Nishant, before leaving for Fatehpur, had asked Prakash, the student leader whose village was in Fatehpur, to accompany Deena, Mayank and Rashmi in the Jeep. She had to be dropped at her parents' village about forty kilometres down the highway from Fatehpur. Kanti had to move to the Annexe to stay with her daughter-in-law and little granddaughter. Rashmi was bringing most of her English reading material with her, and Deena would, while driving the Jeep, tell her about this or that fact of English grammar, test her vocabulary and all. An amused Prakash praised Rashmi's effort.

'The interesting part is,' said Mayank, 'that she's picking it up faster than Deena when he began learning.' 'That's because Rashmi's lucky to have help at hand,' said Deena. 'But that doesn't take away from her being a quick study and her readiness for hard work.' Deena was proud of the way Rashmi had taken to English.

It was mid-afternoon when they reached Fatehpur. Deena and Mayank wanted to meet Baabuji before pushing on to Rashmi's village. It was the last date for withdrawal of nominations. The election office was abuzz with activity. Ram Mohan had just received an important visitor, and then emerged, out of nowhere, two persons, not nobodies, who wished to be involved in the campaign. It was their conscience that had stung them into it. 'Dr Sahab is the most deserving candidate in the fray.'

'Carry on and drop Rashmi first. You'll have your share of the action,' said Nishant.

It took them nearly five hours. Rashmi's father wouldn't let them leave without being properly entertained. He sent for some hot snacks from the market on the highway and had put in the Jeep, a basket of guavas, freshly picked from his own trees. When they got back it was dark. The election office had become calmer. Only those closely allied with the campaign were hanging about. Some were being lodged in the election office, while those who had their homes in the city were waiting for Tiwari-ji to brief them on the next day's plan of action, the first day of the real canvassing to get underway.

But Ram Mohan and Tiwari-ji and Nishant and the local chief of Sanjay Vichar Manch and two other members of the campaign, they all were taken up with the topic of their discussion. It had so much zing that there had to be some good news. The most vocal in the group was Tiwari-ji, who called it a kind of victory. 'It has to do with that very important visitor Nishant mentioned earlier,' whispered Deena to Mayank, as they, along with Prakash, joined the buoyant group, and Tiwari-ji, for the benefit of the newcomers, recapped the development.

It had been none other than the Alliance's Muslim candidate who had dropped by to coax Ram Mohan into withdrawing, putting out a carrot of some position later befitting Ram Mohan's stature.

'Why don't you withdraw and be rewarded later?' Ram Mohan had piped up.

'If the Alliance hadn't picked me, I wouldn't be contesting. My support would be for its official candidate.'

Ram Mohan and Tiwari-ji had pooh-poohed his grandstanding. Now they were exulting at the jitters the rebellion had caused the Alliance.

'Whatever doubts I had about the rationale for our decision, stand annihilated. This request from the Alliance, this meekness, has lifted my heart.'

'We do pose a threat to the Alliance in Fatehpur!' said Nishant.

Tiwari-ji said, 'The advent of Mathura Singh and Agnihotri is another sign that we're seen as a serious contender.' In his early forties, Mathura Singh was a Thakur by caste, while Agnihotri, about a decade younger, was a Brahman. They were friends.

'What could be the reason for Mathura Singh and Agnihotri to come out in our support?'

'Mathura Singh is someone who counts,' said Tiwari-ji. 'Argali should have loved to have him on his team. Why it didn't happen, I can't say. My gut-feeling is that there must be someone close to Argali here with whom Mathura Singh feels a rivalry of sorts.'

'That's plausible,' said Ram Mohan.

Then the conversation turned to how Mathura Singh had become known, and the moment the infamous event was mentioned, Deena sensed who Mathura Singh could be. A year earlier, seven Dalits were butchered by Thakurs for standing up to them in a Fatehpur village. Deena had read in the papers and in *Maya*, a Hindi magazine, that had published an article detailing some other such killings.

* * *

During ten days of hectic canvassing, Deena and Mayank had seen so many villages, far-flung ones, villages forming the entrails of Fatehpur, some inaccessible even by Jeep, the most reliable four-wheeler in that immense rural terrain. If I were to write a proper account of the experience—I was there for a week—it would become a separate volume. I won't go into all that, save that we had been exposed to the full-blown reality of Indian villages, to spectacles of deprivations, to the difference between the mental image of village poverty and its physical version, concrete and tangible, an in-your-face thing.

We were received cordially in these villages. People would be patient with our rhetoric, informed by the logic of caste solidarity. Some elderly people would have stories to tell, stories from Ram Mohan's earlier battles, the kind of enthusiasm his candidacy then had generated. The emphasis on 'then' or 'that time' by many was unsettling, and Deena couldn't hang back from asking, 'What about now? Aren't you enthusiastic about voting for him this time?' The person would say, 'I didn't mean that. We'll vote for him this time, too.' Then, there was the odd person here and there who, in response to Deena's campaign pitch, would blurt something to the effect that when he didn't get the ticket, he should have stayed out. Not only would that discomfit us but also make our endeavour seem risible, denting our sense of purpose. But our despair would dissipate with the welcome we got in the next village.

Nishant and Deena came to be certain that they were out of contention. One of the reasons for that was also the fact that the borders of Fatehpur constituency had been redrawn after Ram Mohan had last contested. The man behind the gerrymandering was Arimardan Singh, whose elder brother Udai Pratap Singh had been elected twice to the Lok Sabha from here, with Ram Mohan as his chief rival.

Now, Dhata, the lynchpin of Ram Mohan's support in his prior battles, stood excluded from the reworked avatar of Fatehpur parliamentary seat, added to which was Tindwari, a territory dominated by the Thakur community, Arimardan Singh's caste. With that, Pratap Singh, the strongman of Dhata, had ceased to be relevant to Ram Mohan's electoral cause. Moreover, he had long felt disgruntled at his friend who, while at the Commission, had failed to help a relation of his get into the state's judicial service.

As for their father's electoral strength to inflict a crushing defeat on the Alliance, Nishant and Deena were hopeful. The constituency still had enough voters of their caste to make that happen. 'Victory for the Congress because of Baabuji's good performance will be the gateway to good things for all of us,' said Nishant. 'We shouldn't slack off on the effort.'

People at the election office always had good things to say about Ram Mohan's prospects. We clutched at every optimistic opinion. Mathura Singh and Agnihotri claimed that among upper-caste villages, at least three they had under their thumb, and could get them to vote for Dr Sahab. Ram Mohan directed Deena and Mayank to take Mathura Singh and Agnihotri in their Jeep to these villages. 'Take Kartik along.'

* * *

It was a different experience visiting these villages, different from the experience we had in villages where Kurmis were the majority. The kind of welcome, warm, almost reverential, to which we had become used was given here to Mathura Singh and Agnihotri. Even the duo's attitude towards Deena and Mayank wasn't the same. Their manner of introducing them was perfunctory, and people, after nodding to our presence, would turn their attention to Mathura Singh and Agnihotri. 'I'll explain later,' said Mathura Singh, on seeing the surprised faces of his people that he was campaigning for Ram Mohan. In the next two villages, Agnihotri would go first, while we, along with Mathura Singh, stayed in the Jeep and would disembark only after his signal. Agnihotri told Deena that Mathura Singh was a famous figure, too famous to appear unannounced.

Famous indeed he was, a kind of celebrity. Thanks to one single savage act of his, he was hailed a champion of the cause of upper castes. 'We're proud of you,' said one elderly fellow in one of the villages. 'They needed to be taught a lesson,' to which somebody else added, 'If we give them their head, they'd become difficult to control. They'll grow wings.' The reference was to the massacre of seven Dalits.

Not once did they ask those upper-caste villagers to vote for Ram Mohan. Mathura Singh explained it away. 'It's complicated. First, we needed to speak to the village elders in private, to help them make sense of it,' he gave a mirthless laugh, while Agnihotri added, 'We told them that Dr Sahab's intellect was that of a Brahman.'

'We felt alienated. They behaved as if we were there to serve them,' said Deena to Nishant after we returned.

'There's something not quite right about the logic of their claim that they're supporting Baabuji because he deserves it.'

Later that evening, after Mathura Singh and Agnihotri had left, Nishant raised it at the meeting held daily, of the core members of the campaign. Deena recounted what had happened in the three villages. Mayank and I pitched in with our inputs. Ram Mohan said, 'I don't find their conduct suspect. There are things they can't discuss in front of you because the people in those villages are hardcore Congress supporters. To have them change their voting behaviour, one would have to put forth all kinds of arguments and put up with all kinds of reactions—'

'But I won't be surprised if these fellows are up to something else,' said Tiwari-ji.

'Can anything be done about it now? Let's not get distracted by it.'

* * *

Every evening, the election office wore a festive air. We all enjoyed the bonhomie on display. There were friendly debates and arguments and a lot of leg-pulling. We all listened to Ram Mohan and Tiwari-ji, with their different but distinct styles of speaking, particularly to Ram Mohan when he was in the mood to regale us with some interesting episodes of his life. Meantime, his nephew, Sateesh, a student leader in Kanpur, paid a covert visit but could campaign for his uncle only at the risk of angering Komal Singh Yadav, to whom he had become close. Ram Mohan asked him to stay away from anything that could imperil his equation with Yadav.

Then came on the scene Jaan Muhammad, who had relations in Fatehpur city. That he could manage some Muslim support for Ram Mohan was just a pretext for having the pleasure of his company. During his stay, Jaan Muhammad lived up to his formidable reputation of someone who wouldn't hesitate about his head-on approach to even questions viewed as sensitive, questions that were supposed to be handled delicately, questions whose gravest challenge to an academic would be how to remain politically correct even in the face of evidence operating against it. Of that Jaan Muhammad never bothered. He was neither an academic nor a politician. Or he could indulge his head-on approach at his own peril.

Jaan Muhammad's presence at the election office was marked by animated discussions. The one that was most absorbing was when the conversation moved from the rally to be addressed by Sanjay Vichar Manch leader, Akbar Ahmad Dumpy—Maneka Gandhi couldn't make it, which Ram Mohan didn't mind, as Dumpy, a Muslim, offered them a better deal as the town had a good Muslim population—to a more fundamental question, the question of the unavoidable Muslim dimension in Indian elections.

'We still have so many Lok Sabha and assembly seats where Muslims can impact the electoral outcome. Many a time decisively,' said Tiwari-ji. His ire at this factor being in play in Fatehpur stood out like a sore thumb. It was because of Liyaqat Argali being the Congress candidate that the Alliance could justify fielding a Muslim. Else, Ram Mohan's ticket was certain. Everybody thought the grievance genuine. Ram Mohan nodded ponderingly, as Jaan Muhammad, sporting his peculiar smile, said, 'For Muslims to have so much political leverage in India even after the battle for Pakistan was won, even after that grisly event called Partition! It makes little

sense . . . And that's the cornerstone of non-Muslim resentment.'
As he tried to elaborate his point, it turned into a long discussion
that I would skip.

* * *

Akbar Ahmad Dumpy's rally was well attended and Dumpy
extolled the effort put up by the local unit of Sanjay Vichar
Manch. Tiwari-ji made a brief speech to lay the groundwork for
his friend's fireworks. Ram Mohan didn't disappoint, making a
solid impression on Dumpy, who spoke last.

After the rally, Dumpy had tea with Ram Mohan's campaign
team at the election office and talked about Maneka Gandhi and his
late friend, Sanjay. 'He was a good person, contrary to how he was
portrayed in public. His only mistake, a big mistake, was that he
let others do his image-building and was fed all kinds of falsehoods
about the situation in the country, about his popularity. You won't
believe, Dr Sahab, how thrifty he was in his personal life. He
would tell Maneka-ji not to buy things she didn't need. Sonia,
on the other hand, is acquisitive. She has a passion for shopping.
Sanjay had said to Maneka-ji right in the beginning, "If you're with
Sonia when she's out on a spree, don't ever show your interest in
anything." Maneka-ji was intrigued. Sanjay explained, "If you do
that, the shop owner will give it to you. He'll be too afraid not to.
Whatever it is, it'll be thrust on you whether you want it or not."'
Dumpy glanced at his watch and said, rising, 'I've to be at another
meeting on my way to Lucknow . . . So long, Dr Sahab. Sanjay
Vichar Manch looks forward to a long association with you. I'll
arrange your meeting with Maneka-ji after the election.'

It was the last day of campaigning, so after seeing Dumpy off,
Ram Mohan and Tiwari-ji, with the workers of the Sanjay Vichar
Manch, made the rounds of the city's Muslim neighbourhoods.
When praised for his effort, the local head of the Manch said, 'Our

party's fortunate to net someone like Dr Sahab, and now through his good offices, we can register our presence here.'

Back at the election office, Ram Mohan ordered tea for everybody. 'I think I should leave tomorrow,' said Jaan Muhammad. 'No, we'll leave together, after the result,' Ram Mohan said .

Tiwari-ji said, 'The crowd at Dumpy's meeting took me by surprise.'

'We all were surprised,' said Ram Mohan.

'More surprising was the fact that the gathering consisted mostly of non-Muslims,' said Jaan Muhammad.

Nishant said, 'Not a single person in that crowd would vote for us.'

'That's what we all noticed,' said Deena, glancing at me and Mayank.

'Barring the people brought by Sanjay Vichar Manch, all were curious onlookers who wanted to see the man who was one of the most trusted lieutenants of Sanjay Gandhi.'

'The most trusted lieutenant of the most powerful man in post-independent India,' said Jaan Muhammad.

'Nishant's right. Dumpy failed to draw Muslims to his rally. The meeting was of no electoral worth,' Ram Mohan said and paused. Everybody waited. 'What next?' he resumed. 'Now I don't know what to make of my being a candidate in this election. Can we ensure the Alliance's defeat here?'

'Of that I'm certain,' said Tiwari-ji. 'That precisely was our objective . . . I discern a shade of regret in your tone.'

'Regret? No way. Regret what? It was a considered decision. I've no regrets . . . Now I wish to revisit the question of my post-election relevance.'

'Dr Sahab's right,' said Jaan Muhammad. 'Fresh stocktaking is warranted, a realistic stocktaking.'

'At the start of a journey, you're more optimistic than realistic. That's a good thing. You must be optimistic as you embark on the effort of getting somewhere. Or it'll be hard to make headway against the odds that are always there. But now, with age, I've become more down to earth and desperate.'

'You can say that again,' said Jaan Muhammad. 'I've long desired to write a novel. Earlier, I used to just romance the idea and relish the thought of such an achievement. No sooner did I start feeling my age than I became conscious of the challenge. That made me a bit desperate too. Now I've a good mind to force myself into writing it. It's not much of an analogy but I know how you must feel.'

Nishant said, 'That we have no Muslim votes isn't surprising one bit. We didn't bank on it in the first place. What's disquieting is that we may have failed to convince Kurmis!'

The silence brought on by Nishant's words was broken by Ram Mohan's laughter. All those present were grinning. All but Tiwari-ji, who, as Ram Mohan wiped his face, said, 'In that case we might end up being of no consequence!'

'The pretence that all's well is hard to keep up,' said Ram Mohan. 'No need for any rhetorical bluster now that the campaign's over. It's time to get level-headed. Nishant's spoken his mind and he's right . . . I'd like Jaan Muhammad and Tiwari-ji to help me decide what my next move should be. Is there anything left for me in politics?'

Tiwari-ji said, 'We don't know what the ballot boxes contain as regards the size of the victory for the Congress. As to the Alliance's defeat, I've no doubt.'

Jaan Muhammad concurred.

* * *

The Congress, enlivened by the assassination, proved a hurricane that left the entire opposition in tatters. Neither Nehru nor his daughter could have dreamt of it, the kind of victory Rajiv Gandhi pulled off, the sheer scale of it, unlikely to be replicated again—404 seats out of a total of 533—because that would take no less than the killing of a leader of the stature of Indira Gandhi.

Argali won by over two lakh votes in Fatehpur. The Muslim candidate of the Alliance came a distant second. The opposition got a big thrashing all over the country and stood decimated in UP, where the Congress bagged all but two seats. The slaying of Indira Gandhi had been sold triumphantly as a great martyrdom in the cause of India.

'If martyrdom at all, it was in the cause of the Congress and her son,' said Jaan Muhammad, a virulent critic of Indira Gandhi's handling of the Punjab problem. Unwilling to let Jaan Muhammad fly off at a tangent, Ram Mohan said, 'Now what . . . ? None of us had the remotest idea of this eruption of support for Congress.'

'Congress itself wouldn't have imagined such a result,' said Tiwari-ji.

'Such a definitive defeat of the opposition has saved me from dismay at being a candidate of no account.' Not only had Ram Mohan lost his deposit but the votes he polled was unmentionable, just over five thousand. No revival of his friendship with Argali. No sense in attempting a reconciliation with Saansad-ji. The Congress triumphing in this fashion had blackened the horizon of any possibility for people like him. Most political biggies in the opposition lay mangled. Saansad-ji, too, suffered an ignominious defeat.

While this conversation was occurring inside the election office, Nishant, Deena, Mayank and I stood outside, discussing the scenario thrown up by the unprecedented poll results. Soon, Rashmi's brother and Prakash, who had been sent to the Congress's election headquarters to see if Ram Mohan could congratulate Argali in person, returned. 'So many people thronged around him it wasn't possible to reach him,' said Prakash. 'When I told one of the workers about my being a student leader from Allahabad, he took my message to Argali—'

'Few would be stupid enough to ignore a student leader,' cut in Nishant.

'That didn't help much, for shortly, I was told Liyaqat bhai was busy, that I should convey his thanks to Dr Sahab . . . Guess who else we saw there? Let's go inside.'

'Tell me first,' Nishant insisted.

'Mathura Singh and Agnihotri,' burst out Rashmi's brother.

'Why should Argali entertain us? We're nobody to him now,' said Tiwari-ji. Nishant asked Prakash to tell them about Mathura Singh and Agnihotri, then to his father, 'I was right about them.' Prakash gave an account of the celebratory atmosphere at Argali's election office and an enthusiastic presence of these two amidst it. 'When I looked surprised, a Congress worker whispered, "They were sent to be part of Ram Mohan's campaign to ensure he didn't withdraw his nomination. His presence in the fray would mean less votes for the Alliance. As it turned out, we needn't have bothered."'

'I feel guilty of these murderers having been part of my campaign,' said Ram Mohan.

Tiwari-ji said, 'Your wily opponents sometimes resort to these stratagems. I'm not surprised that Mathura Singh and Agnihotri were Argali's men all along.'

'It's over and done with. I had better put my mind to what options I've left or where I go from here.'

Tiwari-ji said, 'The Congress is out of bounds for us—'

'How ungracious of Argali to not even want to be congratulated by Dr Sahab,' said Jaan Muhammad.

'My attempt to prove I still enjoy electoral relevance in Fatehpur has ended up a nonstarter. For a hardcore politico like Argali, that's all that matters.'

'No point in going into all that,' said Tiwari-ji. 'Congress is no longer an option and the Alliance leaders like Baran Singh and Saansad-ji are staring political nullity in the face . . . I doubt if you would consider going back to Kanshi Ram—'

'That's not an option either. After the publication of the Phule book, I ditched him and went back to Saansad-ji. Kanshi Ram wouldn't like to have anything to do with me now that I also have lost the support of my own caste. That said, I too think that his dream of welding Dalits, Muslims and other backward castes into a viable political force is unrealizable.' Ram Mohan looked at Jaan Muhammad, who had once argued that the backward or middle castes, also Muslims, behaved like neo-Brahmans and were hostile to Dalits more than the upper castes.

'Just stay with the Sardar Seva Sansthan as its chairman. You can do some writing at the same time,' said Jaan Muhammad.

'I agree,' said Tiwari-ji.

'That's the only option left.'

* * *

Unlike his father, who could put a setback behind him in no time, Deena would brood on adversities, the kind that could have been avoided if things had been done differently. Back in Allahabad, he was at it again, and said to Mayank, 'Why did Baabuji have to contest a poll that had nothing but a defeat in the offing? We had to go to the expense of buying and running a Jeep through the campaign. This, when our resources are so limited. If you ask me, it was just for the thrill of it that he stood in this election, the same as he had by resigning from the Commission four months before retirement, losing that much salary and a big part of his pension. To what purpose?'

'What purpose does your whining serve, except for being a nuisance at a time when we should set our mind to what needs to be done now? What needs to be done is that we find a buyer for the Jeep.'

The same day, they contacted the mechanic from whom they had bought it. He made it clear they shouldn't expect more than sixteen thousand, maybe five hundred more. That meant a loss of six thousand. Nishant said they could get a better offer because the Jeep was still in good condition. When Deena returned to work, he spoke to some of his colleagues and the day after that, the Jeep was sold for a much better price, fetching them three and a half thousand more than what the mechanic had quoted.

* * *

Ram Mohan's return to the Sansthan was greeted with cheers. Patel-ji, like most of the Congress candidates, had won, and was in Delhi. He sent him a note through Singh Sahab, welcoming him back. Nishant, Deena and Mayank were there when Ram Mohan announced to his audience at the Sansthan, 'It's time I made peace with the fact that I'm well past the logic of my Delhi-dream. Now I want to focus my attention on the Sansthan.'

TEN

With the dream of Delhi sliding out of his vision, Deena was awakened afresh to his inability to obtain anything better than his present job. Not sure of the security of his bond with Mayank, he wanted to improve his prospects at work: a BA degree to become qualified for promotion to assistant manager. 'It ill behoves you to have just done twelfth,' Baabuji would tell him. 'You must have a BA and an MA too. To get these degrees from Kanpur University is hardly any sweat.'

Deena wasn't up to it. He couldn't tackle all those questions by himself. If not for Dhata, he might never have cleared tenth and twelfth. He went to the Sansthan.

'In two years, you'll become a graduate,' said Baabuji. 'Go ahead and fill up the form. We have a couple of colleges affiliated with Kanpur University in Allahabad.'

One of Ram Mohan's associates named one such college.

Then Ram Mohan tackled the bane of Deena's wish to possess this degree, the dread that it would end up unavailing. Everybody knew how Deena quailed at having to sit these exams.

'You must be anxious. I know how unnerving it must seem to someone who's been an outsider to the system that seeks to slot students in between the best to the worst. But don't you worry. Just follow what I say.

'First, for each of the three subjects in BA, you buy these booklets with an easy question-answer format. They make a guess at the questions likely to be asked. You don't have to slog away at these booklets. I know your aversion to this sort of stuff . . . You just go through them several times, leisurely, to get the hang of the words and phrases peculiar to each of the subjects, their academic tenor and all. That's about it.'

Ram Mohan looked at those present. 'Continue, Dr Sahab,' said one of them. 'We're enjoying your clarity of how to go about it.'

'Well, after going through these booklets repeatedly, you'll be able to start your answer to any question. Just a hint that you're prepared. Write three or four sentences, using words from the booklets, serious-sounding words, then let go of yourself. Write anything after that, anything that comes to your mind. You can describe the plot of some movie or what you had for lunch, what food you like, about your friends, books that you've read, the authors you like, about your daily routine. You needn't be coherent even in that. Just go on writing about this or that. You must fill the answer-sheets with words and sentences, unmindful of how random or nonsensical they are. The examiner should get an impression that something's written. That's Kanpur University for you.'

* * *

In two years, Deena did become a graduate, passing with a second division. He would write later: *It all worked out so well, totally amazing! In time, when I read about 'stream of consciousness', a much-hyped literary technique, I knew what it was. It was the same technique as Baabuji had in mind. I used it unreservedly, filling the answer-sheets without pausing, writing down any and every damn thing popping up in my mind.*

No sooner did Deena get the final marksheet of BA, than he submitted its true copy to his office. 'You've done it,' said one of the clerks in the Establishment, then under his breath, 'Now you'll be due for promotion when the time comes.'

Still, Deena couldn't make peace with the likelihood of being stuck in this bank job. Baabuji was in no position to help. The only person who could bring him redemption from his doomed world was Mayank. He must become an IAS officer. Deena's angst was relieved that Mayank and I too had become enthusiastic about it. As to his other fear, that one day his bond with Mayank might slacken, Deena gave it a rest. They were years off that moment.

He would be on the lookout for anything that bolstered the importance of being an IAS officer, the kind of life only the latter and his dear ones could lead, a life underpinned by power and perks, in a country that thronged with masses of grovelling, helpless people. That indeed helped steel our resolve. To discuss how to meet the challenge, we often got together.

'Not wise to put all your eggs in one basket,' said Mahavir Wilson, who was in Allahabad to research his paper for some conference abroad. We were at the Sansthan. 'Success in this competition involves a fair degree of chance. The danger of failure is always there. I've seen some bright and serious contenders who, failing to make it, have had to cast about for a new goal and start over. So, it's important to also have some other option in mind.'

'Mahavir's right,' said Ram Mohan. 'You shouldn't be thrown off balance if—'

'Given the limited options, one must be realistic while making a decision,' said Wilson.

'I don't want to become a PO in a bank,' said Mayank.

'You, and also Kartik,' Mahavir Wilson looked at me, 'you both should aim to become a university lecturer if the IAS doesn't come off.'

'Correct,' said Ram Mohan.

'It'll be better if you matriculate at one of the universities in
Delhi as PhD students . . . Or . . . Maybe JNU—'

'First, we need to clear the UGC exam,' said Mayank, 'for
Junior Research Fellowship, which—'

'That'll take care of your financial needs in Delhi,' said
Wilson.

* * *

We decided to prepare for the UGC test and make it a collaborative
effort. But I lived in another part of the city. 'Why don't you move
in with me?' said I to Mayank. Deena endorsed my suggestion.

After filling in the UGC forms, Mayank shifted to my place.
We had two months to get ready for this test. The arrangement was
helpful. The chats we had in between our study sessions kept us
motivated. It was fun. In the evening, we went for a walk. Staying
in my locality were so many other students, talking to whom helped
us keep our eye on the ball. Those who had the UGC fellowship
were dedicated UPSC fighters. In case of losing that battle, they
would set their sights on the provincial bureaucracy. Mayank and I
couldn't lower our sights. It had to be the IAS. Or we would aim
for a university lectureship. We had made up our mind to move to
JNU in Delhi.

'As soon as we clear the UGC test, we'll make our move
towards that,' said Mayank who was much more ambitious than
I. Deena's ambition was to be able to read and write. He was
unrealistic to the core. He visited us twice a week to talk about how
our lives would be transformed after joining this super elite group,
the Indian Administrative Service. One day, he burst in on us,
waving the latest number of *Maya*, the famed Hindi magazine with
a reputation for its well-researched reports. It carried something
of interest to us. Deena went straight to it. Mayank and I peered
closely. Spread over several pages was a feature on JNU.

Deena began to read it aloud. We fastened on to every word. When he finished, we launched into discussing its portrayal of JNU campus, an elaborate and delightful portrayal, that punched up the mental image we had of it. Mayank and I were no less eager for amorous dalliances at JNU. 'Going to this university will augment your chances of passing the UPSC exam,' Deena declaimed. The shadow of despondency he had come under after Fatehpur had lifted.

But only Mayank could sit the UGC test for Junior Research Fellowship. I was felled by a fall down the stairs just the day before the exam and was in no condition to make it. It was a week before I could move out of bed. Mayank's exam went well. He was sure of clearing it and when he did, it gave him a fresh impetus along with a renewed sense of purpose. A beaming Deena said he was confident of him doing likewise in the UPSC exam. I laughed. Mayank said the two just couldn't be compared, not by a long chalk. Like Mahavir bhaiya said, the danger of failure is always there.

'I know. But I also know if you give your best shot, you'll make the cut. Now you must get admission to JNU.'

When the time came, we filled out the application forms for the entrance exam held throughout the country. It's hard to explain why—guess it was the Urdu bug—but instead of an MPhil in history, I applied for MA in Urdu while Mayank applied for a direct PhD in philosophy whose department in JNU was small, offering neither MA nor MPhil, only direct PhD, a five-year thing, aspirants to which had to appear for an interview after passing the entrance test.

For JNU entrance tests, we had to travel to Lucknow. Allahabad had yet to join the group of cities where this test was held. It was the middle of a scorching summer. We did well in our respective tests. Less than a month later, Nisha—JNU is next door to the IIT campus where Nisha and Shekhar lived—informed that we had made the list of successful candidates. Mayank had to appear for an interview. We received the postal communication from JNU at about the same time. Deena reiterated his confidence in our ability to succeed in the UPSC. Mayank reminded him that he had to get through the interview. Deena laughed it off. Mayank and I reached Delhi the day before the interview, and dropping off our things at Nisha's, we were off to the university.

* * *

When we got back, Mayank told Nisha cheerily about the JNU campus. Her response was lackadaisical. Shekhar, on returning from work, asked half-heartedly, 'So, what do you think of the campus?' Mayank answered in the same tepid manner. An hour before we were to head for the station, Shekhar and Nisha had an argument in the kitchen while we sat in the drawing room, talking distractedly to Shivika, who was downhearted that we were leaving.

A moment later, Nisha barged in on us, distraught and angry, then shaking her head, went back into the kitchen. Shivika looked miserable. Mayank tried to comfort her, 'We're going to come to this university to study. Then we can meet every week. We'll have fun.'

We had lost our appetite and were nibbling at the stuffed parathas Nisha had made. She didn't sit with us. Shekhar was trying to have some conversation going, and just as we were leaving, he said to Mayank, 'Your didi is disappointed in you all. She thinks you, each of you, are now too busy making a life for yourself . . .' He didn't complete the sentence and then said, 'You know how much she loves you all . . .' Mayank and I didn't know what the matter was!

When we told Deena, he held forth about his understanding of this behaviour, 'You say they had an argument before Nisha didi stormed into where you sat and left without a word. My guess is that Shekhar Jijaji would have made some comment about us, insidious and insinuating, casting doubt on the sincerity of our affection for her and then came and sat with you as though he had nothing to do with her being upset.'

A few days later, Mayank got mail from JNU. He had been selected for the direct PhD in philosophy. We weren't surprised, but our days of anticipation were over. We went to the Sansthan. 'I never had any doubt about this,' said Ram Mohan, embosoming each one of us. 'My Deena's looking more excited than either of you.'

* * *

Deena told us not to stay on IIT campus this time. Ram Mohan called Mahavir Wilson, who said he would love to put us up at his place—which was at the opposite end of the city—and that it would be hardly a week before we were allotted the hostel. We had been told of this popular phenomenon that hostel residents could have their guests staying either legally or illegally in their rooms. It would be legal if your stay was short, and your host was willing to pay for it, and illegal if somebody put you up in his room without informing the warden's office. The second option was more popular as it didn't just save one the money, but would let a guest stay for a much longer period than permitted. That could mean weeks, months and in some cases even years. Guests of this kind were called PIGs, permanent illegal guests.

Though happy for Mayank, Kanti and Rashmi couldn't but be sad. They were tearful as Mayank hugged them before leaving. To cheer them up, he said, 'I'm going to Delhi to make sure that we live not only together in the future but also live happily and in comfort.'

Just as the Prayagraj Express blew its horn and pulled away, Mayank said to Deena, who stood outside our window, 'I'll write as soon as I get settled.'

Initially, they missed him a great deal. But it didn't obtain for long. Their sense of gloom would give way to a feeling of elation and optimism. After all, Mayank had gone to Delhi to prepare for something that would secure a much better life for them all.

* * *

Dear Deena,

The first list of those getting hostel is out. My name's on it. Kartik's too. By tomorrow, or the day after, I will be allotted my room. I am going to complete the formalities today itself, and tomorrow Kartik and I plan to go down to the local market, Munirka, to shop for the essentials like mattresses, bed sheets, pillows, buckets, mugs, and all. Once settled, I will write you in detail about this place and my experience here thus far. This I am writing in a hurry and about something to which I want you to give a serious thought. I am so excited about the idea and so is Kartik. I think it can well become a reality. The idea is that you and Rashmi Bhabhi both can take admission here, you to do MA in Hindi literature and Bhabhi to do BA in any one of the foreign languages on offer. Given the progress she has made in learning English, and the fact that she's also trying to improve her general knowledge, she, after some preparation, can get through the entrance test. I can send her the photocopies of old question papers. As to your success, I'm certain. You just need to keep to the left while writing your answers. I mean, you must bear in mind the literary perspective, rather, politics spawned by the Progressive Writers Movement in which you are sufficiently versed. In a word, you must tackle the questions from the Marxian point of view. Okay, I now must go finish this hostel business, pay the fee and take possession of my room. Will write after I have got things in order here. Please tell mummy and Bhabhi that things are going to get better.

Love,
Mayank

Deena read the letter out to Kanti and Rashmi, who read it themselves again, several times. Written hurriedly, it had no mention of where Kanti would live if Deena and Rashmi both went to JNU. Mayank would have thought about it. They had better wait for his next letter. Kanti said she wouldn't mind them being in Delhi, preparing for a better future, and could make do with either living with their Baabuji or in the Annexe with Nishant. It was just a matter of two-three years. Compared to a happy life they could lead afterwards, this short-term inconvenience was nothing.

They didn't have to wait long to hear from Mayank again. This time, he wrote in detail, talking about things he found impressive and interesting in JNU, the friends he had made, about political and cultural student outfits active there, about his professor and PhD supervisor who had done her PhD under none other than the philosopher A. J. Ayer, who was a great admirer of Bertrand Russell. Ayer's book on the latter, *Russell and Moore: The Analytical Heritage,* an acclaimed introduction to his life and philosophy, Mayank had bought in Allahabad, a book that Deena now and then picked up to read. Most importantly, Mayank enlarged on how he thought their lives would change for the better if Deena and Rashmi could come to JNU. He also dealt with what it would mean for their mother.

'Of course, mummy can't be left to live alone. We can speak to Baabuji. If he agrees to move in with her, we can retain this place. The cost of living on JNU campus isn't much. We should be able to get by on my fellowship. If there's a need for a little extra, we can always dip into our funds from the Main Building. You know what? JNU also has a married hostel. We have plenty of time to discuss all this. When I come for three-four days, we will put our heads together and straighten the whole thing out.' About two and half months later, Mayank did go to Allahabad. It was some festival, Diwali perhaps. I was in Kanpur with my parents for a week.

* * *

Deena has left a long account of Mayank's visit, talking about the state of excitement they were in during his brief stay, but I would use only this: *We had so much to look forward to. To a world beyond Allahabad! Mayank's optimism about a wonderful time ahead was infectious. I became convinced of being able to live a life of the mind in not so distant a future.*

They all agreed on Deena and Rashmi taking the entrance exam of JNU. Ram Mohan told them not to worry on their mother's account, about where she would live. 'Either I can shift here as you suggest, or she can live at the Sansthan with me, but rest assured, things will turn out excellent. It is time you, all three of you, strove hard and made the most of yourselves.' With every subsequent visit of Mayank's, this idea would grow stronger and stronger.

* * *

Deena couldn't have imagined that the moment when he laid eyes on their landlord's new maid servant, who came to pick coriander leaves from the vegetable patch at the back, next to their rented portion, would lead to something so searing he would be left wounded forever.

'She's the daughter-in-law of their old maid who has got a bad leg and is forced into retirement,' said Rashmi, when Deena asked her casually about the new face.

There was something acutely charming about her face and figure. She was no beauty, this new maid. Not in the general sense. She was a guttering flame beside Rashmi, writes Deena, *yet hardly had I glimpsed her than a flame of lust shot up in me. I took another look that turned into a gaze. She caught on. I knew, the way she met my gaze, I could have her.*

After that, whenever they came across, he smiled and she reciprocated, shyly. To expedite things, he had to open a verbal communication. He began to bide his time. She came to the landlord's house twice a day but her visits to the vegetable patch, hidden from the front side of the house, weren't so frequent. She came to pick coriander leaves once a day or once every other day. Deena wouldn't risk talking to her while Kanti and Rashmi were around. The opportunity he so feverishly awaited, came up a week later.

It was Saturday, his half day at work. After his return, Kanti and Rashmi decided to visit the Annexe. Knowing his eagerness to catch up with his reading, they wouldn't insist on him coming. Rashmi's mother and brothers had shifted to Kanpur, the city much closer to their village. Her *bua*, who was still in Allahabad, she visited once or twice a month.

As soon as they left, Deena, forgoing his usual Saturday snooze, lodged himself in a chair by the closed door that connected the two portions of the house but was kept latched from both sides. This closed door opened into a passage on the landlord's side, next to their kitchen, where the maid spent most of her duty hours. Presently, he could make out her moving about in the kitchen. Getting up, he went to Kanti's room and took up his position by the window overlooking the vegetable patch. His insides were aflutter. He didn't know if she would visit the vegetable patch that day. It was seldom that she wouldn't. Often it would be during her second shift, because it was mostly in the evening that Sardar-ji's family could have dinner together, which had to be delicious, towards which the vegetable patch did its bit by way of some fresh seasonable vegetables and coriander or curry leaves or a sprig of mint.

Relieving his racking anxiety, she came. He was out in a second and gave her a big smile. She knew he was alone. When he beckoned her to come close, she shook her head languidly. Ostensibly a no. But her coquettish glances and smile kept his spirits up and he kept at it through various gestures that made her grin more. Once she finished what she was doing, he came over all desperate, his silent pleading acquiring a febrile urgency. She put her hand over her mouth to keep from giggling. His heart leapt up when she looked around and made for where he stood next to the kitchen just outside Kanti's room.

He took the basket of vegetables from her hand, set it down on the floor against the wall, hustled her into the kitchen and folded the lissom figure in his arms. She kept muttering, 'I've to get back.' Five minutes that they were inside the kitchen—she was leaning on the countertop—he kissed her profusely, his hands tracing the contours of her form, exquisite to the touch. When his feverish fingers contrived to slink into the most tender, sensitive, intimate recesses of her anatomy, she seemed to faint away, and no sooner did he, crouching on his haunches, go down on her, caressing reverently the opulent, luscious set of cheeks than she began to emit a deep moan. He couldn't thank enough that she was always in a sari that made such quick carnal forays possible. Not only on the sly but also at less than a moment's notice.

He promised to help her with money on occasion, before explaining how they could make out once or twice a week with no one knowing. It had to be only after she was done next door. She listened and left. A week later, when Kanti and Rashmi were out shopping, they met again. A blow-by-blow account of their assignation I won't give and just say the experience was a beauty, truly fabulous, the kind that leaves one craving more. Soon, more such opportunities were to come by when Rashmi visited her parents for ten–twelve days and Kanti's visits to the Annexe became more frequent. Often, it was Deena who dropped and picked his mother up. Meaning, he and the maid could have as much fun as possible with no chance of anybody walking in on them.

It became so trouble-free that he grew lax in guarding against the unthinkable. Once succeeding in mating with the maid in the bathroom while Kanti and Rashmi were home, he decided he didn't have to always wait for their absence if the desire got hold of him. That he could have a quickie even when he didn't have the house to himself. His second attempt to pull it off was to end in calamitous discovery.

* * *

On seeing Sardar-ji's wife standing by the boundary wall on their side of the house, Rashmi, who was in the kitchen, thought it was her once-in-a-while visit to inspect the vegetable patch. No, she had something else on her mind. Rashmi got out of the kitchen and gave Sardarni-ji a smile, who said, 'I had to say something to our maid, who just left. I thought she might have come to this side.'

Kanti, who was in her room, watching Doordarshan, asked what Sardarni-ji wanted. 'She was looking for her maid.' Rashmi then went into the main bedroom, attached to which was their only bathroom. Deena was in there. She had caught Deena eying the landlord's maid but had ignored; it was something shared by most men, the tendency to ogle women. Now, she stood cheek by jowl with the bathroom door, fearing the worst but, thanks to the TV blaring in Kanti's room, could hear nothing but the unhurried flow of water into the bucket with the tap at half throttle.

She tapped at the door. 'Deena, how long will you be? I've to go to the bathroom.' He took a second, and said, 'I'll be out in a minute.' She could pick out a faint but hasty movement inside, followed by the toilet flushing, an attempt to drown the noise of the opening of the other door, the door meant, in the manner of those days, for the sanitary person, some Dalit, to come in from outside and clean the commode. She saw the slit at the bottom of the door fill with daylight. She scuttled out, taking the shortcut through the drawing room, and saw the maid trotting towards the gate, her hands still adjusting the shape of her sari. Deena, who heard Rashmi rush into the drawing room, knew his game was up.

A picture of remorse, he seized hold of a glowering Rashmi and had her sit beside him on the sofa in the drawing room and didn't resist when she removed his arm from around her waist. As he began to apologize, tears burst through her eyes. He placed his hand over her mouth. Thankfully, Kanti was still engrossed in watching TV in the adjacent room. He beseeched her not to let his mother know. 'Why did you have to marry me, or marry at all, when you could stay free to pursue any girl you wished?' said she, sobbing in between.

Deena meekly sought her forgiveness, and as she calmed down a bit, said a fling like that meant nothing, had no bearing on their bond. Marriage bound them together in an infinitely serious, significant, important way. It just couldn't be reduced to its physical aspect. If brought to pivot around sex, the idea of marriage would stand belittled and denigrated. 'Marriage is a hell of a lot more than that. It's hell of a lot more about mutual respect and love than lovemaking. It's about companionship.' Rashmi, who had listened with her head down, looked up and said, 'You mean a woman whose love for her husband is beyond question, if she, in a momentary grip of passion, let someone else make love to her—'

'I know where you're going,' struck in Deena. 'That's a question all modern women ask, a reasonable question without a doubt! No man can stomach any such idea. Yet no man with his libido intact would let go of a chance to copulate with other women. Overcome with ardour, some would even be willing to take risks.'

'Someone like you!'

'Don't rub it in,' said Deena, and promised he wouldn't let himself succumb now. He went on to tell her that a large majority of the visitors to red light areas are happily married fellows. 'I've read a book on Indian call girls who all admit that most of their clients are married men,' he paused then hurried to add, 'I'm not justifying it. What I did was bad. It won't happen again.' What he meant was that he wouldn't be caught again.

If he could refrain from taking a chance while Rashmi and his mother were home, the problem would be solved. He forswore the use of the bathroom for the purpose from that day forth. He told as much to the maid—she was scared like hell—when they met next, the opportunity for which presented itself barely three days after the disaster, when Kanti took Rashmi along to visit her friend from the company garden where she went for a walk in the morning. It worked like a charm for about two months as he could revel in erotic ecstasy every week. The maid, going by one of Deena's notes, was delectably sensual.

* * *

It was a Sunday. 'It can't be the postman,' Deena thought when the doorbell rang, striking panic into the maid while he, after a momentary agitation, regained his self-possession. He asked her to stay calm. It could be anyone. Maybe a neighbour or one of his friends, perhaps Vinod. If it was him, she could easily get out of the house through the bathroom. 'I'm sure it's somebody else whom I'll dispose of in a jiffy,' Deena whispered and asked her to gather her things, the sari, the petticoat, the blouse, lying on one side of the bed, and hide behind the bedroom door and stay there till she heard from him.

The doorbell rang again, a little persistent this time, suggesting the vexation of the person. 'Coming,' Deena shouted, sounding irritated at the caller's impatience, and froze when he glimpsed the profile of Rashmi through the narrow window by the main door. Terrified out of his wits, he didn't know what to do. He darted to the maid and told her to get in the bathroom and shut the door.

Deena's pallor and demeanour screamed at Rashmi what the matter was. Her face set, she half ran inside and looked at the state of the bed in the bedroom. She didn't have to go into Kanti's room. She knew where to look. Glowering at Deena, who had given himself over to the situation, she knocked at the bathroom door latched from the inside and asked the maid to come out.

If he hadn't taken off her sari and blouse, she might have been able to get away just in time. But where was the need to be so careful when he was alone in the house? The only regret he had had while having it off in the bathroom was that it denied him the splendour of her nakedness that he could enjoy to the full in its every detail in the bedroom with no bother. 'Come out now or I'll call Sardarni-ji,' shouted Rashmi when she heard the outer door of the bathroom being opened. Deena, moving close to the door, asked her to do as told.

Rashmi grabbed the maid by the arm after she opened the door and stepped out, almost trembling. Just then, the doorbell rang out again. 'Go back in and get out, I'll talk to you later,' piped Rashmi, knowing who it was at the door. 'I just forgot,' she said. It was her cousin, her bua's son, whom she had to give the set of English textbooks Deena had got for her, of which she had long grown out. The cousin was to leave for Kanpur the same day, so he had brought Rashmi back on his father's scooter to get the books. He had been waiting outside at the main gate. She quickly found those books and left, telling Deena to prepare for an altered equation between them. 'I'm going to tell mummy also, your mummy.'

* * *

Neither did she tell Kanti nor broached the issue to Deena again. She assumed a mien so atypical of her even Kanti couldn't but notice. Thinking it to be one of those things between husband and wife, she didn't intervene, as there was no change in Rashmi's behaviour towards her. She was as respectful and courteous as before. And whatever the issue was, they would sort it out between themselves. The target of Rashmi's deadpan manner was Deena. She served him food and tea and discharged her domestic responsibilities as usual but would speak to him only when unavoidable. His reconciliatory moves were met with flashes of anger from her eyes.

When about a week later, on a Saturday evening, Vinod dropped by, Deena was apprehensive about how she would come off. But taking him completely by surprise, she couldn't have been friendlier to Vinod, whom she liked to tease whenever she could, and that day, her attempt to do so enraged Deena, who discerned his friend had taken a bit of offence, though meant there was none.

After the sale of the Main Building, Deena and Mayank would have their mail delivered to Vinod's address instead of the Annexe. Nishant had this incorrigible habit of mislaying things; often his own letters and papers were hard to find, while some would be lost forever. They didn't want anything like that to happen to their correspondence, consisting, inter alia, communications from the companies whose debentures they held. Vinod, a businessman, was careful with any documents or letters deemed important.

Deena visited his friend every two–three days at his shop after coming from work to chat and collect his mail, if any. On Saturday or Sunday, when Vinod came by, he would bring along anything received in between. That day, Vinod had got some letters. Just as he handed them to Deena, Rashmi said, 'Vinod bhaiya, you've become our postman.' It was her idea of a joke that didn't amuse Vinod, who said, 'If that's the case, I'll stop doing it.' Deena, though seething inside at Rashmi's comment, began to talk about something else, but later, after Vinod left, he grabbed hold of her and pushed her on to the sofa, then sitting down beside her and without raising his voice—to keep it from his mother watching TV in the next room—he just fumed and fumed, spewing forth choicest expletives, to which she listened dumbstruck.

He started hitting her, also a first, on the thigh, on the shoulder, on the back, everywhere. 'My remark was in jest,' she mumbled, after which, she bore everything quietly while he went on being unreasonable, speaking quietly but intensely. He would write some years later: *What caused me to have a fit that day was nothing but my sense of insecurity, emotional, social, financial. I feared losing anyone who*

I thought would stand by us, no matter what, and I wanted Rashmi to be
thought of well by all my close relations and friends.

It was getting late for dinner. Kanti called out to Rashmi. No
response. She came to their bedroom and then to the drawing
room, where they still sat. She sobbing silently and he with his
paroxysm of rage over, looking contrite and self-reproachful. Kanti,
thinking it was one of those fights from which no relationship
was exempt, asked them to wash their hands. She was going to
serve them dinner. They moved to their bedroom but when Kanti
returned with two plates, Rashmi said, wiping her face, 'Mummy,
I don't feel like eating at all.' 'Neither do I!' said Deena. Kanti put
the plates on the round table in the middle of the room, scolding
them mildly, 'This food has nothing to do with your quarrel, so eat
and then go to sleep. You'll wake up fine in the morning.'

They went to bed without touching the food. Deena fell asleep
almost instantly but woke up with a start about an hour later and
recalled his behaviour of the previous evening. An unbearable sense
of shame and bad conscience hit him afresh. How disproportionate
my reaction was to Rashmi's postman remark, he thought, and on
noticing she was still awake, an overwhelming feeling of love and
lust came over him. She had her back towards him, nestling against
which, he fastened his right arm around her waist and tried to kiss
her but found her face wet and warm with tears.

If he could arouse her, she would forget what had happened.
His attempts to do so kept being cut dead. He became insistent.
'What do you want from me? You have the maid!' That snuffed
out his desire. He flipped over. He would try and make it up to
her first thing in the morning. At five or so in the morning, he
awakened again and found Rashmi's side of the bed empty. She
must be in the bathroom. He went back to sleep and got up about
an hour and half later, to go to the bathroom. It was busy. Rashmi
was using it. Kanti was in the kitchen. He stepped outside. 'I've
made tea.'

'Not yet mummy, I've to go to the bathroom,' said he and remembered Rashmi was still in the bathroom. Filled with dread, he charged back in. The bathroom door was still latched from the inside. He knocked, waited a second, then rapped on the door harder. 'Please Rashmi, say something,' he yelped and kept knocking. So quiet was it inside, he became stupefied. He called out to his mother, who came bustling. On learning what the matter was, she asked him to break it open, which he did at once. Rashmi was hanging from the hook in the ceiling, her big toes almost touching the floor with a stool beside them.

He howled while trying to free her from the hook, with one arm clasped tightly around her hips, the other untying the end of the sari she had used. He carried her into the bedroom—she had suddenly gained weight—and laid her down on the bed. She felt so warm, he was certain a doctor would resuscitate her and rushed out to fetch the private physician who lived in the same locality, while Kanti, crying and mumbling something or the other, kept vigil. The doctor had yet to be done with his morning rituals but seeing Deena's state and the way he begged him to hurry, he picked his medical kit and followed Deena's Vijay Super on his Bajaj.

Deena, who had hoped Rashmi would have come round by the time he got back, suffered a fresh bout of shock and panic and misery. She was supine, exactly the way he had left her, with no hint of change in her posture. It took no time for the doctor to know there was nothing left to be done. He shook his head and told Deena to inform the police.

* * *

Holding Rashmi's head in her lap, Kanti wept inconsolably, as Deena, feeling hollow with pain and despair, stood in front of the bed, unable to absorb the truth. He wished he were dead, contemplating hanging himself, but his mother's pitiful, distressing state distracted him. He thought of Rashmi's parents and siblings, and felt a dreadful wrench at his soul, a clutch of contrition. How would they take it?

His world had come apart. He couldn't have imagined himself to be confronting not only a terrible personal loss but also that he might be blamed for the same. No wonder he could never be free from a niggling sense of guilt till he, too, would end his life a decade later, though for a different reason. 'Mummy, I'm going to Baabuji,' he said, and headed for the Sansthan and was astonished at the world around him carrying on as if nothing had happened.

Ram Mohan listened imperturbably, having sensed the moment he saw Deena, that he was about to hear something dreadful. *It never ceased to amaze me, Deena would write, how Baabuji could retain his equanimity, even when faced with the most difficult of circumstances, particularly so, when I had seen him losing his cool over minor things, trifles. I would come to realize that the more serious a situation, the calmer, the more collected, he would be. He knew he couldn't afford to be otherwise if he had to address himself to it.* 'Take me to the Annexe first,' said he.

Nishant was downstairs, in his home office, reading some file. He still had half an hour to leave for the High Court. Briefed on what had happened, he instructed his clerk to put off his engagements at the court. Nishant was to call everybody needed to be informed, while Ram Mohan and Deena set off for the office of the police chief, who they saw standing by his official car and other vehicles along with his posse. 'You're just in time. Sahab is about to leave for a tour of some police stations in the district,' said the official, who, recognizing Ram Mohan, had walked up to him just as they entered the gate.

The police chief directed one of his subordinates to tell the man in charge in the concerned police station to deal with the case in a courteous and cooperative manner. 'Now, let's go straight to your place. I've to get Rashmi's parents here by the evening,' said Ram Mohan, and looking at Deena's face, added, 'I'll go there myself.'

* * *

When Nishant and his wife arrived, Kanti began to weep again. Nishant had informed Nisha and Shekhar, who were going to catch one of the day trains and would bring Mayank along. Shortly, the police, a sub-inspector and a constable, appeared and spoke to Ram Mohan, telling him politely that it all now depended on the response of the girl's family. If they decided to lodge an FIR against his son, and maybe some other members of his family, the police would be forced to act accordingly. If they didn't, the case would stand closed.

Ram Mohan directed Nishant to go ask the Junior Engineer to arrange a vehicle for him to travel to Rashmi's village, overhearing which, Vinod, who had just landed, said he would give his Mahindra Jeep and a driver for the purpose. Ram Mohan set off while the police arranged for Rashmi's body to be transported to the morgue. Nishant and Vinod were taking care of everything that needed to be done. Deena could be of no help. He just hung about. His life had crumbled. Looking unkempt and washed-out, he was indifferent to glances thrown by the neighbours gossiping in small groups outside on the street. His landlords, Sardar-ji and Sardarni-ji, were talking to Kanti and Nishant's wife. They had heard nothing the previous night. They were stunned. 'She was so young . . . What a tragedy!' said Sardar-ji.

Deena accompanied Vinod to the morgue at the city's biggest hospital and felt a clutch of revulsion at its condition. Sickeningly filthy and tenebrous, its walls and floor smeared with hard to tell what, maybe blood and other fluids from bloating corpses at various levels of putrefaction. Victims of murders or accidents, waiting for autopsy. The smell was unbearable. Vinod motioned Deena to go outside, as he handed some money to the attendant—grubby and drunk, and looking not far from being a corpse himself—some of which was meant for the man himself, a kind of bribe, and the rest for a big block of ice that he, the attendant, arranged in less than fifteen minutes. The weather wasn't bad. Cold, in fact. But Vinod, given the morgue's state, didn't want to take a chance.

As they drove back, Deena kept quiet, trying to make sense of what had happened to him, to Rashmi, who now lay amidst all those decomposing bodies, in such sordid conditions. Nothing could be more distressing, disquieting. He thought of her efforts, cheered by him, of learning English. She had come to be able to read not only newspapers and magazines but English fiction, having become adept at using Oxford Advanced Learner's Dictionary. All that had been for nothing.

If he hadn't insisted on marrying her, she would be alive today, to which Rashmi's bua would also allude in the evening, in front of Rashmi's parents, her brothers, sister and a couple of their relations who had come with Ram Mohan in Vinod's Jeep. Rajvansh and some others came separately. Nisha and Shekhar couldn't make it as they had had a horrible fight at the last minute, and it would be a week before Sandhya could come. She was a little too far. Mayank and I had arrived and found the scene in the main bedroom, where they all sat, acutely plaintive. Ram Mohan and Kanti were there, with Rashmi's parents and others, while Deena stood outside in the empty space between his mother's room and the kitchen, looking extinguished, forlorn.

Ram Mohan had expressed his deep regret and pain to Rashmi's family, talking about how fond everybody in his family had been of her, especially Deena, who had wanted her to do something in life. Their plan to move to Delhi, to study at JNU, was acknowledged by Rashmi's father and brother to be true, who also mentioned the incredible change her personality had undergone after marriage.

Rashmi had never complained about anything. The father had no intention of going to the police. What could have led to something so terrible? Ram Mohan observed that nobody could know that. There were people who, despite being mightily upset and angry, despite being faced with excruciating circumstances, wouldn't resort to ending their life, while some would rush to it even when their situation wasn't that extreme. The kind of quarrel Deena and Rashmi had had wasn't something unheard of between husbands and wives. Then he doubted if she had really wanted to do it. Maybe she had thought Deena knew of her going into the bathroom with a stool and had expected him to come running and stop her. Maybe she just wanted to give him a scare. What she mightn't have known was that after hanging herself, she couldn't recover. With blood not reaching the brain, she would pass out in no time.

* * *

We were with Deena in the drawing room when there was an upsurge in the hubbub in the bedroom, and Mayank, with a firm look, rose and went in and saw Ram Mohan rebuking Rashmi's bua for her hurtful remarks.

'First of all, you must understand that what's happened is more traumatic and painful to us, to Deena, than it is to you,' Mayank spoke out above the ongoing din and in a voice so compelling everybody stopped talking.

'Deena's no less a victim to this rash act of Rashmi Bhabhi than she was to his behaviour, however bad it might have been. My own didi and jija-ji fight frequently, sometimes viciously, but no matter how distressful it is, I don't think the thought of suicide ever enters her head. There were no serious issues between Deena and Bhabhi. What has happened can't be undone, and it's Deena who would live with it for a long time to come . . . If she was disturbed or had any problem, she could have complained to her parents,' then addressing the bua, 'She could have come to you. She could have gone to Baabuji. She didn't even tell our mother about anything.' Mayank went on talking for half an hour.

After the cremation and all, Rashmi's father talked to Deena alone, and tried to console him. Looking at my friend nobody could have any doubt about the kind of pain and trauma he was in.

* * *

Sandhya came to stay for a month, to take care of her brother and mummy. Deena didn't go back to work for over two months and when he went, it was only to resign. Mayank wanted him to live with him in Delhi, in his hostel room, as a permanent illegal guest, till he himself became a student at JNU. Ram Mohan was all for it. His only wish at the time was for Deena to get over the blow and get on with his life. 'I know what you must feel. The memory of a tragedy of this proportion would haunt you for how long, you don't know. But you can use the pain, the experience, constructively. You can use it to help you not to take yourself seriously. Find a purpose in life and devote yourself to it.'

It was decided that Kanti would live in the Sansthan with Baabuji. Then, one of Ram Mohan's close associates at the Sansthan came up with another idea that made more sense. He, this associate, had a house partially built or half-made in a locality situated two kilometres from the Sansthan. He was building it for his own use but had no plan to move in there in the immediate future. He took Ram Mohan and Deena to have a look. It was like many other houses in the locality, with no flooring or plaster on the walls. One of the three bedrooms and the kitchen had no doors yet, and the ones with doors had windows with missing glass panes.

'It's not your idea of a house, but it's for free,' said Ram Mohan to Deena. 'Your mummy and I should easily survive here.

It's a question of only a year, then we'll shift to the Sansthan . . . Or maybe to Kanpur. Let's see how things turn out, but don't let it bother you. I'll take care of things here. I want Mayank and you to concentrate on making something of your life.' Within a week, they moved into this half-made thing.

Deena was there with mummy and Baabuji for a month before shifting to Delhi. Later, he was to recall the moment of his parting from them.

Most of the day, mummy was busy making snacks for me to take to Delhi. I spent hours on packing my things. Clothes and other essentials weren't a problem, but books were. To decide which ones to take and which ones to leave from my large collection, was agonizing; often, I would fall to reading them, to help make up my mind. It was only in the evening, after I had loaded my luggage into the tiny boot and the back seat of Vinod's Maruti 800—he had come to take me to the station—that I sensed what a lonely life mummy would lead from then on. Baabuji still had an active social life.

She was looking for some pictures in her worn photo album. The pathos of that moment—her sitting before an open old trunk of hers, from which she had taken out the album, some of whose leaves had come loose— was such that I could barely keep from crying. The memory of that, along with that of Rashmi's, never ceases to haunt me. 'Mummy, I'm going.' She got up and walked out with me to the Maruti 800, by which Baabuji and Vinod stood talking. Baabuji, as he hugged me, said he was confident that our Delhi stay, Mayank's and mine, would be a game-changer in the family. Mummy already tearful, began to sob, while holding me close and kissing me repeatedly on the cheeks and forehead. 'Don't cry, Kanti, and be happy for them. These two children of yours are going to make you proud,' said Baabuji. Vinod gestured to his watch and said, 'Let's get a move on.'

Acknowledgements

My thanks to everyone on the Penguin Random House India team who lent a hand. I am specially beholden to Rea Mukherjee, my editor, for steering me through the painstaking process of getting this book in print; to Vineet Gill, the copy lead, who graciously bore with my grumbles; to Aakriti Khurana, for her apt and stunning cover design; to my wife, Bhavna, and daughter, Shinaber, without whose loving support I couldn't have dared venture into fiction writing, which is nothing but 'an exhausting, horrible struggle'; to Ajaz Ahamd, a dear friend from my JNU days, who took an issue with the way I had initially ended the story and made me alter it, for which the book is all the better; and to those of my family and friends who were never close-fisted in giving me encouragement as I laboured over my writing.

Scan QR code to access the
Penguin Random House India website